SECRETS BETWEEN THE SHELVES

4 COZY BOOKSHOP MYSTERIES

CYNTHIA HICKEY
LINDA BATEN JOHNSON
TERESA IVES LILLY
MARILYN TURK

BARBOUR
PUBLISHING

Murder in the Mystery Section ©2025 by Cynthia Hickey
The Secret Passage Bookshop ©2025 by Linda Baten Johnson
By Hook or by Book ©2025 by Teresa Ives Lilly
The Missing Chapter ©2025 by Marilyn Turk

Print ISBN 979-8-89151-031-9
Adobe Digital Edition (.epub) 979-8-89151-032-6

Cover illustration by Begoña Fernández Corbalan

Published by Barbour Books, an imprint of Barbour Publishing, Inc., 1810 Barbour Drive, Uhrichsville, Ohio 44683, www.barbourbooks.com

Our mission is to inspire the world with the life-changing message of the Bible.

Member of the
Evangelical Christian
Publishers Association

Printed in the United States of America.

MURDER IN THE MYSTERY SECTION

BY CYNTHIA HICKEY

"I have said these things to you, that in me you may have peace. In the world you will have tribulation. But take heart; I have overcome the world."

John 16:33 (ESV)

CHAPTER ONE

I unlocked the door to Through the Looking Glass and flipped the sign on the door to OPEN. With a smile and a flourish of my arms, I turned to survey my kingdom.

A dream come true for this Amber Swanson, aged twenty-eight but sometimes feeling closer to forty. A bookstore that resembled the wild world of *Alice in Wonderland* complete with upside-down seating, overly large, brightly colored plants, and shelves of books. Behind the counter waited a new batch of scones to be devoured and coffee carafes and teapots to be filled. The morning sun cast a warm glow through the large front window. Let the swarm of hungry booklovers descend.

I trailed my fingers along the spine of a shelf of rare and antique books on my way to the counter. I'd scoured the country and the internet for months to purchase the fifty out-of-print editions. They were my babies.

Soon, the delectable aroma of freshly brewed coffee mingled with the yeasty smell of baked goods and the comfortable scent of new books. I leaned my elbows on the counter and stared at the entrance.

Why weren't people flocking to my store? I'd been advertising for months in the town's local paper. I'd even purchased a few ads in surrounding towns within easy driving distance. Didn't people want an unusual bookstore in their midst? One that invited a patron to linger and browse?

I grabbed a duster and moved to the window to check the display of new editions of *Alice in Wonderland*. As I pretended to dust, I glanced up and down the street. People strolled in and out of one shop after another. When two women headed my way, I raced back to the counter and busied myself rearranging scones.

The jingle of the bell over the front door sent my heart thumping. I straightened and pasted on a smile. "Welcome to Through the Looking Glass."

The women murmured good mornings and headed to the romance section. A few minutes later, no books in hand, they strolled back out the door.

My smile faded. How could they not stop and read? Purchase food or drink? Had I acted too eager?

Several more customers trickled in and out, some buying a book or a scone, but none lingering at the mushroom-shaped tables to share news. I sighed and plopped on a stool. I'd really thought that on opening day I'd be busier than a one-armed paper hanger. I plopped my chin in my hand and continued to stare at the door then popped up when my best friend, Shelby Downs, entered the store, blond curls bouncing.

She glanced around. "Where is everyone?"

"No idea." I shrugged. "I really had the wrong idea about opening day."

"No you haven't. Folks have been talking about it for weeks." She glanced around again. "Where do I sign up for the drawing? The one for a chance to win a free coffee with every book purchase?"

"Oh no." I reached under the counter and pulled out the sign and the colorful basket for the entries. "How could I have forgotten?" I rushed to hang the sign in the window. "Do you think this is why I've only had a handful of customers?"

"Maybe." Shelby perched on a stool. "I'll take a strawberry-and-cream scone with tea, please. Then I'll take half a dozen assorted back to the office. Once everyone tastes what you have, they'll come in droves."

"I want to sell books. That's where I'd make enough money to keep the doors open."

"You will. Things move slow in this town. You know that. You've lived in Hickory Hill your whole life."

"What if the town isn't big enough to support my shop?"

"Stop thinking that way. Give it time." Shelby took her purchases. "They'll come. God didn't give you this dream only to take it away. He opened all the doors, didn't He?"

"Yes." Feeling mildly better, I wiped the counter as my friend sauntered out the door.

Everything had indeed fallen into place. I'd used my inheritance from my parents to purchase the store. My grandmother, off on one of her cruises, had given me business advice, and any permits I'd needed had been easily taken care of. I'd expected too much too soon, that was all.

Two women entered, ordered tea and scones, and took a seat at one of the tables. Maybe Shelby was right. As the day neared the lunch hour, business picked up in a trickle of one or two patrons at a time. The weird thing was, they all cast suspicious glances my way and kept conversations to a whisper.

I heard the occasional *rumor, book, boycott*. . .none of which made a lick of sense. Nevertheless, I kept the coffee and tea hot. When curiosity got the better of me, I grabbed a tea kettle and approached one of the tables. "Refill?"

The two women seated there startled. "We're good, thank you," one of them said.

I stared at her. "What's going on, Mrs. Stapleton? You act as if we're strangers. You've known me since the sixth grade." The woman had been my teacher, after all.

"Why, nothing." Mrs. Stapleton's smile seemed fake as she cast a glance at the other patrons. "Business looks good. . ."

"Despite what?" I crooked a brow. I felt as if she'd left something out of her statement.

"What do you mean? Ruth, do you know?" She shot a wide-eyed look at her friend.

"Not a clue." The woman concentrated on stirring her tea.

"Ladies. . ."

"Oh, very well." Mrs. Stapleton clutched her purse in her lap. "There is a rumor circulating around town that you've stocked your shelves with stolen goods."

"What?" My eyes shot wide. "That's not true. Who would say such a thing?"

"I can't tell you. Only that. . ." Mrs. Stapleton lowered her voice. "The citizens in this town were ordered not to frequent your establishment. No one will say exactly who told them that, more of a rumor floating around. . . But some of us disagree and, well, here we are."

"Here you are." I couldn't for the life of me figure out who would try to sabotage my store. "If I had stolen anything, don't you think the police would be questioning me?"

"That's what we thought." She nodded. "The scones are delightful, dear."

"My grandmother's recipe." I moved to the next table and heard more of the same ridiculous accusations.

Tears burned my eyes as I returned to the counter to check out a woman who purchased a copy of *Alice in Wonderland*. I couldn't think of a single person who disliked me. Oh, my grandmother, Nina Swanson, had pricked a few feelings in her time with her way of saying what was on her mind, but I thought everyone liked her, despite her sharp tongue.

The bell over the door jingled again. This time, excitement didn't send my heart racing, but the sight of Detective Jack Mitchell did. "What can I help you with?"

"Just looking." With a stern face, he browsed the shelves then asked to be pointed toward the mystery section.

I obliged and watched as he moved up and down the shelves as if looking for something. "I can help you find whatever you're looking for."

"Just browsing."

He could've fooled me. The man was obviously looking for something in particular. When he didn't find what he wanted, he nodded in my direction and left the store, squeezing past a man delivering a box.

"Oh, good." I rushed forward. "The last of my order." I signed for the package and carried it to the counter. Using a box cutter, I opened the box of the last of the vintage books I'd ordered, plus some new fiction releases, logged them into the system, and was able to shelve some of them before more customers came in. The others I stacked on the counter, out of the way.

I didn't expect many of the folks in Hickory Hills to want vintage books, but there were plenty of online shoppers who might, I hoped. Those were my real money makers.

My cell phone rang, and I hurried to snatch it from the counter. "Through the Looking Glass."

"Hello, dear. How is opening day? Sorry I didn't make it home in time. I'll be in late tonight."

"Hi, Grandma. It's okay. How was the cruise?"

"Stormy seas. Good thing I've got the stomach of a sailor."

I laughed and waved as Mrs. Stapleton and her friend left the store. "I need to ask you something. Did you make anyone mad before you left?"

"Not that I know of, why?"

"Just something I heard."

"Well, if those old biddies with the garden club are giving you trouble, I'll—"

"Nothing like that."

"Good. You know I'm like a momma bear where my granddaughter is concerned. See you tonight. Toodles." She hung up.

It was true. Since the death of my parents in a boating accident when I was thirteen, my grandmother had always come to my defense no matter what. Even when I struggled with grief in school, not wanting to face the other students after my parents died, she'd somehow managed to get them to allow me to take online classes for the remainder of that year. Yep, Grandma was a force to be reckoned with where I was concerned. I thanked God for her every day.

Another visitor entered. This time, everyone in the store froze as Mrs. Peabody, gray hair bobbing, marched to the counter. "Where are your rare books?"

"Over there." I shrank back at the malicious gleam in the woman's eyes.

Mrs. Peabody stomped toward the rare books, ran her finger over the spines, then plucked one from the shelf. "This is my book, young lady. You are a thief!"

"You're mistaken. That book arrived today." I reached to take it back.

Mrs. Peabody held it over her head. "I can prove it, Amber Swanson." She flipped the book open. "It's signed by the author to my grandfather. See there?" She tapped the title page. " 'Best wishes to Ronald Peabody.' I intend to have you arrested."

"I assure you, I purchased that book legally." I crossed my arms. How dare the woman accuse me of stealing. "How long has it been missing?"

"Months!" she shrieked. "I knew it would show up on your shelves."

"I have the receipt." I pulled it from my files and waved it in front of her nose. "*What Life Is Made For* belongs to me."

"We'll see about that." Mrs. Peabody slammed the book on the counter. "I'll be back with the authorities to retrieve what is mine and make sure this bookstore never gets off the ground."

"Is that a threat, Mrs. Peabody?" I tilted my head.

"That is a promise!" She whirled and stormed toward the door.

"My grandmother is coming back tonight. She'll take care of this," I called after her.

"Are you threatening me, young lady?" She turned and quirked a brow. "You'll get what's coming to you, mark my words."

I grinned. "No, ma'am, that is a promise."

Once she left, I started cleaning up in preparation to close shop for the day.

CHAPTER TWO

After running late because I'd slept in, a result of staying up talking to my grandmother too long into the night, I rushed to the shop, grabbed a scone, and settled in the storeroom to have a quick breakfast before opening.

Thank goodness, Grandma had agreed to continue making the scones even if it did mean getting up early. I knew how, but my grandmother made them better.

I frowned as the bell over the door alerted me to someone entering. I'd forgotten to lock the door behind me. "We aren't open until eight," I called. "Hello?"

When no one answered, I went back to my breakfast. Maybe they'd simply peeked in to see if I was out front and left.

My mind returned to the heated conversation with Mrs. Peabody the day before. The shocked looks on the faces of my customers. The trickle of customers yesterday afternoon had done little to dispel the uneasiness left behind by the woman's threats.

The door jingled again. I stood, knocking over my coffee. As I stooped to clean up the mess, loud voices, a man and a woman, came from the front of the store. Not the way I'd wanted to start my morning.

I tossed the soiled napkins in the garbage and grabbed my half-empty cup. A blood-curdling scream rent the air. I yelped and dropped the cup, splashing coffee across my ankles. Hissing, I darted to the front of the shop just in time to see the door swing shut.

I turned and froze at the sight of feet sticking out from the store's mystery book section.

Mrs. Peabody lay there with a half-eaten scone in one hand and a knife protruding from her chest.

I knelt beside her and felt for a pulse. Nothing. I got up and grabbed napkins from the counter then tried to staunch the bleeding around the knife as the store bell jingled again. I pulled my cell phone from my pocket to try to call 911 one-handed.

"I know it's early, but I'd like some scones to take to—" Mrs. Winston, the town librarian, gasped, clapping a hand over her mouth before whirling and racing from the store.

Ignoring her, I continued my futile quest to save the life of Mrs. Peabody while staying on the phone with the 911 operator. Once I realized there was nothing I could do, I stood, tears blurring my vision. The woman was difficult to deal with, but for someone to kill her, here in Hickory Hills?

I heard the bell jingle again. Then, "Hands up. Move away from the body." Detective Mitchell shot me a harsh look.

I complied. "I heard loud voices. . .a scream. . . She's dead."

"Stand over there." He motioned me toward the counter then examined the body.

I hurried to stand where he'd commanded. After a few minutes, he spoke into his radio then returned to handcuff me.

"Wait. What? You think I killed her?" This couldn't be happening.

"I detected the scent of almonds, Miss Swanson." He eyed the counter behind me. "The knife sticking out of her chest matches the set behind you."

"Almonds? We don't use them here. My grandmother has a nut allergy." The cold snap of the cuffs had a sob lodge in my throat. "I told you, I heard voices."

"Your knife, and no one else is here. Sit." He pointed to a chair.

Goodness, he thought I'd killed Mrs. Peabody. I sat, tears coursing down my cheeks. "Don't I get a phone call?"

"You aren't under arrest. . .yet."

"Then why the handcuffs?"

"To make sure you stay put." He glared in my direction then returned to Mrs. Peabody.

A while later, two officers in uniform entered the store, both sending accusing glances in my direction. Anyone who knew me would know I wasn't capable of murder.

"My fellow officers have been questioning people outside. We have several witnesses who attest to the fact that you and the victim had an argument yesterday." The detective towered over me.

"News travels fast." I sniffed.

"Did you?"

I nodded. "Mrs. Peabody accused me of stealing her book. Is that what you were looking for yesterday?"

"I'll ask the questions, ma'am."

Ma'am? The man had known me since I was small. "The book in question arrived in yesterday's delivery. It should be on the shelf." It wasn't until then that I noticed the rare book section was in disarray, several of the priceless books on the floor.

"Can I pick those up?" I asked.

"This is a crime scene, ma'am." He marched to the door and shooed a couple of women away.

This would not be good for business. "If Mrs. Peabody was looking for the book she accused me of stealing, why is she in the mystery section? Why were you in that section yesterday?"

"Be quiet, Miss Swanson."

I bit back a bitter retort and hung my head. This was not good. I had no witnesses. "I heard the victim arguing with a man. I didn't know it was Mrs. Peabody until I. . .found her."

He glared at me as two paramedics wheeled a gurney into the store. "I'm not going to tell you again, Miss Swanson. You'll have your chance to talk at the station."

He was going to haul me to jail? Sobs shook my shoulders. I wanted my grandmother.

As if my thoughts had drawn her to me, she backed into the store, a large white box in her hands. "I brought fresh—" She glanced from me to the detective. "What is going on here?"

"Outside, ma'am." Detective Mitchell tried herding her.

She ruffled like an angry goose. "I will not leave." She plopped the box on the closest table and rushed to my side. "What happened?"

"Mrs. . .Peabody. . .is dead," I managed between sobs. "Sherlock here thinks I killed her."

"It's Mitchell." He shook his head.

"Preposterous! You wouldn't kill anyone." Grandma smoothed my hair from my face. "We'll figure this out, sweetie. Wait right here."

As if I could go anywhere.

Grandma marched up to Detective Mitchell.

His face darkened at whatever it was she said.

I bit back a grin, delighted at how she could intimidate even an officer of the law. But my smile faded as the other two officers took me by the arms and marched me outside, through the watching crowd, and into a squad car.

Less than fifteen minutes later, I found myself in a small gray room, unhandcuffed, a paper cup of water on the table in front of me. I glanced at what I suspected was a two-way mirror. Let them question me. I didn't know anything more than what I'd already said.

"Can I get you anything else, Miss Swanson?" Detective Mitchell entered the room and sat across from me.

"No, thanks." I crossed my arms. "You're wasting time. You should be out looking for the person who killed Mrs. Peabody."

"That's what I'm doing." He gave a humorless smile. "Since you were found over the body, your scone in her hand and your knife in her chest, we're starting with you."

"I didn't kill her. I was having breakfast in the back room."

"Then you have nothing to worry about. Start at the beginning, Miss Swanson. Maybe the argument yesterday?"

"Like I said, she accused me of stealing her book. It wasn't even on the shelf until I put it there after the delivery."

"Can anyone attest to that?"

I frowned. "There were several people in the store when I received the package."

"And when Mrs. Peabody arrived?"

"They were there to witness the. . .altercation." Wasn't that what law enforcement called a confrontation?

Wait. What had Detective Mitchell said? Almonds? Cyanide? "Was she poisoned?" I'd read somewhere that cyanide smelled like almonds. Then what about the knife?

"We won't know that until the autopsy." He slid a bag containing the knife across the table. "Recognize this?"

I swallowed against a throat as dry as a desert. "It's one of mine. Since I leave them on the counter to cut scones, it wouldn't be hard for someone to grab one."

He nodded. "Start with your entering the store this morning."

"I took a scone and coffee to the storeroom for breakfast. When the bell jingled, I yelled out that we didn't open until eight. Then the bell jingled again. I spilled my coffee. As I cleaned it up, I heard loud voices. . .a man and a woman. I spilled the rest of my coffee when the woman, Mrs. Peabody, screamed. By the time I cleaned that up and entered the front, I saw the door closing."

"You didn't see who exited?"

"No." But, it didn't take a detective to determine it had to have been the killer. "Then I tried to stop the bleeding." Nausea rose at the sight of Mrs. Peacock's blood on my clothes. "I know how it looked when you arrived, but I didn't kill her." Mrs. Winston hadn't wasted any time calling the police. A good thing. "How did you get there so fast?"

"I was on my way to purchase coffee and a scone when the 911 call came through."

I doubted anyone would be darkening the door of my store anytime soon. Did Mrs. Peabody have any family? I didn't know her well enough to answer that question. "That's about it."

He quirked a brow.

I took a deep, shuddering breath. "Can I go now? You can't keep me without evidence. I read a lot of books."

"I bet you do." He gave a thin-lipped smile. "Enough to know how to commit murder?"

"I didn't kill her," I muttered, feeling like a recording stuck on repeat.

"You're free to go, Miss Swanson. Don't leave town. The store won't be able to reopen for a few days."

My heart fell. "Thanks." I stood and marched for the door.

"Do not talk about the case with anyone, ma'am."

I glanced back, fully intending to talk with a lot of people. I knew from books and television that the police didn't have all the authority they wanted people to believe they had. I needed to clear my name so I could resume business. Instead of saying my thoughts out loud though, I nodded and exited the room.

Grandma waited for me in the reception area. "Let's get you home. I'll cook an omelet." Her answer for everything.

"My car is in back of the store," I said, buckling my seat belt.

"I'll drop you off, but then you come straight home. We have plans to make."

I cut her a sharp look. "What kind of plans?"

"The kind that will catch Ada Peabody's killer."

CHAPTER THREE

A fter a week of my grandmother coming up with one wild scheme after another to catch a killer, I put my foot down. "We'll let the police handle this."

"Where's your sense of adventure?" Grandma pulled a batch of raspberry scones from the oven. "No one is closer to this than us."

"How so?" I taped a box closed.

"You're the number one suspect, or so the rumor around town goes." Grandma grinned over her shoulder. "Business will be booming with looky-loos. Everyone wants to see the killer of Hickory Hills."

"Stop it." I rolled my eyes but didn't discount the suspicious glances I'd received at church the day before. "Let's be happy the store can reopen today. I've got a lot of reshelving to do." Not to mention wiping away the black powder from the police looking for fingerprints. "Bring the rest of the scones when you come, please. My to-do list today is horrendous."

"I won't be long."

After scooping up the boxes of ready-to-be-sold scones, I loaded them in the back seat of my car and drove to the alley behind Through the Looking Glass. I sat there for a moment, nerves threatening to get the best of me. I wanted folks to come into the store to buy things, not gawk and ask questions. But I did have some questions of my own, and maybe someone could fill in a few of the blanks. Grandma was right. I seemed to be the only suspect. At least it didn't appear as if local law enforcement intended to look further than me.

I shot a glare at the squad car parked at the end of the alley. The same car that had been outside our house for the last week. Fine. If they had nothing better to do than watch me live my relatively boring life, so be it.

Inside the store, I loaded the front display case with the freshly baked scones and tossed the week-old ones. Usually, I marked down the ones that were a day old, but these couldn't be salvaged for anything other than hockey pucks.

One by one I tossed them into the trash can, shouting, "Two points!" for every basket. Then I scooped up the ones that had missed and threw them away before moving to the rare book section to examine the books still on the floor. Thankfully, none were damaged beyond repair. Those that had weak bindings, I set aside to fix.

The lack of respect for literature soured my stomach. Didn't people realize books were a legacy? Something left behind for future generations?

After reshelving the rare volumes and taking the ones needing repair to the storeroom, I headed at a snail's pace for the mystery section. Someone needed to deal with the stain on the rug, and that someone would have to be me.

I rolled up the imitation Persian rug and carried it to the dumpster outside. I loved the varnished wooden floors, but they didn't lend the same hushed ambiance a rug did. I made a mental note to purchase a new rug then returned to the site of Mrs. Peabody's murder.

Taking a deep breath, I began the work of reshelving the books dislodged during the woman's struggle for her life. I hadn't cared much for her, but seeing her lying there bleeding to death had given me nightmares. No one deserved to die that way. Not even a crotchety old woman.

Who would want her dead? Lots of people had been on the sharp end of her tongue at one time or another, but murder? I shook my head. If that was the case, my grandmother would be as much of a target as Mrs. Peabody. No, it had to be something more than the woman's personality that got her killed.

Something crinkled as I replaced a book. I removed it and pulled out a slip of typewritten copy paper. I read the words out loud. " 'Do not attempt to find out who killed Mrs. Peabody.' "

What in the world?

"Let me see that."

I yelped and spun around to see Mr. Tall Dark and Handsome glaring at me, one hand outstretched. I put the paper behind me. "Who are you?"

"Brandt Thompson, the deceased's nephew. Let me see the note."

I narrowed my eyes. "How do I know you didn't leave it here?"

He sighed. "I only arrived this morning. Would you like to see my plane ticket and taxi receipt?"

Yes. "No." I handed him the note. "Don't crumple it. I need to turn it over to the police."

He scanned the warning. "Suspicious." He handed it back. "I'm going to assume you own this establishment. I'm also going to assume you found my aunt's body. So, who do you think killed her?"

"I have no idea, but it wasn't me." I folded the paper and shoved it into the pocket of my jeans. "I do intend to find out, despite this warning."

"No need to look at me that way. I didn't kill her."

"I wasn't looking at you in any particular way."

The bell over the door jingled. "Yoo hoo! The sign says closed, but it's past eight."

Pooh. I'd forgotten to flip the sign. "Excuse me. I have a customer." I ducked around the bookshelf.

More than one, actually. A horde descended on Through the Looking Glass, forming a line at the counter and filling every table. Here were the looky-loos. "Have a seat, Mr. Thompson."

"Brandt. We'll be working together to find out what happened to my aunt."

I widened my eyes. "I don't recall inviting you to help."

He crossed his arms. The button-up shirt he wore strained at the seams. "I wasn't asking."

"Good morning, everyone." Grandma sailed into the store, her arms laden with boxes of scones. "Be right with you. But. . ." She arched a brow. "If you aren't here to purchase something, leave. We don't have time for nonsense." She shrugged when no one left.

Brandt chuckled. "Is she always like this?"

"Yes." I excused myself and headed to the back room, which served as breakroom, stockroom, and my office. I called Detective Mitchell, told him about the note, listened to his lecture about not getting involved, and bit my tongue so I didn't sound snippy. "This should prove I'm not the killer."

"It proves nothing, Miss Swanson. Almost everyone in this town has access to a computer and a printer. I'll send someone over to fetch the note. Who has touched it besides you?"

"Mrs. Peabody's nephew, Brandt Thompson."

"We'll need his fingerprints. Tell him not to leave your store or, better yet, have him come by the police station." *Click.*

"Which is it?" I spoke to a dead line. Fine. The detective could do his own bossing around of Mrs. Peabody's nephew.

When I returned to the front, Grandma laughed at something Brandt said. Her eyelashes fluttered like hummingbird wings.

Catching sight of me, her grin widened. "You've met this gorgeous hunk of man?"

"I have." I moved to the register to ring up a purchase of romance novels.

"Then you know he's going to help us."

"So he says." I smiled at the customer. "Thank you. Come again."

Mrs. Winston approached the register. "Do the police have any clues?"

"No, ma'am." I took the book of devotions from her hand. "Will this be all?"

"I was perusing your rare books, hoping to find the one allegedly stolen from Mrs. Peabody."

I stiffened. I didn't recall reshelving that book. Had Detective Mitchell taken it? Had the killer? "I'm sorry. If I find it, I'll give you a call. In the meantime, I can try and find another copy."

"No, I want that one." She gave a stiff smile and marched from the store.

If it was an autographed copy she wanted, I was sure I could, eventually, run across another one. Perhaps she merely wanted it because of the circumstances. The murder of Mrs. Peabody could increase the book's value in the eyes of the town's residents. Sad, but true.

I excused myself again and called Detective Mitchell back. "Did one of your officers remove a book from my store? The one Mrs. Peabody said was hers?"

"No. We weren't able to locate it. I planned on asking you about the book."

"I have no idea where it is."

Not only had the killer gotten away with murder, he or she also had the book in question.

Find the book, find the killer.

CHAPTER FOUR

B y midday, I had a line forming out the door. Rather than a feeling of elation, sadness engulfed me at the idea that people had flocked to my store out of morbid curiosity. Most of them headed straight for the rare book section or the mystery section, where a faint bloodstain could still be detected on the wood planks.

I leaned my elbow on the counter, resting my chin in my hand. "I really need to get someone in here to redo the floors and then order a new rug."

"We can use the rug from our dining room at home in the meantime," Grandma said. "It won't stop folks from wandering down that aisle, but it will cover up the stark reminder of what happened."

"That's a great idea." I forced a smile.

"I'll head home now. Be back in a jiffy." She bustled from the store, car keys jangling in her hand.

"So what's our first move?" Brandt, scone in hand and a bit of cream dotting his upper lip, leaned on the counter.

"What do you mean?" I fought the urge to wipe away the cream.

"To find my aunt's killer and get her book back." He shrugged and grinned. "I heard you asking the detective if he had the book, which means it must have disappeared."

I frowned. "You eavesdropped on my conversation?"

"Sweetheart, everyone in this store did the same."

Was there no privacy in this town? I sighed. "I'm keeping my eyes and ears open."

"What about suspects?" He grabbed a napkin and wiped his mouth.

"Other than me? There aren't any. Well, maybe you." I narrowed my eyes. "What kind of relationship did you have with your aunt?"

"We weren't very close, actually." His smile faded. "She thought I was a bit of a troublemaker, but I spent most of my summers growing up with her, since my parents traveled a lot. I think she meant more to me than I did to her. No." He shook his head. "That isn't true. She left me everything. . .including the missing book. I suppose she cared more than she let on."

"You want the book back."

"And justice served. Since you need to clear your name, we have a somewhat common goal."

True, but I wasn't ready to fully trust him yet.

A tall, thin man with round glasses entered the store. Oliver Dickinson, town artist and eccentric who rarely ventured from his house on the hill. After a stoic glance around the store, he made a beeline for the rare books. A few minutes later, he approached the counter. "Do you have a signed copy of *What Life Is Made For*?"

"No, I'm sorry."

His brow furrowed. "Who purchased it, might I ask?"

"It's disappeared."

His brows rose almost to his hairline. "That is a pity."

"I might be able to find another copy, if you don't mind waiting."

"No, I wanted that one."

What made Mrs. Peabody's copy so special? "You're the second person this morning asking for that very book. What's the attraction?"

A sly smile stretched his thin lips. "A macabre interest. Not many people are killed over a book."

"We don't know that my aunt was murdered over that book." Brandt narrowed his eyes. "Could be a coincidence."

"Do you really believe that?" I asked.

"I'd like to purchase *What Life Is Made For*." Another man rushed into the store. "I'm an avid book collector, and I must have this one. Name is Roger Mulberry."

His name meant nothing to me. I repeated the spiel about the book being gone.

He glanced at Mr. Dickinson. "A book thief runs among us."

"Let's not forget poor Mrs. Peabody," I said.

"Oh, yes, of course. Sad." Mulberry shook his head and pulled a business card from his pocket. "Please call me if you find the book."

"I was here first." Dickinson crossed his arms.

"Actually, someone else asked first." I set the card next to the cash register.

"Then we'll simply bid for it." Mulberry grinned. "May the best person win." He spun on his heel and marched from the store.

I shot a curious look at Brandt. When Dickinson stormed after the other man, I asked, "What is it about that book?"

"I never put much stock in it, but my aunt always said that the book had clues to a treasure map written somewhere inside. Maybe something the author wrote in the margins? Or something in the text itself? She wasn't very clear, but I can see how people heard those rumors and thought it was something specific to her copy."

I gasped. "A treasure map?"

He nodded. "She said the author, Victor Browning, was a good friend of my uncle's and told him about the clues as Victor was dying of cancer. There's never been any evidence of this being true, but it could be why these people are dying to get their hands on the book. Oh, and supposedly with the treasure, or maybe it *is* the treasure, is a list of town founders and their secrets. Maybe that's why people want to get their hands on it?" He wiggled his eyebrows.

I'd lived in Hickory Hills my whole life and had never heard this particular rumor. "That would explain the interest." And a good reason someone might have killed Mrs. Peabody. "We need to find that book."

"Where did you have it last?"

"On the shelf." I sighed. At least I thought so. Could I have put it somewhere else? I had been upset over the confrontation with Mrs. Peabody. "I'll dig around once the store is closed."

"I'll stick around and help."

Right. What would happen if I found the book? Would I be the next victim? I narrowed my eyes at him. How badly did he really want the book?

"Why are you looking at me as if I'd kill for that book?" He tilted his head. "I don't need it, Amber. Not for the money anyway. Like I said, I want to find out what happened to my aunt."

He sounded sincere, but I wasn't totally buying his innocent act. I needed to find the book on my own and turn it over to Detective Mitchell.

"Hey, handsome." Grandma waved from the door. "Come help me with this carpet."

He rushed to assist her. The second he was gone, I raced to the storeroom. If I had set the book somewhere, it would be in there.

I hadn't had but a minute or two to search before I heard Brandt's and Grandma's voices. With a heavy exhale, I joined them in the mystery section.

They'd spread the rug over the bloodstain while several customers looked on, snapping pictures with their cell phones. I shook my head and returned to the counter where a line had formed.

"I heard Mrs. Peabody died with a scone in her hand," one lady said. "And that she'd been poisoned with cyanide."

"I heard that too," another said. "But I'm sure it was the knife in the chest that killed her."

"A combination of both, I'd say." The first one slapped money on the table. "I'll take the same scone Mrs. Peabody had."

"That was strawberry cream, and we're sold out." I handed her back the money.

"Can I place an order for six to pick up tomorrow?" She set the money down again.

"Yes, ma'am." I wrote her a receipt.

"Make that the same for me." The other woman handed me money. "Minus the cyanide."

The two cackled like hens.

"Mrs. Peabody was not poisoned by eating one of our scones." I crossed my arms. "Please, don't spread this ridiculous rumor any further."

"Well, I heard—"

"We don't care what you heard." Grandma glared. "You've placed your orders, now move on. There's a line forming."

They looked back to see one person behind them. Each of them tossed their coifed, silver hair and marched from the store.

"You're too nice, Amber."

"I'm doing business, Grandma."

"We don't need that kind of business."

Actually, we do. I glanced up as the local delivery man entered the store.

"More books?" He grinned.

"Yes, thanks." I signed for the delivery, taking little notice of the next customer to enter. Only that he'd been there the day Mrs.

Peabody died and had browsed the rare books. Wait a minute. I paused in opening the box.

The man strolled down the mystery aisle, then the rare books, then the mystery aisle again before tossing a smile and a wave in my direction and leaving the store.

"Very curious." I watched until he'd crossed the street.

"What?" Brandt followed my gaze.

"He came in on opening day, looked around, took books off the shelf, flipped through them, and left without putting them back. What is he looking for? He searched every section. Most people go to either new releases or the shelves with the genre they want to read."

"He doesn't say?"

I shook my head. "My guess is he's looking for the same book the others are." I really needed to find that book. "Of course, lots of people came in out of curiosity that first day, but he seemed to be looking for something in particular. Almost like he was on a mission."

"After the store closes, ask Brandt to help you with something at the house," I whispered to Grandma. "I need some alone time to look for something."

"I guess I could make something up."

She glanced over her shoulder to where Brandt browsed through the true crime section. "He's too much of a gentleman to say no to his grandma."

"Whatever you think up, make it convincing."

When the last customer left at five o'clock on the dot, I flipped the sign on the door to CLOSED. Grandma asked Brandt to follow her home and check for a foul smell coming from the gutters.

I ducked my head to hide a smile. He gave a slow nod then called to me that he'd be back to help me search as soon as he could.

With a wave after them, I locked the door and skedaddled to the storeroom. *Think, Amber.* What happened after Mrs. Peabody stormed out?

I'd set the book on the counter then started cleaning up. I'd been upset and acting on autopilot. Then I'd shelved the rest of the books from the shipment I'd gotten in earlier. It must have gotten mixed up in those.

Some mysteries, a couple of romances. . . I made my way to the new romance releases, since that was the only section I hadn't searched for the book in.

Voilà! At the back of the shelf was Mrs. Peabody's copy of *What Life Is Made For.*

I closed the blinds on the front window before settling into a chair to start flipping through the pages of the book, looking for handwritten notes. I made sure to look at every page, in between lines, all around the margins. I couldn't find anything. So were all the people who wanted this particular copy wasting their time trying to get their hands on it when they could just use any copy?

I carried the book to the storeroom and made photocopies of the pages so Brandt and I would each have them to dig through. After I finished, I slipped the book in a desk drawer for safekeeping, then headed out the back door with the photocopies, locking the door behind me. The book should be safe until morning. I really needed to find a place to lock it up.

At the house, I exited my car to see Brandt on a ladder. With a gloved hand, he pulled a dead bird from the gutter.

"See, Amber? I didn't have to lie. There was a smell." Grandma clapped.

Brandt climbed down the ladder and faced me. "Why would she have to lie?"

CHAPTER FIVE

U h. . .lie?" Busted. Why couldn't my grandmother keep her mouth shut? I shot a glare in her direction.

Rather than look ashamed, she held out an empty grocery bag for Brandt to drop the dead bird in. "I'll take care of this. Thank you."

Brandt crossed his arms as she went around the corner of the house. "Yes, lie. I would've come help without a falsehood. You didn't want me to help you search, did you? Well? Did you find the book?"

I glanced around to make sure no one was in hearing distance. "I did. Come in the house." No sense continuing the lie.

Since I'd made two copies, I led Brandt to the kitchen table and handed him a set. "I left the actual book in the store, but here are copies. I found the book in the wrong spot. I've already looked through it for anything handwritten. Nothing." After locating two notebooks and pencils, I slid one of each across the table. "Happy reading."

"Not my favorite pastime normally, but this should be interesting." He sat.

"I saw you reading in the store." How could anyone not enjoy reading?

"Passing the time." He bent over the photocopied pages, pencil poised in his right hand.

"Tomorrow I'd like to question the three people who are so interested in this book." I turned to the first chapter and started reading. It wasn't long before my eyes started to glaze over.

"Coffee!" Grandma set a mug in front of each of us. "I'll get supper going. Tuna casserole. Then I'll start reading the pages you're finished with. What are we looking for?"

"Clues to a treasure," I muttered.

"Such fun!" She bustled to the fridge and pulled out a ready-to-cook casserole. "I love treasure hunts. Remember that time the town had a scavenger hunt on the Fourth of July? Your aunt won, Brandt. But then, she'd been the one to come up with most of the hints. What a ruckus that was."

"Doesn't seem fair," he murmured.

"Nothing in the rules said she couldn't play. If anyone could find a loophole, your aunt could." She slid the casserole into the oven. "I've got forty-five minutes." She sat next to me and pulled over the pages I'd already read.

Silence filled the room until the timer on the oven dinged.

I jerked then rolled my head on my aching shoulders. "Maybe we should quit for the night. Pick this back up tomorrow after the store closes."

"I can keep reading tomorrow." Brandt rubbed his hands down his face then narrowed his eyes at me. "Unless you don't want me to."

I didn't but couldn't see a way to say no. "That's fine."

"Doesn't sound fine. I'll compromise and read at the store so you can keep an eye on me."

"Nonsense," Grandma said. "Amber trusts you, don't you, sweetie?" She retrieved the casserole and dished out three servings.

No. I nodded.

"So I don't think this is about gold or anything." She set a plate in front of Brandt. "It's more about secrets. I've made a list of every name mentioned so far. It doesn't state their secret, yet, but everyone has them."

"Agreed. It isn't about gold." I sniffed the food in front of me. My stomach rumbled, and I dug in.

The next morning I carried fresh scones through the back door of the shop and headed for the display counter. I froze.

Books lay tossed here and there. Shelves toppled against each other. Chairs and tables lay on their sides. I dropped the box on the counter and made a mad dash to the storeroom. The destruction there made my stomach roll.

I searched for Mrs. Peabody's book. It was gone.

"Whoa." Brandt came up behind me. "Let me guess. We no longer have the book."

"It looks that way. I need to call Detective Mitchell." A sob lodged in my throat.

All my dreams lay at my feet. Nothing had gone right since the day I flipped the sign on the door to open the first time. A woman dead, a book stolen, and there were no suspects other than me.

I would say the chaos in my store proved my innocence, but I could have done it in order to take the suspicion off myself. At least that's what I would believe if I were a police officer. I pulled my cell phone from the pocket of my jeans and dialed Detective Mitchell, who promised to be there within ten minutes.

"Don't touch anything," Brandt said as I reached for a box. "The detective needs to see things as we found them. Plus, the culprit might have left fingerprints."

"Right." How could I have forgotten?

I stared at my trembling hands. Stress. That's what made me forget common sense. With a heavy exhale, I returned to the front of the store to wait for the detective. I could at least refill the display case with scones. Not that I expected any customers. The detective would once again call my store a crime scene.

A rap on the door announced the detective's arrival. Brandt let him in and introduced himself.

"Interesting." The detective arched a brow.

"Why?" Brandt frowned. "I'm here to settle my aunt's affairs. Nothing strange about that."

"Maybe, maybe not." Detective Mitchell motioned for me to have a seat and righted a table and two chairs. "I'll be with you in a minute, Mr. Thompson. Please wait in the reading section." He returned his attention to me. "You know the drill, Miss Swanson."

I recounted everything since entering the store that morning, leaving out that I'd made photocopies of the book. "So...it's gone."

"It's quite possible that it's buried in this mess, but you're probably right." The bell on the door jingled. "This store is closed for the day," he said to the two women in the doorway.

The women glanced around with wide eyes then backed from the store. The news would be all over town within the hour.

"What are you keeping from me, Miss Swanson?" He gave a tight-lipped smile.

I told him about the rumors. "I guess that might be a reason to commit murder. Either way, it's obvious I'm not the killer."

"Things are looking better for you." He jerked his head to where Brandt waited. "What do you know about the nephew?"

"Only that he's been left everything by his aunt, including the book." Had Brandt broken into the store after leaving my house last night? He might believe it would take suspicion off him. No, it didn't make sense. Especially since he had a set of the photocopies. I told the detective about the three people who had come into the store wanting Mrs. Peabody's book in particular.

"Hmm. Folks are going to gather here, ma'am. Mostly out of curiosity. They'll be talking. I want you to tell us everything you hear, no matter how trivial it might seem." He stood. "Under no circumstances do I want you out there playing gumshoe." With a stern look, he headed for Brandt.

Whatever. If he thought I was going to sit back and allow my store to become a crime scene time and time again, he had another think coming. This was my dream, my livelihood. I needed this crime solved in order to resume business as I envisioned. "Can I straighten up?"

"Not until the crime scene investigators have finished their work," he called over his shoulder. "Then you can open the door. You won't hear anything if you aren't open."

Very true. A small victory at least. I returned to my seat. Three hours later, the crime scene techs had taken photographs and dusted for prints. By now, my grandmother had joined me and watched the proceedings with interest. When everyone had left but me, Brandt, and her, she stood and started righting tables.

A line had formed outside, faces plastered to the window. I flipped the sign to OPEN and went to reshelve books.

Brandt helped. "I'm sorry my aunt's book has caused you so much distress."

"It isn't your fault, but thanks." I worked on the rare books first. One poor Charles Dickens volume now had a loose spine. I set it aside for repair. "It's good for business, I guess."

"Unfortunate advertising."

"That it is." While I loved seeing all the people in my store, I wished it was under different circumstances. "Are you a suspect now?"

"Number one." He grinned. "No worries. I can handle the pressure. Since I'm innocent of any wrongdoing, they'll clear me soon enough. I guess you're off the hook."

I nodded and took the book he handed me. "You didn't say anything about the photocopies, did you?"

"Absolutely not. We won't find out anything if those are taken away."

By the time we'd finished reshelving books and getting the store to rights, Grandma had sold out of scones again. We'd even sold a few books, customers snatching them from the floor before Brandt and I could put them back where they belonged.

I headed for the storeroom. By the time I finished in there, it was time to close up shop. Questioning my top three suspects would have to wait until tomorrow. Hopefully, Grandma could handle the store on her own. Time was of the essence if things were going to return to normal.

I fixed myself a cup of tea and sat at one of the tables in front, not quite ready to go home. The thought of putting a cot in the storeroom occurred to me, but the book had already been stolen.

Besides, if I'd been there, I might have suffered the same fate as Mrs. Peabody.

CHAPTER SIX

L ord, watch over Amber as she ventures out on a fool's quest."
I frowned at my grandmother's prayer. She didn't have a
problem watching the store for me, but she didn't like the fact I'd
spend my day questioning suspects. "Amen, and put a guard on
my grandmother's tongue so she doesn't alienate our customers."
I grinned and opened my eyes.

"You shouldn't be snarky in your prayers." She glared.

"I was being completely honest." Spotting Brandt's car outside,
I grabbed my bag containing a notebook and pen then rushed
out the door.

"Where to first?" Brandt pulled the car away from the curb.

"The library. It shouldn't be full this early in the morning." I
hoped. The last thing I wanted was for someone to overhear what
we were doing and tattle to Detective Mitchell. "Our suspects are
Mrs. Winston, Oliver Dickinson, Roger Mulberry, and the mystery
man who's come into the store a couple of times."

"His name is Rupert Kirkland. I did some digging." He flashed
a grin. "Add a woman named Adelaide Morrison to the list. I
overheard at the restaurant last night someone saying she's been
asking around about my aunt's book."

"Morrison is one of the founding names Grandma wrote down." In fact, all of our suspects' names were. We were on to something about the secrets we had yet to dig up. "It'll take all day to question these folks."

"I've nowhere to be."

"No job?"

"Self-employed." He grinned. "I own a chain of mechanic shops. The managers can handle things for a while."

"Mechanic? Really?" He didn't look like a grease monkey.

"Vintage cars, mostly. I guess I share a love of old things with my aunt. My favorite possession is a 1967 green metallic Corvette convertible. Maybe I'll give you a ride sometime."

"That would be awesome. Where do you live?"

"Seattle, but I'm thinking of relocating. I like this little town nestled in the Ozark Mountains of Arkansas. It's quaint. Plus, I wouldn't have a mortgage now that I own my aunt's Victorian."

True. "It's a nice place to live. Murder isn't a common occurrence here."

"Good to know." He parked near the library entrance.

The hush of the place greeted us. No soft murmurs, no excited squeals of children being read to, only the peace that came from an empty building filled with adventures.

I glanced around for the librarian. "She must be in her office," I whispered. "It's this way."

I led him past the restrooms to a door that had the word LIBRARIAN etched in gold. I paused before knocking and pressed my ear to the door.

"It's not going to be that easy," I heard Mrs. Winston say. "The book isn't in the store. If I did take it, do you think I'd tell you? Not until you've paid the deposit, I wouldn't. I'm not the only one searching for this, you know?"

I motioned for Brandt to join me. The scent of his woodsy cologne as he leaned close wrapped around me like a warm hug from the forest. My gaze locked with his coffee-colored one, and I swallowed against a suddenly dry throat.

The door yanked open, and I stumbled a few feet toward a frowning Mrs. Winston.

She crossed her arms. "Eavesdropping on my telephone conversations?" Her brows shot to the line of her severely pulled-back hair. "I do hope you heard enough, you snoop."

"Not really." I cleared my throat. "You have a buyer for a book you don't have in your possession? Sounds suspicious."

"It's not." She shrugged. "I fully intended to have the book in hand to resell...at a profit, mind you. Now I've got to keep looking."

"The book might have something you don't want to come out?" I arched a brow.

"And what would that be, silly girl?"

"Secrets." My smile widened. "Maybe something you don't want out in the open."

"You have a very active imagination." She shoved past me and headed for the counter, where a woman with an armload of books waited. "I'm busy, Amber. Move along."

"Who's been around long enough to know these secrets?" Brandt asked when we returned to the car. "If we could find out who has the biggest thing to hide, we might find my aunt's killer."

I chewed the inside of my lip. "I suppose there might be someone in the nursing home who would know. Let me call my grandmother while you drive to Roger Mulberry's house."

"That would most likely be Ingrid Olson," Grandma said. "Hickory Hills's oldest resident. She has all her faculties, so what she would have to tell you wouldn't be too much nonsense."

"Thanks." I ended the call and wrote Ingrid's name in my notebook. "Should we visit her before all the others?"

Brandt shrugged. "Since we're already at Mulberry's, we might as well see what we can find out before heading to the nursing home."

"Sounds good." I exited the car and marched to the front door of the small ranch-style home with pristine white aluminum siding and a green metal roof. I glanced at an immaculate flower bed built along the front.

Mr. Mulberry stepped outside before I had a chance to knock. "You found the book?"

"Sorry, no."

"Then what are you doing here?" He frowned at me then Brandt. "I'm a busy man."

"I'd like to look at your book collection," I said, thinking fast. "Maybe purchase one or two from you."

"They aren't for sale." The crease lines on his forehead deepened. "I'm looking to add to my collection, not take away from it. Rather than bothering me, you should be looking for that book."

"I might run across another volume."

"I don't want any other than the one owned by Ada Peabody."

"Why?" I tilted my head. "Because of the rumors?"

"What rumors?"

"That it holds clues to a treasure."

"Nonsense." He stepped back into the house. "Don't return unless you have the book in hand." He slammed the door.

"That told us nothing." Brandt headed to the car.

It could be that we were on the wrong track. Maybe these suspects did simply want the book because of the macabre way it had become available. But... Hold on. I'd purchased the book online.

I dug my phone from my pocket and searched until I found the receipt. "I got the book from Adelaide's Precious Books. I bet that's the woman you mentioned." Which put her name at the top of my suspect list.

"Now, we're getting somewhere." He grinned. "Her address is on the outskirts of town. The nursing home is on the way. We can hit the others on the way back. Maybe after lunch."

The receptionist in the nursing home seemed surprised to see visitors for Ingrid. "The sweet thing hasn't had anyone visit her in ages. She's outlived her family, other than a niece who lives in California. She doesn't make it to town much. I'm sure she'll be thrilled to see you. It's almost lunchtime. Why don't you head to the cafeteria, and I'll bring her to you?"

"That sounds great." Brandt grinned.

We chose a round table for four and settled in to wait. Delicious aromas from the buffet drifted our way as a line of residents started to form. A few minutes later, the receptionist wheeled a frail woman in our direction.

"These lovely people are having lunch with you, Ingrid. I'll go fix you a plate." She patted the woman's shoulders. "Why don't the two of you get your food? You'll have plenty of time to visit."

Once we had our food and sat down, Ingrid smiled. "Now, tell me how I got so lucky to have the two of you visit."

I told her about the book and showed her the list of suspects. "Do you know these families?"

"Of course. Their grandparents founded this town."

"Do you know if they harbored any secrets?" I dug into my Salisbury steak.

"Dear, everyone has secrets. Especially this group. The story goes that they all ran moonshine back in the day. Feuds were fought over land. That's how they got their money to start Hickory Hills. An unscrupulous bunch if I ever saw one. Why do you want to know?"

I told her about Mrs. Peabody and the book's disappearance. "Did any of them ever kill someone?"

"Folks dropped like flies in the day. If you got in their way..." She ran a finger across her throat. "Quite the scandal. No one was ever convicted, but folks learned to stay out of this group's way."

I traded a shocked look with Brandt.

"It appears as if they might have killed again because of this book," he said. "I'm Ada's nephew."

"Sorry for your loss, son." She speared some peas with her fork. "Those days are long gone though. I don't know why those still alive would care much about secrets. Who cares about moonshine and land feuds nowadays? Now, this one..." She tapped Adelaide's name. "Her grandmother, Minerva, and Ada's grandmother both wanted the same man, a salesman named Peabody. That was probably the biggest scandal of them all.

"The two of them acted outrageous, trying to outdo each other. Ada's grandmother won out though. Oh, she was a beauty. She ran off with the man and got hitched. Maybe Adelaide killed your aunt for revenge."

Sounded far-fetched to me. "That would all be water under the bridge by now, wouldn't it?"

She shook her head. "Not considering he'd given a big diamond ring to Adelaide's grandmother then took it back and gave it to Ada's. Like I said, scandalous."

I still couldn't wrap my head around someone killing because of a long-ago fight over a man. There had to be more to the story, and I said as much.

"Think what you will, but while you're searching, I'd look for that ring. It wasn't on Ada's finger when they buried her. It's worth more than an old book."

We needed to have a serious talk with Adelaide Morrison.

We thanked Ingrid for her time with promises to come back and see her then returned to Brandt's car. "This took a different turn than I expected." I clicked my seat belt into place. "A love triangle from the past seems so...out there."

"Maybe it's all about the ring. I wasn't looking through the book for mention of a ring."

"Neither was I." When I returned to the photocopied pages later that evening, I'd be searching with a new eye. "We have two mysteries on our hands."

"Want to help me go through my aunt's things later?" He drove toward their next destination. "Maybe there's something in her. . .my house that will tell us about this ring. I have to warn you though. My aunt had a lot of stuff."

"Sure." I loved digging through other people's things. "I'll bring some empty boxes from the store so you can have keep, donate, and toss piles."

A shadow crossed his eyes. "I won't be keeping much. What she has isn't my style, but there are some valuable antiques."

I put a hand on his arm. "I really am sorry about your aunt. With all that's going on, you really haven't had time to process her death."

"I'll do that when we find her killer."

CHAPTER SEVEN

After stopping at the store to grab boxes, we drove to the next name on our list.

Oliver Dickinson lived in a small redbrick house in the center of town. The shutters and front door were a glossy black, contrasting with the brick. Well, the man was an artist, or so people said.

"I think Ingrid will be our most successful interview." I hitched my bag on my shoulder and raised the lion head door knocker.

"I agree, but we can't leave anyone out." Brandt stepped forward as the door opened and introduced us with a smile.

Dickinson's face darkened. "Unless you have what I'm looking for, I don't have time. I'm in the middle of a sculpture." Mud covered his hands and wrists.

"We'd like to ask you a few questions, if you don't mind." I pasted on a smile.

"Like I said, I don't have the time." He started to close the door.

I stuck my foot in the way. "Are you worried there might be some family secrets revealed in that book, Mr. Dickinson?"

"Why would you think that?"

"We heard about a moonshine ring your ancestors might've been involved in."

He laughed. "That kind of notoriety would only help the sale of my art, not hinder it." He cut his laughter short and narrowed his eyes. "The two of you shouldn't be nosing around. Someone won't like it." He glanced at my foot.

"Who might that someone be?" I removed my foot.

"Do you feel as if your life might be in danger?" Brandt asked.

The man's eyes shot wide. "That's an out-of-the-blue question."

Brandt shrugged. "There's already been one death. The rumor goes that the book contains clues to a treasure. Do you know what that means?"

"The treasure the book might speak of is simply the fact that it is the last of its kind in existence. At least that we know of. Only a few were printed, as I'm sure you're aware. Most disappeared a long time ago. The book is a rare find, indeed."

Could that really be it? These folks simply wanted the book because there were no more, and the real mystery revolved around the ring?

"Do you know anything about a ring and a love triangle between my aunt's grandmother and Adelaide Morrison's grandmother?" Brandt tilted his head.

"No one has seen that ring in ages, but yes, my grandfather spoke of it once and how those two women tore this town apart. Now, please excuse me." He slammed the door.

"Did you see the gleam in his eye when you mentioned the ring?" I asked. "We've been following the wrong trail. He definitely knows about the feud and the ring."

"Looks that way. Let's see what Kirkland has to say, get to my aunt's house, then study those pages again. This time, let's look for any mention of a ring."

"Should we tell Detective Mitchell about this latest development?"

"Not yet. Let's find some actual proof first. Whether this is about the ring or not doesn't take away from the fact my aunt was murdered. Let the detective focus on that for now. I'm still not cleared as a suspect."

Kirkland wasn't home. A neighbor said he hadn't seen the man in a couple of days.

Our last stop before heading to Brandt's was Adelaide's. The fortysomething woman who could pass for late thirties stood from where she knelt next to a flowerbed and wiped dirt from the knees of the pads she wore. "I'm sorry. I wasn't expecting visitors, or I'd have cleaned myself up."

If stylish capris and a fitted top didn't classify as cleaned up, I didn't know what did. Even wearing kneepads and gardening gloves, the woman made me feel underdressed in jeans and a flowered blouse.

Brandt once again introduced us. "We heard you were looking for a book my aunt used to have."

"I am." She smiled, removing her gloves and tossing them on the porch railing. "I love old things."

"Have you heard about the feud between your grandmother and Mrs. Peabody's?" I arched a brow.

She gave a musical laugh. "Everyone knows that old story."

"Do you know where the ring that was given to the long-ago Mrs. Peabody went?"

"Why, I assumed her granddaughter, the current Mrs. Peabody, would have it." Her smile faltered. "Is it missing too?"

She glanced at Brandt, who nodded. "I don't think I've ever seen my aunt wear such a thing," he said.

"Too expensive, most likely. If the stories are true, that ring is worth a fortune. I do hope you find your missing things." The smile remained on her face, but her eyes hardened. "So much loss in a short time, what with your aunt, the book, and now the ring."

"Thank you," Brandt said. "We'll let you get back to your gardening."

Once we were in the car, he turned to me. "She's my number-one suspect. Did you see her gloves?"

"Yes, but I didn't see anything unusual about them."

"They were stained, and not with dirt. It looked like blood to me."

"If she killed your aunt while wearing those gloves, it would be stupid not to destroy them."

"Unless she's super confident."

Maybe, but I didn't see the woman as a killer. Still, there were murderers behind bars that no one had suspected either. "She's as good as any of the others, I suppose. We aren't any closer to finding out who killed your aunt than we were when I found her body."

"I think we are. We strongly suspect the treasure mentioned in the book to be the ring. That changes how we look at things."

"I guess." I stared out the window as we drove down Main Street toward Brandt's inherited Victorian.

The poor house looked sadly in need of a facelift. Faded, peeling gray paint. One white shutter hung on its hinges.

"I have a lot of work to do," Brandt said, cutting off the car's engine. "It'll be fun once I get started." He slid from the car and retrieved the boxes from the trunk. "Ready to work?"

As ready as I would ever be. "You should have a yard sale," I said the second I entered the cluttered house. "Lots of knickknacks and antiques that many folks would like to buy."

"That's a good idea. A lot of this furniture has little cubbies and drawers. We need to search every one then move what isn't going to stay into the parlor." Brandt motioned toward a room on our right crammed with antiques. "If I decide to stay, I'm turning this into my home office, so all of this will go. Let's start in here."

I rubbed my hands together, eager to get started. My stomach rumbled. "I'll order a pizza."

"Sounds good. I've got iced tea in the fridge." He headed for a roll-top desk. "If you see anything you want, let me know. You can have it."

"For free?" My mouth dropped open.

"Absolutely." He grinned. "I can't charge a friend. Same goes for your grandma. If you think she'd like something, take it. Like I said, I don't need the money." He opened the desk and started riffling through drawers while I ordered a mega-meat pizza.

My grandmother would love the desk he was snooping through. I snapped a photo of it and sent it to her. She responded immediately with a yes.

Since my one-thousand-square-foot house wouldn't hold much, I'd have to be picky about anything I might want. I moved to a nightstand and sifted through pens, pencils, a crocheted hankie, and a magnifying glass. No ring or clues as to who might have killed Mrs. Peabody. "Anything?"

"Nothing. How did she find out you had it?"

"I posted online the vintage and rare books I had for sale." Which was how anyone knew I had the book. I eyed the mahogany bookshelves that lined one wall. I salivated at the treasure trove. "I'll make a pile of the books I want and see whether you'll sell them to me. I won't take no for an answer. Furniture is one thing, but books are a whole other story."

He chuckled. "Okay."

Soon, I had a sizeable pile of not-so-new books. I then left Brandt to finish the parlor and headed up a curving staircase to the master bedroom. A four-poster bed took center stage, complete with a white gauzy curtain and a plush comforter.

I ran my fingers along the polished wood. I'd always wanted a bed like this, but there was no way it would fit in my small house. Nor would the matching armoire or dresser.

Feeling like I was doing something wrong, I opened the jewelry box on the top of the dresser. I didn't expect the ring to be on top. Not with it being so valuable. Mrs. Peabody had a few items that looked real, including a fake diamond ring, but most were fashionable costume jewelry.

I lifted the jewelry box and searched for a false bottom. Not finding one, I gave a sheepish grin at my reflection then moved to the closet.

Shoeboxes lined the top shelf. Since a lot of people used them for more than storing shoes, I pulled them down one at a time to search through. Some did indeed hold shoes, some tax papers, and one, odds and ends. After being careful to return each exactly as I'd found it, I went through the woman's clothes.

In the pocket of a black knee-length coat, I found a black velvet box. Inside, the largest diamond ring I'd ever seen winked up at me. "Brandt!"

Footsteps thundered up the stairs. He skidded to a halt, sliding on an area rug in front of the closet.

I held up the box. "Found it."

"Wow." He took it. "I need to put that in a safety deposit box asap."

"There's a fake diamond ring—it's pretty realistic—in the jewelry box. Let's switch them out in case someone comes looking for this one."

"Like a trap?"

"Exactly. We're stirring things up with all our questions. Someone will come looking."

"What happens when they find out we duped them?" He arched a brow. "They could come for us."

"And we'll catch them!"

He sighed. "Sounds dangerous. I don't want you, or me, to end up like my aunt."

"But we'll be careful. Your aunt didn't see her death coming." This would work. I knew it would.

"Okay, for now, but if things get too serious, I'm going to the detective." He switched out the rings and then handed me the box with the fake one.

"Let's see if my crazy idea will work to draw the killers into the open." I stuffed it back in the coat pocket and moved the clothes to hang as they had earlier.

The doorbell rang downstairs.

"That would be the pizza." I rushed to answer the door, my stomach's protests over lack of sustenance increasing.

A young man wearing a perplexed look stood there. "Here's your pizza. And here's a note that was tacked to your door."

A sheet of notebook paper rested on top of the pizza box. In glaring black marker were written the words, *Stop snooping or you'll end up like Mrs. Peabody.*

CHAPTER EIGHT

After showing the note to Brandt, I contacted Detective Mitchell, who arrived in less than half an hour.

He stared at the note after hearing our story. "A ring? This is about a ring?"

"It's one doozy of a ring, Detective." Brandt held up a slice of pizza. "Want some?"

Mitchell shook his head. "Where is this ring?" He eyed Brandt then me.

I shrugged and tried to look innocent.

"Miss Swanson, where is this ring?"

"Fine. Brandt has it in his pocket. We put a fake ring in the closet so we can catch the culprit red-handed when they come to steal it."

"That's the dumbest thing I've ever heard. Give me the ring." He held his hand out to Brandt.

Brandt frowned and pulled the ring from his pocket. He handed it to the detective.

I shot him an apologetic look. Since the detective had yet to focus on a suspect other than myself, mostly cleared, and Brandt, not cleared of suspicion, I didn't know how much I could trust him. I'd read plenty about dirty cops and prayed he wasn't one of them.

Crossing my arms, I glared at Detective Mitchell. "I'm sure Brandt would like this returned to him, since it's part of his inheritance."

"He'll get it back." The detective pocketed the ring box. "The two of you need to stop nosing around. I've had complaints from the people on your list that you're harassing them. Don't make me lock you up." He spun and marched from the house.

"Did he just threaten to arrest us?" I widened my eyes at Brandt.

"Sounded that way." He took another bite of pizza.

How could the man eat at a time like this? "Doesn't that bother you? We can't stop searching for your aunt's killer."

"I don't intend to. We'll have to be more discreet is all." He reached for another piece. "Aren't you going to eat?"

"I had a slice."

"That's all?" He shrugged and kept eating.

"We should get back to work. I have some things to do at the store after closing." I didn't like leaving the tallying up of receipts to my grandmother. She usually rounded things up and left the money in the cash register, saying the lock on the store door should deter any thieves. That was proven false. Also, she'd like to know the latest developments.

"Okay. I can work on the rest later. We can finish up in the parlor, unless you want to go now?"

Since we'd found what I'd come for, I nodded. "If you don't mind."

"Not at all." He tossed the empty pizza box in the garbage and followed me outside, locking the house behind us. "The people we've questioned wasted no time tattling to the sheriff. I find that odd."

"Me too. They're wanting the attention off them and on us. One of them is the killer, Brandt."

"Don't worry. We'll catch them."

I wished I could be as confident.

"Look how much we've already discovered. That the book is only the key to the real treasure. . .the ring."

We entered a full store where a happy grandmother greeted us. "Been busy, busy, busy today. If someone asked a nosy question, I wouldn't answer unless they bought a book." She grinned.

"You didn't tell anything of importance, did you?"

"How could I? I don't know much." She smiled at the next customer. "I've been here all day while the two of you have been playing Sherlock."

"Find out anything?" the woman at the counter asked. "I can't sleep at night knowing a murderer is running loose."

"Not much, Mrs. Jones. Don't worry. The police are doing their job." I smiled and headed to the back room to check emails. Sweet. I'd sold a rare book. I grabbed a box off the top shelf, found the book, and boxed it up for tomorrow's mail.

The phone rang. When it became obvious my grandmother wasn't going to answer, I did. "Through the Looking Glass. This is Amber, how can I help you?"

"You can help by staying out of what doesn't concern you," an electronically altered voice said. "Learn a lesson from Mrs. Peabody and mind your own business."

"This is my business. She was killed in my store, and one of my inventoried books stolen."

"Heed my warning, lest you be next." *Click.*

Lest? A learned murderer, it seemed. I rushed to find Brandt and told him about the phone call.

He glanced around the store. "Can't be anyone here. No one is on their phone."

"They had plenty of time to put their phone away. It has to be someone we've questioned. It sounded like a man, but since it was altered, I can't be positive." I plopped into a plush reading chair. We'd worried someone. That meant we were getting closer. The fact that I'd received two warnings in one day, within the span of a couple of hours, chilled my blood. Someone had just threatened to kill me.

My heart rate increased, and my breath came in gasps.

"Put your head between your knees." Brandt helped me into position. "Concentrate on your breathing. Have you had panic attacks before?"

"No. But...then...no one...has wanted...to kill me...before."

"Let me get you some coffee." He rushed away, returning a few minutes later with my favorite blended mocha drink. "You'll feel better soon."

"Thank you." I waved a hand to let Grandma know I was okay.

Slowly, all the customers who'd been watching returned to their conversations. It would be all over town by morning that I'd cracked. The killer would know he or she had frightened me.

"Feeling better?" Grandma placed her hand on my forehead.

"I'm not sick." I shrank back.

"Good. Brandt, how do you feel about taking two hot ladies out for a night on the town?"

He grinned. "I wouldn't say no."

"Grandma, what are you talking about?" I narrowed my eyes.

"I've heard something delicious." She lowered her voice. "Rumor has it that Adelaide Morrison and Oliver Dickinson have been frequenting the Watering Hole most nights."

"We don't go to bars," I hissed.

"We'll order sparkling water. Let's get spiffed up and go see whether the rumor is true."

"What does this have to do with finding out who killed Mrs. Peabody?"

She looked at me as if I were dense. "They're two of our top suspects. They could be in this together. I also heard someone say that Detective Mitchell should look at the family tree of some of the people in this town. I'm still working that one out. Most folks are related in some way or another if you go back far enough."

"I'm game." Brandt stood and held out his hand. "I'd be honored to escort the two of you anywhere." His gaze warmed as it landed on me.

"Okay, but you'd better behave yourself, Grandma. Let Brandt and me take the lead on asking any questions. I don't want you in danger." I filled her in on the phone call.

"You should let the detective know about the call. If he finds out you're withholding information, it won't look good for you. Pick us up at eight, Brandt." She rushed back to the counter.

"This could be fun," Brandt said. "We can start a rumor of our own. Let folks think we're dating. They won't think so much of seeing us together so often that way."

A man darted so hard into the store, the door banged against the wall. "Robert Kirkland was found dead in his car! Right down the block."

Brandt and I sprinted in that direction with the shop customers on our heels. Red and blue flashing lights showed us the way. Officers blocked the entrance to the alley.

Detective Mitchell spotted us and came our way. "You can't go any farther."

"I got a threatening phone call," I blurted out. "I was going to call you, I promise."

He took a deep breath and released it slowly. "You're taxing my patience, Miss Swanson. Tell me about the call."

I did and then asked, "How did Kirkland die?"

"Knife to the chest while he sat reading a book. Or so it appears." He glanced back. "There's something else. I'm only telling you, since it seems you may be a target."

"Spill it." I squared my shoulders. "I can take anything you have to say." What could Kirkland's death have to do with me?

"Hold on." He returned to the entrance to the alley.

My mouth dropped open. How could he leave me hanging?

Brandt pointed. "He's bringing something back with him."

The detective carried something in a plastic baggie. "Ever seen this stationery before?"

I glanced at the page rimmed with comic books. "That's from my store. I keep it in the top drawer of my desk."

"You haven't given any to anyone?"

I shook my head. "No. How did you come across it?"

"Read it, Miss Swanson."

I glanced at Brandt then read, " 'One-by-one they fall, toppling like a tower of books. The treasure is mine. No one will get in my way.'"

I swayed against Brandt. "The killer took this." I straightened then dashed back to the store and into my office. I yanked the desk drawer open.

The pad of stationery was gone.

CHAPTER NINE

At five minutes before Brandt was due to pick us up, my hair in a messy bun, a little makeup on my face, and dressed in black skinny jeans with flats and a flouncy blue blouse, I joined Grandma downstairs. "Let's get this over with."

"You clean up nice." She grinned, dressed in slacks and a multicolored sequin jacket. "Do try to have fun, won't you? We're out for a night on the town with the added bonus of trying to solve a murder. Two murders, actually. Plus, we're being escorted by a handsome man." She opened the door to Brandt, who was wearing jeans and a black polo shirt.

"The two prettiest girls in Hickory Hills." His gaze settled on me.

Face heated, I breezed out the door. "Let's go. We get up early to make scones." Well, I didn't, but Grandma did.

I had no reason to be surly but couldn't shake the bad attitude. I hadn't dated anyone in a very long time and didn't want the town to think Brandt and I were an item if we weren't. Might not make sense to some, but there it was.

Grandma climbed into the back seat, leaving the front for me.

Brandt slid into the driver's seat and glanced my way. "You okay?"

"Yes. I have to admit that I've never been to a bar in my life." My childhood Sunday school teacher, Mrs. Hobbs, would roll over in her grave if she saw me.

"No one is going to bother you. Think of me as your guard dog." He flashed a grin.

"The handsomest guard dog ever," Grandma piped up.

Brandt laughed and drove us to the outskirts of town to the Watering Hole. The parking lot was full, and country music blared through the doors whenever anyone entered or exited.

My heart thumped in time to the beat. What if Brandt asked me to dance? I didn't know how to dance anything other than the waltz that I'd learned while playing the part of a lady-in-waiting in a fourth-grade play. I was bound to make a fool of myself somehow before the night was through.

With me on one side and Grandma on the other, Brandt escorted us inside. No one spared us more than a cursory glance. Some of the anxiety ebbed, replaced with a bit of excitement when I caught sight of Adelaide and Oliver seated at a table in the corner looking very cozy together.

I nudged Brandt.

"I see them." He led us to a table with a clear view of the lovebirds and ordered three sparkling waters from the waitress.

I turned my gaze back to the two in the corner.

"Don't be so obvious," Grandma said. "Inconspicuous, remember? You are not a good detective."

"I'm not a detective at all." I'd been thrust into this investigation. I wouldn't have gone looking for a murder case.

"Let's dance." Brandt stood and held out a hand. "Playacting, remember."

"I don't know how to dance."

"It's a two-step. I'll teach you. Just follow my lead."

"I'll hold down the fort," Grandma said.

I put my hand in his, my traitorous heart turning a somersault. Grandma clapped, and I shot her a glare, mouthing, "Stop it."

Within minutes, Brandt had me two-stepping. If I'd known how much fun country dancing could be, I would've tried it a long time ago. A grin spread across my face, fading as I spotted Grandma approaching the table with Adelaide and Oliver.

Sparkling water in hand, she joined them as if they were fast friends.

"What is she doing?" I hissed.

"Digging for clues, most likely." Brandt twirled me as the song ended. "Let her have her fun. Nothing can happen in a crowded bar."

The words had no sooner left his mouth than a fight broke out. Keeping himself between me and the two men throwing fists, he led me back to our table and scooted his chair closer to mine.

"I don't mind your grandmother sitting over there for a bit." He entwined his fingers through mine. "It's nice to have you to myself."

There went my face again. "We've spent a lot of time together lately," I said softly.

"But not to have fun."

Could he actually like me? As someone other than a person trying to clear his name?

"Here comes trouble." He jerked his head toward the entrance, where Detective Mitchell, dressed in plain clothes, stood surveying the room.

The detective frowned and marched in our direction. "Tell me you aren't investigating."

"We aren't investigating." I smiled.

"You have a smart mouth, Miss Swanson." He took a seat.

"What are you doing here?" I tilted my head.

"Same as you, most likely. Heard two of our suspects would be here. Three, if I count Mr. Thompson."

Brandt's face darkened. "You seriously still consider me a suspect?"

"Where were you about an hour ago?"

"Getting ready to pick up these two ladies?"

"What's Mrs. Swanson doing with our suspects?"

"Why are you asking, Detective?" I crossed my arms. "You should be over there questioning them instead of harassing us."

"A commotion was heard outside the library about that time." He leaned back in his chair. "Someone called 911. When law enforcement arrived, we found Mrs. Winston dead, a knife to the chest. . .same as the others."

I gasped. "My knife?"

"No, ma'am. Why would you assume so?" He quirked a brow.

"Because Mrs. Peabody was killed with my knife."

"Kirkland wasn't."

"Was there a note left again?" Brandt asked.

"Yep. On the bookstore stationery. It said 'Two down, a couple more to go.' Seems like our killer is eliminating either witnesses or the competition. It's unfortunate you don't have an alibi, Mr. Thompson."

"I do. I was with Amber. I'm not sure even I could get ready to go out for the evening, kill someone, and pick up these ladies on time."

"Maybe with careful planning you could." The detective crossed his arms and glanced up as Grandma joined us.

"Hello, Detective." She sat. "Nice of you to show up, since I've been doing your job for you."

"Do tell."

"Those two were whispering when I joined them and stopped when I sat down." Grandma grinned. "They were discussing a book, clues, and a treasure. Now, we all suspect what the treasure is, don't we?"

"I know all that, ma'am."

"Well, I bet you didn't know that Dickinson is kin to the man that Adelaide's grandmother and Ada's grandmother fought over, did you?"

"You heard all that?" His brow furrowed.

"Sure did. Not only that, but right before they stopped talking, I heard Dickinson tell Adelaide that he would marry her once he has his uncle's ring." Grandma looked very proud of herself. "After that, I joined them, and we talked about the weather and once in a while the murders, but they didn't say anything else of interest. You should put me on the force, Detective. People talk around old people. They don't expect us to comprehend much, I don't think."

"Not thinking you're capable is a grave error on their part." He stood. "Please, stay out of my investigation before the next victim is one of you."

"If you suspect Brandt, then you shouldn't be worried about us." I lifted my chin. "He wouldn't hurt us."

"Don't let down your guard, Miss Swanson." With a nod at Brandt, he left the building.

"I can't believe he still suspects me." Brandt shook his head.

"He's just getting under your skin," Grandma said. "You're the new fella in town, and your aunt was murdered. I don't think he really thinks you killed her. He's got two dead bodies—"

"Three." I filled her in on the latest.

"Three dead bodies and no solid suspects, but I bet those two over there are at the top of the list now."

"You did it, Grandma." I gave her a one-armed hug.

"They're leaving." Brandt stood. "Let's follow them."

"Yippee. A road chase." Grandma set aside her half-empty glass.

By the time we got to the car, they were pulling from the parking lot.

"Don't let them see us." Grandma jumped into the back seat.

"I know the drill." Brandt squealed the tires pulling onto the highway.

We followed them to Adelaide's house, passed by, and then parked a few houses down. Darting from shadow to shadow, we approached the house. *Lord, please don't let me see something I won't be able to forget.*

Brandt motioned to an open kitchen window. Voices drifted through the screen, beckoning us like moths. We hunkered below the windowsill.

"They weren't there to dance, Adelaide. They're on to us," Dickinson said. "I'd bet my last dollar they have that ring."

"Of course they do, Ollie. Mrs. Peabody had it, last anyone knew. With her dead, her nephew got everything. We need to get into that house." Glasses clinked.

"Tomorrow when he's at the bookstore?"

"Has to be at night. Too many nosy neighbors."

I clapped a hand over my mouth. If they broke in at night, Brandt would be there. He could be the next victim.

Grandma elbowed me hard enough to steal my breath. Her wide eyes glittered in the moonlight as she put a finger to her lips.

"Did you hear something?" Adelaide asked.

"Probably the neighbor's cat again. I'll take a look."

The three of us took off, crashing through the neighbor's hedge. Once we reached the car, Brandt sped away.

Nervous giggles escaped me. "That was close. If only we could prove what we heard."

Brandt held up his cell phone. "I recorded their conversation."

"Good man!" Grandma leaned forward and patted his shoulder. "At least one of us was thinking ahead."

"I'll call Detective Mitchell and ask him to meet us." I had some trouble pulling my phone from the pocket of my tight jeans and pulled a muscle in my shoulder when I did. I told the detective what we'd heard, listened to his lecture about us not heeding his advice, then ended the call. "He said to meet him at the station."

"This should take me off the suspect list." Brandt switched directions and headed for the police department.

Detective Mitchell met us outside, arms crossed, a glare on his face. "Let me hear."

Brandt played the recording. "If you have someone stake out my house, you should catch them."

"I'll send someone over to pick them up right now. Waiting to catch them puts you in grave danger, since I'm pretty sure you don't intend to sleep somewhere else?"

"No, sir. I've got a lot of work to do at the house." Brandt shook his head. "Besides, I'd be expecting them. The others didn't know death was coming."

"These people won't hesitate to kill again," Mitchell said. "I strongly suggest you find somewhere else to stay."

"Our place," Grandma offered.

"That would bring my trouble to your door."

"Trouble is already here," I said. "It came when they killed your aunt. Please, don't stay in your house alone." It hadn't occurred to me until that moment how much he had come to mean to me.

"Two against one, son." Grandma clapped him on the shoulder again. "Mind your elders. We've got a comfortable guest room, and I keep a gun in my nightstand."

"Heaven help us all." Mitchell marched into the police station.

"That man is wound tighter than my aunt's perm." Grandma leaned into the front seat. "He needs to have a little fun."

"Maybe when this is all over." Brandt drove us home. In the parking lot, he faced me. "Maybe I will take you up on that offer. There's nothing in my aunt's house worth dying over."

"Except you," I said.

CHAPTER TEN

Having a man seated at the breakfast table, surrounded by the aroma of freshly brewed coffee and baking scones, felt familiar yet strange. Not since my grandfather had a man sat at this table.

"This is nice," Grandma whispered in my ear as she set a cup of coffee in front of me.

"Thanks." Somehow, I needed to put a stop to her matchmaking. If something developed between me and Brandt, I wanted it to happen naturally. Not with meddling.

The doorbell rang. I froze, my gaze locking on Brandt's. No one came visiting at six a.m.

Grandma answered the door and returned with Detective Mitchell. "Would you like some coffee?"

"I never turn down coffee." He glanced at Brandt. "You stayed here last night?"

"Yes, sir." Brandt frowned.

"Likely saved your life. Someone broke into your house and ransacked the place. Morrison and Dickinson are nowhere to be found. Cars gone from both houses, doors left unlocked as if they left in a hurry." He took a seat. "We suspect they packed up and hit your place before taking off. They weren't at Miss Morrison's house when our officers got there. When you've finished your breakfast, I need you to come see if anything is missing." He took a sip of his drink. "Gotta warn you, they made a real mess. Since they've fled, we'll need to have an officer stake out your place."

Some of that mess might've been from us poking around. Hard to tell with all the possessions his aunt owned. "I'll come with you, if you want."

"I'd like that." Brandt gave me a soft smile.

"I can handle the store," Grandma said. "But it would be nice if you came in by lunchtime. We're getting quite the crowd." She grinned. "I have someone making us sandwiches now. A big hit."

"Why didn't you tell me?" I glared. "It is my store."

"You were busy." She shrugged. "Since I footed some of the money to open the place, I figured I get some say."

Fair enough.

"I'll meet you at the house." The detective finished his coffee and left.

We finished in a rush, leaving Grandma to take care of the scones. I felt a bit of remorse at leaving her to handle it all again, but the need to support Brandt when he saw the state of his home lured me more.

"This is bad." I stopped right inside the door of the old Victorian, glancing over my shoulder at the squad car out front, then back to the house.

Overturned chairs, broken picture frames, drawers upended and tossed. I followed Brandt through each room then upstairs. The master bedroom suffered the worst. Mattress slashed, clothes tossed from the closet. Every shoebox from the top shelf of the closet had been emptied on the floor.

"I'm so sorry." Tears burned my eyes.

"It'll make it easier to go through." Brandt sighed. "I'll sort things as I pick up. Don't cry. It's just stuff."

It would take a long time. "I'll help." I knew he didn't want the stuff, but seeing how callously a dead woman's things had been treated hurt.

"You have a business to run. I can't ask you to help with something of this magnitude."

"There's something in the bathroom you need to see." The detective jerked his chin in that direction.

I followed Brandt and paused at the threshold of the bathroom. In peach lipstick someone had written a warning on the mirror. *We're coming for the ring.*

We. The one word pointed to Adelaide and Dickinson.

"Maybe we should give it to them." I glanced away from the ominous words.

"Never." A muscle ticked in Brandt's jaw. "If they contact me, if they want to meet, I'll meet them gladly. Justice needs to be served, and if facing them helps the authorities catch them, then so be it."

"You'll let the authorities handle things," Detective Mitchell called from the bedroom. "Once you've determined if anything is missing, we're going to consider this a crime scene. Take what you need, Mr. Thompson. You won't be coming back for a while."

The unspoken "Until the killer is caught" hung in the air.

"I don't know all that was here, so I can't determine if anything is missing. The ring is safe with the police. That's all that matters at this point. I'll pack a few more things." He marched from his aunt's room and down the hall, leaving me alone with the detective.

"I guess there's no way of knowing where these two went?" I asked him.

He shook his head. "We've issued a BOLO. Hopefully, someone will spot one of their cars. I've got someone digging into what other property they might own. We're doing our best, Miss Swanson."

"I suppose you are." I moved to the living room and started righting furniture.

"Leave things as they are until the house is cleared, please." Mitchell frowned.

"Oh, right." I sighed, wanting to sit down and knowing I shouldn't. I moved to the front porch and lowered myself to the top step.

Adelaide and Dickinson had pulled flowers from posts and dug holes around the rosebushes. How had no one seen them?

I looked at the house next door and saw an older woman in a housedress with rollers in her hair. I stood and waved.

"That's quite the mess." She motioned to the flowerbed with her water hose.

"Did you see anyone here last night?"

"I did, but it was early this morning. I don't sleep late. Bad hips, you know?"

"Can you tell me what you saw?"

"I heard a car running and somebody talking. By the time I got to the window, I could see lights on in the house. I thought it was the nephew and didn't think much about it." She gave an apologetic smile. "I thought maybe he had a date, since there were two cars."

So far she hadn't told me anything new. "Did you hear anything the two were saying?"

"Lots of banging around at first. That's what made me suspicious. So, being the nosy woman I am, I came out here and peered in the window. Saw a man and woman trashing the place and laughing. Looked like they were up to mischief, so I called the police." She shook her head. "If they hadn't come with sirens on, they might've caught the idiots. Once they heard the sirens, though, they took off and headed west."

Detective Mitchell joined me. "You're sure it was west?"

"Yes, sir. I do know my directions. I've lived here my entire adult life." She turned off the water hose. "Sorry I can't be of more help."

"You told us which direction they went, ma'am. That's a big help." He unclipped his radio from his belt and walked off as he talked.

"You know, now that I think more on it, they mentioned Ada. Not by name, but they said the old lady had put up quite the fight. That made me quite proud of my friend." She wiped a tear from her wrinkled cheek. "She was a tough old bird."

"Yes, she was. Be careful, ma'am. If these two know you called the police. . ."

"I've got a gun, and I know how to use it. They won't get anything on me." Some of her friendliness vanished. "I don't know what this town is coming to. It all started with your bookstore, you know? We were doing just fine with a library."

Ouch. "Most folks seem to enjoy my store." Now that their morbid curiosity had been satisfied and they'd tried the scones. "Books are never a bad idea."

"I like books same as the next person, dear. But it was a book that got Ada killed." With a stern look the type a schoolteacher would give an unruly student, she went into her house.

"None of this is your fault." Brandt stepped onto the porch. "With these two wanting the book and the ring, it would've happened in another way."

"Yeah, but it didn't." I sniffed. "I'm so sorry for getting you into this."

He dropped his bag and wrapped me in a hug. "Like I said, it would've happened anyway."

"But who originally took the book and sold it to me?" I'd researched the person and found nothing but an online book reseller. I'd given the information to the authorities, and they'd come up with a dead end. "Whoever originally stole it found out about the ring!" I stepped back. "That's how the whole thing started. It has to be."

"Dickinson," we said in unison.

"He collects books. He would've known about my aunt's volume."

"No, Mulberry was the collector. Dickinson is an artist. He must've stolen it from Mulberry."

"Or stole it first. We won't know until we catch him."

"How?" I frowned.

He grinned. "I'm working on an idea. I'll let you know when I have the kinks out." He lowered his voice, his gaze on Mitchell next to the detective's car. "I grabbed my aunt's stationery. Do you think your grandmother will write a letter if I dictate one to her?"

"Absolutely." Excitement welled. "Let's get to the store."

Once Detective Mitchell gave us the okay to leave, we sped to the bookstore. I took over manning the counter even though curiosity overwhelmed me as Grandma and Brandt headed to the back room.

"Did you hear that Ada's house got broken into?" a woman I didn't know but had seen around asked me after ordering a scone.

"News travels fast."

"My Harvey has one of those scanner radio thingies. We hear all that goes on in this town. Well, if it goes across the police radio anyway."

"Heard anything else on it lately?"

"Not since the latest killing." She sighed. "Horrible news, that one. Our dear librarian's family were founders, you know. So were Rupert Kirkland's. Makes me glad to be a relative newcomer. Only been here thirty years." She paid for her purchase and stepped aside for the next in line.

Grandma was right. The sandwiches were a big hit. I needed to know who made them so I could put a sign in the window giving them credit.

When the line died, I leaned my elbows on the counter and rested my chin in my hands. I loved that my store seemed to be a success but hated how it all started.

Finally, my grandmother and Brandt returned. He handed me two pages of stationery.

I glanced at the writing. "This isn't your handwriting. It's messy." My grandmother's writing was always neat and meticulous. Girly even, with circles over the *i*'s.

"Mrs. Peabody had a tremor. I had to write shaky for anyone to believe this letter was written by her to Brandt." She perched on a stool behind the counter.

"Smart." I laid the letter on the counter and started reading.

My Dear Nephew,

If you're reading this, that means I'm gone, and you've been through my things. Not something I would allow under different circumstances, but well, there it is. If you have this letter, then you've been to my safety deposit box at the bank. Other than some stock, this should be the only thing in the box.

I glanced up. "Sounds like you nailed what she would say." Brandt grinned. "Keep reading."

As you know, I own some things of value, but there are a few you know nothing about. I have a signed copy of What Life Is Made For. Silly title, I know, but it was given to your grandfather. The book is worth only the sentimental value and the fact it's a rare edition.

The real thing of value I have is a diamond ring. An infamous ring given to my grandmother after quite the scandalous love affair.

I've left you everything in the house, but this ring isn't in the house, dear. I've hidden it away so only you can find it. But not without me telling you where I've hidden it.

You know your favorite place when you would come to visit? You left a green coffee can up there perched in the branches. Inside that can, you will find the ring. Keep it safe. Hopefully, you can use it someday to adorn some lucky girl's finger.

Aunt Ada

"This is brilliant." I smiled up at him. "I guess there is such a place? A treehouse, maybe?"

"Exactly a treehouse. I'm going to put the fake ring in that can."

CHAPTER ELEVEN

I don't understand why all this is happening." I closed the box on a new batch of chocolate scones the next morning. "All I wanted was a successful business. One that people were happy to enter. To instill a love of reading."

"Sometimes, God allows such things so we can find out what we're made of. Find out how strong our faith is." Grandma rubbed a hand across my shoulders. "Something good came out of this. Brandt is here."

"We're just friends, and he lost his aunt." I closed my eyes and leaned into her touch.

"It could turn into something more." She kissed the top of my head and removed the next batch of scones from the oven. "This is the last one. When are the two of you going to place the letter?"

"During a lull in the store's traffic." I'd fallen asleep the night before thinking about Brandt's brilliant scheme. We'd stake out the treehouse later that night.

The sound of the shower turning off downstairs let me know Brandt would be ready to leave soon. He'd apologized for sleeping in, said he planned on working on the house today while I was at the store, then mentioned where he thought it best to put the letter. I thought it best he keep it in his car with the doors unlocked. Less suspicious.

"You're right." Brandt, hair still wet, entered the kitchen. "I thought over your suggestion. I'll leave the letter on the floor of the passenger side as if I dropped it. You've got a good head on your shoulders, Amber." He grinned. "Maybe you should write a mystery book."

I laughed. "Don't think I haven't thought of writing a book of my own." I'd thought about it since I learned to read at the age of five, but I didn't have the confidence. Maybe, when this was all over, I'd actually give writing a shot.

After all, I was living an adventure. I could write about this whole ring thing.

While Grandma took the scones to the store, I accompanied Brandt back to his house. We followed a trail from the back yard into the woods until we reached a treehouse that had seen better days.

A frayed rope with knots for climbing led to a weathered platform. Splintered plywood made up the walls.

"This looks like a death trap. That rope will break under your weight." I eyed the rope with disdain.

"I'm tall enough to climb the tree now." As if to prove his point, Brandt grabbed a low branch and swung himself up. His first step onto the platform sent his foot through it. "I'm okay!"

"Be careful." I waited for another foot to come through.

Before I grew too worried, Brandt swung from the tree like Tarzan and landed with a thud beside me. "Piece of cake. I'll drop you off at the store and head to the house. The detective texted me last night that I could go in."

"Again, be careful. These killers won't stop just because it's daylight."

"I'll keep the doors locked. I want to make the place at least habitable by the time this is over. Which shouldn't be too long with our new plan in place. Besides, there's a squad car parked out front."

I hoped.

A slow day of customers made the time drag. I kept glancing at the door, expecting to see Brandt. With every hour that passed and he didn't show, my anxiety grew.

"Relax. You're making me nervous." Grandma shot me a glare. "Do inventory or something. Go online and try to see whether the book is being sold again. Anything."

"What if something happened to him?"

"Then we'd hear. If you're that worried, call the detective and ask him to send an officer by the house."

Good idea. I rushed to my office and made the call.

He echoed Grandma's words but promised to send someone by. "I'll let you know if there's anything to worry about."

I thanked him and hung up. I took Grandma's second advice and browsed the internet to no avail. Mrs. Peabody's book didn't surface.

The hours continued to pass with no sight of Brandt or word from the detective. "I'm going over there." I waved my fingers at Grandma. "Car keys, please."

"Fine. Won't you feel silly when you find Brandt knee deep in his aunt's clothes?" She dropped the keys to her car in my palm.

"I'd rather feel foolish than continue to worry." I marched from the store.

As I drove, I called the detective again. "You didn't call back with news."

"Because Mr. Thompson is fine."

"Okay." I hung up. Maybe they were right, and I was overreacting. Still, the niggle of worry at the base of my skull wouldn't go away. I needed to see for myself that Brandt was fine.

I parked behind his car. Both front doors hung open. I glanced at the floorboard as I headed for the house. No sign of the letter. My worry grew.

The front door swung open with a slight push. "Brandt?" Goose bumps peppered my skin. "It's me, Amber."

I glanced in each room as I passed. Furniture had been righted, broken pieces picked up and placed in a large trashcan. I headed upstairs. "Brandt?"

A moan came from under the four-poster bed. I dropped to my knees and lifted the dust ruffle.

Dark eyes met mine. "Someone hit me over the head. I rolled under here in case they came back to finish the job."

"Why aren't you dead?" I moved back so he could get out.

"I don't think I'm a target." He slid out and put a hand to his head. "No blood. That's good."

"The letter is gone from your car."

He grinned. "The plan is working."

I narrowed my eyes. "You were attacked."

"But still breathing." He got shakily to his feet. "Look. A note." He grabbed a sheet of my store's stationery from the nightstand. "'Stop snooping. Let us get what we want, and we'll be gone.'" His grin widened. "We'll catch them red-handed tonight."

How could he grin at a time like this? Tears welled in my eyes. "You could've been killed."

"True, but again, I wasn't. Like I said, I don't think I'm a target. The ones who are dead, other than my aunt, were all relatives of town founders. I think Adelaide and Dickinson are eliminating the competition. The question is, why? Did they all believe they have a right to my aunt's ring?"

I sat back on my haunches. "Maybe. But the ring was given to your great-grandmother. That means it belonged to your aunt. No one else."

"People don't always see reason where money or love is concerned."

"Hmm. We need to call Detective Mitchell again." The man was going to get tired of hearing from me.

"Mr. Thompson called me. From under the bed, I presume." The detective stood in the doorway with arms crossed. "The two of you are going to give me gray hair. What's this I heard about a letter?"

"Were you eavesdropping?" I got to my feet and matched his stance.

"Best way to learn things." He didn't look the least bit ashamed.

Brandt explained our plan.

"You put a fake ring in a treehouse?" The detective's brow furrowed.

"Come on." I put a hand on his arm. "I'll take you to the clinic and get you checked out."

"I want to go to the treehouse tonight."

"Absolutely not," the detective and I both said.

"I'll send an officer to watch the place," Detective Mitchell said. "You stay out of this." A faint smile tugged at his lips. "Good plan, though." He marched from the room.

"Wow. I got kudos." Brandt allowed me to lead him to my grandmother's car, which told me he hurt more than he let on.

"I'll close your car doors and be right back." Before I did, I made sure the letter was indeed gone then drove Brandt to the clinic.

After an examination, the doctor said he had a mild concussion. She gave him a pain pill that would help him rest.

Two hours later, we arrived back at the store, where I settled Brandt onto one of the cushy reading chairs. "I'll get you something to eat and drink. Don't move from that spot until it's time to go home."

"Home," he murmured. "I like that. Especially since I'm going with you."

"You're on drugs." I smiled on my way to the coffeepot.

"He okay?" Grandma turned from the cash register.

"He'll be fine. I'm glad I went with my gut and checked on him." He'd come to mean a lot to me. I couldn't lose him now.

"You like him." She wiggled her eyebrows.

"What are we, twelve?" But yes, I did. I ducked my head and smiled.

"I think we should go to the treehouse tonight," she whispered.

"The detective explicitly told us not to."

"I know for a fact that you don't always do what you're told." She crossed her arms.

True, but I tried to follow the rules. "Brandt is in no condition to go out there."

"We'll leave him sleeping like a baby at the house and sneak out. I've got black clothes and beanies we can wear. No one will be the wiser. Besides. . ." She grinned. "The cops need us. We might see something they miss. I haven't had this much fun in ages."

"Death and murder is not fun, Grandma." I smiled at a customer who approached the counter. "How may I help you?"

"I'm looking for a first edition of *Girl of the Limberlost*. Do you think you can help me?"

"I can sure try. Give me a moment, and I can look for you now. Maybe you could enjoy a cup of coffee while you wait."

The woman smiled. "That would be great, thank you."

After asking her how much she was willing to spend, I hurried to my office and booted up my computer. Ten minutes later, I'd located the book she wanted and made my bid. Five minutes later, it had been accepted. I returned to the front of the store to give the woman the good news.

"It says in good condition, which means there might be some wear and tear." I quoted a price over what I'd paid. "It should be here by early next week. If you leave your number, I'll give you a call." I slid a notepad over to her.

"That sounds wonderful."

"It never ceases to amaze me how folks don't know they can find things on the internet themselves." Grandma shook her head.

"Not everyone is as smart as you." I chuckled. "Besides, we'd have lost a sale if she knew. It's faster if I do it. I know where to look." I glanced at Brandt. "Let's get him home and fed. It's closing time."

I tallied up the till and locked the money in the safe in the storeroom. After making sure the back door was locked then locking the front door after me, I followed Grandma to her car. We could pick up Brandt's car tomorrow.

As we drove home, I tried to convince Grandma that defying the detective's orders would get us in trouble not to mention be dangerous.

She was having none of it, convinced we could be of service.

I sighed and mentally prepared myself for a night of Something Could Go Terribly Wrong.

CHAPTER TWELVE

"What are we doing?" A groggy Brandt leaned heavily on my shoulders.

"Putting you to bed." Grandma plopped him onto the sofa. "Now, lie down like a good boy, and I'll turn on the TV."

"Are you sure it's safe to leave him?" I asked. "What about his concussion?"

"It's been long enough that he'll be fine. Get a glass of water to put on the coffee table then change into the clothes I put on the chair in your room." She set the TV remote within Brandt's reach. "He'll be asleep in five minutes. I guarantee."

"How long have you had this planned?"

"Well..." She gave a sheepish grin. "The last few days, I reckon. I figured we'd go spying at some point. After almost getting caught peeking in those scoundrels' window, I thought we should be better prepared the next time."

"I'm not cut out to be a sleuth," I muttered on my way to my room.

I dressed in black leggings, a long-sleeved black tee, and beanie. I felt ridiculous. Like an imposter cat-burglar or something.

"Why are we doing this?" I asked when I joined Grandma by the front door. "None of us are suspects."

"Because it's fun and I consider it a civic duty to help our small police force apprehend the people who committed murder in our place of business." She handed me a backpack. "Snacks and water."

I widened my eyes. "How long do you expect us to be out there?"

"As long as it takes or until I have to use the bathroom."

I sure hoped she'd drunk a lot of liquids. With a sigh, I headed out the door, locking it behind us and sending a prayer heavenward that Brandt would be okay without us.

What if Adelaide and Dickinson broke into our house? He'd be in no condition to defend himself. And Grandma would be heartbroken if some of her antiques were ruined.

"Let's not do this."

"Nonsense." She climbed into the driver's seat. "Too late to back out now. I drank coffee. I'll be up for hours."

Good grief. I rolled my eyes and buckled myself into the passenger seat, hoping the coffee would go right through her. If we were out too late and I didn't get a good night's sleep, tomorrow would be a very long day.

Grandma parked behind Mrs. Peabody's house and shoved her door open. "We move quietly from here. No idea when those scoundrels will show up."

"I hope they don't."

"They will. They want that ring."

Ugh. I quietly closed the car door. "Follow me. I know where we're going." At least we had a full moon to light the way.

Every step we took seemed too loud. Twigs snapped, leaves rustled, my heart pounded. Grandma had a smile on her face.

"I'm putting you in a home. You've obviously lost control of your mental faculties."

"Shh. No talking."

I exhaled heavily, wishing again I could've thought of a way to stay at home but also knowing she might have gone by herself if I'd refused. I didn't think there was a more stubborn woman in the whole country.

I did want this whole ring murder thing behind us. Maybe we could help in some way. At least we could foil the plan of the two cold-blooded killers. Get in their way. *Lord, please don't let them kill us.* "If I get murdered, I'm going to haunt you."

"I'd probably be dead too. Besides, there's no such thing as ghosts."

"Then I'll ask God to give you fewer jewels in your crown."

"Shh."

As we neared the treehouse, I held up a hand to stop her. I motioned to a thick, leafy evergreen bush.

Grandma nodded, removed her backpack, and sat on it behind the bush. She removed a pair of night-vision goggles then pointed at my backpack.

Where in the world had she gotten those? I shook my head and pulled out another pair then put them on. Amazing how clear they were. I could see everything.

Maybe no one would come, and Grandma would grow bored. I sat on my own pack and settled in for what I hoped would be a short wait.

Time ticked by at the speed of a caterpillar's crawl. My eyes grew heavy, and my head bobbed against my chest.

The snap of a twig jolted me upright. Detective Mitchell? For once, I hoped to catch sight of him. Anyone in uniform would do. When no other sound came and no one stepped into view, I started to relax again.

Grandma, on the other hand, swiveled her head from side to side, on constant watch. Occasionally, she'd sigh in frustration, her shoulders slumping, then some little sound would perk her up.

I scooted my back against a tree, crossed my arms, and settled in to take a nap, convinced this had all been for nothing. Another twig snapped. The sound of a footstep behind me sent my heart into my throat.

"Boo." Brandt's teeth flashed in the moonlight.

"How did you know we were out here?" I slapped his shoulder. "You scared me."

"Where else would you be this time of night?"

"Shh." Grandma put a finger to her lips.

"How did you get here?" I removed my goggles.

"Called for a ride."

"Did you see anyone else around here?"

"Nope." He settled against the tree with me and took the goggles. "Cool."

"How do you feel?"

"Just a slight headache. The nap did me good." He put on the goggles and stared at the tree house. "The rope is down."

"Give me those." I took the goggles. Sure enough, the ragged end of the rope lay on the ground.

"I'll be right back. I need to see if the ring is still there."

"I'll keep watch." Now alert, I kept my focus on him as he jogged to the base of the tree and picked up the rope. He glanced upward then dropped the rope and swung up as he had earlier that day.

After what seemed like forever, but was more like a few minutes, he returned. "The can is gone. Someone went through the floor like I did. Whichever one it was cut themselves on a nail, so they left behind some DNA." He grinned.

"You're as bad as she is." I jerked my chin toward Grandma. "Both of you are enjoying this."

"It's definitely not something a person does every day. Not unless you're law enforcement."

"Which you are not."

I shrieked and whirled as Detective Mitchell stepped from behind a large oak tree. "I'm getting tired of people sneaking up behind me and giving me a heart attack."

"And I'm getting tired of the three of you not listening to me. Get up. I'm taking you to the station."

"You're arresting us?" I bolted to my feet.

"This is your fault." Grandma gathered her things. "I told you to be quiet."

"The three of you do make a lot of noise, but it was seeing Mr. Thompson climbing the tree that alerted me to the fact you all disobeyed my direct orders and snuck away from the officer watching the house."

Grandma shrugged. "Not the first time I've been sent to the slammer. I protested the war in Vietnam. Got locked up a few times. Don't worry, Amber. We'll be out by morning."

"It is morning," I hissed.

"Then by daylight."

"Please don't put this over the police scanner," I said, remembering the customer who'd heard about the break-in at Mrs. Peabody's. "It'll be all over town within an hour."

"Let's go, or should I cuff the three of you?"

"Do you have three sets of cuffs?" Grandma tilted her head.

"No."

"We could try to run."

His brow furrowed. "I know where you live and work, ma'am."

"Okay. I'm too old to run anyway. We'll come peacefully."

Who was this woman? I shook my head and followed the detective to his car.

"I'll get us bailed out." Brandt took my hand. "He's only trying to make a point."

"I'll have a record." My eyes burned.

"I doubt he'll book us." He gave my hand a gentle squeeze. "Look at this as another adventure."

"The three of you have had enough adventures." The detective slammed the door. When he settled into the front seat, he glanced back. "You keep getting in my way. Let me solve this crime so your lives can return to normal."

"You aren't doing a very good job." I glared. "They've already come and taken the fake ring."

He glanced at Brandt. "That true?"

"Yep. One of them cut themselves on a nail. I spotted a few drops of blood."

"Maybe they'll die of blood poisoning," Grandma said. "It would serve them right."

The detective shook his head and drove us to the station. "I doubt this will do you any good, but I'm holding you for a few hours so we can search for Morrison and Dickinson."

The sound of the heavy door clanging shut behind us chilled my blood. Not how I intended to spend a Saturday night. I eyed the hard stainless-steel seat. It would be an uncomfortable few hours.

"Hello." Grandma settled next to a rough-looking, rail-thin woman. "What are you in for?"

"Selling stolen goods. You?"

"Not following orders. We're trying to catch a couple of killers, and the police think we're stepping on their toes."

"Leave her alone, Grandma." She could talk the hind leg off a mule.

"No, Amber. A woman in her profession hears things. Right?" She turned back to the woman.

She nodded. "Sometimes. I've heard about the murders."

"I need my one phone call." Brandt clutched the bars of the window in the door.

"I haven't arrested you," Detective Mitchell called. "Sit down, shut up, and think about what could've happened to the three of you, and leave Lacey alone."

"I don't mind," Lacey said. "Talking will relieve the boredom. I'm in here a couple of times a month. It's a hazard of the job. I don't work in Hickory Hills much, only coming by a few times a month, but Mitchell nabs me every time."

"You seem like a nice girl." Grandma patted her hand. "One of these days, you come by the bookstore, I'll give you a coffee on the house, and you can tell me how you got into your profession. When you're done, I'll tell you about my God."

"You'd let me into your store?" Lacey's eyes widened.

"Of course. Now, tell me what you know about these murders."

I nestled against Brandt and let my grandmother work her magic. She could make friends with a concrete wall if it would enter into a conversation with her.

"A couple of friends I work with in Wilson Falls met up with the dead guy once in a while. You know, the book freak? Anyway, he talked about a book and a ring, they said. Told them the ring was worth a lot of money and that there was some arguing between him and others in his "group." She made finger quotes. "About who the ring really belonged to. I guess it's pretty old."

She shrugged. "We really didn't think much about it until a couple of people died. Then, Frank, one of my friends, said he remembered him saying something about eliminating the competition. That's about it."

It looked like someone was indeed eliminating the competition, but she hadn't told us anything we didn't know. "That's it?" I asked. "No other word on the streets?"

"Oh, yeah. There's a lot of money hidden somewhere. Bootlegging money."

Could there really be a ton of cash hidden in the walls of Mrs. Peabody's old Victorian? I thought hard about the pages of the book I'd copied. There had to be a clue there about where the money was hidden.

"We need to read those pages from the book again."

CHAPTER THIRTEEN

I t was hard to focus on the pastor's sermon Sunday morning. My mind kept drifting to the photocopied pages of Mrs. Peabody's book.

Instinct told me we'd missed something of importance. How many people suspected Mrs. Peabody's house might've been a moonshine house?

Even after Grandma telling me there had to be a reason that these recent events landed in my lap, I struggled with the why. Until the pastor said something that made me start paying closer attention.

"'I have said these things to you, that in me you may have peace. In the world you will have tribulation. But take heart; I have overcome the world,'" the pastor said. "John 16:33."

Surrounded by death definitely fit in the tribulation category. As the pastor spoke, peace settled over my shoulders like my favorite blanket. I could do this. Together with my grandmother and Brandt, with God's guidance, we would find out the truth and stop the killing.

That might not be exactly what the verse meant, but I felt better and less stressed. I smiled and pushed aside thoughts of the book to be returned to later.

After church, reading was prolonged further by our traditional noon meal of pot roast and potatoes. Grandma sighed, handing me the three plates. "Relax. Those pages aren't going anywhere, and the afternoon stretches before you. There's plenty of time to eat then read."

"I'm just excited. We're getting so close to putting an end to this nightmare." I set the table with Brandt's help.

"We're going to find something today." He grinned. "Something huge that will help."

"When we do, we'll let Detective Mitchell know. That way, the trouble might not come knocking on our door."

"I agree with that plan."

I ate quickly and waited impatiently as the others ate. After the last bite went in Brandt's mouth, I jumped up and started clearing the table.

"I'll wash, you dry." Brandt tossed me a dishtowel.

"The dishes can wait." I really wanted to start reading.

"Let's get them done so they aren't hanging over our heads." With a sigh, I took the towel. "Wash fast."

He laughed and filled the sink with hot soapy water. "If you're in such a hurry, you might want to think about buying a dishwasher."

"I'm not usually in such a hurry." Normally, I enjoyed the relaxation washing dishes gave me.

Finally, the last dish had been dried and put away. I hung up the towel and thundered up the stairs to gather the copied pages. When I returned, a plate of cookies sat on the table, along with three filled coffee mugs.

"Let's get to work." I dove in. After a few pages, I frowned. "Was Victor Browning a poet?"

"Not that I know of." Brandt glanced up. "You're the book expert."

"I don't think he was, but right here in the middle of his book is a poem." One that sounded very familiar.

I sat back and thought over what poetry I had read in the past, which wasn't very much. "Got it. This poem is by a poet named Philip Larkin and it's about money. Listen to this." I read the part that seemed like it could be linked to the mystery.

> "'So I look at others, what they do with theirs:
> They certainly don't keep it upstairs.
> By now they've a second house and car and wife:
> Clearly money has something to do with life.'"

"And this part." I continued reading.

> "'I listen to money singing. It's like looking down
> From long french windows at a provincial town,
> The slums, the canal, the churches ornate and mad
> In the evening sun. It is intensely sad.'"

How could I have missed this? I'd been looking for something much more subtle when the clue we needed was in plain sight for anyone to see. When I finished, I glanced up. "We need to find out where Browning lived. I bet the money is hidden there." I tapped my fingers on the part I'd read. "I bet it's in an upstairs room with french windows."

"That's quite a stretch." Brandt's brow furrowed. "My aunt has a room that matches that description. It's her sewing room. We should check there first."

"Do you have the blueprints to your aunt's house?" Grandma asked. "We might be able to tell whether there are secret passages. A lot of bootleggers used them during Prohibition."

"There might be some in her safe." Brandt got to his feet. "Let's go, ladies."

We grabbed our purses and followed him out the door. Soon we stood in the foyer of his aunt's—his—house.

"The safe is upstairs." He led us to the master bedroom and removed a large landscape painting of a mountain lake from the wall. A few turns of the dial, and he pulled the safe open.

I peered around Brandt. "The safe is packed."

"Stocks and bonds, mostly." He riffled through the items then pulled out a folded blueprint. "Voilà."

"Follow me." He opened a door I'd thought was a closet to reveal a narrow set of stairs that led to a turret room. "This is the only room that might fit the poem. Let's search here, then I'll spread the blueprint out on her sewing table."

It didn't take long to search the small room. Grandma looked in the one closet while I lifted rugs to see whether any hid a trap door. Nothing. I started to think the money wasn't here. Which meant our best bet was Browning's home.

I sat in a rocker and searched the internet. "Browning was from Oakdale. That's only an hour from here. This article says he lived modestly in a cabin on the mountain but doesn't give an address."

"Detective Mitchell can find that information." Brandt spread out the blueprint. "This doesn't show any hidden tunnels or rooms, but I guess it wouldn't. I'd need to compare this to each of the actual rooms to see if they add up."

"That'll take a long time." I didn't think we should spend the time satisfying our curiosity but soon found myself outnumbered.

"We don't have time today to go to Oakdale," Grandma said. "It's almost suppertime."

"We work tomorrow."

"I'll mind the store while you and Brandt drive up there."

I shrugged. Looking for hidden rooms did sound like fun. "Okay, let's do this."

"We'll start downstairs. If there's a tunnel, that's where we'll find one." Brandt folded the blueprint and tucked it under his arm.

We stood in the parlor. I studied the bookcase. That was where tunnels and secret rooms were in the movies I'd watched and books I'd read.

I pulled out books and moved knickknacks while Grandma knocked on the rocks making up the fireplace and Brandt measured the room.

I started to lift a bronze cat. Something clicked, and the bookcase slid a couple of inches. "Look!" I shoved against the bookcase.

Brandt joined me, putting a hand on each side of me, which pressed his chest against my back. My breath hitched as the woodiness of his cologne washed over my senses. I smiled. There were worse ways of spending a Sunday afternoon than being close to a handsome man and looking for hidden rooms.

Reminding myself that we'd been together every day since his aunt's death, I shoved my foolish girly emotions to the side and stepped into a small concrete room.

Canned food covered with dust and a shelf of water bottles lined one wall. "This looks like a safe room or fallout bunker."

"Could be either, I suppose." Brandt circled the room. "How did I never find this as a kid? I thought I'd been all over this house on my visits."

"The bronze cat opened it."

"Right. I wasn't allowed to touch anything in the parlor. That room was off limits to a rowdy boy." He opened a door at the far end. "I need a light."

I found a flashlight in a box on the shelf. "A tunnel?"

"Yep." Excitement laced his voice. He took the flashlight and turned it on. "Let's see where it goes."

"You first." Grandma motioned me forward. "I don't like dark places."

"You can stay here."

"And miss out on the fun? No way." She stayed close on my heels.

A chill permeated the air of the tunnel. Rough beams held the dirt back from falling on our heads. Still, I didn't think the tunnel was safe enough to spend a lot of time in.

We eventually came to another room. This one was full of mason jars with a clear liquid in them that I didn't think was water.

Brandt opened one and took a sniff. "Whoa. That's some strong stuff."

"Why would your aunt hold on to this?" I took a whiff and grimaced. "Smells like turpentine."

"You can tell by the looks of the house she didn't get rid of much. Look around for the money. I want to make sure it isn't here before we head back to your place."

I nodded and set the jar on a shelf. You could kill weeds with that stuff.

There were no hidden doors in the dirt walls. No trapdoors. No boxes that hid money. Nothing but jars and jars of moonshine. "Have fun getting rid of all this."

"It won't be fun carting it all out, that's for sure." Brandt shook his head. "Maybe that's why it's still here. No one wanted to bother."

"There's a small fortune on those shelves," Grandma pointed out. "Sell it and have the buyer take it out."

"Maybe. I'll think on it. Ready to head back? My stomach's growling. What's for supper?"

"Sandwiches," Grandma said. "On Sunday, our big meal is in the middle of the day so I can relax and watch taped recordings of Lawrence Welk. Reminds me of being a kid."

And bored me to tears. I usually used Sunday evenings to get lost in a book. Having Brandt around would make the evening more enjoyable.

"I'll watch with you," he said.

Okay. Good thing I had a book.

"Let's head to Oakdale early in the morning," Brandt said as soon as we got in his car. "That'll give us a lot of time to do some digging. We can ask around to find out where Browning's house is."

"What about Detective Mitchell?"

"I'll give him a call and tell him we're headed up there to see the author's house and about the poem. It might be a wild-goose chase, but at least he'll have the information so he can decide if he wants to come along."

I nodded. "Sounds like a great plan. Play it up like we're sightseeing so he doesn't throw us in jail again."

"We did learn about the money from our time in the slammer," Grandma said from the back seat. "Well, sort of. We kind of guessed."

True, but I didn't want to repeat the experience. The four hours the detective had held us had seemed like an eternity.

Brandt called him via the Bluetooth in the car and explained our theory about the poem.

"I guess it can't hurt anything for you to go see the house," the detective said. "I doubt anyone will let you in anyway. Knock yourself out. I think the idea of money hidden there is a long shot. Why would he tell Peabody about his fortune?"

"Did Browning have a family?"

"He had a brother, now deceased. No one else that we've been able to dig up."

Brandt pulled into the driveway. "Uh-oh."

"What?"

"There's a sheet of paper taped to Amber's front door. I bet it's another warning, Detective."

CHAPTER FOURTEEN

Y OU'RE NEXT. The warning flashed from the front door like a highway motel sign over and over in my mind while I tossed and turned, trying to sleep. I couldn't stop thinking of how my usually peaceful small town had changed because of greed. I wanted things to return to normal, when most days bordered on me being bored.

Gritty-eyed from lack of sleep, I crawled from bed and stumbled to the kitchen. Brandt thrust a cup of coffee into my hands. I mumbled a thanks and dropped into a kitchen chair.

"I made you a ham and cheese omelet." He set a plate in front of me. "You up to visiting Browning's home?"

"Yes." Barely. "Grandma?"

"Already taken a batch of scones to the store."

I glanced at the clock. Eight o'clock? I didn't feel as if I'd slept in, but the time told me otherwise. "I'll be ready in half an hour."

"No rush. The house isn't going anywhere." He sat across from me. "Today might be the day everything is revealed."

I nodded. "Doesn't the warning last night frighten you?"

"A little, but they've had a few opportunities to kill me and haven't yet. They need something from me."

"The location of the money."

"Yep."

I glanced up from my breakfast. "They'll kill us once we find it."

"They'll try." He grinned. "I don't plan on dying anytime soon, Amber."

True, but I still wanted to live a good long time. I ate, finished my coffee, then rushed to shower. No amount of hot water and floral-scented bodywash could erase the dread that hovered over me. Something was going to happen today. I prayed it wasn't something bad.

When I returned to the kitchen, Brandt had done the dishes and waited with keys in hand. "Let's catch some crooks."

"Leave your phone on so the detective can find our bodies." I stepped from the house and headed for the car.

"Don't be such a pessimist." He chuckled, pulling the locked door closed behind him.

As I reached for the car door handle, a van turned into the drive. Dickinson slid from the driver's seat and aimed a gun in our direction. "In the van. Now, or Adelaide shoots Amber first."

Brandt took me by the elbow and led me to the van. "Very cliché, buddy."

"Shut up and get inside."

"Who'd you steal the van from?"

How could Brandt carry on a conversation when we were about to die? My blood chilled as I climbed in the back to be met by Adelaide's icy stare.

"You should've minded your own business," she said. "Hold out your hands."

I obliged and hissed as she tightened zip-ties around my wrists then Brandt's. "You made it my business when you killed Mrs. Peabody."

"That was Oliver, not me." She shrugged. "I guess she should've told him where the treasure is."

"Maybe she didn't know." I hitched my chin.

"But you do." She grinned and climbed into the front passenger seat. "And you're going to take us straight to it. No more false leads like the fake ring. Did you really think someone of my intelligence couldn't tell the difference?"

"Don't talk to them," Dickinson ordered, returning to the driver's seat. "Where are we going?"

"To jail." Brandt grinned.

Dickinson aimed his gun at my head. "Talk, or she dies. We don't need both of you."

"Victor Browning's house." Brandt rattled off the address.

"Sit back and enjoy the ride." Dickinson squealed out of my driveway.

Why had I thought we could do this? Get into the house, find the money, hand it over to the authorities, and get away without harm? Stupidity! I sighed. I'd been caught up in the excitement despite my reservations. Now I might not live long enough to discover whether anything could happen between me and Brandt.

My gaze settled on his lips. I really would've liked to know how it felt to be kissed by him. To see whether we could be more than friends. To know whether he wanted to be more than friends.

"Chin up. We'll get out of this," Brandt whispered. "I sent a text to Mitchell."

"When?"

"Just now. Big mistake not securing my hands behind me or taking my phone. Not sure how much sense I made with a bumpy road and trying not to get caught, but help will come."

"What if the money isn't there?"

"We'll think of something. Stall until help arrives."

"No talking!" Adelaide tossed an empty plastic cup at us, bouncing it off my head.

I wasn't a violent person, but at that moment I would've enjoyed slapping her. I nestled against Brandt for the remainder of the hour-long drive. We'd get out of this. I held on to God's promises. If we perished, I knew where I'd end up.

"There," Adelaide said. "It's used as a museum of sorts and it's closed today. Perfect."

I peered through the front window at a sprawling Victorian similar to Mrs. Peabody's, except this one had two tower rooms. The money had to be in one of them. "Yours can look that great one of these days, Brandt," I said.

"Absolutely."

"Fools." Dickinson laughed and parked behind the house. "Where's the money?"

"Inside somewhere," Brandt said. "That's all we know. We'll have to look for it. Try not to act like your usual selves and make a mess, all right?"

Dickinson's face darkened. "I'm going to enjoy shutting you up for good. Get out."

"Can't." I held up my bound hands. "You'll have to open the door for us, and unless you want to do all the searching yourselves, you might want to cut these ties."

"I just painted my nails, Oliver. Untie them so they can do the work." Adelaide smiled in his direction.

"I'm surrounded by incompetence." He shoved his door open. A few seconds later, the back of the van opened, and he cut our ties. "Don't try to escape, or I'll shoot."

"Wouldn't dream of it." I rubbed my wrists and stared at the house in front of us. Unfortunately, there was no way in except to break in.

Dickinson picked up a ceramic gnome and tossed it through the back door window. He reached inside and turned the lock. "You two first."

I thought back to the poem. It stated the window looked down on the town. "This way." I led them upstairs to the tower that looked down on the garden. Anything to stall for time. Why hadn't the detective arrived yet?

"Why up here?" Adelaide frowned. "Shouldn't we start downstairs?"

"I think we know more than you do." I glared over my shoulder.

"Fine." She swept her arm in front of her. "Lead the way."

We could spend a good hour in this tower before heading to the other one. By then, help would have arrived. Right?

"Look for somewhere to hide a bunch of cash," Brandt said.

"The two of you look." Oliver shook his head, keeping the gun trained on us. "I'll watch to make sure you don't try anything stupid."

"So the two of you really weren't sure what the treasure was, were you?" I asked.

Adelaide studied her nails. "We thought it was the ring, but then you left the fake one and kept snooping around, so we knew it had to be something else. The ring is rightfully mine, you know. It was given to my grandmother first. Won't it look wonderful on my left ring finger, Oliver?"

"Yeah, sure."

She narrowed her eyes. "You said you wanted to marry me. Was that a ruse? Do you plan on leaving me once we find. . .whatever it is we're looking for?"

"Money, Adelaide. Pay attention." He waved the gun at us. "Start looking."

Adelaide pouted. "Are you going to marry me?"

"Yes! Once we get to Mexico, I'll marry you, unless you keep jabbering."

"The Bible says a nagging wife is like the dripping of a leaky roof in a rainstorm," I said. "Proverbs 27:15."

Brandt grinned. "When you look into your heart, you see what you're really like. Death and the grave are never satisfied. People's eyes are never satisfied either."

"Shut up." Dickinson's face darkened. "I know the Bible."

"Sure, buddy, but you might want to rethink any upcoming nuptials." Brandt tossed me a wink and shoved aside a large armoire.

"What are you doing?" Dickinson scowled.

"Looking for a hidden panel in the wall. You don't think Browning would stash the money in a drawer, do you? It would've been found a long time ago."

"How do we know it hasn't?" I asked.

"We don't."

"Either way, you're going to die." Dickinson leaned against a table. "Hurry up. I don't want anyone to notice the van when the museum is supposed to be closed."

"Nope, wouldn't want that." I studied a bookshelf, taking my time pulling the books out one by one and then replacing them. Where was Mitchell?

"You sure headed to this tower fast enough." Dickinson tilted his head. "Which makes me think you're stalling. Let's go to the other tower, shall we?" He motioned the gun toward the door. "Move."

I sighed and replaced the book in my hand. My plan had worked longer than I thought, but not long enough for help to arrive. Maybe Brandt's text hadn't gone through after all.

Our captors followed us through the museum of antiques to the second tower. This one overlooked the town and had been used as the author's office and library. A perfect hiding place, in my opinion.

It didn't take long to find the money. I moved the rug under the leather office chair and revealed a trapdoor. After lifting it, I pulled out a bag of the kind used by carpetbaggers after the Civil War. Inside lay a large amount of cash.

"Voilà!" Adelaide clapped her hands. "Mexico, here we come."

"Not so fast, dear." Dickinson waved the gun at her. "Over there with them. Did you really think I'd marry such a self-absorbed woman?"

Her eyes widened, and she pulled her weapon from the belt around her waist. "A stand-off." She grinned. "What fun!"

Brandt gripped my hand and slowly pulled me toward the door. "Don't drop the bag."

"Wouldn't think of it." The money belonged to the museum, not to any of us. If I could help it, those two wouldn't get a dollar.

In unison, Adelaide and Dickinson aimed their weapons in our direction. "Stop," Dickinson ordered. "Drop the bag."

"Drop the guns." Mitchell and two officers stepped into the room.

"About time." I shot him a glare.

"Your boyfriend should've sent a text that made sense." He took the guns from the crooks and ordered them to be handcuffed.

"What did my text say?" Brandt handed the carpet bag to the detective. "The road was bumpy, and my hands were bound pretty tight."

"A jumble of letters. We finally figured out that two of the words were 'Browning house.' Took us a bit to figure out what that meant, then a call came through about a stolen van. We put the pieces together. Sorry it took so long."

"We could've been killed in that time!" I crossed my arms, glaring up at him.

"Again, I apologize. Go outside and wait by my car."

Gladly. I couldn't get out of there fast enough.

Brandt leaned against the car and pulled me into his arms. "That went well."

"It could've gone so very wrong." His embrace held comfort and safety. "Thank you for being with me every step of this crazy adventure."

"It was my pleasure." He straightened as the authorities escorted Adelaide and Dickinson to the waiting squad cars. "Those two are going away for a very long time."

I laughed. "I hope Adelaide likes orange."

The woman shot me a glare. "It looks hideous on me."

I laughed louder. "Should've thought of that before entering into a partnership with Dickinson."

"Let's get you two home." Mitchell opened the back door to his car.

Brandt smiled down at me. "I like hearing those words."

"Me too."

EPILOGUE

After a week of not seeing Brandt, I decided the adventure of bringing down Adelaide and Dickinson was all I'd had with him. I propped my chin in my hands and watched my customers enjoy their coffee and scones while browsing through books. Thankfully, business hadn't slowed since the end of the crime spree. My store was a success after all.

Then why wasn't I happier? Because I missed Brandt far more than I wanted to admit.

Grandma patted my shoulder. "Cheer up, dear. Life is back to normal."

"I wanted that normal to include Brandt." Tears burned my eyes.

"If it doesn't, then he wasn't the man for you."

True, but I wanted him. Every time the bell over the door jingled, my heart leaped, only to fall when it wasn't him.

And then it was. I straightened, hope rising.

He approached the counter. "Hello."

"Hey."

His gaze warmed. "Can we talk?"

"Sure." I led him to my office. "Where have you been, Brandt?" I searched his face for answers.

"Clearing up some things. I'm going to stay in Hickory Hills. I can run my businesses from almost anywhere. Is that okay?"

I shrugged. "It's your choice."

"I'd like that choice to include you." Uncertainty flickered across his face. "Would you give us a chance? See what the future might hold for us? Maybe someday wear my aunt's ring?"

My mouth dropped open. "Are you proposing?"

"Not yet. Just tossing out the idea that I might someday. What do you think?" He opened his arms.

"That sounds wonderful." I stepped into his embrace and lifted my face to his. "I've been wondering what it would be like for you to kiss me."

"Let's find out." He lowered his head and claimed my lips.

The kiss was everything I'd dreamed. Full of sweetness and promise.

Multipublished and bestselling author **Cynthia Hickey** has taught writing at many conferences and small writing retreats. She and her husband run the publishing press, Winged Publications, which includes some of the CBA's best well-known authors. They live in Arizona and Arkansas, becoming snowbirds with two dogs and one cat. They have ten grandchildren who keep them busy and tell everyone they know that "Nana is a writer."

THE SECRET PASSAGE BOOKSHOP

BY LINDA BATEN JOHNSON

CHAPTER 1

"I should have listened." I offered my most apologetic expression to the three people at my bedside.

"Never listened before, have you, Abby?" Ben True's droll remark didn't hide the concern in his eyes.

Dressed in faded jeans, a denim shirt, and a ball cap advertising his Rocking T Ranch, Ben shifted his weight from one foot to the other, and his eyes darted toward the door as if planning an escape. At six feet tall and with a stocky build resulting from years of hard outdoor work, the man became antsy when cooped up inside, yet he'd been in my hospital room each time I'd opened my eyes.

What an anchor Ben turned out to be. A man with an open heart, he welcomed stragglers and strays like me to join him in his work helping with young "guests" on the ranch. Apparently, he had an arrangement with Sheriff Hawthorn to allow youthful offenders to work off their fines or community service obligations.

Ben, about the same age as my parents, had served as my mentor, boss, and landlord for the past three years. I guided hiking trips, led trail rides, mucked the stalls, and made beds at his ranch, located in a small town nestled at the base of the Teton Mountains.

After I received my master's degree in library science, I immersed myself in research at the Oklahoma State Library. My sweet parents, eager for grandchildren, thought a vacation with them might awaken me to life outside library shelves. They hoped I might fall in love, and I did, but with a place, not a man. The grandeur of Wyoming's skies, mountains, and streams awakened a desire I never knew I had.

By the time the vacation ended, I'd secured Ben's promise of a job at his Rocking T Ranch and resigned from my job. I'd been happy with my decision until I found an opportunity to combine my love of books and Wyoming by opening a bookshop in my adopted town.

Today, I was rethinking that decision as I lay in a hospital bed with a huge gash in my head. I'd entered the dilapidated building alone, despite advice not to, and had been attacked.

Sheriff Hawthorn cleared his throat and leaned forward. "Abby girl, you feel up to talking?"

"Don't know how much I can tell you." Trying to recapture the events of the day I'd been attacked, I reached up to run my fingers through my unruly reddish curls but felt smooth flesh instead. "What happened to my hair? Bring me a mirror, please."

The sheriff shook his head. "You're fine, girl, and that's the important thing. Hair regrows. At least yours will." He tapped his bald pate. "We need your help to figure out what happened and why."

I rubbed my hairless head. "Why did they cut off all my hair?"

Ben patted my hand. "You insisted. They took about half your curls to clean and stitch the wound, but you told them to take it all. Told the nurse you didn't want to look lopsided."

"I said that?"

The sheriff sighed. "Abby girl, what do you remember about the accident?"

"It wasn't an accident. Well, you know I'm buying Secret Passage, the derelict building at the end of Main. It used to be an escape room, but that didn't work out for the owners. Not enough business, so I decided to purchase the—"

Ben held up his hand. "Stop rambling. Sheriff Hawthorn doesn't want your life story."

"Right. Sorry. Well, I wanted to look around again and see what changes I needed to make for the space to work as a bookshop. Jolene, the real estate agent, gave me a key so Zach and I could look at it. You know how good he is at renovations. His woodwork is amazing." I nodded to Zach Cooper, who sat in the room's only chair.

"Abby—" Ben's voice carried a touch of annoyance.

"Right." I turned to the sheriff. "I got impatient. Even though Zach hadn't arrived, I went into the building. I'm calling it the Secret Passage Bookshop because books can offer a surprising introduction to people, places, and events in the past, present, and future. It's perfect for me. Setting up a shop here allows me to hike, bike, ski, and live in beautiful Bailey surrounded by books. Don't you think the business will be the perfect addition to the town?"

Now Sheriff Hawthorn glared at me.

Zach leaned forward in his chair. "Sheriff, I can tell you I didn't see any other person or unfamiliar car when I found Abby unconscious with a nasty bump on her head and an open wound that was bleeding buckets."

"Zach, I appreciate your conciseness. Now, Abby, focus on the time you were in the building. Did you see or hear anyone? If so, how many? One person? Two? Did you see who hit you?"

"No. I was fiddling with the flashlight. Shaking it. You know how you do when the battery doesn't work? The light would come on, then go off. Think I moved closer to the front window, but I'm not sure. I never carry extra batteries in my car, and I thought about calling Zach to see if he had batteries. Zach keeps his van equipped for any emergency because we take kids from our church group on hiking trips. Zach and I are the youth leaders, but you already know that since you and your wife attend the same church. Well, anything we need on an outing with the kids, Zach has it." I babble when I'm nervous, and today, senseless words spewed from my mouth.

The sheriff's clenched jaw told me he was not happy with me. Sheriff Hawthorn is a large man with a fighter's face marked with multiple small scars, a broken nose, and a crooked smile with gleaming white dental implants he'd purchased after his career as a semi-pro hockey player ended. His considerable paunch required him to hitch up his pants frequently. In my opinion, he needed a larger uniform, but I wouldn't tell him so.

On cue, he tugged his pants up and started the questions again. "Try to remember the day—even trivial details are important. Let's start over. You went in the front door, right? Did you hear anything? See anything? How about smells? Anything unusual?"

"I'm sorry, Sheriff. I didn't notice any new sights or sounds. As for smells, well, the place smelled dank, damp, and mildewy because the building has been boarded up. Nothing unusual. Sorry," I repeated.

"I don't like attacks happening under my watch," Sheriff Hawthorn said.

"I don't either, since this one happened to me." My remark didn't elicit a smile from any of the three men.

"If you remember something, let me know immediately." The sheriff pivoted toward the exit, where Ben hovered half-in, half-out of the doorway, ready to bolt.

Zach stood. "I wanted to stay until you woke up. Now that I know you're all right, I'll go to work. The old Abby Scott has returned, the one who can't stop talking. And don't worry about the hair thing. You rock the bald look."

"I doubt that, but I'd like to see for myself. When you leave, could you ask the nurse if there's a hand mirror available?"

Of the invitations that came to spring me from the hospital on that bleak January day, Jolene Roussel's was the one I accepted. She was the real estate agent who arranged the purchase of Secret Passage, and I wanted another look at the property to see if something triggered a memory I could share with Sheriff Hawthorn.

Jolene was a Bailey icon because she had grown up in the area. Before her husband died, he'd sold their ranch to a Hollywood couple—now no longer a couple—and that sale left her with more money than she could spend in two lifetimes.

Though she never needed to earn money, Jolene worked like I talked—incessantly. She offered a drop-in sunrise yoga class, sold real estate, volunteered at the National Museum of Western Art, and served on every board in town. At about five eight and very slender, she seemed to exist on the rarefied air of Bailey, because I'd never seen her eat anything more than raw vegetables. Her only brother operated a successful design studio in LA, and she visited his business quarterly to purchase furniture and art for her rental units and for clients.

"Brought you something." Jolene waved an aqua fleece head covering with the Rocking T symbol embroidered in black. "I have five in the bag, all different colors to match whatever you choose to wear."

"You know my attire is sweatshirts and jeans," I said. "And head coverings? I don't think so."

Jolene pushed them toward me. "You will. I had a friend who suffered through chemo, and she said she needed something, not to cover her baldness, but because the skin on her head was so sensitive to temperatures."

"I have my ball cap." I grabbed the bill of the cap and settled it on my head. "Do you have time to take me by the property again? And to the Chapel of Transfiguration?"

"Of course. I'll clear my schedule. I'll be in the hall." Jolene whipped out her phone.

I signed papers and received my clearance to leave. Hospitals didn't like healthy people to dawdle, and once the staff decided I'd live, they were ready for me to go. So was I. They'd sewed up the back of my head and watched me for three days for concussion symptoms.

"Don't take it personally, but I hope I won't be seeing you in the near future," I said to the nurse at the central station. Then I followed Jolene, still talking on her phone, out the front door and into the parking lot, which provided an impressive view of the Teton Mountains.

"Which first? Chapel or Secret Passage?" Jolene shoved her phone in her pocket and unlocked her Range Rover.

"Secret Passage." I secured the seat belt. "Zach will need access to the property sometime. He ended up taking me to the hospital instead of taking measurements of the place."

"I know. I gave him a key." Jolene edged into traffic filled with cars sporting rental franchise stickers.

I expected to feel exuberance at the sight of the Secret Passage sign over the door, but instead a sense of dread filled me.

Jolene flipped on the light switch. "We winterized the property. You have electricity, but you'll have to arrange for the other utilities after you take ownership."

"I have electricity? You mean I was fumbling around here in the dark when all I had to do was turn on the lights?"

"I told you about the electricity, Abby. As for the other utilities, I'd wait until Zach is ready to start work. Heating an empty building in January is costly."

"Heat would feel good today," I said.

Jolene moved through the building and pulled back the blackout curtains the escape room owners had added. "That makes it a little brighter."

I wrinkled my nose. "Those curtains will be the first thing to go. A bookshop needs to feel open and welcoming." The rooms constructed by the previous owners would serve as sections for used books, new stock, a children's area, and a spot for reading and refreshments. The upstairs would eventually be my apartment. The picture in my head was clear, but the reality looked nothing like my vision.

Jolene straightened things as she moved from room to room. I turned in the opposite direction, retracing where I'd been the morning of my attack.

"Looks like there's blood where I plan to shelve the mystery books," I joked. "Maybe I could use my attack for a bit of publicity. What do you think?"

"You could." Jolene checked her watch. "Why did you want to stop here after what you've been through?"

"I promised the sheriff I'd try to remember details from that day. Thought a visit might jog my memory. Hmm, I don't remember that pile of stuff by the back wall." I pushed at the heaped blankets with my foot and uncovered empty food containers from Maria's Meals, the town's new Mexican restaurant.

"Kids," Jolene said. "Zach will have a dumpster for the demolition and reconstruction. He'll take care of the garbage."

"Should I tell the sheriff?"

"No. I'm sure the sheriff examined the whole building." Jolene edged toward the front door. "You won't have trespassers once Zach starts his work. When do you hope to open?"

"My goal is April 1, but that will depend on Zach's other commitments. I'm not his only client," I said.

"April Fool's Day?" Jolene asked.

"That's appropriate. I feel a bit foolish for sinking my savings and part of the future inheritance from my parents into this venture. But as I told myself and them, this business will allow me to stay in Bailey. I can't work for Ben at the Rocking T forever. Bailey is the perfect home for me. People here love the outdoors like I do. They pick up trash, pull plastic bags off fencing, use drinking containers with metal straws, and look out for each other. That's what has me baffled." I followed Jolene to the door.

"What? What has you baffled?" She held it open so I could go outside.

"My being attacked. Who would do that?"

Jolene shrugged and locked the door behind me. "You were in the wrong place at the wrong time. I talked to the sheriff about increasing surveillance. I don't want squatters in a property I represent. My guess is that kids were camping or partying in the empty building and wanted to scare you off."

I rubbed my bandaged scalp. "They didn't have to bash me over the head."

Jolene opened the car door for me then went around the car and got in on her side. "I'm sure they'll stay away once you take possession. You also wanted to go to the chapel?" She started the car and pulled forward.

I could tell Jolene had a busy agenda for today, and listening to my fantasies about what might have happened in a neglected building wasn't on her list.

As she pulled out, Zach drove up, opened his window, and dangled a key on an extra-large ring. "Glad I caught you two. Jolene, I'll return the key to your office in about an hour. And Abby, I should have your estimates and a timeline by midafternoon. How about dinner at Maria's at six?"

I gave him a thumbs-up signal through Jolene's open window before she closed it and drove to our next stop, the Chapel of the Transfiguration.

The chapel was one of my favorite spots near Bailey. The small worship site sat on part of the Wyoming acreage purchased and later donated by John D. Rockefeller Jr. to the United States for a national park area. The wealthy New Yorker claimed a special pew in the modest church with a large window showcasing the magnificent Tetons behind a simple cross on the altar.

The site evoked spiritual feelings. The vista reminded me of God the Creator, the cross on the altar of Jesus the Savior, and the quiet reminded me to listen for the promptings of the Holy Spirit. Today, I would pray and listen for the answer to my questions.

Was I doing the right thing by opening the bookshop?

Was someone against the idea? If so, who and why?

Did someone intend to harm me to keep me from buying it?

Jolene pulled into the chapel parking area behind a van from Paxton's Ski Lodge that belched visitors armed with binoculars and guidebooks.

I shook my head. "Guess I wasn't meant to use the chapel today. Just take me to the ranch, please. Then you can get on with your day's agenda. Thanks for picking me up at the hospital."

"Not a problem. We're all glad you're okay. Forget about the accident," Jolene urged.

I touched the bandage on my head and resisted the impulse to say it wasn't an accident. "I don't think I'll be able to do that, not until my hair grows back."

"At least fight the impulse to play detective. Leave that to the sheriff." Jolene glanced my way.

I didn't meet her eyes. I knew myself too well.

CHAPTER 2

S mells of garlic, onion, and chili powder welcomed those entering the two-story building with a winter clothing shop on one side and a general store/souvenir shop on the other. The walkway between the establishments led to stairs to restaurants above the businesses.

The aroma of cilantro wafted from Maria's Meals—a small, cheerful café decorated in aquas, reds, and yellows. Our friend's Mexican food restaurant was opposite the Burger and Dog, a fast-food place frequented by families with young children. Maria's Meals offered selections for all ages, and seating was at a premium.

Zach waved at me from a table in the back, the only quasi-quiet spot in the restaurant. He stood behind a painted green chair with a woven cane seat. He helped me sit then took the chair across from me. A basket of nacho chips next to bowls of salsa and cheese sat in the center of the table.

"Hi, I'm glad you got us a table, because I'm starving. I'm like Pavlov's dog. When I open the door downstairs, my mouth starts to water." I dipped a chip into the queso and then popped it into my mouth before picking up the menu. "Have you decided?"

"Chile rellenos. That's my go-to dish."

I turned to watch Daniel Zapata deliver a sizzling platter of grilled chicken, onions, and peppers to the next table. The smells confirmed my choice, and I closed the menu. "Beef fajitas for me."

"Be with you after I deliver the rest of their food." Daniel returned to the kitchen.

When Maria Zapata opened a restaurant using her grandmother's recipes and her family's money, Maria's Meals quickly became one of the preferred eating establishments in town. With flirtatious brown eyes, dimpled cheeks, and a broad smile, she had charmed the town's mayor, Rodney Paxton, to fast-track her permits but made an enemy of the mayor's wife, Carol.

Daniel, fresh out of high school, had joined his cousin Maria in Bailey last summer to work in their family restaurant. He frequently reminded folks that he'd been eager to move to Bailey when Maria asked for help, but he didn't expect to be waiting tables. People in the community knew that the cousins, Daniel and Maria, had lived in an affluent Los Angeles suburb and skied in Bailey during their childhood and teen years. The switch from being served to serving seemed to bother the young man.

Daniel approached the table, swiping beads of perspiration from his forehead. "Zach, Abby, what would you like?" He took our orders for beef fajitas and chile rellenos and refilled our water glasses.

After he left, I reached for the chips again. "I can't leave these alone. You want to tell me the bad news about renovation costs now or after dinner?"

"How about good news? The Secret Passage building is structurally sound." Zach opened his laptop and showed me schematics of how he envisioned the final look of the bookshop with a tea shop downstairs and my living quarters upstairs.

"Oh, I like these freestanding bookshelves. When I was a kid, I always peeked through the shelves to see what might be on the other side. All kinds of horrible things happened in the next aisle, at least in my imagination."

"Nothing good?" Zach asked.

"Of course not. Drama's part of my DNA, but in my bookshop, I only want good things."

"Let me make a note of that." He tapped on the keys then said, "I emailed you my estimate. Think about any changes you want before I begin. If you approve, I could start before the end of the month. The kids from the youth group want to help with the initial demolition as a thank-you to us."

"Oh, that's sweet. They don't have to, but I would appreciate it." I grabbed another chip. "The heat isn't on."

"Heat would be nice, since we haven't had a day above thirty-two degrees this year. How about the thirty-first of January for a start date?" Zach grinned.

I raised an eyebrow. "That's the end of the month for sure. If the estimate works with my budget, I'll transfer money to your account for half the invoice. You're paid half up front and the remainder at completion, right?"

"I could make an exception for you," Zach said.

"No special treatment. Oh, here's our food." I leaned back so Daniel could put the hot skillet and other fajita goodies in front of me.

Zach turned to the waiter. "We're celebrating tonight, Daniel. I'm starting work on Abby's bookshop, the Secret Passage."

"When?" Daniel asked.

"Last day of the month," I said. "Our church youth group is going to help us with the cleanout."

"Sounds like fun, but I doubt I could join you. I'll mention it to Maria. She might send over free tacos. Last day of the month, huh? Well, don't let your food get cold." Daniel turned to the table beside us and handed them their check.

We took Daniel's advice about not letting our food cool. Zach cut his peppers open and began eating right away, while I had to build my food, starting with Maria's handmade tortillas. I didn't skimp on the fixings, and my concoction bulged with lusciousness.

"Mmm. I made an excellent choice." I wiped my hands on the napkin and then blotted my mouth. "These are so good. You should try them." I dabbed at an errant crumb on his cheek.

Zach and I spent quite a bit of time together, but we weren't linked romantically, as many locals assumed. We'd become friends on the winter ski slopes and summer hiking trails in the early mornings before starting our regular workdays. People sometimes asked why I'd given up my librarian's job for a menial job that included scooping poop, but the breathtaking view of the Tetons each day paid immeasurable dividends.

Zach's work was construction and renovation. His father taught him the carpentry trade, and he excelled in woodworking. Even though he was an expert craftsman, he preferred hiking, boating, or skiing. In one of our first conversations, he told me his philosophy was "work to live, don't live to work." He loved his vocation, and he loved living, and he did both with zest.

In the church youth meetings, teenage girls queued up to be in his group instead of mine. Zach's deep brown hair matched his beard and mustache, and those dark, almost black eyes always twinkled with an expectancy of fun. He was handsome, didn't drink or smoke, loved the Lord, and was in awe of God's creation. In other words, he was perfect spouse material, and he attracted the ladies without even trying.

As if agreeing with my thoughts about the man opposite me, Maria Zapata, her eyes smiling, approached our table. "How was your meal?" Maria made an appearance at the tables each night.

Zach patted his stomach. "I may have to quit coming here. You're going to make me fat."

"You're a man who will be slim and handsome when you're eighty. Don't you agree, Abby?" Maria's flirtatiousness caused Zach to blush.

"Oh, I don't know. He might grow to be fat and bald." I touched the hot-pink fleece covering the stubble on my head. I appreciated Jolene's thoughtfulness in providing me with colorful selections, but I felt frumpy as I watched Zach and Maria's banter. The three of us were in our early thirties and often joked that we were too busy to date. Tonight, I wondered if my two friends had changed their minds.

Maria's hand was on Zach's shoulder. "That's not true. I have an instinct about such things. I'm counting on this man staying single until I'm independently wealthy and ready to marry. When are you starting work on the bookshop?"

"End of the month," Zach answered.

"So soon?" Maria's eyes widened then she turned to me. "I'm sure your business will be more successful than the escape room. The previous owner liked my cooking too. I think a bookshop will work better. There's not much for people to do here after dark. They soak in the tubs after overexerting unused muscles or watch reruns on television. When do you plan to open?"

"April." I didn't mention April 1 because I'd heard enough jokes about that being a foolish day to open. "Thinking of doing the official opening on tax day, April 15."

"If you have a grand opening, I'd love to cater." Maria looked for a response.

But I only shrugged, letting her know I'd consider her offer. The woman was an excellent businessperson. No mention of the free food Daniel had suggested. Just an offer to cater for the opening. Even though Maria's Meals had only been in Bailey a couple of years, the restaurant had a sterling reputation and never lacked customers. I should ask her for advice on how to garner positive attention for the bookshop.

"I must visit my other customers. Nice to see you two again." Maria slid her hand from Zach's shoulder to the back of his neck before she left.

"You too," I said, but she'd already moved on to the next table.

———

At the Rocking T Ranch, Ben babied me by assigning easy chores. That wasn't fair to the others, so when I recognized his footsteps in the dorm's hallway, I hurried to the door.

"Ben," I called. "Have a minute?"

When he stepped inside my room, he shook his head. "When are you moving out?"

My dorm area at the Rocking T Ranch looked like a hoarder's refuge as I'd been receiving donations for the used book section after I'd announced my plans to offer new and next-to-new books. I'd accumulated a selection of romance, mysteries, nonfiction, biographies, and children's books. Ben, although not the neatest of people, grimaced each time he glimpsed the books stacked inside my room.

"I'll be out of your hair by the end of March. Zach says the bookshop will be ready April 1, and I want to move into my upstairs apartment before the shop opens. Look at these plans. Since you're one of my investors, I'll keep you informed on the progress." I showed him Zach's drawings and explained where furniture would go in my apartment and where the different book sections would be downstairs.

Ben tapped his watch. "Abby, you asked for a minute."

I laughed. "I'm sorry. Wanted to remind you that I expect to do my share of the work here until the day I leave."

Ben grinned. "I don't need your help making the work schedules. And the bookshop proposal looks great."

"Zach's starting this month...Well, the last day of the month. Talk about God opening a window. I wanted to share my love of books, and I can do that right here in Bailey, one of the most beautiful spots in the world. I'm signing the papers and getting the keys today. You helped make my dream possible."

"Glad to help. If that's all, I have work to do." Ben, a sentimental softy, never showed affection with words.

After I signed the contract in many places, Jolene handed me the keys to my property. Well, it was my property, with strings. I had put up a large down payment, but the purchase required personal loans from my parents and Ben True. My "investors" professed confidence that the bookshop would be an enormous success. I agreed with their assessment and planned to repay them in jig time. What could go wrong?

Before embarking on my dream of living a carefree life of skiing and hiking, my constant companions were books. My enthusiasm for the written word began in elementary school. Instead of toys or stuffed animals, I requested books for holidays and birthdays. Some of my favorite people lived inside the book covers. Laura from *Little House on the Prairie*, Fern from *Charlotte's Web*, and Annie and Jack Smith from the Magic Treehouse series were all friends. I longed to share my love of reading with all of Bailey's citizens and visitors.

Eager to begin, I phoned the gas company. The woman told me they could have a tech come out late afternoon but stressed someone must be there to let them in. I grabbed a burger from Burgers and Dogs and headed off for the first step of my dream adventure.

My dream turned into a nightmare when I unlocked the door to my new property and saw the interloper.

CHAPTER 3

You can't sleep here. This is not a hotel!" I stomped toward what appeared to be a person snuggled under a pile of blankets.

He or she hadn't roused when I turned on the lights and shouted. Bedding pulled down over the forehead and up over the nose left only closed eyes visible.

The form was a "she," and she didn't respond even when I threw the top cover off, knelt beside her, and shook her shoulder. "Wake up. Are you okay?"

The building was freezing, and so was she. Noting her blue lips, I reached inside her ski jacket to place my fingers on her neck. I'd been trained in CPR, but in the pit of my stomach, I knew those skills wouldn't help this woman. I checked her wrist and again at the carotid artery. She looked so peaceful.

Someone banged at the entrance, so I covered her body with the blanket before opening the door to a tall man I didn't recognize.

"Are you Abby Scott?"

"Who's asking?"

The broad-chested man wearing shiny sunglasses pointed to the name on his jacket. "I'm Frank, I'm here—"

I stopped him midsentence. "I don't know any Frank." My voice held a panicky timbre. "I want you to leave."

"It'll cost you."

"Cost me?" I stepped outside and searched up and down the street. Where were all the people?

"Yep. My boss said I had to take care of Abby Scott this afternoon. The company will not be happy if I disappoint them."

"Stay away from me!" My head whiplashed around, looking for someone, anyone, to help me.

"I'm here. You're here. Let's take care of your problem."

"I don't have a problem." I heard the fear in my voice.

"Let's go inside, Miss Scott."

"No. I'm not going back inside." Was this man responsible for the death of the person in my bookshop?

"You're not the only person on my list. This will be quick." He nodded toward the front door.

When I lurched backward, he snorted—not a moose-sized snort, but a snort, nonetheless.

"I'm not going to let you 'take care of me' like you 'took care' of her." The view of myself in his reflective lenses looked brave enough, although my pounding heart betrayed me.

"What are you talking about?" Frank took a step back in our macabre sidewalk dance.

"I'm quite sure she's dead."

"Dead? Who's dead?" He glared at me.

"That girl. I don't know who she is. Do you?"

"If there is really a dead person, why don't you call the police?" He moved two steps to the right, trying to peek inside the building.

I followed his lead. "Did you kill her?"

"No! Is there really a dead person in there?" He didn't seem so macho now.

I lifted my chin. "A dead woman. I know Sheriff Hawthorn, and I'm calling him right now." I fumbled with my phone and failed to find the phone number the sheriff gave me when I was in the hospital.

"Your knowing the sheriff doesn't surprise me." Frank had lost all his swagger, and he stepped away from me.

When Zach pulled into the lot, I raced to him and threw my arms around his neck the moment he got out of the car. "I think she's dead."

"Dead? Who's dead? Do you have a gas leak?" Zach pulled my arms away from his neck, turned me around, and pushed me toward the building.

"I found her body when I unlocked the building."

"Found who?" Zach grabbed my elbow and pulled me to a stop.

"I don't know who she is. Then that man showed up saying his boss sent him to take care of me."

"What man?"

I nodded toward Frank, who leaned against his van. "Zach, I'm so glad you're here. How could someone die in my bookshop?"

"Sit down." He guided me to the bench on the wooden sidewalk.

My hands shook. "Maybe she isn't dead. Maybe I'm wrong. I was so scared, and then Frank showed up. What if he's the murderer? Do you think he meant to kill me, not that poor woman inside? Maybe he's the one who sent me to the hospital with a concussion."

"Calm down. Take a breath."

I filled my lungs with air then exhaled slowly. "Who would want me dead?"

"I bet there's a list somewhere," Frank murmured loud enough for me to hear.

I ignored him. "Why did you ask about a gas leak?"

"Because Frank's here." My friend patted my shoulder and then turned to the man. "Want to check things out? I'm not sure she should go back inside."

Frank grunted his agreement, and I noticed for the first time that the logo on his coat matched the emblem of the gas company on the van.

"I don't want to stay out here by myself." Curiosity won out, and I hurried to join them. I looked at the woman more closely this time. She had shoulder-length brown hair, high cheekbones, and penciled-in eyebrows above closed eyes. Her bluish lips, stilled by death, appeared to have a hint of a smile.

After finding no pulse, Zach called Sheriff Hawthorn. Then Frank "took care of me" by connecting the gas. Then he offered his contact information for the sheriff.

"I'm sorry... I don't..." I mumbled.

But Frank held out a fully extended arm with palm facing me in that "don't speak, don't come any closer" gesture. I doubted he'd frequent my bookshop.

———

Sheriff Hawthorn had earned his reputation in the hockey league as the defensive enforcer. Whenever a player from the other team interfered with Bailey's star forward, the coach sent his best defensive player into the game. He body-checked the offender into the boards, slashed him across the back with a high stick, or dropped his gloves and pummeled him. Sheriff Hawthorn was a legend in Bailey, and his record of penalty minutes was unmatched, as was the number of the team's championships.

With that same ferocity he exhibited on the ice, the sheriff protected this town. As a result, Bailey didn't have many law violators. The angry expression on his face when he returned from checking the body made me wish for the sanctity of a penalty box.

I leaned against the front door, shivering. I didn't know if my chill came from the lack of heat in the building or from the dead body in the back of my bookshop or from the scrutiny of Hawthorn's stare.

"I called the coroner. Now, Abby girl, how many people did you invite to view the corpse?" He unzipped his jacket.

I feared this meant we would be here a long time, not that he was too warm.

He glared at me and rephrased his question. "Why'd you call your boyfriend instead of me?"

"Zach's not my boyfriend, and I didn't call him."

Sheriff Hawthorn put his hands on his hips.

I continued, "I didn't want to believe she was dead. I was scared, and then this big guy threatened me."

He tilted his head forward, and my uncensored comments spilled forth.

"Jolene believed kids were using the building. She called you about that, right? But today, I saw a person under the blanket and freaked. Then Frank threatened me, so I panicked. Sheriff, what's going on?"

He shushed me. "Abby girl, you know this doesn't look good. First, you're knocked unconscious, and now a body turns up in your place. And the victim was next to a walled-over corridor. Take a look." He approached the wall and pointed to a very small, half-opened door. "There's an opening in the wall. Can't see it when it's closed. Were you aware that space was behind your interior wall?"

"No."

He gestured toward the deceased woman. "Do you recognize her?"

I rubbed my pounding temples. "I don't know anything about that wall, and I don't recognize her."

"I'd like both you and Zach to take a second look." The sheriff cupped my elbow and directed me toward the woman's body.

"She doesn't look any older than I am." I pretended she was sleeping instead of dead. She had unblemished skin, a slightly upturned nose, and cracked lips—the kind one gets from being out in the cold too long. Her dark hair emphasized the pale pallor of her skin. "I don't know her." I wanted to turn away, but I couldn't stop looking at her.

"Found a driver's license. Name's Isabella Diaz, address listed is in Los Angeles."

I shook my head. The immensity of the situation washed over me. Who was Isabella Diaz? How did she get here? What happened to her? Where were the people who loved her? Her face looked unlined, innocent. Because it was my property, I felt a sense of responsibility for her.

The sheriff turned to Zach. "You can't start work until we get this wrapped up. Abby girl, you be careful, and call me—not your boyfriend—if you notice anything unusual or if you feel you're in danger."

I opened my mouth, ready to remind him that Zach wasn't my boyfriend, but then decided to let it go.

Zach snapped his fingers. "I've seen her."

His words made me glance at the woman's face again. "You have? Where?"

The sheriff glared at me then repeated my question. "Where?"

"LA. She helped at the mission church where our youth group worked last summer."

"I didn't go on that trip," I said.

"You were doing river raft trips for the Rocking T Ranch. Carol Paxton took her car, and I drove the church van." Zach nodded again after studying her face.

The officer scribbled on a notepad. "Carol Paxton? The mayor's wife?"

Zach nodded. "That's right. The mayor and Carol initiated the connection with our congregation and the LA mission church. People there called her Belle, not Isabella. She headed a program to keep kids off the streets. The Paxtons supported her outreach program. You should talk to Rodney and Carol."

"I'll do that. You two can leave. Abby, I'll let you know when you can go back in the building."

"Thank you." My teeth started chattering, and I shivered involuntarily.

Zach put an arm around my shoulder. "How about hot chocolate with lots of marshmallows?"

"Please." My one-word answer surprised us both.

At the warm coffee shop filled with living people, we sipped from steaming mugs topped with marshmallows.

"Was she married? Did her family go to that church? How long had she been working with street kids?" I asked.

Zach shrugged. "You know how those mission trips are. As counselors, we work on specific projects requested by the host church, corral the kids, and make sure they're fed physically and spiritually."

"I know. Hey, I have an appointment with Rodney Paxton at three tomorrow. You could come with me. We could ask if they know why Isabella Diaz was in Bailey."

"The death investigation belongs to the sheriff," Zach reminded me.

"But I already have an appointment about scheduling a ribbon cutting and the grand opening. We could ask some questions while we're there."

"I'm pretty sure the sheriff won't like it." Zach picked up my mug. "Refill?"

"No. Please go with me tomorrow. If Isabella Diaz was active in our church's mission outreach program, we should find out why she showed up in my unheated bookshop."

"That's a job for professionals."

"I know, but we could help. Rodney and Carol must know more about Isabella's story." I stood and deposited my ceramic cup in the dish receptacle. "Will you help?"

"Not willingly," he said. But his smile told me he'd support my sleuthing. "I remember you wanted to keep the name of Secret Passage because you believed books could offer a surprising introduction to people, places, and events in the past, present, and future."

"True."

He tossed his head to get the hair out of his eyes. "Well, there's a surprising person and a secret passageway, so I guess your name fits."

I shivered again, this time not from the freezing temperature. My hope for my bookshop had come true, but not in the way I wanted.

CHAPTER 4

The next morning, I punched in the number for Bailey's municipal offices. "Mayor Paxton, this is Abby Scott. We have an appointment at three. I wondered if your wife might join us, and I'd like Zach Cooper to be there too."

His answer came quickly. "I assume this has to do with the dead woman in your building. Zach's welcome, and I'll ask Carol to join us."

News in our tightly knit community spreads quickly, so I wasn't surprised the mayor knew about the death. Bailey, located in the shadow of Jackson, Wyoming, maintains its unique identity. Visitors see us as one sprawling town, but we aren't. Bailey is a separate entity, and that's the way we like it.

Both towns are located in what's known as the "hole," a dip in the landscape before the Teton Mountains rise straight up from the banks of the Snake River. Old pioneers dubbed Jackson as Jackson Hole because it's literally in a geographical hole. The nickname stuck. Tourists overran that city, and the four-antler archways to Jackson's city park is a favorite photo spot. Bailey residents view Jackson as commercially minded and our town as laid back and homey.

Businesses in both towns flourish, but there isn't much expansion room for either municipality, as half of Wyoming is earmarked as public lands. We have the benefit of those wanting to visit the Grand Teton National Park, the National Elk Refuge, and Bridger National Forest, but there's not much growing room left. With limited space in town, I considered myself fortunate to purchase a storefront for my business. I was confident it would thrive—that was, until I discovered a dead body on the premises.

I spent my morning at the Rocking T Ranch, going over Zach's drawings and wondering why I hadn't noticed a hidden passageway in that wall. Jolene and I had inspected the property multiple times, and the previous owners hadn't mentioned the secret corridor in the disclosure statement. What baffled me was how the body of Isabella Diaz appeared next to the open door to the secret corridor. Had she known about it?

Sheriff Hawthorn informed me that the space behind my interior wall and next to the Pretty Nails shop ran the length of the building. Perhaps the escape room owners added it to enhance their adventure experience, so the passageway represented nothing clandestine or nefarious. Studying the drawings, I debated using part of the newly discovered secret section as a children's book nook or a mystery book alcove.

After lunch, I packed the papers I needed for the meeting with the mayor, checked the time, and drove to Jolene's office. My Realtor was putting on her coat when I arrived.

"Have you heard?" Of course she had. I knew the question was foolish.

"Yes, and that you found her. That's awful. How are you doing?" Jolene pulled me close.

"Shaken up. Zach recognized her as a member of our LA mission church."

"Heard that too. I usually visit the mission when I go to LA on my quarterly shopping trips, but I focus on the art galleries and picking up decorative items for my unoccupied listings. I have a trip planned in February. Want me to look for anything for your apartment?" She secured a scarf around her throat.

"Not now. My mom will want to help with decorating. I'm curious. Did you know anything about a hidden section behind the wall?"

"No. If I'd known, I'd have told you. The footprint of the building matched the measurements we took. Sometimes builders leave a gap between walls to add more insulation. The room measurements didn't seem off enough to start banging through walls." Her clipped words told me she was not pleased with my questions.

"I didn't mean to question your integrity or your representation of my interests in the purchase."

"Anything else? I'm meeting a client." She didn't say goodbye, just waved a gloved hand and left.

My visit with Jolene gave me no information except that she went to LA several times a year, which meant she could have known the dead woman too. Why hadn't Jolene asked me for the woman's name? Had she learned the identity through the gossip chain? Or had she not wanted to acknowledge their acquaintance?

While driving to the Paxton Ski Lodge, I tried to analyze Jolene's testy behavior, a side of her I'd never seen before. She was always upbeat and cheerful. Busy? Yes, but she'd never been curt or dismissive.

A car exiting the first row of parking at the lodge made me forget Jolene's actions. Getting a prime spot was unusual in Bailey, and I saw the open slot as a good omen for my upcoming visit with the mayor and his wife.

As I entered Rodney Paxton's office, he was placing Legos, toy trucks, and board books into bright red canvas bins by his bookcases.

"How old is your grandson?" I joined the mayor's efforts by collecting tiny blocks, wheels, doors, and windows.

"Five, and he's a handful. I keep him when his parents are busy. I love having him around."

"Has your daughter gone back to work?" I asked.

Rodney tilted his head. "Maria's Meals took a lot of their business, so Elsa's concentrating on marketing to get more customers. Our girl blames me for encouraging Maria Zapata to open her place in Bailey instead of Jackson. I didn't expect Maria's to take so many clients from my daughter and son-in-law's restaurant."

"Bailey's Best Food has been around for years. Maria's Meals is new, something different to try. Things will work out."

"Hope so. I don't like having both Carol and Elsa mad at me. Thanks for the help in toy pickup. Terrible business, the death in your bookshop." Rodney surveyed the office, hands on hips. The mayor's body was a series of spheres—round shoulders, round face, and round stomach. Bailey voters had elected the genial man to six terms as town leader. As a former teacher and now manager of a successful ski lodge, Rodney Paxton preferred people over processes.

Carol and Zach arrived together but stayed outside the glassed-in office, intent on a private conversation. I longed to know what they said, but I wasn't a lip reader.

After a final look around the room, Rodney opened the door, kissed his wife on the cheek, and gestured to the chairs.

Carol hugged me. "Poor dear, how horrible for you to find a dead person in your future place of business."

"Zach identified her. He told Sheriff Hawthorn you knew her. Carol, do you remember Isabella Diaz from the LA mission church?" I jumped right in with my wannabe-detective questioning.

She shrugged. "I vaguely remember Belle. She was passionate about rescuing kids who felt threatened living in their own homes. She also had a plan to rescue them from the streets. I admired her zeal. She was a determined woman." Carol pushed her oversized, black-rimmed glasses up at the nosepiece.

"You didn't know she was in Bailey?" I pushed.

"We didn't, did we, Rodney?" She looked at her husband for confirmation.

He frowned. "I don't think I knew her. We sent money for her program, didn't we? I'm a sucker for anything dealing with kids."

After what he'd experienced, it was no wonder he had a heart for children. Rodney had been part owner of the daycare center destroyed by the horrible Oklahoma City bombing of the Murrah Federal Building. Paxton rallied for the empty chair memorial but later left Oklahoma and moved to Wyoming. He often spoke at church and civic meetings about how the event made him an advocate for children, and he encouraged those in the audience to find and act for a specific cause.

Carol took Rodney's hand but spoke to me. "As I told Zach, I don't know why Belle would show up in Bailey. Didn't you suspect local mischief-makers had camped in your building?"

"Jolene and I found boxes from Maria's Meals and a pile of navy-blue blankets. When I saw the form under the covers, I thought it was a vagrant. I didn't realize she was dead until I pulled the blanket off." I choked up, as I did each time I pictured the woman's face.

"Have they determined a cause of death?" practical Carol asked.

"The sheriff suggested hypothermia. You know how cold it is here, and someone visiting from southern California might not know the warning signs," I said.

"What a tragedy. I wonder why she didn't contact me or Zach," Carol said.

I'd been wondering the same thing. Did I want this to be a mysterious death rather than an unfortunate accident? Since the Paxtons didn't seem to know anything, I got down to business. "My appointment concerns the bookshop. My savings and the loan agreements I've made with Ben True and my parents are tied to its success. With the pending investigation, I don't know when I can open, but I want to schedule a ribbon cutting by the mayor."

Carol picked up a red marker. "Surely Sheriff Hawthorn will allow you to go ahead with your plans. I doubt the woman's death had sinister connections."

"Isabella's death," Zach corrected.

"Yes, Belle's unfortunate death. Rodney and I will continue to fund her program, of course." Carol's response sounded dismissive to me.

Even though I didn't know the dead woman, I wasn't ready to push forward with my plans until I knew how and why she died in my bookshop, cold and alone.

Carol tapped on the oversized wall calendar. "About the grand opening, shall we put it on Rodney's calendar?"

Ever the businesswoman, Carol had married Rodney Paxton shortly after he arrived in Bailey. Her parents ran a successful ski lodge and handed it over to the newlyweds, and Carol and Rodney changed its name to the Paxton Ski Lodge. Although Rodney's surname was on the door, everyone knew Carol ran their commercial business and scheduled her husband's public appearances as Bailey's mayor. It wasn't that Rodney was incapable, but he didn't mind giving up control, and Carol thrived on it.

"Let's pencil in April 15." I emphasized the word *pencil*.

Her red pen hovered over the date. "What time?"

"Between four and six? I'd like to catch the day and after-work crowd."

"Rodney and I will be there at five o'clock on April 15." Carol noted the time in red.

"I hope to open on April 1, work out any glitches, then use the grand opening for book sale promotions. I'd love to invite an author for a book signing, but they probably book up a year in advance." I stared at the date square marked in red.

"In order to be successful, you must make your plan and stick to it. You're booked." Carol let the calendar sheets fall back down.

"We'll work around your schedule, Abby. Let us know what works for you. If you need to postpone, that won't be a problem." Rodney winked at me to assure me he was flexible, even if his wife wasn't.

"Is there a fee for your appearance?" I asked.

"No, openings are a public service, but don't ask me to do a closing. We want Bailey businesses to succeed." Rodney chuckled.

"Well, if you want food catered, I hope you'll consider Bailey's Best, Elsa's restaurant. Have you eaten there recently?" Carol asked.

Ah, so Carol knew Zach and I had shared dinner at Maria's Meals. "I've been trying to eat out less. That was one of my New Year's resolutions. Plus, I'm saving money so I can pay my contractor."

"Glad to hear that," Zach said enthusiastically. He rose, indicating he was ready to go.

Carol pressed on with her agenda. "Well, Rodney and I would appreciate you supporting Elsa's restaurant, just as we plan to support you in your new venture."

Rodney placed his hand on Carol's shoulder. "Abby, we'll support your bookshop, no matter your taste in food."

"Of course," Carol agreed.

Interesting. Carol could be a bit pushy, but Rodney seemed to be in charge. He'd denied knowing Isabella Diaz, but I was positive that if Carol knew the woman, Rodney had too.

Why hadn't he admitted it?

CHAPTER 5

I raced through my chores, eager to visit one of my favorite trails before twilight. The doctor had discouraged me from downhill skiing for a month after my head injury but agreed I could handle cross-country. Today was perfect.

I parked my old CR-V by the Sunrise Trailhead, unloaded skis and poles, and checked the weather app that predicted snow for late afternoon. Sunrise Trail was a three-mile loop, so I'd be back before the snow arrived. Thankful for the fleece hats Jolene had given me, I tugged a red one on my head then secured my ski jacket hood. Without my long, unruly curls, my head got cold quickly.

I soon found my rhythm in the kick-and-glide sequence, forgot about the skiing process, and relaxed into the sweet sounds of nature. Sunrise wasn't a challenging trail, which was why I enjoyed it. I could feast on my surroundings, the crisp air, and the occasional bird calls. Winter quiet had a unique stillness I found comforting. The trail's halfway point, a lean-to cabin, was in sight when the flakes began to fall. The weather app had been wrong.

As I approached the shelter, a small form dressed in black scurried out of the shack and into the thickening snow. Why was the person running?

The flimsy building served as a wind break and as protection from rain or snow. On the back wall was a fireplace, but the only furniture was a lopsided bench. Today, a small fire burned and hastily discarded blankets lay by the hearth. These were the same style of navy-blue blankets that had covered the dead woman in my bookshop—practical and cheap, plain navy wool fabric with gray stitching around the perimeter, no labels, no designs. The recent visitor had eaten and, just as in my bookshop, the food of choice was from Maria's Meals. The restaurant's biodegradable bags sat next to the fireplace.

"Come back," I shouted out the door. "The snow won't last. Don't stay out in the cold. We can share the fire." Had I just invited the anonymous person who hit me on the head and sent me to the hospital with a concussion to enter this secluded shack? Not likely. The departing form looked more like a child than a threatening adult, and I didn't want anyone out in the cold.

The trail shacks always had wood. It was the neighborly thing to do, leaving the place ready for someone in need. On any hike outing with the youth group, we checked all cabins and ensured they had abundant supplies of papers, twigs, wood, and matches. The small figure who fled from the shack had taken advantage of the fire-building supplies. The weather forecaster predicted snow for less than an hour. Although I wasn't chilly, I feared for the person who'd run out of the building. I opened the door and yelled my invitation to come into the shelter again.

No response.

Then I switched into pseudo-detective mode, picked up the food bag by its base, and stuffed it into my backpack. The attached order indicated the breakfast tacos were purchased today, but that clue wouldn't help. Maria's did a brisk business from two outdoor stands near the ski lifts. Nevertheless, in the detective shows I watched, they always found fingerprints on items left at the scene. Forensics might identify the mystery person by prints on this taco bag.

Even though the snow arrived before its expected time, the white flakes stopped after an hour as predicted. After dousing the fire, I slid my feet into the bindings and headed out for the second part of the trail loop.

My Tuesday assignment for the Rocking T was supervising an outing at Paxton Ski Lodge. The first-time skiers would need help selecting equipment before I gave them basic lessons. I enjoyed working with newbies. In my experience, some caught on immediately while others tried once and returned to the lodge to sip hot chocolate and watch their friends through the big windows opposite a warm fireplace.

I answered questions on the drive to the lodge. The younger ones expected to be able to soar down the slopes, while older first-timers worried about losing control, taking a serious tumble, and breaking bones.

Carol Paxton was in the ski rental shop when we arrived. "I didn't know you'd be here today, but I'm glad. Could Rodney and I have a word over lunch? You do take a break between sessions, don't you?"

"I do. What's up? Does Rodney have a conflict with my grand opening date?"

Carol's laugh came out too loud. "No, no. Nothing like that. Rodney and I will be in his office from twelve to one. Pop in when you have a minute."

Her suggestion must have distracted me, because I rushed through my explanation of ski etiquette with the skiers. Luckily, my group didn't seem to notice. For Rodney and Carol, who were organized, methodical people, to suggest a "pop-in" conversation was unusual. I racked my brain and couldn't imagine a reason for the meeting request. After I dismissed my group for lunch, I hurried to Rodney's office.

Carol opened the door and offered me a bag from Bailey's Best Food. "Thank you for coming. Have you tried the wraps from Elsa's restaurant?"

I accepted one and fiddled with the paper. "We don't take a long lunch, and the skiers often ask me questions during the break."

Rodney took the hint and leaned forward on his elbows. "Abby, I know you've taken out loans from your parents and Ben to purchase the Secret Passage."

I hadn't hidden the fact, but why would my friends bring up my personal finances?

"Carol and I would like to do you a good turn. We believe Bailey needs a bookshop. But we worry about you risking so much. We'll purchase the bookshop property from you for the same amount you paid."

I stopped fiddling with the sandwich wrapping and placed it on the desk. "Why? What would you do with the property?"

Carol moved next to Rodney. "We'd do what you're planning—offer a bookshop on one side and a tea shop on the other. If you want to be involved, we'll lease the bookshop half to you with an option to buy after a certain term. Our Elsa could add a satellite business at the bookshop. Her family needs more income. As you know, Maria's Meals added a couple of morning taco stands by the ski lifts."

I shook my head, confused by their proposition and the last statement, which had nothing to do with anything. "Which half?" I asked.

"What do you mean?" Carol tilted her head as if trying to grasp my question.

"Which half would you want for the tea shop?" I repeated.

"Oh, we'd take the side where you found the dead woman, dear. You wouldn't have to worry about that bizarre hidden corridor.

I know this is sudden, but we wanted to meet with you before Zach started working. If you take the offer, we'll finance the renovations," Carol said.

For once, I was without words.

Rodney filled the silence, "It's a cash offer. You could pay off the loans and lease from us. The shop would be smaller, but you'd have more money to spend on your book inventory."

Carol lifted her shoulders. "We just want to help."

My mind reeled. "I was in this very office less than a week ago to schedule the grand opening of 'my' bookshop. This offer comes as a shock. If you'd been interested in expanding Elsa's business, why didn't you do that before I purchased the property?"

"We feared your opening a new business where a dead person was found would discourage customers. We don't want you to take that financial risk," Rodney said.

"Or perhaps a corpse in a bookshop might intrigue customers to come in. They might want to see the spot where a body was discovered." I folded my arms. "Wouldn't the business you plan to open have the same stigma?" A glance at my watch showed I still had thirty minutes until I met my group.

Carol sighed and pushed her glasses up. "I didn't want to mention it, but as you know, we are well-positioned financially. Abby, you could continue working for Ben or lease the bookshop until you have more funds. If you want us to take the whole building, we can."

"Your offer is generous, but I spent months making my decision. My answer is—"

Rodney placed his hand on my shoulder. "Shh. Don't say anything. Think about it. You could still have your bookshop, but we'd be the ones paying for it. We're willing to buy the whole building for the use of half. As such, we can offer you a long-term lease or sell half of the building back to you. Which would you prefer?"

Jolene had told me offering two items could be a real estate presumptive closing technique. Offer two choices, and the hapless buyer will choose one of them. The Paxtons offered me half the building or a lease. Why would I choose either? I owned the whole building.

Carol glanced at her husband. "Rodney and I hate that you found that woman. Although her death appears to be an unfortunate incident, the sheriff is investigating. Who knows when the coroner will release his findings? We decided this was the best way to help you. Sleep on it. We'll talk later this week."

I rewrapped the sandwich in its paper, since I hadn't taken a bite. My appetite had disappeared, but I knew not to refuse a chicken wrap from Bailey's Best Food.

———

Sunday should have been a day of rest. It wasn't.

A week ago, conversations at church centered on the body found in my future bookshop. Sheriff Hawthorn, Jolene Roussel, Ben True, and Rodney and Carol Paxton all belonged to our congregation. Today, I sought out Rodney and Carol by the coffee and doughnut station.

"I appreciate your offer, but I'm not selling." My words didn't seem to shock them.

"Have you talked with the sheriff?" Carol asked.

I nodded. "He told me that Zach could start work anytime. He also said the coroner ruled the woman's death as accidental."

"Accidental death?" Rodney stirred his coffee with the skinny wooden stick. "Doesn't answer questions about why she was found near that secret passageway with the door open, does it? Abby, we're fond of you and want to help you out of a tough situation."

"Well, I can't allow myself to worry about unknowns. I'm not selling."

"Did you tell Zach about the offer?" Carol asked.

"No. Why would I? Excuse me, but I'm late for my Sunday school class."

When I walked into the youth room where Zach and I were co-teachers, the students were discussing ghost sightings. At least they weren't discussing the dead woman. Then I realized the "ghost" they saw matched the description of the person I'd encountered on my snowy cross-country outing. However, their chatter indicated they knew nothing more than I did. They'd seen a form dressed in black who appeared, then disappeared. There had been sightings on Main Street, near the ski lifts, and in Bailey's town square. I had told no one about my encounter at the cabin on Sunrise Trail and kept silent now.

During prayer requests before the lesson, one student asked for shelter and protection for the ghost person. Zach turned to face me, and I mouthed "later" to him. After opening prayer, Zach directed the discussion to the devastation Nehemiah saw when he returned home. After class, he reminded the students of their cleaning commitment at the bookshop on Saturday so his work crew could start the transformation of the derelict building into a beautiful bookshop. He joked that there wouldn't be time to search for ghosts.

We didn't have to look.

CHAPTER 6

Z ach and I met at the Secret Passage the night before the youth group's scheduled work day. I'd taken on extra chores at the ranch since I wanted to be on site as much as possible when Zach began turning this shambles of a place into a magnificent bookshop. He carried tools and supplies inside the building, and I walked through, imagining the finished product. Whenever Zach described his projects, whether a single piece of furniture, a renovated bathroom, or a whole condominium, his eyes took on a certain look, and I knew he saw things I couldn't. My Secret Passage Bookshop was the same. I saw the blueprints, but I couldn't visualize how it would look. Neither of my parents had passed on an artistic gene to me. Even my stick figure drawings were awful.

All I saw were remnants of the escape rooms—deserted sections with different themed decorations—a western saloon, a mountain cabin, a bedroom, and a country store. Last year, when I'd visited the country store escape room with some of the Rocking T customers, we'd failed to unravel the clues to escape within the time allotted. And therein lay the problem. The escape room business needed confined quarters; my bookshop required expansiveness.

I followed Zach toward the wall opening where we'd found the body of Isabella Diaz. I'd been so shocked by the discovery of a dead person that I hadn't wanted to return. But with Zach here, I felt braver and was ready to see that hidden area for myself.

Zach's phone flashlight illuminated the corridor between my bookshop and the wall of Pretty Nails, the nail spa next to my property. The width of the tunnel-like walkway was about a yardstick's length, and it stretched from the front wall of the building's street-side exterior to the alley's outside wall, creating a forty-foot by three-foot rectangle. The area smelled musty, and both long interior walls felt cold, but light came from the alley area. The sheriff believed the dead woman had entered through an opening in the back wall. I stayed put while Zach walked the length of the corridor.

"This hidden passageway was created deliberately. You can see the marker on the front wall where the property line between the two buildings should be. There is approximately eighteen inches from your side to that spot, and the same distance from the nail salon side to the mark," Zach said.

"I estimated the width of this corridor to be about a yard, so I guessed right."

"Let's check out the back of the building, the place where the sheriff thinks Isabella entered. Sheriff Hawthorn had his men cover the opened area, but you can see how large it is—easily big enough for an adult or a child to enter." He shined the flashlight beam on the plywood pieces taped to the back that blocked an opening about two feet square. "I can see how a person could enter, but why would anyone want to come into this cold, dark corridor between the businesses?"

Zach studied the back wall. "Maybe Isabella was told to enter this way. The sheriff said the city dumpster obscures a view from the alley and there were wooden crates covering the outside entrance."

I sensed Zach knew more than he was telling me. Everyone seemed to want to protect me, which I found quite annoying.

He lifted a shoulder. "A person could enter this passageway between the two buildings and then get into your bookshop through that small door in the wall. I wonder. . ." Zach began tapping on the Pretty Nails side.

I followed close on his heels. "The Paxtons offered to buy my bookshop."

Zach turned. "What did you say?'

"I told them no. I thought it was weird. The Paxtons wanted half the building for a sandwich shop for Elsa to manage and offered to lease the other half of the property to me for a book-shop. Isn't that crazy?"

"They already own half of Bailey. Maybe they want more." He resumed tapping on the nail salon wall. "That's odd."

"Isn't it? But why wait until I'd purchased the building? Why didn't they come forward earlier?"

"Are you going to hire someone to operate the tea shop?"

"I was leaning toward Maria, but the Paxtons' surprise offer made me feel guilty. It never occurred to me their daughter might be having financial problems. They're rich, they could give Elsa money instead of another restaurant to run. Do you think they intended to sell it back to me?"

"Stop. You don't know what they were thinking, and it doesn't matter, because you refused their offer—you told them no. But I'd like to know if there could be legal complications about the corridor space. You should settle that issue before I start work."

"Jolene's drawing up a document about the ownership of the passageway. She says a piece of paper and amicable parties can fix any problem." Zach removed his gloves and touched the wall with his fingers. "What are you looking for now?"

Hinges screeched as a lower section of the wall moved into the nail salon, revealing a stock room filled with towels and hair products.

"I thought we might have an opening into the Pretty Nails business. You did say the Paxtons only wanted this side, right?"

I shivered. "Yes. This is weird. It's like one of those haunted houses with secret passages to my bookshop and to the nail salon. Anyone who entered the corridor could get into either business. Why would building owners incorporate something like that?"

"For extra storage? For added insulation? Noise abatement?" Zach shrugged.

"I believe the sheriff thinks it was used for something wicked," I said.

"Did he tell you that?" Zach asked.

"No, but he wouldn't. You know how he always calls me 'Abby girl.' He uses it as a term of endearment, showing me even a big ex-hockey player can be kind and protective, but he considers me young and naive. This opening on the nail salon wall makes me even more curious about the purpose of this space."

"You should ask the sheriff." Zach pulled the nail salon door flush with the corridor. "The Pretty Nails side doesn't appear to have been opened recently, but the latch release still works."

I knelt and searched for the latch Zach had discovered. "Do you think the sheriff noticed this spot?"

"Maybe he did but didn't tell you," Zach teased.

"Why wouldn't he?" I asked.

"Because you like to talk too much?"

"I'm aware I chatter when I get nervous. Do you think the person who hit me on the head could have hidden in this corridor?"

"It's possible." Zach aimed his flashlight toward the end of the corridor on the Main Street side. "I forgot to tell you, but I saw more blankets up front."

"Were they navy blue with gray stitching along the edge?"

"I don't know. They were blankets, cheap ones that felt rough to the touch."

I sighed. "When Jolene gets the papers filed, I want you to make certain the back wall and the entrance to the Pretty Nails shop are sealed."

"My plan exactly." Zach stood and stepped into my property near the spot where I'd found the dead woman. "If we left support beams intact, you could open the passageway and use the extra three feet of space for more books, maybe mysteries."

"But that's my tea shop side, according to your plans," I protested.

Zach laughed. "Right, I forgot. You could sell bookmarks, small reading lamps, and touristy items—maps, key chains, magnets on the tea shop side. I could add shelving."

"Let me think about that another day. I have a lot on my mind."

One thing I learned while serving as a youth leader was that teenagers love to eat, and Zach and I promised breakfast and lunch for them on Saturday. Daniel Zapata assured me he'd bring the tacos to the bookshop before the youth group's arrival time at nine. And Zach's lunch treat for them would be buckets of burgers.

As the sun peeked over the horizon, I stopped by the church for the first aid kit, work gloves, and tools we used on environmental work and home repairs. Our youth's outreach program offered "helping hands" to those in need locally as well as when disaster struck. We designated one Saturday every other month for changing light bulbs, installing smoke detector batteries, doing yardwork, and hauling away clutter. I was proud of the love and commitment the young people showed through their actions, and their concern about the "ghost" in town proved their compassion.

Zach beat me to the building and was staging projects so the teenagers could get right to work. As I unloaded flats of water and assorted snacks, I saw a darting movement out of the corner of my eye. I placed the container of snacks on the sidewalk as bait and went inside the building. Through dirty windows, I watched the person edge forward toward the waiting food.

I opened the door and held out a bottle. "Water?"

The "ghost" was a girl, younger than anyone in our youth group, and frail. Frightened brown eyes debated accepting my offering.

I extended the bottle by its base, and when she grabbed it, I inched forward to the snack bag and offered a cracker packet and a bag of trail mix. "I'm Abby. I stopped in the cabin on the cross-country ski trail. You had a fire going."

The girl maintained a distance of about five feet, although the look in her eyes said the treats tempted her.

"We're having tacos from Maria's soon. You've had those before, right?" I remembered the bag in the cabin.

She gave a slight nod.

"Daniel's bringing them." At the mention of Daniel's name, her head bobbed up. I continued, "You know Daniel? He'll be here soon. What's your favorite breakfast taco? I like the egg and potato one best, but I'm not fussy. They're all good."

She twisted off the water cap and drank.

My phone beeped an incoming text. "Daniel's on his way. You should stay to see him and have a taco."

Her body sagged, and she slumped down on the sidewalk bench. Exhaustion seemed to rise from her like steam from a hot mud spring.

When Daniel arrived, I went to the driver's side and offered to unload the food if he'd talk to the girl.

The lyrical rhythm of Spanish wafted through the crisp air. Daniel and the girl spoke rapidly, then she ran to Daniel and buried her face in his jacket, her shoulders shaking. While Daniel consoled the girl, I phoned the sheriff.

Daniel patted her arm gently and glanced my way with a "what do I do now" expression on his face. I nodded toward his car then opened the back door and slid across the seat, leaving space for the girl. Daniel took the driver's seat.

"Her name's Felicia. She's supposed to be going to a new home, and Isabella Diaz or her friend was to meet her in Bailey to take her on the next leg of the journey. But no one showed up. She's scared," Daniel said. "I asked her if she speaks English, and she said she can, but so far, she hasn't."

I pointed to myself. "Abby, no Spanish but *hola* and *amigo*." I turned to Daniel. "Can you find out how old she is, who brought her here, where they left her, and if she knows Isabella is dead."

My questions frightened Felicia, who grabbed the door handle. Daniel's soothing Spanish reassured her, and her panic eased. With eyes focused on Daniel's kind face, she answered his questions in bursts.

Teenagers emerged from packed cars before the sheriff arrived, and Zach came out to meet them. I hoped the girl would stay calm, and motioned for Zach to keep our curious young workers away from Daniel's car.

Daniel paused before filling me in on Felicia's latest conversation. "She came with a man in his truck. She's only twelve. That's the same age as my little sister. I can't imagine my sis on her own. Felicia recognized me because she bought tacos from me earlier this week. She has a little money, but it's almost gone," Daniel said.

"Why did she leave LA?" I pushed.

"Because anywhere was better than her home in California. She latched on to Isabella at the mission church. The word circulated that Isabella rescued people in desperate situations."

"But Felicia's a child. That's illegal. Isabella could have been in serious trouble if she'd been caught." I couldn't imagine anyone helping a runaway cross state lines. Kidnapping was a felony that meant a long prison term. Did she know the man with the truck?"

"No. She was told she'd be going to Canada, where someone would love and take care of her. What's going to happen to her now?" Daniel asked.

"Not sure. I called our friend, Mr. Hawthorn." I avoided saying the word "sheriff," in case Felicia might recognize it. "She'll probably go to a home approved by child protective services until he can find a relative in LA."

Felicia's fingers snaked across the back seat and touched my hand. "Amiga Abby?" she asked.

"Si, Felicia and Abby amigas," I said, but the hope shining in the girl's eyes intimidated me. Could I protect her?

The sheriff, dressed in regular clothes instead of his uniform, opened the passenger door and slid inside. I stroked Felicia's hand to reassure her that things were okay, and Daniel explained what he'd learned to the lawman.

"Felicia, I'm Mr. Hawthorn. I'm glad you're safe. My friend in LA knows three other people who came here on a similar journey. Would you like to go home? Back to your friends and family?" I could tell from Felicia's face that she understood what he was saying.

Felicia remained calm until asked about going home, then her eyes grew large. "No. No! I need to go to Canada." At least now she felt safe enough to speak English with us.

The sheriff turned to me. "An escape from intolerable home situations in California appeals to these youngsters. However, the travelers don't end up in Canada in a nice house with a cookie-making granny and a feisty cocker spaniel in the yard."

The girl cried again and spoke to Daniel in rapid Spanish.

"Felicia says they'll kill her if you send her back. She wants to wait here for Isabella. Can I go now?" Daniel asked.

"Not yet," the sheriff said. "Where did you meet her, Daniel?"

Daniel's eyes shifted away. "The larger of our taco shacks near the ski slopes, not the restaurant. I really need to leave. Maria will kill me if I'm not at the restaurant to help prep for the lunch rush."

I didn't like Daniel's word choice since I'd been bashed on the head and a woman had died inside my building, but the phrase didn't seem to bother the lawman.

Sheriff Hawthorn nodded. "Thanks, Daniel. Do you think your cousin Maria might know anything about this girl?"

"I doubt it. Maria's a workaholic. She doesn't notice anything except food prep and profits." Daniel positioned himself behind the steering wheel, a not-so-subtle hint.

After Felicia and I got out of the car, the girl latched onto my hand with a white-knuckled grip.

The sheriff leaned on Daniel's car. "Felicia can stay with Abby. Appreciate your help, Daniel. May I call you if we need your language skills?"

"Sure, but I might go back to LA soon. I'm not crazy about working for Maria." Daniel turned and spoke to Felicia in Spanish before driving away.

What if Felicia stopped speaking English again? I regretted taking French instead of Spanish in high school and college. I should make learning Spanish a long-term goal.

"Abby girl, Ben is an approved care provider with local children's services. I'll ask if he'll offer quarters for her at the Rocking T. Felicia's bonded with you, and I don't want her running off until we can gather some more puzzle pieces."

"More?" I asked.

"I have some leads in LA and here, but I'm not ready to make an announcement."

"Can you tell me what you know?"

Sheriff Hawthorn shook his head. "It's not a story I'm eager to share, especially with someone as sweet as you, Abby girl."

My imagination jumped into overdrive as I studied Felicia's frightened, vulnerable face.

CHAPTER 7

Felicia lived with us at the Rocking T Ranch because child protective services listed Ben True as a short-term host. The "us" turned out to be me, as she slept in my dorm-style quarters. She avoided the male wrangler employees and stuck to my side, helping me clean and change linens in the ranch's guest rooms.

Trying to build her confidence, I asked her to teach me Spanish words while we worked. Days passed quickly, but nights terrified Felicia, and she woke me with her screams or crying. In the dark hours, I held, rocked, or sang to her until she could rest.

Sheriff Hawthorn visited regularly, but he maintained a grim visage and was tight-lipped about progress in his investigation, only saying he wasn't happy about the direction it was taking.

Zach's renovations of the bookshop moved quickly. After only two weeks, he had the old interior walls down and the new framing up. His plans included a rock wall on the interior perimeter to match the outside of the building. He believed the stonework would reflect the rustic atmosphere associated with the name Secret Passage. The wall symbolized strength, solidarity, warmth, and adventure—at least I thought so. He completed the stairs leading up to my future apartment but had done nothing on that level.

Each day, Felicia and I stopped in to see the progress.

"Wow, this is shaping up," I said.

Zach removed his safety goggles and scowled. "Abby, Felicia."

"Jolene filed the paperwork signed by the Paxtons, giving me ownership rights to the Pretty Nails wall. There's a legal term for it, but I thought you would want to know as soon as possible. You can work on the tea shop area too. After my firm refusal to their offer, they've been cooperative."

"Are you going to ask someone to handle the food area or manage it yourself? I'll need to talk to that person about where the plumbing and electrical hookups should go."

"I decided on Maria's Meals. Her sweets and the upbeat ambiance of her restaurant are more compatible with the bookstore. Felicia and I are meeting with the Zapata cousins tomorrow afternoon. Do you want me to ask them anything?"

Zach shook his head. "I want to sit down with you and Maria later to coordinate the piping for your apartment upstairs with what's needed on this level in the food area." He sighed. "Abby, I'm putting your project on hold for a week."

"Why?" I asked.

"Emergency at the Paxton Ski Lodge. A water leak. Since it's their high tourist season, I promised to help. They're going to LA for Isabella's memorial service next week, and repairs will be easier without Carol looking over my shoulder." Zach stuck his chin out as if daring me to contradict him.

"You have other crews, don't you?" I asked.

"I do. All are busy. I'll finish your project by the date I promised."

For some reason, Zach helping the Paxtons irked me. And why were the Paxtons going to LA for Isabella's service when they claimed only a fleeting acquaintance? I considered myself easygoing, and contradicting others was not in my nature. So the words that came out of my mouth surprised me. "I feel you're taking advantage of our friendship by leaving my bookshop to work on another job."

The lines around Zach's mouth tightened. "I said I'd get it done on time. Work would go faster if you didn't constantly check my progress."

"Well, we don't want to stop your progress. Let's go, Felicia." I grabbed the girl's hand and stormed out.

Zach's behavior and his words seemed out of character for him. Or was I the one behaving differently? I touched the short stubble on my head. Had my concussion changed me?

———

That night, Felicia went to sleep early. Her peaceful face reminded me of my first glimpse of the dead woman. As I replayed that day in my mind, hoping to remember an overlooked detail, a tap sounded on my door.

Ben looked past my shoulder to Felicia's relaxed slumber. "Can we talk? In my office?"

"Sure. I'll let Felicia know in case she wakes up." I grabbed some paper and wrote her a quick note.

Ben's office rivaled my room for messiness. Three boards on the wall listed daily, weekly, and monthly schedules on an oversized calendar. Folders and boxes weighed down his three file cabinets, and photos of former workers and guests filled the corkboard.

He emptied a chair of boxes and motioned for me to sit, but he remained standing. "Felicia's settling in, isn't she?" The comment was a statement rather than a question.

"She's still scared. I can't imagine a home life that would leave a child so terrified," I said.

"I can," Ben said softly. "Abby, I need you to take care of the Rocking T for a week. I want to go to LA and see what's happening there. I don't want to jump to conclusions, but with Isabella dead and Felicia's fears, I want to check out that mission church to see if it's legit. I'd hate to discover they're exploiting children."

Ben's statement, long by his standards, showed he was troubled.

He shrugged and continued, "I've been grooming Jason to take on your responsibilities, but he's not ready yet. I'll miss you around here, Abby." Ben didn't show his sentimental side often.

"I'll be less than a mile away. You won't even know I'm gone, except that you'll have room for another wrangler."

He didn't respond to my statement, so I asked him a question.

"Does the sheriff know you're going?" I asked.

"No. The trip's for me. Well, I'm doing this for the little boy I used to be." Ben gazed into the distance.

"I'd like to hear about that boy."

"Abby, happenings in your bookshop reminded me of the pain of my early years. I don't like to talk about those times."

"You listen more than you talk. Let me return the favor." I leaned forward.

"My dad left shortly after I was born. Mom tried, but I ended up in foster care, bouncing from one house to another. Those hopeless kids from LA remind me of myself. I ran away when I was fifteen. Since I'd never seen snow and I figured Wyoming had it, I hitched here from Texas."

"At fifteen? And nobody attempted to track you down?" I struggled to picture Ben as a runaway teenager.

"Not that I know of. My last ride let me off at a gas station down the road, the best day of my life. Jonathan True was filling up his truck and wearing his Rocking T Ranch cap. I asked if he could use an extra hand."

I interrupted. "Was Jonathan True a relative?"

"Only through love. That big-hearted man took me in and gave me the only real home I ever knew. When I was twenty-one, I asked his permission to change my name legally from Ben Harper to Ben True. He was the father I never had, and I wanted to show him how much I appreciated him. When he died, Jonathan willed everything to me, including the Rocking T Ranch. I was shocked. He'd never mentioned an inheritance."

"You don't say much either. Guess in that way you're like your chosen dad. What you do here would make him proud," I said.

"I'd like to think so. That's why I partnered with the sheriff's department, offering work assignments for youth offenders, and I applied to offer a temporary home for kids from child welfare awaiting placement. I identify with the forgotten kids. I've walked in those shoes. I feel like I'm honoring Jonathan True when I help."

"Does the sheriff know your story?" I asked.

"Some, not all. He knows I understand how desperation can drive kids to do crazy things. I want to check out that mission church in LA personally. Phone calls and emails only offer so much information." Ben rubbed the back of his neck and then tapped the weekly board. "I've talked too much. Anyway, will you manage the Rocking T for a week?"

"Yes. The timing's perfect," I said. "Zach's putting my bookshop renovation on hold for a week while he takes care of an emergency at the Paxton Ski Lodge."

"Heard something about that," Ben said. "Thought it odd. People in Wyoming know how to protect pipes in winter months."

"What are you saying?"

Ben shrugged. "Nothing. Just that burst pipes aren't usually a problem in Bailey."

"You're right," I said. "I'll make sure we don't have any pipes burst. Go to LA and don't worry about the Rocking T. I'll take care of things for you. My parents were relieved that you took me under your wing when I ditched my sensible librarian job to become a ski bum."

Ben grinned. "Managing you is a tough job, but someone has to do it."

I gave Ben an impulsive hug, and he patted my back three times, the way he told his horses he appreciated them. I regarded those slaps as high praise.

Even though Zach had left to work at the ski lodge, I invited Maria and Daniel to meet at the bookshop and talk about the food area. Felicia and I had time to examine Zach's progress at our leisure without his disapproving glares.

Maria, followed by Daniel, entered the shop carrying a white box with a red bow. "I made you a Valentine's Day package of treats, a sample of what I'd serve in your bookshop. We won't offer a wide selection, which will mean greater profitability because of less waste. Everything will taste wonderful."

I believed her. Maria was not modest about her exceptional culinary skills. I followed her around as she took photos. "Zach wanted to talk about the plumbing and electrical connections."

"He and I shared coffee and dessert last night." Maria smiled as if savoring the memory. "We have another appointment tomorrow. I think Zach and I can decide."

"Oh," I said. So, Zach had time for two dates with Maria but didn't have time for my bookshop.

"Daniel will be managing the shop here," Maria said.

I glanced at Daniel, who stared out the front window. He'd told the sheriff that he planned to return to LA. "Daniel, are you excited about managing your own place?"

"I guess so. Maria will do the real cooking. I'll just make sandwiches and wait tables."

"Weren't you thinking of going back to LA to live?" I asked Daniel the question and watched Maria for a reaction, which was immediate and disapproving.

Daniel lowered his chin and avoided my eyes. "I'll see how this goes. Might like having my own shop."

"You'll stay?" Felicia asked.

Maria looked at the photos on her phone then answered for him. "Daniel can visit LA, but I need him here, and the two of us won't get homesick, because we have a visitor from someone in our large family every couple of months. Our clan's excuse for coming is to bring ingredients I need for my grandmother's recipes or decorations, but the truth is they like to stick their noses into everyone's business, even when they're miles away. You will allow me to decorate the food section, won't you?"

"I'd like to see what you have in mind before you do it," I said to the steamroller known as Maria. I felt sorry for Daniel, whose cousin expected him to obey her every command.

"You don't have to worry, Abby. The tables, chairs, and decor will be perfect." She gave my hand a dismissive pat. "I have the contract you sent over, and I'm signing it, which specifies that I'll take over my part of the space in mid-March." Maria pulled a pen from her purse and scrawled her name across the last page of the contract.

I took the papers she'd signed. "I'll look over it again. I hope the Paxtons won't be too mad at me."

Maria continued, "Carol and Rodney told people they wanted the Secret Passage tea shop for Elsa, but that's their dream, not hers. Elsa loves her life the way it is. She wants no additional involvement in the restaurant business, and her husband has his hands full. Carol's the one who needs something to do. Don't you agree?"

I didn't comment, since gossip moves faster than a fall forest fire. Instead, I held up the contract she'd signed. "I'll send you a copy."

"No rush. I'm going to LA to check on family recipes for this place. I need a mini vacation."

"What about the restaurant?"

"Daniel can manage."

I could tell by Daniel's expression that Maria's trip was news to him. Daniel followed his cousin out the front door, his shoulders slumped. Didn't the young man have any options other than working for Maria?

As the Zapata cousins left, Jolene breezed in.

"So glad to catch you here. Zach's making progress, isn't he?" she asked.

"He is. Do you know Felicia?" I motioned to Felicia, who was occupied with a Spanish to English book I'd purchased for her.

"I know of her, but we haven't officially met. Hello, Felicia. I'm Jolene. Now, Abby, I owe you a housewarming gift. I give something to all my clients, and I've come up with the perfect idea. You know your slogan about the Secret Passage and how books can introduce you to surprising people, places, and ideas? Well, I thought I'd have something made that uses that. Do you like the idea?"

"I do. But you don't need to get me a gift."

"I want to. Anyway, I might find something I like better this week. I'm going to LA to buy artwork and pick up furniture to stage a couple of empty houses. Staging properties decreases their time on the market."

"You're going to LA this week?" I asked. Seemed everyone was going to California. The Paxtons were attending Isabella's memorial service. Ben was investigating the mission's outreach program, Jolene was visiting art and furniture shops, and Maria was checking on recipes for the bookshop.

With everyone in LA, I could do some sleuthing here in Bailey. The idea sounded like fun.

It wasn't.

CHAPTER 8

I'd managed the Rocking T Ranch in Ben's absence for a couple of days at a time but never for a full week. Ben didn't take vacations. He considered Bailey the most beautiful place on earth and claimed he never wanted to leave even for a few days.

Despite the chaos in Ben's office, his scheduled activities ran smoothly, making my job as replacement overseer easy. We offered ski trips to Paxton Ski Lodge and snowshoeing excursions that culminated with a campfire meal of burgers, dogs, and s'mores. Our sleigh rides to the National Elk Refuge were fully booked, and we often had to send people to other outfitters. Even though the weather in February rarely topped the freezing point, the Rocking T had a core of winter visitors returning year after year.

With Felicia's help, the housekeeping chores went quickly, and my Spanish improved. I also tutored her on schoolwork using lesson plans sent by the local elementary principal. With Ben's status as a safe place for children, those in his temporary care were allowed home study. On Wednesday, while I worked in Ben's office on staff assignments for the rest of the week, Sheriff Hawthorn showed up at the ranch unannounced.

"How are you doing as the boss, Abby girl?" he asked.

"All guests are accounted for, and none have visited the hospital since Ben left me in charge. I'd say I'm an enormous success."

The sheriff nodded. "Got two bits of news. Thanks to forensics, we determined that Isabella was the one who knocked you on the head. We took a big rock from that passageway that had blood on it. Blood was yours; fingerprints were hers. You must have surprised her."

"She didn't have to hit me so hard." Reaching under my ski hat, I realized my hair felt like hair instead of stubble. I should check the mirror when I returned to my room.

"She might not have meant to hurt you. When people are scared, their adrenaline is high, giving them extra strength. My guess is she panicked when she saw the amount of blood and returned to the hidden corridor."

"I'm lucky Zach showed up to save me," I said.

"You are. I saw Felicia walking a horse over to the barn. Looks like she's put on a couple of much-needed pounds."

"She's acting less skittish. We're working on language skills as she helps me with housekeeping chores, and the wranglers let her brush and feed the horses. She thinks horse grooming's fun, not work." I remembered the glow in her eyes as she leaned her head against Maverick's shoulder. He was the gentlest of our horses and always stood completely still when Felicia approached him.

"Don't get too accustomed to having her around," Sheriff Hawthorn said. "That's my second bit of news. We've located a relative, an uncle. The networks showed Felicia's picture as a missing child, and a person came forward. Child Services in LA thinks he's a relative, not a crackpot."

I shivered. "You promised you wouldn't send her back to LA."

"I didn't promise that. Felicia's not a stray cat you can adopt. She has family."

"And she has nightmares about that family. You can't return her to the life she left," I said.

"I don't have a choice. I explained to the Child Services worker how frightened Felicia was, and he's promised to do a thorough investigation of the relative and the home environment."

I lifted my chin. "Even if the person who came forward is honest, Felicia could be passed to a different family member, one not so upstanding. Sheriff, the day we met her, Felicia told Daniel they would kill her if she went back."

"She might have been exaggerating. Kids do that..." His words trailed off as if he were trying to convince himself.

"And we wouldn't know she'd told us the truth until she turned up dead, would we? Please give her more time here," I begged.

"Abby girl, my hands are tied. I have to follow the law. Thought you should know what's going on. I need to get back to the office."

"This all revolves around my bookshop, doesn't it?"

The sheriff hitched up his belt. "Seems to. This has the hallmarks of a people-smuggling ring with your bookshop as one of the stops. Working with the LA law, we've found that the travelers received food, a little money, and a promise of a new home. We haven't yet determined who does the transporting or what happens to the youngsters, but I'm quite sure it's not good. The backgrounds of the missing children are similar, and all had attended that mission church in LA where Isabella worked. It seems the runaways looked for a painted green stick outside a location indicated on a map stop to tell them it was safe."

"Then Isabella showed up here. Was she trying to stop the ring, or was she a part of it?"

"I don't know, but her death threw a wrench into the operation. When she died in your bookshop, your place was no longer an option for the runaway travelers. I'm praying they've shut down the ugly business."

"What if we—"

The sheriff interrupted me. "Stay out of this, Abby girl. There's a chance someone you know is involved."

I thought about Zach leaving the bookshop, Jolene's sudden trip to LA, Ben's trip to LA, Maria and Daniel's family deliveries to Bailey from LA, the Paxtons' crazy offer to buy the bookshop followed by them going to California for Isabella's memorial service. I didn't want to think any of those people might be involved. That old nursery rhyme about the man going to St. Ives came to mind. Well, all my friends here in Bailey seemed to be going to LA.

The sheriff interrupted my woolgathering. "We found Felicia, but there may be another runaway looking for a painted green stick outside a "safe" space. There were four who disappeared about the same time Felicia did. I've placed extra surveillance on the streets, but in a resort town, families with kids come and go. We don't want to alienate money-spending tourists by questioning every child we don't recognize."

My mind raced. Maybe I could do something on my own. With Zach working at the Paxton Ski Lodge, I could post a green stick outside the back of my bookshop and leave food and blankets inside with instructions for the person to wait for me. It was a long shot, but if I could persuade another child to come inside a warm safe place instead of struggling outside in the frigid Wyoming winter, it would be worth the risk.

The sheriff coughed. Was he reading my mind?

He wagged a finger at me. "I'll let you know what we find out, but this uncle is pushing to meet Felicia. I'll do my best to make certain it isn't a trap."

I walked the sheriff to his car. "You'll tell me the specific date you'll be taking her, won't you? I'll need time to prepare her to leave."

"I'll definitely let you know ahead of time." The sheriff climbed in, placed his gearshift in reverse, turned around, and tooted his horn as a goodbye.

No matter what the sheriff said, Felicia's night terrors were rooted in happenings at her home. I couldn't let her return to that environment. Had the sheriff hinted for me to hide Felicia?

———

With the day organized, I asked Jason to cover the ranch office for an hour while I visited the bookshop and delivered advertising flyers to local businesses. Jason eagerly agreed, proud to be in charge.

Felicia joined me, and we made quick work of our deliveries, then I drove toward the bookshop and parked behind the building. Even though I felt guilty, I began to question her.

"Felicia, when you first came to my bookshop, what did you do?"

"I was left at the cabin and had a map to your place." The girl inhaled deeply before getting out of the car. "Each place has a stick. If it's green, we can go in. If it's red, we can't. There's supposed to be a bag with instructions near the stick. It's not always easy to find."

"Do the instructions tell you where to go?" I knew the sheriff had asked Felicia the same questions, but I hoped I might learn something he hadn't.

"Yes, usually they used words and pictures—where the food and blankets are, a map, and how far to the next stop."

"What did you do with the stick and the bag?"

"We leave the stick, rock, and bag inside the safe place. If no one comes after two days, we go to the next stop," Felicia said.

"Were there instructions at the cabin? The place you made a fire?"

She shifted in her seat. "No. There wasn't a green or a red stick there. I looked everywhere. I waited, but no one came for me."

Felicia, a vulnerable child, had been dumped in a strange place with no resources. Such a situation would be challenging for an adult. My anger boiled up at the people who were tricking young boys and girls into taking such a treacherous trip. Who would do such a thing? I couldn't allow myself to imagine what the children might face at their journey's end.

Like Felicia, I wanted to believe the children would end up in homes where they would be loved. I knew my attitude was Pollyannaish, but it was difficult for my mind to grasp the alternative.

Felicia continued her story. "I went to the bookshop but saw the police, so I returned to the cabin." Tears trickled down her face.

I wrapped my arms around her. "You must have been scared."

"I didn't know what to do. Then I remembered the taco shop man who spoke Spanish."

"Daniel," I said.

"But then you gave me water and food." Felicia's arms tightened around my waist, binding me to her and to her problems.

"Felicia, did you come alone or with others?" I prompted.

"I don't know any others." She pulled away from me.

"Were they going to Canada too?" I asked.

Her lips tightened. "I don't know."

"I heard there were four of you." I watched as her eyes widened in disbelief.

She picked at her fingernails. "Two before me, one behind. Isabella said not to talk to them."

If Sheriff Hawthorn had received this information from Felicia, he hadn't told me. My heart ached for the other child still looking for a green stick, shelter, and hope. I changed the subject. "Do you have a relative you can trust? Maybe an uncle?" I prodded.

"No one. Miss Isabella asked many times. She asked if there were people who would miss me. She said the Canada people don't take children away from happy families."

Felicia's speech was as long as the lies she'd been told. There was no Canada, no people waiting to love these children who had experienced fear, heartache, rejection, and possibly physical or emotional abuse. I wondered about Isabella Diaz. Was she a saint or a sinner?

Felicia reached for my hand, which made up my mind. I sucked in a deep breath and committed myself to a course I might regret. But if it saved this little girl, I wouldn't feel remorse. I didn't tell her about the relative the sheriff had mentioned, but I wanted a rescue plan ready.

"Felicia, I'm going to give you directions to the Chapel of Transfiguration. I've told you about it. It's one of my favorite places. I'll leave things for you there in case you need to get away. If I can't meet you, I'll send someone else."

She gave me a puzzled look then nodded her agreement.

"Today I'll take you to see the place, and I'll draw a map so you can get back on your own, if necessary. Other buildings near the chapel can provide shelter or a hiding place."

I wasn't sure what Sheriff Hawthorn's plan for Felicia might be. I only knew this girl with the sweet brown eyes trusted me.

CHAPTER 9

Felicia said there were three other travelers. Two had gone before her, and one was to come after. That meant a child might be wandering around in the cold near Bailey.

"Did you know any of them?" I asked.

She shook her head. "No, but all of us were to go to Canada. Miss Isabella said we must be brave. She said we would ride in a truck to Bailey. She gave us food, money, and a map in case. The two ahead of me were girls. I don't know about the last one. Miss Isabella helped both boys and girls."

Since my bookshop was the center of this operation, I felt obligated to help the missing child find safety. I needed sticks to paint green, large rocks, bags, and a message with directions in simple words and pictures. Two places used by the runaways were the cabin on Sunrise Trail and my property, the Secret Passage Bookshop. I would put items there to draw the child from the streets to safety.

After Felicia fell asleep, I placed drawings in a waterproof bag along with instructions to wait for a woman named Abby. My self-portrait wasn't glamorous. I had no artistic aptitude, but I added a picture of my car, my Rocking T Ranch hat, and the pink puffy jacket I wore. Luring a lost child to safety wouldn't be easy, but I had to try.

I hadn't thought past rescuing the child in need. The sheriff reminded me that Felicia was not a stray I could adopt, but that didn't stop my imagination. I was a responsible adult, but adopting any child, especially one from another state, would be a monumental task. This "relative" who turned up requesting Felicia's return concerned me, but tonight, I'd focus on the unidentified child.

The moon was high in the dark sky when I slipped from my room to place the items behind the cross-country cabin and at the back of my bookshop. I arranged the food bags with protein bars, sealed snacks, and water bottles next to the blankets. After I laid the painted stick and bag next to the plywood covering the passageway entrance outside my shop, I went home.

Sleep didn't come quickly, and I was groggy the next morning. Fortunately, Jason, my Rocking T helpmate, was alert, and strong coffee helped me focus as we coordinated the day's activities. The Rocking T Ranch had welcomed late arrivals last night, and I agreed to include them in the day's excursions, which meant juggling the schedules.

During our morning housekeeping routine, I showed Felicia my phone and pictures of all the people in Bailey with a connection to the LA mission outreach. I asked if she recognized them. She knew Zach, Daniel, and Ben.

Then I showed her pictures of Carol Paxton, Rodney Paxton, Jolene Roussel, and Maria Zapata. I didn't want her to point anyone out. These people were fellow church members, friends I'd learned to love since I'd moved to Bailey. She touched Jolene's picture. "Your friend?"

I nodded. This picture thing wouldn't work. She'd seen every person I'd shown her because she'd been in Bailey for over two weeks, and none of my friends were slinking around in the dark. These were upstanding citizens of the town. I was torturing myself by wondering if one of them was guilty of the unimaginable. "I want to find the other person in your group," I told the girl.

"No. My friends are in Canada. I'm the only one here." Felicia spoke firmly, as if willing me to believe her.

I didn't. Because of her response, I decided to go alone to see if anyone had taken the bait. Sleep eluded Felicia, and it was ten before I slipped out to check on my green-painted sticks and the rocks with clues underneath. I hoped to see a hint the child who was traveling behind Felicia had been at one of the places. At my building, I saw no disturbance around the makeshift entrance the police had temporarily repaired with plywood and tape since Zach's crew would do the final closure before finishing my bookshop. The Sunrise Trail cabin items were also untouched.

As I drove through the deserted streets, I considered the people who were suspects, hoping I could discount them. Rodney Paxton couldn't be a suspect. He'd worked in Oklahoma when the Oklahoma City bombing took the lives of so many children in the daycare center. Nor was his wife a likely suspect. Carol Paxton admitted her relationship with Isabella, who advocated for children in difficult situations. Then there was my dear friend Ben, my mentor and boss, who confessed his past as an unwanted child.

Zach had never expounded on his desire to work with youth, but why should he? I didn't have a story in my background either, only my awareness of the benefits I'd gained by participating in my church's youth group as a teen. As an adult, I wanted to provide that same spiritual base for today's teens. Zach's story was probably similar, but I should ask him.

Then there was Jolene. She went on regular shopping trips to visit her brother's design studio in California. My real estate agent didn't seem to have the "kid" connection others did, but because she visited LA and the mission church, I couldn't rule her out. She also received truckloads of furniture and decorative

pieces from LA three or four times a year, and Felicia said they'd
traveled by truck.

Could Daniel be a suspect? He translated for Felicia and
sympathized with her situation because she was the same age as
his sister. But Daniel appeared more worried about himself than
a runaway girl. He seemed self-involved, trying to find his way in
the world without being in his cousin's shadow. And Maria? Well,
I wasn't exactly impartial, because of the way she flirted with Zach,
and he flirted back. I didn't like some of Maria's behaviors, but I
loved her cooking, so I wanted to discount her involvement.

All those Bailey residents who went to LA should be back soon.
My goal was to rescue the missing child before everyone returned.

Tonight's journey was fruitless. The warmth of the car caused
me to close my eyes a couple of times, and I fought to stay awake
on the drive back to the ranch. Snow fell lightly as I pulled into my
spot, grateful again for the garages Ben provided for his employees.
I couldn't wait to put my head on my pillow and drift into a deep,
delicious sleep. The days at the Rocking T Ranch started at six,
and I needed my rest.

Sleep came in an unexpected form. Before I unfastened my
seat belt, my door opened, and a cloth with a sweet-smelling odor
covered my face.

"Abby girl, come on. Get your feet under you. I can't lug you around
forever." Sheriff Hawthorn sounded like he was at the bottom of
a deep well—not that I'd ever heard anyone from a deep well, but
he sounded far away, and his voice echoed.

I squinted and tilted my head.

"That's it. Open those eyes. Breathe deeply. The ambulance
will be here soon."

"Buh-lance?" My attempt to say "ambulance" sounded strange.

The sheriff had one arm around my waist and was dragging me. I blinked twice, trying to get my bearings. I was outside my garage space at the Rocking T, and the moon was still overhead.

"What's. . ." Again, I only forced a single word out.

"Save it. Concentrate on breathing and walking."

My walking consisted of the sheriff dragging me back and forth across the parking area in front of the garages.

Sirens split the frosty night and made my head throb. Then the place filled with people rushing here and there. I leaned against Sheriff Hawthorn's shoulder until he handed me off to the EMS workers.

Why were people shouting? The crew loading me in the ambulance yelled at me just as the sheriff had.

An EMT with red hair leaned over my face. "Stay with us. I'm going to put you on oxygen. Open your eyes. Abby, can you grip my finger?"

Something squeezed my arm. How could I grab her finger when my arm was being squeezed?

Then I saw Felicia's terror-filled eyes and reached for her. "Felicia, you okay?"

The sheriff put his arm on the small girl's shoulder. "I'll make sure Felicia's okay. We'll see you tomorrow. Tonight, do what these people tell you."

The ambulance door slammed, and the sirens sounded again. This time, I closed my eyes. I didn't know what had happened, but I knew I was on my way to the hospital—again.

———

The same three men who had been in my hospital room in early January waited there in late February, but this time, Felicia was with them.

"I shouldn't have asked you to run the ranch while I was gone. I feel responsible." Ben didn't smile.

I wondered why he felt responsible, but instead I asked, "When did you get back?"

"Earlier," Ben answered.

Even in my groggy state, I considered "earlier" a strange answer, but I was more curious about why I was in this hospital bed. "How did I get here?" I vaguely remembered a cloth being put over my face and then the sheriff lugging me around the Rocking T Ranch parking lot.

The sheriff said, "You fell asleep in your car. Fortunately, Felicia woke up and went looking for you. She found you in the garage with the car engine running. She switched off the ignition, opened the garage door, and called me. You're lucky you survived."

"I didn't just fall asleep. Something was placed over my mouth. I think someone tried to smother me," I insisted. In Ben's absence, I'd worked extra hard during the daytime and spent my nights trying to find the missing child. Even so, I couldn't believe I wouldn't turn off the car before closing the garage. That was an ingrained habit.

Sheriff Hawthorn sighed and shook his head. "Abby girl, I know you're concerned about Felicia, but we're worried about you. Do you want to talk to someone about your troubles?"

"You mean like a shrink? No. I'm not depressed. Someone tried to kill me." This time I said it louder and more emphatically.

The room went silent, and my visitors avoided looking me in the eye. Fortunately, a ringing phone broke the quiet.

My parents, frantic that I'd landed in the hospital again, asked if they should fly out immediately. I suggested they not make the trip from Oklahoma to Wyoming until the bookshop's opening in April. I glibly told them of Zach's progress with the food area and that my upstairs apartment had framing.

"Send us pictures of the progress," Mom said. "Then we'll be able to watch your bookshop and your new apartment take shape."

"I'll need you to help me get everything in the right place, Mom," I said.

My dad answered, "Your mom loves organizing people. We should drive out, then I can bring my tools."

I laughed, quite sure Dad wouldn't win the fly-or-drive argument. "I can't wait to see you both. Don't worry about me. I'm surrounded by good people," I said, even though my friends didn't believe my version of last night's events.

After I clicked off, I looked around the room. "I didn't try to commit suicide. I would never do that," I protested. Seeing Felicia's frightened expression, I spoke directly to her. "Felicia, I'd never leave you without a helper. You must know that."

She glanced at Zach, and I could tell she didn't believe me.

Zach twirled his ski cap then sighed. "Abby, I knew you were upset when I left your bookshop project to work a week for the Paxtons. When I told you, your response was not typical. I should have realized something was wrong at the time."

"I was annoyed with your choice, Zach. Wouldn't any customer have felt the same?"

Felicia stroked my hand. "You showed me the chapel. You said if you didn't come, another would." She wiped tears from her eyes. "I thought you were saying adios. *Por favor*, don't go away."

Although my head still pounded, my mind was clearer now. "Good grief. It's me—Abby Scott. You must know that I'd never attempt to take my own life! How could you even think that?"

"All signs point that way, Abby girl," Sheriff Hawthorn said.

"Well, you should look for some different signs!" I pushed the call button for the nurse. I wanted out of this hospital, away from these people who had such little faith in me. I intended to find the person who left me in the garage to die.

CHAPTER 10

I felt like my life was on display in a storefront window with everyone watching me. Zach returned to work in the bookshop and now welcomed me and Felicia when we showed up, unlike before when he'd seemed annoyed that we'd dropped by to check his progress.

Ben shuffled most of my assignments to other staffers, saying he'd have to do it when I left anyway. Felicia stuck to me like glue. I didn't mind her presence, and I hadn't heard any more about the supposed uncle. She insisted she'd never met other family members, which raised a red flag in my mind.

By the end of the week, I felt guilty about my light workload, and Felicia and I stopped by the Rocking T office to see if we could help with the horses. I knocked twice and then opened the door. Ben and Jolene Roussel stood close together, shoulders touching. Ben quickly stepped away. Both looked surprised and embarrassed.

"Jolene's here on business," Ben stammered.

"What? What business?" I stuttered. "I mean, are you buying another property?" My first thought was that he might need me to pay off my loan to him sooner than I expected if he planned a purchase himself.

Jolene recovered her composure first and offered her real estate agent's wide smile. "Ben's building a new home. I brought information about local builders."

"You're going to build?" Had Ben stated he planned to grow a second head, I couldn't have been more surprised. He'd never expressed a desire to leave the home he'd inherited from Jonathan True, located only feet from the offices and buildings that made up the Rocking T Ranch.

"Thought it was time," Ben said. "Guess I got the building bug from you. You're starting over, why shouldn't I? Planning to put it on the ridge. Jolene thinks that will be perfect. It's a beautiful spot."

"Everything around here is gorgeous," I said. "All you have to do is lift your eyes to see God's magnificent handiwork."

Jolene rested her hand on my shoulder. "Abby, I was sorry to learn about your. . .difficulties. I hope you're feeling more optimistic now. I had the housewarming gift for your bookshop made in LA. May I drop it off at the Secret Passage this afternoon, or does tomorrow afternoon work better?"

I chose option two, and she set the time. I guess my "difficulties"—the attempted suicide I had not even remotely considered—was common knowledge in Bailey. Once gossip spreads, it's impossible to stop the flow.

Jolene asked if Felicia would like to show her the horses, and the girl eagerly agreed.

After they'd gone, Ben looked at his boots. "I asked Jolene to distract Felicia. Wanted to tell you about my findings in LA. The missing-persons unit has opened cases on twenty kids who have gone missing over the past two years from that section of the city. I nosed around the mission too. Everyone considered Isabella a saint. I attended her memorial service. The little church overflowed, and people stood outside. They're renaming the mission in her honor."

"I guess Isabella was trying to help children. Did you check on Felicia's uncle? Felicia says she doesn't remember meeting any relative of her mother's."

"I didn't ask about him. I focused on the kids who disappeared. Kept putting myself in their shoes. Thanks to Jonathan, my life turned out great, but the LA youngsters who've vanished may not have been so lucky." Ben was speaking in longer sentences today, a rare occurrence.

"Did you find any link between LA and Bailey? If Isabella was the good woman people say she was, could the whole thing have been legitimate? Maybe there was a Canadian connection where endangered children could find a new home." I heard the hopeful tone in my voice, although I feared the opposite was true.

"No connection I could sniff out. Law officers down there have hit a brick wall." Ben lifted his chin. "I'll be concentrating on kids around here. I'm building myself a home so I can turn the old ranch living quarters Jonathan gave me into a halfway house for kids or young adults. It'll be a tribute to the man who saved me. Having Felicia here convinced me I must act, and Jolene's on board with my plan."

"Jolene approves?" I couldn't think of anything else to say, unusual for a chatterbox like me, but his saying Jolene approved shocked me into silence.

The woman was a force. She'd planted the bug in sweet, affable Ben's head for him to build a new home, which would net her a hefty commission from the selected builder. I shook my head to rid my mind of the notion. My friends were right to worry about my personality changing, as I realized I was becoming a cynic.

My natural tendency toward trusting people and expecting them to act honestly and honorably changed after I'd been hit on the head in January and then left in my car to suffer carbon monoxide poisoning in February because someone put a rag over my face laced with some sort of knock-out drops. I knew I hadn't left the car running. I didn't have a death wish, but someone wanted me dead, and I hadn't a clue as to who or why. The phrase "three's a charm" entered my mind. Would the third attempt on my life be successful?

———

By the end of the week, Zach had a full crew working in the bookshop with hammers, saws, and enthusiasm. The vision he'd seen for the bookshop was now obvious to my eyes. I wanted to be excited, but my nightmare of children seeing my bookshop as a beacon of hope and having their dreams dashed clouded my happiness.

"Felicia, do you want a job?" Zach asked.

The young girl skipped over to check on the task, and he showed her how to stain baseboards. She seemed happier to learn carpentry skills from Zach than social studies and language arts from me in her daily tutoring sessions.

Jolene knocked loudly to announce her arrival then made her way inside, holding a large parcel. "Oh, it's so dusty in here! I don't know if you'll want to put this up or store it at the Rocking T Ranch." She placed the parcel on top of a freestanding bookcase on wheels, one of Zach's beautiful handcrafted pieces. She pulled scissors from her bag and snipped the twine. "I followed the rustic theme, since you're using exposed stone in the interior. I asked them to use reclaimed barn wood."

My eyes filled with tears as I stared at the sign with the letters burned into the wood. Line one read: THE SECRET PASSAGE BOOKSHOP. Underneath, in a smaller font, were two more lines. The first of those said, WORDS OFFER A SURPRISING INTRODUCTION TO PEOPLE, PLACES, AND IDEAS, and the second line read, IN THE PAST, PRESENT, AND FUTURE.

The etched border showed books, both open and closed.

"Jolene, it's perfect." I grabbed her in a big hug and surprised myself by bursting into tears.

Jolene, embarrassed by my emotion, picked up the sign. "The information shows on both sides, and the wood is sealed for outdoor use. You can drill holes and hang it from the roof extension covering the walkway out front. That placement would make it visible to vehicles and pedestrians." I pictured her gift on the wall behind the vintage cash register Carol Paxton found on a neighborhood exchange site, then in the front window or over the door's entry. I wiped my eyes. "I'm not sure about the placement."

Jolene began rewrapping her gift. "You have options. Zach can suggest where it should go."

"What?"

"Well, after people have. . .uh. . .hospitalizations, sometimes it's hard for them to make decisions."

"I'll figure it out. Thank you. The present is generous, and I love it." What I didn't love was Jolene's patronizing attitude or my zigzagging emotions.

"I'll leave it in Ben's office at the Rocking T for you." Jolene gave me a finger-roll wave goodbye then went to whisper in Zach's ear before leaving.

Her actions made me feel more paranoid. As Jolene left, a scowling Carol Paxton entered.

"I hear you're going with Maria's Meals instead of Elsa's restaurant." Carol didn't preface her remark with a "hello."

"Carol, neither Elsa nor her husband ever contacted me about having a spot in my bookshop."

"Rodney and I spoke on their behalf." Carol blocked my exit, arms crossed.

"This was a business decision," I said.

"It feels personal to me. Food is food, and friendship is friendship." Carol uncrossed her arms to push up her glasses.

"Are you sure Elsa and your son-in-law want to expand?" I asked.

"They need to. Rodney and I understand they need to branch out, but they refuse to talk with us about expansion or changes to the restaurant," Carol said. "They've even said they might sell this restaurant and move somewhere else. They can't. Not seeing our grandson two or three times a week would break Rodney's heart and mine." She removed her glasses and wiped her eyes.

"I'm sure you'd miss all of them." I realized now that the Paxtons' pushiness centered around a relationship issue.

"And she's expecting another one, which I hope will be a girl. I told Elsa she could go back to work and that I'd stay home and care for the baby and our precious grandson. That wouldn't be easy on me, but I'd do it. Do you know what Elsa said when I offered?"

Of course I didn't know, but the question was a rhetorical one, and Carol promptly informed me.

"She told me she could take care of her own children. Rodney and I did everything for that girl, and now she won't listen to a word we say."

I doubted Carol and Rodney listened to anything their daughter and son-in-law were trying to say. At that moment something from the training course for youth ministry came to mind that might help Carol. "Do you remember when we attended that workshop about working with teenagers? The presenter reminded us that students don't want us to solve their problems. They just want someone to listen and to treat them respectfully as they consider their options."

Carol gazed off as if recalling the seminar. "That course was before our LA trip. I listened to a lot of kids on that outing. By the time we reached LA, my ears were tired."

"Have you thought about trying that listening technique with your daughter?"

"I listen. Rodney listens. Elsa and her husband are the ones who don't listen." Carol waved a dismissive hand. "Well, you're busy. I need to talk to Zach for a minute, if I can get him to turn that saw off. He did a wonderful job at our place. We only lost a couple of reservations since he was able to work at our place instead of yours."

My heart ached for Carol, who didn't realize that she was driving a wedge in the relationship with her daughter by trying to control her. With Carol and Zach in discussion and Felicia occupied with her staining assignment, I ducked out the back door to check on the green stick and packet of supplies. Both were as I'd left them. Felicia and I would stop by the Sunrise cabin on the way home to see if my other "bait" items were still there.

My phone rang. It was Ben, asking me to return to cover the office for him. As soon as I ended the call, my ringtone sounded again. My heart sank when I saw Sheriff Hawthorn's number. He'd promised to phone before he came to the ranch to pick up Felicia. I feared this message was the call I'd been dreading.

CHAPTER 11

W as the call bad news? Are you okay?" Felicia asked as we headed back to the Rocking T.

"Felicia, I'm fine, thanks to your actions last week. You're smart." I reached over and touched the tip of her nose.

Felicia grinned. "You helped me, I helped you."

Jolene waited on the porch and spoke as soon as we got out of the car. "Ben and I want to look at our building site." She giggled. "I mean, Ben's new house site. He's found plans he likes. We need to do basic measurements."

"Okay by me. I should work on my housekeeping list."

"I've taken you off that duty," Ben said.

"But housekeeping is my responsibility," I protested.

"We're expecting a couple of families, so I'd like you in the office. Jolene and I won't be gone long," Ben said.

"Would you mind if Felicia and I took one of the horses out for a ride when you get back?" I asked.

Felicia squeezed her eyes shut and crossed her fingers on both hands.

Ben nodded. "Maverick could use the exercise. Good idea."

Felicia had fed and brushed the horses, but this would be her first time on a horse's back, so we rode double. Her slight frame fit in front of me, and I gave her the reins after showing her simple commands. I directed Maverick to the Chapel of Transfiguration and reminded Felicia that this place would be our meeting spot if anything unusual happened.

We walked around the area's buildings and went inside the chapel. As usual, I was awestruck. Even though I saw the same scene when outside, somehow seeing it through the window behind the altar's cross always took my breath away. I pointed out hiding spots in the nearby buildings, but Felicia kept tugging me toward Maverick. I prayed she'd paid attention to what I'd said.

When we returned to the Rocking T Ranch, Sheriff Hawthorn's car sat next to Jolene's vehicle.

Felicia grabbed my hand. "Why is the sheriff here?"

"He told me he might come visit," I said.

Felicia grabbed a curry comb after I took off the horse's saddle.

"Do you know the term 'don't borrow trouble'?" I asked.

"Borrow trouble?" Felicia repeated as she brushed the horse.

"It means don't worry about imaginary things." I squeezed her shoulder after we finished in the barn and then led her toward the office.

The sheriff stood up when we entered the reception area of the Rocking T. "Abby, Felicia. We have good news. Why don't you take a seat? I have a surprise arranged for you."

"I don't like surprises," I said, and remained standing.

"No surprises," Felicia repeated.

"This is a good one, I think." Sheriff Hawthorn smiled. "The police in LA did DNA tests and compared yours to the man claiming to be your uncle. He's a close match."

"I don't know any uncle." Felicia scooted behind me.

"Please sit, ladies. Let me tell you what we know. We think this man is your uncle, your mother's younger brother, Ralph Garcia. He and his family live in the Sacramento area and were visiting friends in LA when they saw the newscast with your picture. He called the station because you and his youngest daughter look enough alike to be twins. I've arranged a televisit. We can leave our camera off if you prefer. You'll be able to see them, and you can ask questions. The family knows your situation, and they want to go slowly. Are you okay with looking at them and hearing what they have to say?"

Sheriff Hawthorn had explained the plan when he'd called earlier, and he'd told me firmly that this would be happening and not to say anything to Felicia before he got there.

When Felicia looked at me, I nodded, sat on the sofa, and patted the seat by me. "I'm curious. Can Felicia and I both ask questions?"

"All the questions you want. Today you'll get to see the uncle, his wife, and their two daughters, Alexis and Julia. Julia is the younger one. With your permission, I'd like to give them a call."

I held up my hand. "Sheriff, what have you found out about Felicia's parents? Have you located them?"

"The stepfather and his sons have left California." The sheriff paused. "Felicia was born in the United States, so she is a citizen. We've not been able to find records for citizenship for any other family members." The sheriff gave me a "don't ask any more questions now" stare.

I nodded. "So, her stepfather and stepbrothers are out of the picture, right?" I asked.

"I've grown fond of this little gal too. We only want her to go to a place she feels safe." The sheriff stood next to the computer.

I turned to Felicia. "Then I think we should hear what the Garcia family has to say. The sheriff said he'd leave the camera off on our side. They won't be able to see you, but we can see them and ask questions."

"Okay." Felicia grabbed my hand and snuggled close.

Sheriff Hawthorn pushed keys on the computer, and soon the screen filled with a family seated at a kitchen table.

Both Felicia and I gasped.

"The resemblance is uncanny," I said.

"She looks just like me," Felicia said. "What's her name? What does she like to do?"

"You can ask her yourself—if you're ready to talk," Sheriff Hawthorn said. "I'm going to turn on this microphone now so we can talk to them." He pushed the unmute button and greeted the waiting family.

"If Felicia is with you, I'm sure she'll see why we knew we were related. Our daughter Julia is also twelve. We were visiting friends in LA when we saw Felicia's picture on television." Mr. Garcia laughed. "I thought someone had posted Julia's picture by mistake."

The girl named Julia looked into the camera. "They said you could come live with us, but it would be your choice. I hope you will. I've always wanted another sister, one closer to my age. We live in Sacramento. My daddy works in an insurance office, and my mother works in the school cafeteria. Alexis is in high school." Julia pointed to the older girl seated next to the mother. "My room has two beds. We can share."

The sheriff asked Felicia if she wanted to ask questions, and she nodded. This family seemed perfect. After the girls talked, I'd have questions of my own to ask.

"My name's Felicia. What is your favorite color?"

Julia giggled. "Purple, but I like pink too. How about you?"

"Pink and purple are my favorites. Why do you want me to live with you?"

I was shocked that Felicia went straight to the important part. The father answered, "My wife and I came here from Mexico when immigration was easier. We are proud Americans. I even have a flagpole on the side of our house, and I fly the flag every day. We are grateful for the life we can live here. It took a long time, but we became citizens, and we want to share our good fortune with my niece."

His story sounded good, but I had my doubts. "Didn't you stay in touch with your sister, Felicia's mother?"

The man shook his head. "The short answer is no, but it's a long story. My sister met and married a young American, really a boy, when he was vacationing in Mexico. They returned to the US, and Felicia was born here. Not long after Felicia's birth, the man found someone else and divorced my sister. She returned to our parents' home in Mexico with Felicia. She was desperate to find a husband to help her raise her daughter. Our family didn't approve of the man she chose. He had three sons from a previous marriage, and neither the man nor his boys treated my sister or Felicia with love and respect. We all tried to dissuade her, but my sister was a stubborn, determined woman. She married him despite family objections."

I looked at Felicia. Perhaps her mother's strength had been passed down, which might have saved her life. "Didn't anyone keep in touch?"

"No. My mother never heard from my sister after the wedding. Our mother died last year, and my dad's been gone for ten years. There were no other siblings."

Sheriff Hawthorn spoke. "The people in LA haven't been able to locate any relatives. Neighbors where Felicia lived said it was only the father, his sons, and Felicia. They'd never seen a woman at the house."

Felicia looked down and whispered so only I could hear, "No mama."

I sighed. That she couldn't remember her mother made me doubly sad, since I'd grown up in a home with two loving parents.

"I want Julia to see me." Felicia sat up straight and lifted her chin.

Sheriff Hawthorn looked my way, and I nodded. He clicked the mouse to enable the camera.

Julia clapped her hands. "Felicia, look at us! We could tell people we're twins. I might have to let my hair grow."

"Or I could cut mine," Felica said softly.

"Felicia, we want to visit you. I have a cat named Snowball. He's all white. If we come to Wyoming, would you like for us to bring him too?"

Sheriff Hawthorn must have noticed how Felicia held on to me. "Why don't you two girls exchange emails for a couple of weeks? Abby, you could correspond with Julia's parents."

"I'd like that." I wanted Felicia to have more time to get acquainted with the Garcia family.

Mrs. Garcia spoke for the first time. "Felicia, we would love to have you live with us, to be part of our family. I work at the school and know teachers who could help you catch up with your studies."

Felicia didn't speak, but her shoulders relaxed. I waved to the Garcia family, and Felicia followed my lead.

Julia blew kisses and shouted, "Goodbye, future sister."

The sheriff spoke to Mr. and Mrs. Garcia and then closed the video-chat session.

"They seem nice," I said to Felicia. "Would you like a sister?"

Felicia smiled shyly. "Maybe. She has a cat, but here we have a horse."

"When Julia comes to visit, she can show you her cat and you can show her Maverick."

Felicia popped up. "Maverick's probably ready for a carrot."

"You know where they're kept. I'll be with you in a minute."

After Felicia left, I turned to the sheriff. "They seem too good to be true."

"Kid deserves a break. Child Protective Services interviewed Mr. and Mrs. Garcia and their two daughters. The family wants to move forward with the process. We have no idea what happened to Felicia's biological mother, but her brother doesn't believe she'd abandon Felicia." The sheriff hitched up his pants.

"Felicia remembers only cruelty from her stepfather and his sons. I'm not sure she ever went to school. Her education consisted of classes at the mission church where Isabella Diaz worked."

The sheriff blew out a frustrated sigh. "The counselor explained to the Garcias about Felicia's past, and that made them want her even more. I feel good about this, but paperwork and court action can take time. The Garcias and Felicia must have visitation sessions so both parties feel comfortable before their family can apply for custody."

I looked out the window at the girl who had wormed her way into my heart. "Well, I'll miss her. I was thinking of adopting her myself."

"Then you'll be happy she has a biological family who already loves her. I think the Garcias will encourage you to visit—if you can get away from your new baby, the Secret Passage Bookshop."

"Yes, I'll be busy getting my bookshop up on its feet and running, but I'll always find time for Felicia."

Things looked good for Felicia, but there was another child we hadn't found, a child desperately wanting a home.

CHAPTER 12

By mid-March, changes were happening so fast in the bookshop that I wanted them to slow down. Zach was acting more like himself these days, so I chalked up his previous behavior to stress. I didn't realize the number of projects he had. He was doing my bookshop, a condo renovation, and, during his evening hours, he'd built my rolling bookshelf cases. He was on schedule to have my marvelous bookshop and apartment ready for April 1.

"Zach, this place is wonderful. When can I start bringing my stuff? Ben tells me my dorm room at the Rocking T resembles a maze with all the new and used books stacked as high as I can reach."

"Box them up and bring them over. I'm ready for the final plumbing installations in your apartment and down here, then after the painting and final city inspection, you're done. Are you going to ask Jolene to help you with the decorations?"

"I doubt she'd have the time. She's incredibly involved with Ben's new house. She never mentions her real estate business, and she's stopped volunteering at the art gallery."

"That's not like her," Zach said. "How about dinner tonight? We're painting your apartment today, and I'll be ready to get away from the paint fumes."

"Maria's?" I asked.

He shook his head.

"Really?" I hoped he hadn't heard the delight in my voice.

"We weren't a good fit. She has different priorities."

"Oh." I waited for him to explain, but he didn't, so I filled the conversation void. "She and Daniel are coming here in about thirty minutes, aren't they?"

Zach checked his phone for the time. "Yes. I asked for both to be here. Maria's the boss, but maybe she'll allow Daniel to decide on paint colors, counter placements, and what to call the food section. Think Maria would allow him to call it Daniel's Delights?"

I laughed. "Maria? Never. She might tag it Maria's Meals Two, but nothing with Daniel's name. We could go with a book or reading theme or use the name of the bookshop. How does Sweet Secrets or Passage Pastries sound?"

"Good possibilities. We could ask the youth group on Sunday. You know they'll have suggestions. They're as excited about your new business as you are."

"They offered to help me move books and furniture when I'm ready," I said.

Zach inclined his head toward the door. "We have company."

Maria, trailed by Daniel, marched to the counter where Zach had arranged paint samples, and opened a folder she was carrying. "Abby, we'll soon be in business together. I have the menu offerings and the hours the shop should be open. I've given the pastries and the teas and coffees literary names. What do you think?"

The names were clever. Maria suggested Jane Austen's Tea, an English theme with scones and tarts, a Mad Hatter's Tea, with a mixture of fruit tea blends and sandwiches cut in playing card shapes. She had names for items such as Writer's Block, Mystery

Muffins, Child's Delight, and Satisfying Conclusion. Maria even suggested the tea and coffee offerings be named for authors. I loved the ideas, but it would require a menu board to list the ingredients in each drink.

"Interesting. I think bookshop customers will like these. Daniel, what do you think? Did you come up with some of these ideas?"

He shook his head. "Wasn't asked."

"Well, since you'll manage the shop, do you have suggestions for its name?"

Maria answered for him. "I'm thinking Bookshop Maria's or Secret Maria's."

"Let's keep brainstorming." I intended to hold my ground about not having "Maria" in the name but wondered about my motive.

"We didn't agree on a name when we signed the contract. That was an oversight on my part," Maria said.

"Since your business will be part of my bookshop, I think I'll select the name."

"Sounds like I don't have a choice. Well, Zach invited Daniel and me to select paint colors. We do have a say in that, don't we?"

I didn't like the way I was behaving, baiting Maria into a confrontation, so I reined in my impulse to be sharp and critical. I should appreciate what she offered. The names and menu items took thought, and they would appeal to customers.

Zach spread the paint samples in groups. "Any of these groupings would work with the bookshop's dominant color scheme. Which combinations do you prefer?"

Maria pointed at a few of the samples. "I like the blues and purples. Purple will attract children, and blues are soothing. You want your bookshop to have a relaxing vibe. For my restaurant, I use bright reds, yellows, and aquas to stimulate conversation, buying, and eating."

"Daniel, what do you think?" I wanted the young man to voice his opinion.

"Blues and purples will be fine." He looked at his shoes.

Zach tapped him and pointed to the plan drawings. "This is what the final layout will be. You'll have a sink, plugs for your coffee and tea machines, and your microwave."

"Isn't that the hidden passageway area?" Daniel pointed to a spot on the plans.

"Part of it. I opened half the corridor's wall to the bookshop and your coffee shop but left a wall to hide a work area on one side and space for the refrigerator on the other."

Daniel smiled. "That's a great idea. Are you adding a work counter where I can make sandwiches?"

"Yes. I plan to build upper cabinets for plates and cups with a counter underneath. I'm also putting the dishwasher behind the wall as well. We don't want your customers looking at dirty dishes."

For the second time, Daniel smiled. Zach had a way of developing a rapport with people, young and old.

Maria scowled. "That's all we needed to do today, right?"

"Right." The word sounded cheerful when I said it. "I'm moving in some books by myself this week, but the big move will be a week from Saturday. Zach promised to finish the painting today. I look forward to being in my apartment, since I've lived in a small dorm-style room at the Rocking T for the past three years."

"Your choice, wasn't it?" Maria asked.

The decision had been mine, but Maria made it sound like a demeaning accusation.

That evening, Felicia and I packed some of my belongings. She didn't want me to leave, but she was also thinking about her new future. She looked forward to meeting the Garcia family this weekend and getting to know Julia. It helped that Julia would bring Snowball when they visited. Sometimes animals provided a bridge between people.

The conversation with the Garcia family alleviated my major concerns, and I'd exchanged many emails with the uncle and his wife. My heart told me that Felicia would be happy with them, that God had arranged Felicia's future. Our heavenly Father cared for His children in the most amazing ways. The fact the Garcia family was in LA when Felicia's picture appeared on a specific news show and that they happened to be watching that channel was no coincidence. Those "chance events" were part of God's plan.

"Right now, I'm just packing a suitcase. I'll pretend I'm vacationing at the Rocking T until my official move. Each night I'll take boxes of books over."

"You'll make many trips." Felicia winked at me.

She felt comfortable teasing me, something I couldn't have imagined a little over a month ago.

"Ben does call me a pack rat," I said.

"Pack rat?" Felicia asked.

"I save things." I motioned to the room.

Each bunk room had a chest, nightstand, and bed, but I'd added other items. Now my space resembled a jumble sale as I'd filled every nook and cranny with merchandise for my shop. Boxed books and piles of fiction, nonfiction, teen selections, and early reader material made walking through my room a challenge.

"I'm going to take a load to the bookshop. Want to come?" I gestured to the chaos I called home.

"Do you want me to?" Felicia asked.

"You don't have to. What do you have planned for tonight?"

"A talk with Julia. Mr. Ben will help me get connected. She wants to show me pictures of Snowball, and I'm showing her Maverick's picture." Felicia looked at the clock. "She wants to talk at eight."

"Then that's what you should do." I hoisted a box on one hip and opened the dorm door.

"I'll help you." Felicia picked up a small cardboard container and followed me.

After we packed my car, I asked Felicia to tell Julia hello from me and then I headed to the bookshop and my future home.

I parked in the back, unlocked the door, and flipped on the lights. What was that scurrying sound? "God, please don't let my bookshop have rats," I whispered.

The noise didn't come again, so I lugged the containers inside. I took them to the far side of the bookshop because I wanted used books toward the back, hoping my customers would first select from the newer, more expensive fiction and nonfiction offerings.

After my final trip, I used my flashlight to check for the green stick and bag under the rock. Both were gone. I turned the bright beam toward the secret entrance and found it undisturbed. Perhaps someone entered the bookshop while I was unloading.

I went back inside, closing the door behind me. "Hello? Don't be afraid. My name is Abby. I'm the one who left the food and water for you. Hello?"

As I walked through the bookshop, I listened for movement or sounds. Nothing.

Zach had told Daniel and Maria about the hidden corridor's change and new purpose. I went to the archway entrance and flipped on a light. Inside was a child rolled up in a blanket crouched in a corner. I remembered Felicia's fear of strangers and kept still. "I'm Abby. I see you've found the food and blankets. It's cold in here. We leave the building heat on a low setting. Mind if I sit?" I eased down to a spot in the doorway, blocking the child's escape route.

The blanket was pulled up so I couldn't even see the child's eyes.

"My friend Felicia started on a journey from LA. She lives with me in a dorm room at a ranch where they have horses. Her favorite is one named Maverick. She gives him carrots each day. Do you know Felicia?"

I heard no answer, so I kept talking. "She'd been hiding out for days. I gave her food, water, and a place to stay. No one came for her. No one came to take her to Canada. Want to meet her?"

"No." The covers muffled the child's response.

"I first saw Felicia at the cabin on Sunrise Trail. Have you been there?" I asked.

"No." Small hands pulled the blanket down.

"I put water and food there too because I wanted to find you, to help you." Pulling my knees to my chest, I wrapped my arms around my legs. "Want to go to the ranch with me?"

"I don't know. I don't know what to do." Sobs and coughing followed the child's words.

"You could meet Felicia. She's twelve and came before you. We'll give you a bed to sleep in and hot chocolate to soothe your throat. How long have you been coughing?"

"Don't know. I should stay here." The child pulled the covers down, revealing a young boy who looked small and scared.

"Didn't the instructions say to wait for Abby?"

He nodded.

"I'm Abby. What's your name?"

"Pete."

"Hello, Pete. I'll unlock my car, and then we'll go to a place where you'll be safe." My promise sounded hollow even to my ears. But God revealed His plan for Felicia, and I believed He had one for this boy too.

When I opened the back door to my shop, the Paxtons' black Mercedes entered the alley. The driver blinked the headlights, letting me know I'd been seen.

CHAPTER 13

Hoping the child would stay inside, I hailed the car, wondering whether I'd find Rodney, Carol, or both. Rodney was alone.

"Good evening, Rodney. What brings you out tonight?" I feared my tone sounded too cheerful, but I was nervous.

"I could ask you the same."

"I asked you first." My retort sounded like a fourth grader's, but Rodney laughed.

"My tenant at Pretty Nails told me she had an electrical problem in one section. If it's a breaker, I can fix it. If it's something more, I'll ask for Zach's expertise."

"How long will you be here?" I thought about the boy waiting inside.

"Don't worry. I'll stay here until you're ready to leave. With your recent experiences, I understand why you might not feel comfortable alone." Rodney slid out of his car. "Want to come in the nail shop with me?"

"No," I said too loudly.

Rodney gave me an inquisitive look then held up his hands. "Your call. I won't be long."

As soon as the lights came on in the building next door, I hurried to the secret corridor and urged the boy to come with me. I opened the back door of my car and motioned for him to stretch out on the floor. "I don't want that man to see you," I said.

As soon as the words left my mouth, Pete spun around and raced off into the night.

"Wait!" I yelled.

Rodney appeared at the back door. "Abby? Is everything okay?"

"Yes, I left something inside. Sorry, I didn't mean to startle you. I'll be out in a jiffy."

I went back inside to search for a "forgotten" item, grabbed a hammer from Zach's toolbox in case I needed a weapon, and returned to my car. I saluted Rodney with the hammer and climbed in my CR-V then followed him out of the alley. On the way to the Rocking T, I drove slowly, searching the dark streets for the little boy, knowing he'd already squeezed into another hiding place.

———

With the Rocking T Ranch back under Ben's management, I allowed myself to worry about the happenings in Bailey. First was the visit from Felicia's potential future family scheduled for this weekend. Add to that there was the young boy I'd discovered, the unexpected appearance of Rodney Paxton, and the boy's hasty exit when I mentioned the presence of a man. What didn't concern me was the completion of my bookshop.

When Zach's plans became reality, they were more practical and aesthetically pleasing than anything I'd imagined. Zach had completed my apartment, and I itched to get in there with a hammer and nails to hang artwork, decorate with personal items, and make it feel like home. Moving day would be next Saturday when Zach and the youth group would transport my things and the remaining books from the ranch to my upstairs home.

On the bookshop side of things, the coffee/tea shop received an official name—Refresh. The softer pastel versions of purples and blues complemented the stronger hues present in the rest of the bookshop. Furniture in the food area would include small café tables and chairs and one comfy, stuffed armchair with a small table next to it. I wondered if the armchair would be an oddity or if customers would claim it when they entered the shop.

I'd been making runs with books from my dorm to the shop and could now walk into my room without fear of toppling a tower of tomes. Wednesday evening, Felicia begged off going to the bookshop with another load of books, saying she had scheduled another chat time with Julia. The two girls had formed a bond. I wanted to like the uncle and his wife as much as Felicia liked the daughter and the cat. The Garcia family would be visiting this weekend, so I intended to get as much done as possible during the evenings.

I borrowed a dolly from Ben and placed it in the passenger seat. My muscles would ache tonight, but the pain would be a good omen, meaning I was one step closer to realizing my dream of opening a bookshop and living in an apartment on the premises.

The temperature had dropped, so I drove to the Sunrise Trail cabin before going to the shop. The stick was where I'd left it, and the water and food had not been touched. Had the child recognized the Paxtons' car, or was he afraid of men? The children all knew Isabella from the LA mission church and trusted her. I'd put my name in the note, hoping the child would trust another woman.

No one ever explained why Isabella had been in my bookshop. Had she accompanied other children to Wyoming? Or did she have a base in LA and an accomplice in Bailey? Was she the one smuggling children out of California? If the answer was yes, then the question was why? I faced my old quandary. Was Isabella Diaz a saint, or a vile parasite feeding off the sale of innocents?

At the bookshop, I backed in by the building's rear door to make unloading easier. After unlocking the building, I turned on the inside lights and the back exterior floodlight. I didn't want to label myself as a fraidy cat, but I had been bashed on the head when in the bookshop alone, then left to die inside a running car in a closed garage, again when alone. As I wrestled the dolly from the front seat, headlights blinded me.

"Abby, it's me. Your place is lit up like Christmas, so I thought I'd stop by. Mind if I look around?" Maria's smile reminded me of the one she wore when flirting with Zach.

"Sure, I have several boxes to unload. I might even put you to work," I said.

Maria laughed. "Can't stay that long. I needed cilantro and was going home to get some when I saw your lights on in the bookshop. I've been carrying around two copies of the lease for the Refresh food area."

"They've been filed," I said.

Maria stepped out of the car with a briefcase. "I prefer contracts with original signatures instead of copied ones. Do you mind signing in ink above your name on the contract?"

"Of course not. Come in. I'm officially moving into the apartment next weekend, then I'll start concentrating on my bookshop instead of being an amateur sleuth."

"No offense, but what do you know about detective work?" Maria walked around the Refresh food area, nodding her approval of the layout. She stepped through the arched doorway to look inside the secret corridor. "Daniel will have ample storage. The public won't see anything back there."

"And Daniel won't have to leave the restaurant in search of cilantro," I joked.

"Why would he?" Maria asked.

Alarm bells went off in my brain because she'd just said she was on her way to get cilantro. Why was she really here?

"Tell me what you've learned as an amateur sleuth. I work long hours and never have time for gossip."

I grabbed a box of books and headed toward the moveable bookshelves. "Well, we don't know much more than we did three months ago. Apparently, someone in LA finds vulnerable children with no home support and offers them the dream of a new life in Canada. The person transports the children from LA to Bailey. I don't know if Bailey is a destination or only a stop." I moved behind one of the bookcases, peering at Maria from between the shelves.

Maria smiled her cat-eating-the-canary smile. "Makes sense to me. If you want to sell children to the highest bidder, this is the place. Consider all the rich people who come here for short periods."

I sucked in my breath. Maria had just voiced the horror I'd refused to consider. "Children are being sold? What kind of person would do that?"

"A practical one. Think of the lives endured by those children who came to Isabella's mission church—"

"I didn't know you knew Isabella," I said.

"Our paths crossed. I know that area. Life is tough for kids who live there. What's happening with Felicia and the boy?" Maria asked.

"There's a boy?" My heart pounded so hard I knew Maria must be able to hear it. I had told no one about the boy I'd found hiding in the secret corridor. If Maria knew, then—

Maria tilted her head. "Did I say 'boy'? I guess I assumed there were boys and girls involved. Is Felicia still with you?"

Maria and the whole town of Bailey knew Felicia lived with me at the Rocking T Ranch. I gulped past the lump in my throat. "Yes, but not for long. An uncle has come forward. He and his family seem nice, and they're eager to take Felicia into their home."

"What?" Maria stared at me.

"Yes, the situation was like divine intervention. When the uncle visited LA, he saw Felicia's picture on television as a missing child and contacted the station. Everything fell into place. The family is visiting the ranch this weekend. If all goes well, Felicia will become a part of their family within the next few months." I avoided saying "Garcia." Maria didn't need to know the surname.

Maria walked from Refresh to the much larger bookshop area, her eyes narrowed. "Why are you involved with these children?"

Her glare made me back up. "I've been blessed all my life. Guess I feel compelled to help those in need, don't you?" When I moved to the far part of the Secret Passage, I realized I'd backed myself into a corner. I felt uneasy and didn't know why. This was Maria, a friend who managed a high-quality restaurant. Could she be an enemy?

"Since you're moving into the apartment soon, I could watch Felicia until she joins the other family. You'll have your hands full with moving and unpacking," Maria said. "Why don't I pick her up tonight?"

"Ben's the one who legally provides custody; I'm just helping. Are you concerned about Felicia's welfare?" Maria had never visited the girl, and Daniel said his cousin had discouraged him from visiting her.

Maria placed her briefcase on an empty bookshelf. "I'm interested. You must realize Felicia wouldn't be in Bailey without my connections."

"Really?" I moved behind one of the movable bookshelves Zach had made and gave it a slight push. I breathed a prayer of gratitude that the wheels weren't locked.

"You're so naive, and you're much too nosy."

"I am?" My voice squeaked, but my fingers locked onto the end of the bookcase.

Suddenly, Maria opened the briefcase and pulled out a gun. "Sorry, Abby. This will be the end of your dream before you destroy mine."

"What? What was your dream?" I shivered, and my hands trembled. The gun in Maria's hand looked bigger than any gun I'd ever seen.

"I was getting rich. The kids we offered to buyers had no future in LA. They were eager to get away from their situation."

"You lied to them. You told them they were going to loving and caring adoptive homes. Wait. You said 'we' offered children to buyers." I thought of Mayor Paxton's visit to the bookshop and how quickly the boy had run.

"No one local, and I've had to shut the business down, thanks to your interference. Isabella was a great partner—until she had an attack of conscience. She told me she was finished." Maria laughed. "So I saw to it that she really was finished."

"I thought she died of natural causes," I said.

"Oh, she did, with a little help from some sleeping pills in her last supper—a delicious broth I made for her."

"You poisoned her?"

"No. I simply gave her something to allow her to sleep. She died of hypothermia. Isn't that what the coroner said?"

"Did you leave me to die in the garage with the car running?"

"Maybe." Maria aimed the gun at my heart.

The gun kept me from thinking clearly, but I chattered to delay the inevitable. "How did you find people who wanted to 'buy' children?"

Maria laughed again. "Not everyone is a do-gooder. It's not hard to find people on the internet who will pay for anything."

"Why did you do it?" I asked.

"I like money, lots of money. Although I enjoy cooking at the restaurant, I'll never make the fortune I want from that business. I want more, and this undertaking is profitable. Isabella was the

LA liaison and sneaked the children into the back of the van when my family visited or brought supplies. I stored the children in the secret corridor in your deserted business or at the cabin as a holding spot until I could place them." Maria seemed proud of herself.

"Does your family know? Does Daniel?"

Maria emitted a bitter laugh. "No. My family is as pious as you are. Why would I share my profits with anyone else?" She took another step toward me.

"But how did you know about the hidden passageway? How did you know you could hide children here?"

"The escape room manager was a friend who made the opening directly into the passageway from the exterior. He thought it would be romantic. Can you believe that? A dark, damp, dirty corridor is not romantic, but it was the perfect hiding place for my products."

My shivering started anew. "Products? They're children! You'll never get away with it."

She stepped toward me. "That's where you're wrong. I came here tonight to have you sign papers, and then—oh, no. I found you dead, or maybe I couldn't find you. I'll leave you in the storage area for Zach to find."

"Do you still want me to sign the papers?" I needed to keep her talking.

"No. If anyone notices my car, I'll say I came here to get you to sign, but you weren't able to lift a pen." Maria chuckled at her sick joke, and her eyes gleamed as she surveyed the bookshop. "Maybe I'll make a deal with the next owner to keep the restaurant—with its corridor for children waiting for a new home."

Suddenly I used all my might to push the bookcase toward her with a strength far superior to my own. The bookcase moved quickly, pinning Maria between it and the wall. The gun flew from her hand, and I raced to grab it.

CHAPTER 14

I tried holding the gun steady while fishing for the phone in my pocket and pushing my full weight against the bookcase. I'd never shot a gun and didn't want to.

"Let me out of here." A rustling came from behind the shelves as if she was trying to move down the wall toward the end of the case.

I braced my feet and leaned back against the bookcase. "Pick up. Answer my call," I shouted into my phone.

"Sheriff Hawthorn here. This better be important, Abby girl."

Relieved to hear his growling voice, I shouted, "Maria Zapata is behind the child-smuggling ring. I have her trapped in my bookshop. Please hurry."

"On my way."

Left with a person who wanted to murder me, I sought answers while keeping her trapped between the bookcase and the wall. "You were the one in my garage. I remember someone grabbing me from behind."

"A touch of homemade chloroform to let you relax, followed by a nap in a car with the engine on." Maria snarled. "I just wanted to frighten you."

"You know how to make chloroform?" The idea shocked me.

"One can learn anything on the internet. That skill came in handy with the children too," Maria boasted.

"Why me?"

"Because you were interfering with my goals. I planned to discontinue the operation for a brief time, but you wouldn't let it go. What are these kids to you, Abby?" She twisted her body and shoved, causing me to stumble.

Regaining my position, I said a prayer of thanksgiving when I saw the sheriff's car. I waved with my gun hand for him to come through the back. I didn't want the town's ex-hockey player to destroy my new front door.

———

The sheriff kept me long past midnight, and office lights at the Rocking T Ranch were on when I returned. Felicia, Ben, and Jolene all rushed toward me when I opened the door.

"Jolene, what are you doing here?"

Jolene held up a hand. "No questions for us until you tell us where you've been and what you've been doing."

When I retold the evening's happenings, they didn't seem all that scary—since I had survived—but my friends treated me like an invalid. Ben pushed me into his overstuffed chair, Jolene draped a blanket over my shoulders, and Felicia sat on the arm of the chair and stroked my hand.

"Does the sheriff think it's over?" Ben asked.

"There's still a missing child." I looked at Felicia. "The children Miss Isabella said were going to loving homes in Canada didn't go there. They were probably sent to a situation worse than the ones they left."

Felicia's face blanched, and her eyes widened. "Was Miss Isabella bad?"

"Not at the end. Isabella realized what she was doing was wrong. She came to Bailey to rescue you and the others."

"But you saved me instead," Felicia said.

"You saved yourself. You were the brave one, and the sheriff wants you to be brave again. He's asking you to help the boy. His name is Pete. Could you wait at the cabin for him? He must be as scared as you were."

"Will you be there too?" Felicia asked.

"I will. The sheriff wants us to try the plan right away. He's worried about Pete, and so am I."

"When will we go?" Felicia asked.

"After I've had a shower and after Jolene explains why she's here in the middle of the night."

Jolene laughed. "You're slow to catch on, aren't you, Abby?" She laced her fingers through Ben's and leaned against his shoulder. "Well, Ben and I have been friends forever, but you starting a new life by buying and opening your bookshop made us think about our lives. Your bookshop project threw Ben and me together, and we liked the idea."

Ben shocked me by kissing the top of Jolene's head. "My trip to LA wasn't all about investigating. Valentine's Day was during the week Jolene and I happened to be in LA. I met her brother and asked for his blessing, then gave Jolene a ring."

Jolene held up her left hand, which sported a large round-cut diamond in a stunning setting. "The house we've been designing is for us. Ben and I planned to delay any announcement until your business opened, but with the bookshop mystery solved, I want to tell everyone."

"How could I have been so blind? Congratulations to you both." I admired her ring. "Jolene, you said you'd never remarry, and Ben, you said you were too ornery for any woman to put up with you. You're two of my favorite people, and I think you're perfect for each other. When's the date?"

"We're thinking of October. The house should be ready for occupancy, and that month is one of the slowest for both our businesses." Ben gazed at his bride-to-be with loving tenderness.

"Want me to throw you the bridal bouquet?" Jolene teased.

"No way! I'm not getting married anytime soon. But I'm glad you are." I gave both my friends a congratulatory hug.

Jolene released Ben's hand. "I don't think anyone will go back to sleep, so why don't I make breakfast?"

"Breakfast sounds fantastic. I'll grab a quick shower, eat, and then Felicia and I will try to rescue a lost boy."

As I turned, I heard Ben say to Felicia, "While they're busy, let's see if Maverick is awake."

Felicia's giggles made my heart sing. Earlier that evening I'd been terrified, and now friends surrounded me. But we had to find Pete.

———

Even though Felicia and I stuffed ourselves with Jolene's breakfast, we stopped at the taco shack. Protein bars were okay in a pinch, but an egg, potato, and cheese breakfast taco would appeal to a hungry child. I prayed Pete would come out to see Felicia. Sitting in a camp chair in front of the cabin, Felicia held a sign that said TACOS.

Thirty minutes passed before we saw a boy edge from the trees on the other side of the trail and into the opening.

Felicia held the two tacos over her head. "For you," she said.

"Is it okay?" the boy asked.

Felicia nodded, holding the wrapped tacos out to him.

He sprinted toward her, grabbed the tacos, retreated to the path, and devoured the food.

"I have water," Felicia said. "I came from LA too. Miss Isabella died, but she lied about the Canada families. My Abby can help you."

I studied him from my hiding spot behind the cabin. When he heard Miss Isabella was gone, his face crumpled. Felicia was twelve, but the boy didn't look older than ten.

"Abby looks out for me. I'm safe. She'll help you too." Felicia stood and inched toward him.

The boy hesitated then slowly walked toward Felicia, who handed him a bottle of water.

"Want to meet her?" Felicia asked. "I stay at a ranch. I feed Maverick, he's a horse. I even rode him once."

The slump of Pete's shoulders told me he wanted to quit searching for food and a warm place to sleep. "I'm tired. You really trust her?"

"I do. You'll meet her?" Felicia asked.

Pete nodded.

"Abby, he wants to meet you."

I came from the back of the cabin so Pete could see me. "I'm Abby. We've met before. Let's go to the ranch where you can bathe and then sleep in a real bed." I turned and walked to my CR-V, hoping both children were following.

———

Felicia paced on the Rocking T Ranch porch, looking for the uncle she'd never met to arrive with his wife, two daughters, and a cat named Snowball. Inside the dining room, I waited with the sheriff, Ben, Jolene, Zach, and Pete. None of us paced, but we showed our anxiety in separate ways. I chattered to the sheriff, who rocked back and forth on his heels and hoisted his belt repeatedly. Zach ran his fingers over the tables and chairs, as if searching for a needed repair. Ben and Jolene studied their house plans, and Pete sat in the corner of the room with a graphic novel I'd found in my donated book supply.

"They're here!" Felicia shouted.

The uncle honked the horn as he pulled into the parking spot. A little girl in a purple sweatshirt bounded from the car and grabbed Felicia in a bear hug.

"Same," Felicia said, glancing down at her own purple sweatshirt.

Julia giggled. "When you come live with us, we can dress alike and pretend to be twins. Want to see Snowball? He's in the car. Snowball doesn't like to travel. When we take him in the car, it's usually to the vet, and he doesn't like that. Come meet him."

I sighed as I watched the two girls race off together. I'd tried to make Felicia happy, but I'd never seen the joy her face showed now.

Sheriff Hawthorn initiated introductions, and Ben invited everyone inside for coffee. Before we sat, the door opened and Felicia and Julia told us they were going to visit Maverick.

Felicia seemed excited, but I had questions. I began with Mrs. Garcia and grilled her about her willingness to take another child into their home and what her expectations were.

Zach put a hand on my arm. "Mrs. Garcia, you don't have to explain your parenting style to us."

"Good. I'm not sure I could. I love my children, and I'm teaching them responsibility. I'll treat Felicia the same as the others. Of course, I expect my girls to be respectful, keep their rooms clean, and help with chores. And church attendance is not optional. The whole family goes every week. Our girls participate in the youth programs at church, and Julia is in the junior choir. Does Felicia sing?"

"I don't know," I said.

When the exuberant strains of "Old MacDonald Had a Farm" came from the corral, we all laughed.

"She sings," Ben said.

By the end of the day, we'd all agreed that Felicia should visit the Garcia family at their Sacramento home and meet with school personnel for placement. I feared she might be grade levels behind, but she was smart, and I knew she would thrive. The paperwork would take a long time, starting with supervised visits then temporary custody with drop-in visits by Child Protective Services.

Before they left, Mr. Garcia took my hand. "Abby, our door is open. Visit Felicia whenever you wish. Thank you for taking care of her."

For once, I was speechless. I nodded, but the lump in my throat prevented me from answering. I turned and saw Pete look at me. He had both fear and hope in his eyes. Would such a happily-ever-after situation happen for him?

The next weekend, I left the dorm-style room I'd called home for the past three years. The teens from our youth group had my furniture arranged and the boxes unpacked before noon. From the whispers and laughter, I figured I might discover my belongings in unusual places, but I'd sleep in my new home tonight.

Ben loaned Felicia a camp cot and a sleeping bag, so she'd be company for me until she left for her home with the Garcia family. She and Julia stayed connected with texts, emails, and Facetime videos, sometimes using filters to change their faces to look like animals.

Despite my doubts about Zach completing his work, as well as my own problems with hospital stays, finding lost children, and being attacked by a child trafficker, my Secret Passage Bookshop with its Refresh coffee/tea shop would open on schedule. All the pieces were in place. My stomach growled when I saw Daniel's car arrive.

"I have the tacos you ordered for your bookshop volunteers," Daniel said as he carried large bags in both hands. "And I brought my mom to help serve. She's moving to Bailey and taking over Maria's Meals, since Maria...well, since Maria will be gone for a long time. Our family didn't know what she was doing. We're all ashamed of her actions."

An older, feminine version of Daniel stepped out of the car, and she approached me with open arms, offering a hug.

"Mrs. Zapata, welcome to Bailey. You'll love our friendly town," I said.

"I already do. You should know we're changing the restaurant's name from Maria's Meals to Zapata's. We don't want reminders of Maria's actions to taint the family business." Mrs. Zapata released me from her embrace. "Daniel's excited about operating Refresh. He's thankful for the opportunity, since his cousin did try to kill you."

"Your son was cleared of any connection with Maria's trafficking ring. The people of Bailey know Daniel's innocent of any wrongdoing. Now, we should feed these hungry teenagers. They've been working hard." I waved to get Zach's attention and clasped my hands together in front of my lips to indicate he should offer a blessing so we could eat.

Silence followed Zach's ear-splitting whistle. "Abby's thank-you for helping her move is a taco lunch. Let's ask God to bless this food and Abby's new business."

"Ask God's blessings on my business too," Daniel said.

"You got it, Daniel."

Even though I'd ordered twice what I thought the youth group would eat, there weren't many tacos left when Sheriff Hawthorn showed up with Pete in tow.

"Looks like we're too late," Sheriff Hawthorn said.

Daniel held up foil-wrapped tacos. "Four left. I put them aside for an emergency. You two look like you need them."

"We do, don't we, Pete?" The sheriff took all four in his large hands then handed three to the youngster. "This boy can eat."

My heart constricted. "You're not here to check out my new business, are you?" I asked.

"Nope." The sheriff unwrapped his taco. "I'm here with good news. Pete will be under Ben's care, just as Felicia was. And Rodney and Carol Paxton offered to help with the school tutoring."

I raised my eyebrows. "Really? Will they have time? Won't Elsa need help with the restaurant since she's expecting another baby?"

"Just between you, me, and the fence post, Elsa would be delighted to have Carol occupied with something other than their lives. Neither the daughter nor her husband is as ambitious as Carol and Rodney. With Pete visiting the Paxtons frequently, they won't be able to be overly involved in Elsa's life. That's a win for everyone." The sheriff hitched up his pants and took his first bite of taco.

Zach came up behind me and put his arms around my waist. "Look at everything that's happened, Abby. Your Secret Passage Bookshop has already brought people together, and it's been the site of unusual events even before your official opening."

He didn't release me, so I turned to face him. As I did, a surprising thing happened. Zach cradled my face in his hands and kissed me.

I blinked and pulled back. I've always said that I don't like surprises, but I did like Zach's kiss. Then I surprised him by throwing my arms around his neck and kissing him.

I guess I do like surprises, at least the pleasant ones.

Linda Baten Johnson loves visiting our national parks, and one of her favorites is Grand Teton in Wyoming, the area that serves as the setting for this book. Linda grew up in White Deer, a small Texas town where everyone knew and looked out for each other. After retirement, she and her husband volunteered in national parks, where they met interesting and unusual people and were awed by the parks' history and beauty. Linda now lives in Frisco, Texas, and serves as a museum docent, volunteers with several organizations, and conducts Grandkid Camp for her grandchildren. Her squeaky-clean romances, cozy mysteries, and historical fiction for young readers are available in print, e-book, and audio. Visit her website at: www.lindabatenjohnson.com.

BY HOOK OR BY BOOK

BY TERESA IVES LILLY

CHAPTER ONE

It was late September, the trees in town were at their peak, and the lovely shades of yellow, orange, and red glistened along the streets. However, I could feel the freezing air beginning to form along the coast, especially early in the mornings. Before long, the water would be so cold no one would be able to even wade in it. I didn't mind though. I was used to this type of cold, having lived in Boston for so many years, but I was beyond glad to be back home in Harbor Inn, Maine, where somehow the cold didn't seem to cut through to one's bones quite as much as it did in downtown Boston.

The town hadn't changed much since I was a child, with the exception of the addition of some new stores, including a few on the Harbor Inn Courtyard, where I was headed. As I walked along the sidewalk from the parking lot, I could feel the cold mist from the ocean. The Harbor Inn Courtyard is an open-faced square that looks out over the ocean, and this early in the morning, it was nice to see that several of the old-timer beach-combers were still braving the weather and the frigid waters.

I'm not much on beach bathing, but a good walk along the coast in spring or fall is always invigorating. Many days I could spend an hour walking a half mile in either direction, just to relax, but I was in a hurry to get to the square, because even after being back in town for three months, I was still excited to open the doors to my little bookstore each morning.

By Hook or by Book is the name of the shop. I chose a pirate-themed decor to go along with some of the local folklore. Pirates are always a draw for visitors, and I've been intrigued with them since I was a young child. I decorated the inside of the shop with spyglasses, eye patches, a tricorn hat, and several treasure chests filled with gold doubloons, jewels, and books. I even have plans for an almost true-to-life-sized anchor to be placed in the main store area, though currently, it's in my storeroom. I stocked the shop with an entire rack of books about pirates for adults as well as children. All in all, the ambience is amazing, if I do say so myself.

So far, in the first month since I opened, I've been happy with sales, even though they are mostly from the last of the summer's-end visitors, who stay in the quaint bed and breakfasts that are scattered up and down the coast. I've yet to see too many of the locals coming through my doors. I'm hoping that as winter settles in, more of them will be needing a good book to read during the winter months and will stop by.

I know that change in a small town is often difficult; however, I plan to reel in the local customers one book at a time. I have plans for book readings for kids as well as adults. I'm hoping to host the local mystery book club and once a month offer an evening of fun and entertainment for those who want to dress up as pirates. My mind is constantly trying to come up with ideas, and I've got a long list written out. It's just making it all happen that will take time. Just thinking about it gets me excited. Of course, these things take time to set up, and making the right contacts is the most important thing. For that reason, I even plan to attend other local events to meet people and encourage them to come by the shop. This town is filled with all kinds of groups. The Red

Hat Society, The Butler Did It Mystery Club, the Ladies Quilting Guild, just to name a few. I'm not sure how many I can join, but I plan to visit them all, with coupons to pass out.

It's strenuous, trying to start a business and pinching pennies all the time. Not that I'll go broke, at least not at first. I have money I've been saving for over fifteen years in hopes of opening my own bookstore one day. Still, the shop can't survive forever without the patronage of the townspeople.

A few of the locals remember me, and most of them know my mother, who is very much a part of the town when she isn't traveling. She's kept my memory alive in many of their minds by telling them inflated stories about my exciting life in Boston as a librarian. How she turns that into excitement, I will never know. As far as I remember, nothing exciting ever happened to me until I moved back to Harbor Inn, Maine, to open my own bookstore.

The month seems to have flown by since I opened the store, but I feel as if the dreamlike state I've lived in the past thirty days is beginning to lift off of me. This is my life now, and I'm very happy, but I'm also becoming much more realistic about things and recognizing the truth about how slowly things change in a small town like Harbor Inn.

As I drew closer to the shop, I noted Penny London, my friend and owner of the Cup 'n' Cake Coffee Shop, standing in front of my store along with a police officer. I wasn't sure why, since it was a police officer and not a firefighter, but images of fire destroying all my books flooded my mind. I ran up to them and stopped beside Penny.

"What's going on?" My voice trembled, and I tried to move closer to the door, my eyes flashing back and forth.

Penny grabbed my hand and gave it a squeeze, holding me back, which only served to bring my heart's palpitations up to pounding in my chest.

The officer, a startlingly handsome, dark-haired, dark-eyed man, turned to face me. His demeanor seemed pleasant, not concerned. "Are you the owner of the bookstore?" His voice was strong and steady.

I nodded, almost unable to speak, my stomach turning in knots and reminding me I hadn't eaten yet.

"We got a call this morning from your neighbor, Penny London." He tilted his head at Penny. "She believes she saw someone trying to break into your shop."

I turned to Penny, questions wanting to flow, but still trying to gasp a breath.

She nudged closer to me. "I was heading into my place when I saw a man dressed in all black—including a black hoodie—pulling on your door." She pointed at the By Hook or by Book's front door, which was situated between two large windows where I had set up a very appealing display of pirate books. Seeing it reminded me that I would have to change the decor soon for Halloween, then Thanksgiving, and finally, because the store owners in the courtyard usually voted on a Christmas theme, I would have to really put some time into my Christmas display.

Penny continued. "At first, I thought it was an early shopper, but he didn't seem to want to shop. He kept pulling at the door, until I was afraid it would give way. I yelled at him, and he ran away. I must have scared him."

I stepped closer to the door and examined it. There didn't seem to be any damage, so at least the stranger hadn't broken anything, which I guessed was a plus. Replacing a door wasn't in my budget.

"Do you have your keys?" the officer asked in a kind voice. I looked up, and our eyes met. I'm not sure how to explain the feeling that took over, but it was something like a warm tingle, slipping up and down my spine. As though in a trance, I slowly reached into my purse and pulled out a lanyard that was decorated with pictures of books. It had my car fob and shop keys attached to it, plus several smaller keys that opened drawers and boxes in the shop. I handed it to the officer and, after a moment, he opened the door.

"I'll go in first." He stepped inside. He wasn't gone for ten seconds when I turned to Penny.

"Do you really think this person was trying to break in?"

She nodded. "I can't imagine what else he was doing."

I shook my head. "That's weird. I mean, who breaks into a bookstore? They aren't generally known to have much cash on hand."

"Do you have any rare books?" Penny asked, but I wasn't able to answer because the officer stepped back outside.

"There's no one in there. I'd like you to look around. Make sure nothing was disturbed." He smiled at me, and I felt as though I was going to faint. Of course, it could have been from the lack of food and all the excitement.

I stared at him incredulously. "If the man didn't get in, how could anything be disturbed?" I immediately wished I hadn't said anything, because a mask of irritation quickly dropped over his face.

"I'm just doing my duty." Any trace of a smile was now gone.

I realized my words had been a bit harsh. "Sorry," I mumbled, and stepped into the shop. I reached to the right and flipped on the lights. One switch brought the entire store to life. I'd used all sorts of twinkle lights to highlight different items in the shop. There were also old lanterns one might find in a captain's cabin that I'd turned into lamps, and they lit up certain sections of the store along with several other lights.

A long whistle made me turn. The officer was standing there, hands on his hips, looking around. "Wow, when lit up, this is something." I could see the admiration in his eyes. My spirit warmed to him again. I followed his gaze around the shop. I especially loved the reading corner I'd made with part of an old rowboat. I'd fashioned it into a place where a customer could sit in the boat to read, but I'd made the seats a bit more comfortable by upholstering them with foam and some worn-looking leather. So far, it was a favorite spot for those who came in and stayed to read.

"Now, Miss. . .?" He feigned a stern look.

"Carter. Lily Carter."

He nodded and actually gave me a small wink. "Miss Carter, I'm Officer Forgione. Dwayne Forgione." His eyes met mine again, and for a moment I felt that same warmth spread up to my cheeks. If I didn't know better, I'd say the man was flirting with me. "Do you see anything out of place?"

I looked around then began to move slowly through the store. I didn't believe there could be anything out of place if the hoodie man hadn't broken in, but I wanted to be sure. After about ten minutes, I shook my head. "No, I don't see anything that looks out of place or even tampered with."

He walked to the back room and entered it. I watched as he maneuvered around the large anchor I'd bought in Boston. It was very large and heavy, and I still needed it to be placed in the store somehow. "This is a beauty," he said, and I could tell he was impressed.

"Thanks. I'm trying to find someone to help me move it to the front." My words tumbled out. He turned and with a big grin asked, "How do pirates like to cook their steaks?"

I was a bit taken aback and tilted my head. "What?"

"It's a joke." He grinned again. "How do pirates like to cook their steaks?"

I shrugged. "I don't know." I thought it was a weird time for jokes, but his endearing grin was enough to get my attention.

"On the barrrrbeque." He emphasized the word in just the right places, using a pirate-like voice. Then he laughed at his own joke.

I guess I just blinked. After a few seconds he shrugged. "Sorry, my childhood dream was to be a stand-up comedian. The jokes just slip out sometimes."

Not sure what to say, I stood there for a moment. Penny was still hovering around the door out front. I felt bad because she looked cold. "Everything's fine," I called out to her. She nodded then moved off. I knew she needed to get back to her shop because there were sure to be more people buying coffee early in the morning than there were people buying books.

"I guess everything's okay here then," Officer Forgione stated. I nodded, hoping I could soon open for the day. The break-in was obviously a mystery that might never be solved.

Before he left, Officer Forgione handed me a piece of paper. "That's my cell phone number," he said. "Just in case." He gave a little crooked smile. "And, if you don't mind, I'll be back sometime when I'm off duty. I love reading, and your pirate-themed shop is a wonder."

I smiled, looking forward to his return but unable to even squeak out an answer. When he was just a police officer talking to me, I had no problem, but when he was a man who seemed as if he might be interested in me, I couldn't think of a thing to say, and my shy awkwardness took over. I could feel my face flush and a bit of sweat form on my brow.

He must have realized I was uncomfortable, because he suddenly turned and headed toward the front door. He glanced at the lock once more, I assume making sure it really hadn't been damaged, then disappeared.

Once Officer Forgione was gone, I closed the front door and locked it. I leaned my head against it and said a little prayer, thanking God that no one had actually broken into the store. I wasn't even sure I believed anyone had really been trying to break in. I mean, aside from some petty cash, what could anyone want in my little bookstore?

For a moment I stood still, and a thought, or a whisper of a thought, traipsed through my mind. Perhaps there was something in the shop worth stealing, but what was it? As quickly as it came, the thought disappeared, and I had to shake it off.

After a few minutes, I began to organize the counter for the day. I was early, so I didn't need to unlock the doors for customers for about fifteen minutes. That gave me time to open some of the boxes from the storeroom. There was a shipment of books about pirates that I'd bought at an estate sale in Boston right before moving here. They'd arrived in the mail two days ago and were still sitting in the back. I was interested to see if any of them were first editions or special at all.

I made my way to the back room and started searching the box labels. I'd written ESTATE SALE on the two boxes. After a few minutes, I located them, pulled one into the front room, and lugged it up onto the counter. It never ceases to amaze me how heavy books are, and I'm glad media mail is available for shipping, or I'd go broke buying books for the shop.

Garage sales, estate sales, and thrift stores are places I frequent. Not that I usually sell used books, but if it's something that has a pirate theme or is worth something and I can get a great deal, then I'm going to purchase it.

So, with box cutter in hand, I slit the box and opened the flaps. A musty smell wafted from it. I don't love the smell of old dusty books as some librarians do, but a little bit of mustiness doesn't bother me. I started pulling the books out one at a time and scanning each with the Lens App on my phone to see what its value was on eBay.

After fifteen minutes, I'd set aside four of the ten books I'd looked up that seemed to be worth a bit more than the others. I was happy with the outcome of my purchase so far and hoped that the second box would yield even more promising items, but now it was time to open the shop.

I turned on the OPEN sign and unlocked the door. Then I returned to the counter. I consulted my calendar book and frowned.

There still weren't any events filled in, and I knew without them I didn't have much chance of making a real go of things.

I sat down to brainstorm and wait for customers, making notes about some ideas I had that might pull in the community. One thing that looked interesting in town was the Cocoa Festival. There were many events held during the week, all which had a cocoa theme. There was even a cocoa craft and antique show. I had the date circled on my calendar because I wanted to get a table at the show. I could display some of my oldest books and pass out flyers and coupons at the same time.

An hour later, the door opened and a woman came into the store. She noticed me at the counter and smiled with a wave, making her way across the room. I was surprised by her behavior because I had no idea who she was.

"Good morning," I said, giving her a curious look.

She smiled. "You don't know me, but I'm one of your mother's friends. She's told me so much about you, I feel as if I've known you your whole life. I've been waiting for you to get the shop opened, then I was out of town, so this is the first chance I've had to stop in." She turned around and allowed her gaze to take in the entire ambience of the room. "This is fantastic. I believe it's the most unique bookstore I've ever been in." She turned back and gave a flashing smile.

I was proud of the store, and it was nice to hear someone saying such a positive thing about it. "Thank you."

"I'm Katie, by the way. I own the Aunties' Attic Thrift Store."

I remembered my mother talking about someone named Katie. "Oh, yes. I've heard of you."

"Yes, and now you've converted the old bookstore into a glorious new bookstore." The woman gushed like a schoolgirl. I recalled Mother telling me that Katie had lived with her elderly aunts for years, as a recluse. That was probably why she seemed so childlike. When the aunts had passed away, Katie had converted the mansion into a thrift store and become an active member of several groups in town.

"Well, Katie, I'm glad to meet you. I believe you're one of my mother's very best friends."

The older woman nodded. "Yes, she started shopping at the thrift store, and before long we were talking. We've become great friends."

"I was glad when Mother told me about you. She tends to be a loner, and as she's getting older, it's nice to know she has a good friend." I was a bit surprised though. Katie was obviously older than me, but still, much younger than my mother. Come to think of it, I was even more surprised that my mother had gone on a cruise that week. She liked traveling, but never alone. And she was off on a Jamaican cruise by herself. We had always spoken every week, but something about her had obviously changed since I'd moved away.

Katie reached over the counter and gave my hand a squeeze. "And she's so happy you're back in town."

I laughed. "Well, I can't get any closer than living in the apartment over her garage. Of course, now that she's run off on that cruise, I won't see her for a week or more."

Katie agreed. "I just wanted to stop in and tell you that I often get donations of books at my shop. I really don't have a market for them unless they are true antiques. If you'd like, I could send them here and maybe you can sell them at a discount?"

An idea of wrapping them in plain brown paper and giving them as mystery gifts came to mind. That might be something that would draw in new customers. Or I could even wrap them in orange and black paper and give them away at Halloween.

"That would be lovely, if you're sure."

"Yes, I have way too many donations coming into the store, and I'm always looking for other outlets rather than just the trash. I sell the vases to the florist for twenty-five cents each, and I donate the towels and blankets that aren't in good condition to the humane society for them to use with the dogs. I love spreading it all around. I'll send a few boxes over next week. In the meantime, now that I've seen your shop, I'll tell all my customers to swing by. All you have to do is reel them in." She laughed at her play on the name of the shop.

"Thank you, Katie." I felt like giggling. I could see why my mother liked her so much. "It's my goal to do just that, by hook or by book."

Katie smiled. "I can only hope things go better for you this first month than it went for me and my store." Her voice sounded rather mysterious.

I looked up at her. "Why? What happened?"

"A woman was killed outside my shop. I was sure it would put me out of business before I even got started."

I felt a shiver run down my spine.

"That's a story I need to hear." I remembered my mother telling me that Katie had helped solve a murder, but I didn't realize it happened at her thrift store.

Katie nodded. "Another time. We can get together when your mother returns, and I'll tell you all about it. In the meantime, I'll try to send you customers."

I was sure Katie telling her customers about my shop was one way the locals would begin to feel comfortable enough to stop by and visit the bookstore. I asked her if I could give her some coupons and flyers to hand out. She agreed then wandered around the shop for a few minutes, brought a book of poetry up to the counter, and purchased it. "I'm in The Butler Did It Mystery Club, and I attend monthly poetry readings. I'll tell them all about your shop."

When Katie left, I found myself lifting up prayers of thanksgiving for the woman.

CHAPTER TWO

L ily, I'm so glad that guy didn't break into the bookstore," Penny said as she handed me a cup of coffee to go with one of the blueberry bagels she offered as a staple at Cup 'n' Cake. "Especially since you only just recently opened." She gave me a wink. It was the day after the mysterious break-in attempt, and I had joined Penny at her shop for a quick chat and cup of coffee before opening the store.

I lifted the Blue Willow floral cup and took a sip followed by a long sigh. "I'm glad too. It's scary enough to be opening the shop so recently, without worrying about having anything stolen. I don't think my insurance company would look too pleasantly on that."

Penny agreed. "I'm just glad you're finally getting the chance to have a bookstore of your own." She wiped the counter out of habit not need.

"Yes, I've waited my whole life for it. Ever since I was a little girl, I loved going to the Turn the Page Bookstore here on the courtyard. It nearly broke my heart to hear they'd closed down eight months ago."

"It was sad, but when Turn the Page closed, it gave you the chance you've always wanted—to open your own bookstore."

Penny laughed. "I mean, you didn't want to go on being a librarian forever, did you?"

I shook my head. I was now thirty-five and had almost begun to believe that owning my own bookstore would never happen. "You know I didn't. And moving back to Harbor Inn has always been my dream, but there was no need for a librarian here. Still, if I couldn't own a bookstore, then working at one of the Boston public libraries was the closest thing to a dream come true." I lifted the bagel and took a bite. Penny and I have been friends for such a long time. We grew up together, and when I moved I became her long-distance friend on the internet. I was her greatest cheerleader when she met her now-husband, Kyle, the famous mystery writer. The two of them combined their coffee shops and settled down here in Harbor Inn. I, on the other hand, hadn't had a steady boyfriend for over five years, much to my mother's dismay.

My mother has always lived in Harbor Inn, and before I moved back, she'd kept up a steady flow of weekly texts with photos of different men from town who were available. However, I don't remember her sending one of Officer Forgione. *Don't think about him,* I told myself. I glanced up at Penny, changing the subject she hadn't even been aware had come up in my mind.

"Do you think the town will accept the name change? I mean, By Hook or by Book, it's quite different." I tilted my head. I didn't like questioning my own decisions, but opening a bookstore was a huge undertaking. When the previous owner closed shop, she didn't want to have the store called by that name any longer. I had scrambled for a name until I went to see a pirate-themed dinner show in Boston. I knew immediately I had to have a pirate-themed bookstore.

"Sure, plus your shop is very different. You're offering a children's department with all sorts of readings and craft time for the little ones, which no one's done in this town before. And you've added an entire mystery section." She pressed on enthusiastically.

"The whole pirate theme will really go over with the vacationers. Everyone loves pirates, and the way you play off the old lore of Harbor Inn's pirate history is unique."

I had to agree; however, I was apt to worry about things. I'd put my life savings into redecorating and reopening the bookstore, and there had been a few older people in town who'd frowned at me changing its name.

"And Lily, I appreciate you dedicating a whole shelf to Kyle's books." Penny smiled at me.

"He's one of the best mystery writers I've ever read, and the fact that he's local is all the better. I'm hoping he'll plan to do some readings from time to time." Nothing wrong with getting in a few hints, I thought. Even though I was a rather intimate friend of Penny's, I only knew Kyle in passing and hadn't ever spoken to him about his books.

Penny swished the cloth over the counter again. "He'd love to do it. You know, he's been in The Butler Did It Mystery Book Club for a few years, and they've never asked him to do readings. I believe that bothers him."

I felt my pulse speed up. This was good news. I would talk to him as soon as possible and set up a reading. Maybe even once a month, if he drew a large enough crowd. He had at least twenty books out. He could do a reading every month for nearly two years and discuss a different book each time. Surely that would be a big draw in this town. We could advertise in a few of the nearest towns as well.

"I wonder why the club never asks him to do a reading?" I spoke out loud, although I was actually only thinking. I looked up and saw a flash on Penny's face, which I knew to be a sign of irritation.

Penny dropped the cloth. "Oh, something about not letting anyone in the group be more important than anyone else, which I can understand, except that the club is all about them talking about other murder mysteries. After three years, you'd think they could have discussed one of his books. But I'm not in charge, so I guess my thoughts don't really matter." She looked at me with a frown. "But he doesn't write about pirates," she said, a tone of sadness in her voice and her enthusiasm waning.

I laughed and patted her hand. "Not a problem. It's a pirate-themed store, but not everything can be about pirates. There are plenty of other things I want to offer, including Kyle London's mystery books and, if possible, readings by the author."

Penny leaned over and gave me a hug. "Thanks. Kyle's been a bit down lately. He can't come up with an idea for his next book, so I think an offer to do a reading would really help him."

I nodded and promised I would look over my calendar and call him as soon as possible. In my mind I was already planning how to advertise and where to set him up in the store. Kyle London could be one of the biggest highlights of the upcoming year.

Just then the bell over the door rang. Penny and I turned our heads. A group of students who attended our local college entered the shop and sat at one of the tables near the front window. They were laughing but not causing a ruckus. I wondered if I'd ever been so young. My days in college were so long ago, I could hardly remember them, and gathering at a local coffee shop hadn't really been the thing to do back then.

"I better get busy making some caramel macchiato," Penny said. "That's all these college students want." She turned away and moved into the back of the shop, giving me a wave as she went.

I finished my coffee, set my cup down, and stood. I was glad I'd stopped in. Talking to Penny always lifted my spirits, but it was time I got to my own shop. I liked to open at nine, just in case there were any early birds who wanted to peruse the books.

The shop was in the Harbor Inn's Courtyard, which faced the ocean shore, and there were many people who walked on the beach early in the morning. Several would end up at the coffee shop and then the bookstore. I didn't want to miss any of them.

I began to walk past the group of students but stopped when I heard part of their conversation.

"Aye, mate, I'm going to make you walk the plank. Argh!" The young man imitating a pirate had dark hair and olive skin. Judging by his looks, I assumed him to be at least partially Greek.

There were two young women, who started to giggle. The young man who'd been speaking bowed and without the pirate voice said, "Thank you, thank you. Just throw money, please."

One of the girls, who had coal-black hair and wore her eye liner in a way that made her look like a feline, smirked. "Good one. I don't want to walk the plank though. I'd like to join your crew." She spoke in a voice that, oddly enough, sounded like a cat's meowing. I found myself imagining her hissing and scratching someone with her sharpened fingernails.

The young man pretended to pull out a sword and swish it around. He nodded at her. "Well, shiver me timbers, wench. I'll have you know as captain of this ship, I will not abide any felines frolicking around."

The girl swiped a hand at the imaginary sword, like a cat. Then she sat back down, and the banter ended.

I tried to hide a smirk behind my hand. It was all good fun. The librarian in me wanted to approach them and explain how pirates would usually welcome a cat on board. They would keep it well fed and content, because they believed that cats could start storms with the magic in their tails. Looking at this group, I doubted they would want to hear my ramblings, so I began to move toward the door again, when an idea came to my mind, and I turned back and moved closer to the group. "Excuse me." I directed my words to the one who had been doing the acting. "I heard you speaking like a pirate."

The young man turned to face me. "Aye, mate, that you did."

"I own the By Hook or by Book bookstore, and it has a pirate-themed decor," I began to explain.

The entire group gave me their full attention, which was encouraging, and they all seemed interested in what I had to say. "Yes?" the young man said.

"Well, I overheard you speaking in a pirate voice, and it gave me an idea. I'm interested in having someone do some readings at my shop, in a pirate voice. You know, for the kids."

The young man's eyes lit up. "Is it a paying part?"

I nodded, not wanting to overcommit. "Not much, but I'm sure we can work something out."

The girl who had the catlike eyeliner brightened. "I, for one, could use the money."

Another young man stood up. His hair was lighter, and he had dark green eyes. "We can all use some money, but Nico, your attention needs to be on the play." His brows were drawn together, glaring at me. I wasn't sure what I'd done to make him angry.

"Relax, Greg. I just tried out today. We don't even know if I got the part. And even if I did, I can handle both."

I wasn't sure what to do. I didn't want to be cause for contention between the two of them.

The dark-haired girl nodded. "Yeah, Greg, Nico can do it all. Have you ever seen anything he can't do?" I thought her words sounded rather spiteful, which seemed strange for a group of friends. But maybe this was their normal dynamic.

Greg didn't respond.

"That's not true, Kat," Nico said. I could see he was uncomfortable with the conversation. "But I could use the extra funds. My treasure chest is almost empty these days." Once again, he pulled a pirate theme into the conversation. I was sure he was just what my shop needed.

Both girls giggled again, although Kat's smile seemed forced and I noted that Greg didn't smile at all.

"There are others who could do the readings just as well." Greg looked at me, almost daring me to argue.

I wasn't really sure what to say. I thought Nico was great, but perhaps there would be someone even better out there. I was a bit amazed at the competitiveness between them all.

"I could hold tryouts," I suggested, thinking I could ask someone else to help me judge so that I wouldn't be partial to Nico.

The entire group thought that was a good idea. "That's fair enough," the second girl said. "Would you consider female pirates?"

I nodded. Girls might work with the younger kids better anyway, but Nico's performance earlier had already spurred my imagination.

"I can make a poster and hang it up at the college in the drama department," Kat offered, her eyes sparkling. "Can you interview in two days?"

"Yes, the sooner the better," I assured her.

I looked at Nico again. "I assume you just tried out for the college play *Pirates of Penzance*?"

Nico nodded and waved a hand around, indicating the group. "We all did." Then he looked at the other young man for a moment. "You weren't there, Greg."

Greg shrugged. "Why waste my time? Everyone knows you're going to get the lead."

Nico frowned. "Man, that's not right. I mean, we talked about it all summer."

Greg stood up. "Let it go, Nico. It's no big deal. I gotta get going." He turned abruptly and left the coffee shop without having ordered anything.

The other young woman, a girl with coppery auburn hair and light blue eyes, called out, "Wait, Greg." But the young man was gone.

What's got into him?" She hurried out the door after him without waiting for an answer.

Nico's dark eyebrows were drawn together. "I don't know about Greg. He's been a bit moody since the semester started." He faced me again. "Sorry about that, but we'll all be here for the tryouts."

Kat nodded in agreement, picked up her purse, and slid out the front door.

I reached out and shook hands with Nico. "I'm looking forward to these tryouts. It should be fun."

He seemed a bit distracted, so I left the coffee shop, hurrying now, not wanting to be late opening my own store. I headed across the courtyard, passing Roses Are Red Florist and Good Old Days Antiques.

This town was filled with quaint places, all with quaint names. I could only hope that By Hook or by Book would fit right in, and that everyone in town could forget the old bookstore.

When I reached the storefront, I noted that Greg was standing outside with a taller man. They were looking in the window. From what I could see, the man was speaking to Greg in a rather aggressive way and Greg was shaking his head back and forth. The girl with the blue eyes must have left, but I saw Kat. She seemed to be hovering at the edge of the building, not wanting to interrupt Greg and the man's conversation. I wasn't sure she could hear what they were talking about, but from her stance, she was trying hard. I wondered if she was an eavesdropper in general or just when it came to Greg. He was a good-looking young man.

I turned my eyes toward Greg again. Whatever it was the other man was saying, Greg wasn't happy about it.

As I drew near, Kat noticed me, turned, and walked the other way. I thought she seemed like a person walking in a trance and ignored me. The man who had been speaking to Greg was turned so I couldn't see his face, but I wondered if I'd ever seen him before, although nothing about him rang a bell. I noted that he wore a black hoodie. He turned on his heel and disappeared between two buildings in the courtyard.

I stepped up beside Greg and opened the door. "Want to come look around?" I asked.

His head whipped up, and I could tell his jaw was clenched. "No!" He turned and stomped away, leaving behind a cool chill running up and down my veins. How someone who had just moments before been rather charming in his own way turned into such an angry person, I didn't know.

I bowed my head. "Lord Jesus, I don't know the issue with Greg, but it seems as though there's something upsetting him. Please help him, Lord." I ended the quick prayer with an amen then moved into the shop. I wanted to add Greg to my prayer list, so I rushed over to my counter and pulled out a leather journal I kept stashed there. When I opened it, there was an almost full page of names.

These were people I prayed for throughout the day; people I'd met in the store, or on the beach, or in town. People who had no idea I was praying for them. I always jotted little notes beside their names to remind me what their special needs were.

I wrote Greg's name on the bottom empty line in the journal and beside it wrote: "seems troubled." I could only hope that whenever I had a moment to pray for him, I would remember exactly what it was that I thought he was troubled about. Before closing the book, I also jotted down Nico's name and Kat's, plus a blank line for the other girl whose name hadn't been mentioned. I wasn't sure what to write beside those three names, so I left them blank, hoping I'd find out more about them when they came to audition.

CHAPTER THREE

Two days later, I walked along the beach early in the morning bundled up in a warm, fur-lined coat and felt invigorated as I moved into the courtyard, planning to open early and prepare for a few students to come and try out for the readings. I was more than surprised when I turned the corner and saw a long line of students, most of them dressed in pirate garb, waiting for me. I was aware that Harbor Inn's college had partnered up this year with our local Carousel Theater to put on the *Pirates of Penzance* play. The theater was much bigger than the one at the college, and the play would probably pull in a large crowd.

It was exciting to think of the college putting on that particular play. I'd heard rumors that the mayor wanted to host a Pirates on the Beach festival that would coincide with the performance, and I hoped the play would inspire people in town to check out my pirate-themed bookstore.

The students who wore costumes had not necessarily tried out for the play, but I guessed those who dressed up thought it would help them at my tryouts. I actually hid a giggle behind my hand when I noticed some of the rather thrown-together costumes. I wasn't even sure they were all pirates, as some looked more steampunk or Goth.

Nico and Kat were in the crowd, but I didn't see Greg in line. I'd hoped to have him try out for the reading job. There was something rather appealing about the young man, but I didn't have time to think about that right now. I had hoped to get this over in an hour; now I could tell it would take all day.

At the front of the line, I noticed Katie from the thrift store. She gave a big wave. I'd asked her if she would help me with these tryouts. I wanted a very unbiased opinion, which I felt she would be able to do. She didn't know any of the students. I only knew the four I'd met the other day, but that alone made me biased.

"Morning, Katie." I grasped her hand. We weren't really on hugging terms yet, but I did like her a lot. I could see what my mother liked about her. She had such a fresh look, and her eyes were filled with excitement. I looked at the long line again. I didn't think my eyes were lit with excitement.

Her cheeks were rosy from the cool air. "Morning. What a turnout!" She pointed at the group.

"I know. We have our work cut out for us." I wanted to go home and crawl back in bed, but instead I turned with a forced smile and faced the group. "Good morning. I'll have to have you in one at a time, so everyone can sign your name on the chart." Reaching into my purse, I pulled out a clipboard that had a chart attached. I handed it to the closest "pirate" and then moved into the shop's doorway. "If your number is ten or greater, it could be a half hour or more. Maybe run over to Cup 'n' Cake and get some coffee. If your number is over twenty, it could be an hour. I don't want you hanging around and getting cold. So put your cell phone number on the sheet too. If you aren't here when it's almost your turn, I'll give you a call and about ten minutes to get here."

I could see that plan pleased the group, especially the ones toward the back of the line. So as the clipboard was sent around,

I opened the shop and got Katie set up in the far back corner where there was a small stage. That way the auditions wouldn't interrupt any customer's shopping.

The day progressed slowly as one student after another gave a short reading. A few did a great job, some almost made me laugh, while others were completely inadequate. I could easily read Katie's expressions and hoped the students didn't notice it. She was like an open book. After the first hour, I was rubbing the frown lines between my eyebrows and could feel a headache coming on.

Two hours in we took a short lunch break, eating our own bagged lunches in my back room, along with the boxes and the big anchor.

Katie looked around. "This anchor is just too big for this room," she announced.

I laughed. "Yes, I need to get it moved out. Maybe I'll write down a few of the strong boys' names and numbers and call them sometime to help me move it."

Katie thought that was a grand idea. She was like that. She didn't just say, "great idea," she said "grand idea." There were many times I could see or hear the influence her elderly aunts had on her. She was sweet and very old-fashioned.

I was glad when the last student finished their reading. It had taken several hours. A few of the students were very good, however, none were as talented as Nico, in my opinion. But I was leaving that decision up to my unbiased partner.

"So, what are your thoughts?" I asked Katie. She handed me a list with names and numbers written on them. She'd used a one-to-ten scale and had created three categories. Once totaled, the highest score was circled. Nico's name, as I suspected, was circled twice and had a star drawn next to his perfect score of 30.

"Nico was the best." Katie's smile flashed. "That boy is a born actor."

I agreed and looked at the other names. Kat's score was the second highest and was followed by three other names I didn't know, but I was in complete agreement with Katie's scores. I debated on whether I should give Nico the job, though, especially since he was hopeful of getting the lead role in the play, but he did mention again that he really needed a job.

I selected the top five in case I ever needed an extra to fill in for Nico and put their names in my address/phone book. Not many people use those these days, but I still like to write the most important numbers in my book in case I ever lose the contacts on my phone.

I had promised to post the winner's name at the Carousel Theater doorway the following day and so, once Katie left, I locked the door to the shop. It was almost closing time anyway, and I did have some receipts to count, since many of the students had taken time to look around the shop after doing their auditions and several bought novels or small gifts like bookmarks and note cards. By Hook or by Book was now known by many of the college students.

That gave me an idea to consider advertising in the college's student newspaper. I could offer a coupon for those who attended the school. I jotted that down on my idea list and closed shop for the night. I was tired and could barely drag myself to the car.

I was very weary driving home. My mother's house was dark and would be for another day or two until she got home from her cruise. I pulled into the garage, turned off the car, got out, and headed up the stairs we built inside the garage. The apartment over the garage was cozy and inviting. In minutes I was ready for bed and cuddled down and reading my Bible. I try to read it in the morning, but most of the time, I have to finish up before bed.

"Lord, I'm not sure why we had to go through all those tryouts today, just to end up choosing Nico, but I appreciate all the sales we had. Please help Greg with whatever is bothering him and, once again, thank You for my very own bookstore." I'm so grateful to God for the opportunity to open the shop that I never forget to mention it in my prayers. My last few words were barely audible as I drifted off to sleep.

———

Two days later, Nico showed up at the shop. He was glad to have been chosen to do the readings and promised to be the best bookstore pirate available. We had a nice chat. He was actually taking college courses for computer programming but loved acting. He explained that his father used to live in Harbor Inn but had long ago moved away. However, all the tales he'd told over the years made Nico want to come and see the town. Once he did, he decided to stay and go to school here.

"This town is just. . .what can I say, it's the only place I want to call home." Nico's words agreed with my own thoughts.

"I grew up here but spent many years away in Boston. I was very glad to move back," I explained. "I won't ever leave again, if I can keep the bookstore going."

Nico beamed. "It's a great town. I love the coast and, so far, most of the people have been wonderful. It's the type of place I'd like to settle in. Not too sure if my computer skills will be of much use, but I can always work remotely."

"And we have a wonderful new bookstore," I joked.

Nico smiled. "By the way, Miss Carter, I got the lead in *Pirates of Penzance!*"

Hearing him call me by my last name made me feel so old. "Please call me Lily. That's wonderful news. It's a fun play." I'd seen it done in college, years earlier. "Are you sure you have time for school, the play, and doing book readings here?"

A big bright smile crossed his face. "Lots of acting students carry full-time jobs, participate in plays, and carry full class loads.

I think I'll be okay, so long as my programming classes don't get too overwhelming."

I recalled having much more energy in my college days than I did at thirty-five. "Okay, but if you need a break, let me know. I have the numbers for a few others who could possibly fill in for you."

He nodded. "That's good to know, just in case."

I showed Nico a few of the kids' books with pirate themes and suggested he read them through in his dorm. Then we could decide which would be the best to have him read aloud to the kids. "There's one by Melinda Long called *How I Became a Pirate*," I told him. "That one, I for sure want you to read. The kids will get a kick out of the pirate who wears two eye patches."

He took the books, interest showing in his eyes, and headed out of the store, but before he left, I stopped him. "I didn't see Greg the other day. I thought he would try out for the readings." I tried to keep my tone friendly. I knew there were a few issues between them and didn't want to start something.

He shrugged. "I don't know. Greg has been MIA since the day we met you. Well, at least he's locked himself in his dorm room. I've tried to talk to him, but he won't communicate with anyone. I was really shocked that he didn't try out for the lead in the play. He would have been my biggest competition and maybe might have even gotten the part."

I remembered seeing Greg arguing with the man in front of my store. "Before he locked himself in the dorm, did you ever see him with a tall man?" I wished I had more details, but that was really all I'd noticed about the man. "Maybe dressed in all black?"

Nico crossed his arms over his chest. "As a matter of fact, I saw someone like that talking to him outside the cafeteria. I don't know everyone on campus, but he looked too old to be a student and too young to be a professor. They were in an animated conversation."

I was intrigued. "Really? Anything you can share?"

"All I heard was the guy telling Greg, 'You'd better find it, if you want your money. Don't even think of going back on your word.' I didn't like the way he looked at Greg, and I headed that way to see if Greg needed backup, but the guy disappeared, and Greg headed off before I could reach him."

"That's strange," I said. What did the man want Greg to find?

While I was brainstorming, Nico moved toward the door. I shook off the thoughts running through my mind. "I hope Greg is able to work through whatever's bothering him." I smiled and waved as Nico left the shop.

As he headed out the door, a middle-aged man walked in. As they passed one another, Nico nodded, but the other man hesitated for a moment, staring at Nico as if he knew him. I had no idea what the man's reaction was about, so I turned back to some books I was organizing on a cart to put on the shelves.

The man walked up to the counter and cleared his throat. I turned and realized I knew him although I hadn't seen him for several years. "Bill! Good morning." Bill was the local cab driver. But since there was very little call for taxis in the town, the older women who didn't drive anymore kept him busy most of the day taking them to hair appointments, grocery stores, and luncheons. He was about forty-five, balding, and had piercing blue eyes. I remembered things about him my mother had told me over the years, and I was pretty sure everyone liked Bill. He always had a smile and a kind word.

That was why I was surprised at the look on his face. "What's wrong, Bill? Looks like you just saw a ghost."

I noted him clenching his fists. "I think I did. Who was that kid that just left?" He nodded over his shoulder in the direction of the front door.

"Kid?" My brow squinted in confusion. "Oh, you mean the college student?"

Bill crossed his arms over his somewhat extended midsection. "Looks like a kid to me. Up to no good, I suspect." Bill's voice was harsh.

Now I was really taken aback. This was not like the Bill I remembered or that my mother had told me about. "His name is Nico."

"Nico Slate?" Bill almost shouted.

I wasn't really sure what Nico's last name was, but I did have his application in front of me. I glanced down. "Yes, Slate is his last name. Why?"

Bill suddenly slammed his fist down on my counter, causing pens to jump in their cupholder and a few papers to fly off the counter.

My heart jumped a beat as well, but I jammed my hand on my hip. "What's gotten into you, Bill?"

As quickly as his anger had taken over, a calm spirit seemed to envelop him. He ran a hand over the bald spot on his head. "Sorry. Don't know what came over me. It's just that I had a big problem with that kid's father years ago. He cheated me out of about three thousand dollars and then left town. I was never able to get my hands on him."

I could understand Bill's reaction under the circumstances. "Yes, but this is his son."

"Yeah, he's the spitting image of his old man. For a minute there I felt like I'd gone back in time. I swore, back then, if I could ever get my hands on Nicholas Slate, I would. . ." Bill stopped speaking. He looked at me rather meekly. "That was before I gave my life to God."

I'm pretty sure my expression was one of shock. "I see. Well, Bill, what brings you into the shop?" I thought changing the subject might be best.

He turned around and perused the entire store with a long sweep of his eyes. "Heard you'd redecorated the place. It's unique for sure." He wasn't smiling as he spoke. I didn't think his comment was meant as a compliment. "Not anything like the old shop."

"It's pirate themed, to go along with some of the local folklore." My gaze took in the small store. I had pictures of famous pirates framed and hung on one wall, a porthole, a ship's wheel, some oars, and netting hung over the kids' reading area. I found it to be appealing and friendly.

Bill seemed to consider the room a bit longer, and a small smile began to take over his face. "I like it, and I believe Miss Sylvia will like it too. As a matter of fact, I know she had an old diary, written by a pirate's wife, in her diary collection. Might be something interesting you could use here."

Miss Sylvia was the owner of Good Old Days Antiques on the square. Her competition, Hatty Schuster, had owned the Blue Willow Antiques across from Good Old Days Antiques, but Hatty had finally retired, and now Miss Sylvia's business was thriving. Not only did she have the best antiques, she had a collection of rare and unique diaries. I wondered if she'd be willing to share the pirate's wife's diary with the bookstore. I might be able to get an evening crowd if Nico agreed to do a reading from the diary. I thought a minute and realized it would be better if I had Kat do the reading, since it was a woman's diary. "That diary sounds interesting," I commented. "Where did she find that?"

"I'm not sure, but she gets boxes of items donated all the time. You never know when there is a real treasure in the box."

The image of the boxes of books in the back room ran through my mind. The first box had a few good deals, but I wondered if there was going to be something especially good in the second box.

Bill cleared his throat. "Well, what I really came here for is to see about trying to set up The Butler Did It Mystery Book Club's date on your calendar. We've been meeting at different members' houses, however we all voted that meeting at a bookstore would be better. Ever since we got your invitation, that is."

I grabbed my calendar. This was something I was very interested in setting up. I wanted to join the group myself as well. I suggested a twenty-five-dollar meeting fee, which he agreed to.

Bill and I looked over the calendar. The group usually met on the first Thursday of the month, and I didn't foresee any problems with that. It was good to know, because Kyle London attended that group, so Thursdays were out as far as book readings for him.

We scheduled the first two months of The Butler Did It Mystery Book Club meetings, and Bill paid up front. "We can vote at the end of two months and decide if we'll continue to meet here or go back to members' homes."

"Sounds good." I handed him the receipt and watched as he walked out the door. I was very glad to have this group on the calendar, but looking at Bill, I had a strange feeling in my stomach and wondered if his feelings toward Nicholas Slate would somehow be taken out on Nico. I hoped not.

CHAPTER FOUR

Two days later, Nico sat on a small chair, reading to a group of children. He was not only speaking in the voice of a pirate; he'd come dressed as one. I was very impressed with his acting ability and wasn't surprised he'd been chosen for the lead in the play at the college.

"Where did you get your costume?" I asked him later in the day. "It's the real deal."

Nico nodded. "It's from a costume shop in Boston. I find them to be more realistic than what the college has to offer. I wore it for tryouts for the play." He ran a hand through his hair. "I think it helped me get the part."

I laughed. "I doubt it. You do an excellent pirate's voice, and I'm sure your acting is just as good."

Nico smiled. "Thanks. I've dressed up like a pirate since I was a kid. It's always been my favorite part to do." His voice grew quiet. I assumed he was a bit embarrassed by this admission.

The bell over the bookstore door jingled. Nico and I both looked up. It was a slim man dressed in black jeans and a black hoodie. His eyes scanned the room then settled on Nico. He stared at him for several long seconds.

"Can I help you?" I called out.

Nico didn't seem to notice the man, because he'd gone back to getting ready for the next reading.

The man shook his head. "No, just looking." He moved away and began to peruse the shelves. I watched him for a while, and Nico finished up his reading. The kids and their parents all left for the day, and Nico headed out the door.

The man was still in the shop. He didn't seem to be looking for a specific type of book, because he went from shelf to shelf, area to area. He moved toward my special pirate book collection. Here, he became more interested. After a short time, I started to feel wary as the man continued to pull out one book at a time, open it, page carefully through it, and replace it. I even picked up my phone, thinking of calling Officer Forgione.

But the man must have suddenly felt my eyes on him, because he glanced up, turned, and hurried out the front door without another word. Only then, seeing him from the back, did I connect him with the man I'd seen speaking to Greg. This seemed to be too much of a coincidence as far as I was concerned. I decided to follow through and call Officer Forgione.

When he answered, I explained about the man in the hoodie and his strange behavior in the shop. Officer Forgione, or rather, Dwayne, as he pressed me to call him, tried to assure me that I'd done the right thing, but I was worried that I'd done the wrong thing. The man could have been a perfectly normal customer. Dwayne did not agree with me.

"I'll come over, maybe see if I can get some fingerprints," he said.

I hesitated but then decided that was probably the best thing.

"Had any dinner?" Dwayne asked.

I was a bit confused, wondering what that had to do with fingerprints. "Um, no," I murmured.

"I can pick up some Chinese takeout on my way over. You like sesame chicken?" His voice was so enthusiastic, I felt like a fish being reeled in, but for what, I didn't know.

I really wasn't sure what to think or say. Was I presuming he meant something by the dinner offer? I was confused, but I was also hungry. "Sounds good. I've got some books from an estate sale in Boston I need to get out and record. I'll work on that until you get here."

I began to pull more books from the first box. If the second box was as full of great books as the first one, I was going to be able to list them on eBay and probably make enough money to pay my rent for a month at least. Those worth a little less would still be a great addition to the store.

I gave a small sigh, releasing the breath I felt I'd been holding ever since I decided to call Dwayne. I pulled another book from the box. It was just a few minutes after closing and already dark outside, but some kind of noise caught my attention. I looked up at the front door and saw a face pressed against the glass.

As any face would appear distorted if smashed against glass, so was this one. I stepped back, gulped, and gave a frightened squeak. It must have been loud enough for the person to hear, because their eyes met mine. The person took a step back and turned away. Again, all I could see was the back of the person fading away, and whoever it was, was wearing a black hoodie. Yet there was something different about this person. I tried to put my finger on it. Maybe shorter, maybe thinner. Maybe I was just imagining things.

My hands were shaking as I held the book I'd been looking at, and I tried to see out the door. My other hand was reaching for my phone in case I needed to call 911. After a few seconds, I realized the person was gone. I stood for another full minute, squinting at the door in hopes of being able to see. . . Actually, I hoped to see nothing. I didn't want there to be anyone outside the door. Still, I needed to get a grip. Once more, I questioned my own reaction.

Perhaps it had just been a late-night customer hoping to get in and shop.

I bowed my head and began to whisper a prayer for protection and also for clarity. I needed to be able to keep a clear head and not start making up stories about mysterious people. A few minutes later, I felt calmer, but when Dwayne knocked on the door, I jumped halfway out of my skin and realized I wasn't the slightest bit calm.

I looked up and could see Dwayne outside, standing in front of the door. He was holding up two bags with Chinese writing on them. My stomach growled. I rushed over and opened the door.

"Hi," he said, looking around. "Shop closed?"

"Yes." My voice had a strange squeak to it, which was a sign I'd been upset recently. Dwayne didn't know me well enough to catch that.

"Well, I have a joke for you. Why doesn't a pirate need to take a shower before he walks the plank?" He set the bags on the counter and waited for my response.

I just stood there for a minute, wondering if he was seriously telling me another joke. "I. . .I don't know."

"Because he'll wash up on shore later." He clapped his hands together and gave a most charming grin.

"Funny, very funny," I said dryly. I noticed he looked a bit dejected at my reaction. Men were a rarity in my life, but I had been told by one friend, long ago, that men were often silly when they liked you. I wondered if that was why Dwayne told jokes.

I thought about it and realized it was kind of a cute joke.

"Well, come on in and wash up yourself, before I make you walk the plank," I joked playfully. His countenance cleared, and he smiled. "Let's eat in my workroom," I suggested.

Dwayne nodded agreeably. "I wonder if pirates like Chinese food?" he said as he headed toward the back.

Penny leaned on the bookstore's checkout counter the next morning. She'd stopped over with a cup of coffee for me. I didn't think anything of it, although most mornings I stopped in and got my coffee at her shop, but today I'd been running a bit late.

She whispered, "So, I left the shop late last night and saw something interesting."

My head shot up. "Did you see someone standing outside my shop?"

She nodded. "Yes, and he was carrying two bags of Chinese food." She snickered and gave me a wink.

My shoulders sagged. "Oh." That one word dripped with disappointment.

She tilted her head. "What's wrong? I know it was Officer Forgione, but maybe it wasn't a date?"

I felt my cheeks burning and crossed my arms over my chest. "No, it was not a date. I called Officer Forgione because I saw someone lurking around outside last night. There was the weird break-in the other day, then I saw a man talking to one of the college students named Greg, and I thought it might be the man you described. Then, someone who matches that description came into the shop yesterday and was acting pretty strange, pulling every single book on the shelves out and going through them, like he was looking for something."

Penny's eyes had widened as I spoke.

I continued. "Then, last night, I saw a face at the door, and it frightened me. I'd already asked Dwayne to come by and take fingerprints." I feigned a glare at her. "So, no date."

Penny looked straight at me for a few seconds. "I'm sorry about all that, but, Lily, I know you. You like him."

There was no getting around it. Penny wouldn't leave the subject alone. I huffed and dropped my shoulders. "Yes, I do. He's really nice, and he brought Chinese for dinner. The whole time he was dusting for fingerprints, we talked, and he's so easy to talk to."

Penny smiled. "I'm glad. It's about time you found someone. Officer Forgione has only been in town for about a year, but he's settled into a nice house."

Once again, I wondered why my mother had never mentioned Officer Forgione. If he'd been in town and single for a year, I figured my mother would have set me up on a date with him the first second I got to town. I looked at Penny and wondered how she knew so much about him. Still, this was a small town, and everyone knew everyone. I held up a hand. "Hey, I wouldn't start thinking that. Like I said, he came to take fingerprints."

I turned away from Penny. She was able to read my expressions too well. I did like Dwayne, and it seemed he liked me, but I wasn't ready to consider it a relationship. I knew better than to jump to conclusions. The last time I assumed I was dating someone, I found out he already had a girlfriend, and I wouldn't want Penny saying anything that could somehow get back to Dwayne. "Besides, all I'm interested in right now is getting my bookstore going strong. As a matter of fact, I bought a box of pirate-themed books at an estate sale in Boston and, so far, I think I'm going to be able to sell them for a good profit." I was set on changing the subject.

It must have worked, because Penny straightened up. "That's great. Who would have imagined books about pirates could be worth anything?" She turned, and with a final glance at me, she strolled toward the door. "Well, I'm off. Oh look, here's Nico now."

I looked up and saw someone enter the shop, dressed as a pirate. It wasn't Nico though.

"Oh, Greg, is that you?"

The young man nodded. "Yes."

"Nice pirate costume," I stated in a tone that asked questions.

"Oh, yeah. I. . .I got a part in the *Pirates of Penzance* and just came from practice. They want us to wear our costumes all the time so we really feel the part. I thought I'd like to look at some of your books about pirates. Maybe get some ideas to pull into my character." He tilted his head and grinned.

I realized that Greg had a very disarming smile. "I thought you didn't try out?"

He ducked his head. "To be honest, I wasn't going to, because I knew that Nico would get the lead part. He's really great, you know."

"He is good," I agreed. "But I never got to see you audition."

"I'm not as good as he is, and it's sad because acting is what I want to do for a career, while all Nico wants is to be in this one play for fun while studying computer programming." His voice held a tinge of malice. "But after he left that day, I decided to go ahead and try out. I just changed the part I was trying out for, and I got that part. I'm happy with it. Sometimes the best parts aren't always the lead. But I still want to do some research, so I can be authentic."

"Go ahead and look around then," I suggested, thinking that once he was more comfortable, I could ask him about the man I saw him speaking to the other day. I wanted to assure myself there wasn't someone sinister following Greg around and trying to break into my shop.

The bell over the door jingled again, pulling my attention off Greg. Nico walked in, dressed in his pirate outfit. He waved at me then noticed Greg. "Hey, dude, I've been wondering when you would come out of your room."

Greg glanced at him. "Had a cold." He dropped the book he was looking at, and I realized he'd pulled it out of the box that held the books I'd bought at the estate sale in Boston. Then he moved toward the door. "Not really your business," he called back. It was obvious that Greg held no love for Nico, yet when I first met them, I would have sworn they were friends.

Nico's back straightened, and I saw his hands clench. Then he walked over to the pile of kids' pirate books and began looking through them. He didn't seem to have any further interest in Greg.

Greg immediately decided to leave the shop. I watched as he walked out, wondering what he'd really been doing there. He hadn't been in the shop long enough to look at any of the pirate books except the ones in my box. I recalled that Nico said the man told Greg he had to find something. Was Greg looking for something for that man? If so, what? There wasn't anything in my bookstore that could be of any value worth all this mystery, and I was pretty sure nothing of great value was in the boxes I'd bought in Boston.

I could picture the shelves on which I'd found the books. There were a few other items on the shelves as well. Of course, I had only been interested in the books. When I saw that a few of them were about pirates, I knew I had to buy the lot. I'd told the woman who was working the desk, and she'd boxed them up for me.

Before I left the estate, I'd looked back and noticed the bookshelves were completely empty, which meant she'd either moved all the knickknacks off of them or had put them in my boxes. Like I said, so far all I had found were books, but could there have been something of value?

My thoughts were interrupted by the front door opening again. Kyle London, Penny's husband, strolled into the shop. He stopped long enough to scan the entire room then moved toward me. "Lily, this place is amazing. Sorry it took so long for me to stop in." His words were genuine. I'd only met Kyle a few times over the years, but I'd always thought him to be a nice and very down-to-earth sort of guy.

"Thanks, it's a dream come true." I couldn't help but be pleased whenever anyone said nice things about my bookstore.

"Well, I stopped by to talk about doing a reading. Penny said you might be interested? Of course, if not, I don't mind." A bit of red crept up his cheeks. I found that amusing. I'd had many famous authors visit the Boston Library, and in general they were all sort of conceited. Kyle, on the other hand, was a bit shy.

"Yes, I'd love to have you do that! I've got a whole shelf of your books, and many of my customers have been interested in them," I answered enthusiastically. I grabbed my calendar book and flipped it open. Kyle leaned over.

"You're hosting The Butler Did It Mystery Book Club?"

I nodded.

"They never want to have me do a reading." His voice grew softer. "I understand their reasoning, but do you think I should do it anyway?"

"Well, this won't affect that group at all," I encouraged. "We'll set your reading on a different night." I was afraid he was going to back out, and I had some great plans for his readings.

Kyle pointed at a date on the calendar. "That works for me." He sounded very happy. It made me think that maybe there were other authors who lived within an hour's drive who might be happy to do readings here.

I took in a deep breath. "Great. I'll send you some information on how we can advertise this and some of my ideas. I think it will be fun." I kept my voice steady. He looked like a rabbit in a snare, and too much enthusiasm on my part might cause him to flee.

Kyle smiled shyly. "I'll be happy to do it. You know, being in here has given me an idea for a new mystery novel. Maybe one that includes a pirate."

"Or a pirate-themed bookstore?" I asked with a laugh, thinking it would be fun for him to write a book that took place in By Hook or by Book.

He gave a big chortle, turned, and walked toward the bookshelves. I wondered if he really would write a mystery that would involve pirates or a bookstore.

I noticed that as Kyle passed the children's section, he stopped in his tracks and stood watching Nico reading through a few of the books. After several minutes, he walked up to Nico. I wasn't close enough to hear what he said, but I thought Nico's face turned into a hardened mask. Whatever Kyle said had made Nico angry, but it didn't get any more heated, because Kyle walked away and began looking at books.

Nico watched Kyle then returned to his stack of children's books. I let out a breath I didn't realize I'd been holding. It seemed that several people had issues with Nico. So far, Bill, Greg, and now Kyle. The young man didn't seem aware of it though.

I sidled up to him. "Nico, is there anything wrong?" I nodded at the door as Kyle walked out.

The boy tucked his head. "The other day, some old guy came up to me at Cup 'n' Cake and started telling me I needed to get out of this town. For a minute, I thought he was going to hit me or something, then all of a sudden, he just turned and walked out. Everyone heard him, and a couple guys from the group I was with started joking about him and getting silly. A few of them started clowning around. A table got knocked over, and I guess a few cups got broken. Everyone got up and ran out." He shrugged. "I'm not sure why I didn't stay and pay for the damage. I guess I was caught up in the moment and followed the crowd. But Mr. London saw me run out. He was just informing me of that."

I met the young man's eyes with mine. "Nico, I can't have you working here if you've got that hanging over you."

"I know, I know. I plan to go over today and pay for the broken things." His words rang true.

I felt a wave of relief knowing he planned to pay for the damages. I'd hate to lose him. The kids loved hearing him do the readings, and I had the children's pirate stories scheduled out for a while. "Good, but what about the others? They need to pay their part of the damages."

"I'll just take care of it all. But I'd like to know who that guy was and what his problem with me is." Nico looked like a small boy in need of a mother for just a moment. I wasn't sure he would take kindly to me as a fill-in, but I moved closer and gave him a quick hug. I could feel him relax slightly.

The moment passed, and Nico moved away. I had to be content with his promise to go and pay Kyle, so I headed back to the front and finished emptying the first box of books from the Boston estate sale. The next box would have to wait. As I worked, I mulled over the question of who the man was that had bothered Nico in the first place.

The front door began to open and close as several mothers, fathers, babysitters, and even an older sister entered with children in tow. It looked to be a full house, however the last one through the door was without a child.

"Dwayne?"

He nodded at me and moved closer. "Is that Nico?" He pointed at my pirate.

Dread surfaced again. "Yes, why?"

"Seems he and his friends broke a few things at Cup 'n' Cake yesterday. Kyle London called it in." He stood with his hands on his hips and arms akimbo.

I nodded. "He just told me. He plans to go over there and pay for the things later."

"Yeah, well, I need the names of the other kids involved." He sounded apologetic but determined.

"Can it wait? He just started his reading for the day."

"I suppose so, but Kyle is very upset. He wants those kids to pay for what they did."

Dwayne sounded stern. He placed his hands on his duty belt, which housed his gun, a flashlight, radio, handcuffs, and who knew what else.

My voice dropped so Nico couldn't hear me. "He wants to pay for it himself. I think he'll protect the others. It seems there was someone else in Cup 'n' Cake who was antagonizing Nico in the first place."

"Hmm, so long as it gets paid, I'm sure I can calm Kyle down. He was angry enough to hurt someone. But I can't do anything about it until Nico pays. I hate to see there be any issues between the college kids and the townspeople. We all need to live in harmony."

"Dwayne, I've got a cold soda in my mini fridge if you want a drink while you wait," I said, hoping to get his mind off of Nico.

"Sounds good." He sat down on one of the chairs I had in the shop for readers and gave me a smile. My heart skipped. As I walked away, I wondered why him being there made me feel that way. He hadn't indicated anything more than wanting to speak to Nico, and there I was, as giddy as a schoolgirl.

CHAPTER FIVE

As most businesses were in Harbor Inn, By Hook or by Book was closed on Sundays, so I had time for church. Since moving back, I'd only attended once, but now that the shop was open and running, I felt it was time to begin getting involved with my community of other Christians.

The great thing about the Harbor Inn Church of Hope is that it's the most centralized church and pretty much everyone in town attends. Sure, there are a few other churches, other denominations, but this is the one nondenominational church in town. Penny and Kyle attend the church as well my mother and a few other friends. I also appreciate that they still offer good old-fashioned Sunday school classes before the main service, which I had not attended yet but wanted to start today.

When I arrived at the church at nine, I was hoping to meet Penny and Kyle. The few times I'd attended so far, I'd come later, for the main service only, and I'd sat alone, and Penny had given me a talking-to about it. However, now that I wanted to get plugged into a Sunday school class, I would have to worry about that later.

I strolled down the hall and noted Penny heading into the women's restroom, so I scooted that way and stood outside the door.

It was a great place to watch people. Bill, the taxi driver, passed me, as did several of the students from the college. The owner of the Carousel Theater stopped long enough to ask if I would order a dozen copies of *Pirates of Penzance* because she believed there would be a call for the book once the play was finished. I assured her it was already on my list of things to do.

Then, out of nowhere, Dwayne Forgione stopped beside me. "Hi, Lily. I didn't know you attended this church." His smile, as usual, was disarming, and I felt my tongue freeze up. Something I needed to get over.

"Y-yes. I mean, I've been a few times."

He tilted his head. "Glad to have you here. Chosen a Sunday school class yet?"

I shook my head. "Nope. Are there any good choices?"

"Yes, there are all sorts of groups. Some for singles, couples, teens, or they have classes by subjects. Right now, there's one on the book of Daniel and another titled Hope in the Lord."

I wondered which class Penny and Kyle were in, but the last class he'd mentioned sounded interesting. "I think I'd like to go to the Hope in the Lord class."

Dwayne nodded with his disarming grin. "Follow me."

I figured I could catch up with Penny before services, so I walked with Dwayne. Once we reached the room, I was surprised when he walked in with me. "I think I can find a seat. You don't have to stay." I sat down.

He hovered for a second then sat down beside me. "This is the class I've been attending. You've only missed two weeks out of eight, so it should be easy to catch up."

I noticed several people in the class looking our way. I swallowed and could feel my cheeks blush. I was glad he hadn't told me up front that this was the class he attended. At least I knew I didn't choose it because of him. However, having a familiar face beside me was nice.

Outside the classroom, Penny and Kyle walked by, not looking into the room. A few minutes later, Greg walked by. He did look in, and when he saw me, he gave a quick wave. I waved back, but he moved on. A few seconds later, a tall man, dressed in black jeans and a hoodie, walked by. Without thinking, I grabbed Dwayne's arm. "Did you see that?"

He glanced around. "See what?"

"The tall guy in black pants and a black hoodie."

Dwayne shrugged. "Nope."

"I think he's following Greg." I tried to keep quiet, but I could feel an urgency in my voice.

"The college student?" Dwayne asked, giving me his full attention.

"Yes. I saw him talking to Greg the other day, and Greg wasn't very happy about it. Nico also told me that he heard the man ask Greg if he'd 'found it' yet."

Dwayne sat up attentively. "Found what?"

I shook my head. "I don't know, but the conversation happened outside my shop."

Dwayne stood up. "Should I follow him?"

I shook my head. "No, it's time for class." I looked out the door anxiously and saw Kat rush by. She must have been late for whatever class she was attending. I thought how nice it was to see a few college-aged kids attending church. "I'm not sure about anything with Greg and that guy, so let's just forget it for now." I patted the seat beside me, and Dwayne sat back down.

Just then the teacher stepped into the room, so we gave him our attention. But about halfway through, Dwayne leaned over and whispered again, "I want to talk to Greg as soon as possible."

I nodded.

I didn't see Dwayne once I sat with Penny in the morning church service. I scanned the room, but I didn't want to appear as if I was looking for him, if he saw me. I gave my full attention to the singing and then the pastor. It was a great service. I gleaned a lot from it.

Penny and Kyle asked me to join them for lunch when the service ended, but I wanted to catch up on the lessons from the two weeks of Sunday school class I'd already missed. The information was very interesting, and a real day of rest sounded good to me. I planned to order a pizza that would last me two meals and just relax.

I wasn't sure if Dwayne was going to talk to Greg after church or not, but I left it in his capable hands. All I wanted was a quiet day.

The following morning, I rolled out of bed slowly. A full day of rest had been wonderful, but it made wanting to get up the next day more difficult. I looked at the clock and gave a squeak. It was twenty minutes later than I usually woke up.

This jarred me into action. I jumped up and headed for a quick shower. Being late would mean a quick protein drink and no stop for coffee and a talk with Penny. I slipped on a comfortable pair of jeans and a T-shirt with a picture of the Cheshire cat from *Alice in Wonderland* on the front. I'm not only into pirates, I love many different books and authors, and most of my clothes reflect this.

I grabbed my coat, ran out the door, and jumped into the front seat of my car. The air was frigid and the ground covered in a light layer of snow, which meant I had to drive slowly to be safe because the roads hadn't been cleared yet. It was frustrating, but I didn't think there would be a huge crowd beating down the door. Most of the day's activities wouldn't start for a few hours.

I had hoped to get that other box from the estate sale out this morning, but now it might have to wait for yet another day. I pulled the car into my regular parking spot, turned off the engine, and slid out of the car. It was silly at this point to run to the shop. I was late, and if there was anyone waiting, another minute wouldn't matter.

As I turned the corner, I looked out at the beach with longing. I could use a brisk walk. There were the regulars taking their morning strolls. Just then, I noticed someone walking away from the square. Although his back was to me, he looked familiar. I stopped and watched, trying to figure out who it was.

Ah, Bill, the taxi driver.

Many people from town could often be found on the beach, but I do have to say that I'd never seen Bill there before. He's the sit-in-a-taxi-or-coffee-shop type guy. Could it be that he'd started dating and decided to get in shape?

I didn't have time to speculate. I was really late. So I strolled quickly and reached the front door but then came to a dead stop. The glass was completely shattered and the door slightly ajar, as if someone had broken the window, reached in, and opened the door.

My first instinct was to rush in, but as my hand moved toward the door, my phone rang. I pulled it out and saw Dwayne's name appear, which gave me a wake-up call. I shouldn't be entering my store when it had obviously been broken into.

I clicked on the phone. "Hello, Dwayne."

"Hello, Lily. I just wanted to say I enjoyed sitting with you in church yesterday." His voice was friendly.

"Thanks." My answer was short and clipped. "Dwayne, there's a situation at the store."

He must have heard my concern, because he was immediately attentive. "Yes?"

"The glass on the front door has been broken, and the door is open. Should I go in?"

"No!" Dwayne actually yelled into the phone, causing me to hold it away from my ear.

"Okay, I won't."

"I'm on my way." The phone went quiet. I looked around but didn't see anyone. I wasn't sure if I should stand guard by the door or not. I began to walk toward Cup 'n' Cake, thinking to get a cup of coffee and see Penny, but what if a customer came along and tried to enter the shop?

I stopped and turned then paced back and forth in front of the door. I was so confused. What could anyone possibly want in my bookstore? Surely everyone knew it was a new shop and there wouldn't be much money inside. There were a few books worth about a hundred dollars each, but I just couldn't imagine someone breaking in for that.

In the distance I heard the sound of police sirens. Not sure that was a good idea, I glanced at the shop. If anyone was in the store, that would warn them. I expected someone to run out, but no one did. Finally, Dwayne came rushing toward me.

He stopped at the door and pushed me back gently. "Did you go in?" His voice was rather accusatory.

I crossed my arms over my chest. "No, I've been standing here waiting for you."

He must have noted my stance and my tone. "Oh, sorry. Good. I was pretty worried. I'm going in, so please stay here. I called for backup." He turned, pushed the door open, and disappeared inside.

I stood there, shivering from the cold and fear, straining to hear anything. I didn't notice that Penny had come out of the coffee shop until I looked up. She waved and jogged toward me, calling, "What's going on? I heard the sirens but didn't think anything until I saw Dwayne running this way."

She reached my side. "There's someone in the shop," I told her. "At least, we think so. The front door was broken, and Dwayne went in."

Penny grabbed my hand, and we stood side by side, waiting.

A few minutes later, Dwayne came back out the front door. He was pale.

"Was there anyone in there?" I asked.

He held up a hand as if to ward us off, which made me move forward. "What is it?"

He stopped me at the door. "You can't go in there, Lily."

"Why, what is it?"

He didn't speak, so I stomped my foot. "Tell me, Dwayne."

He ran a hand through his hair and gave a very deep sigh. "There's a young man on the floor. He's been killed."

My mouth opened and closed. "What? Who?"

"I don't know, but he's dressed in a pirate outfit."

I covered my mouth. "Oh, my. Is it Nico?" I began to move toward the shop door. Dwayne tried to stop me, but I pushed past him and entered the store. I expected to find whoever it was on the floor right by the front door, but instead, the shop was empty.

Dwayne walked in behind me and grabbed my hand. "I don't think you need to see."

I pulled away. "Where is the body?"

"Behind the counter, in the back room."

I moved in that direction, and when I leaned over the counter, I almost screamed at the sight. From where I stood, I was sure it was Nico. The costume was the one he always wore when he came to do the readings, and the person had dark hair like Nico. The young man lay in a pool of blood near the large anchor, and an oar, which I'd also bought to decorate with, was beside him as well. It looked as if he had been coming out of my back workroom. His arm stretched out, as though he had been holding something. But whatever it had been was no longer in his hand.

"Oh, no. I think it *is* Nico."

Dwayne shook his head. "No, I looked at his face. It's someone else. It looks as if someone hit him with that oar, and he fell and hit his head on the anchor."

I stepped around the counter and leaned in. With almost a breath of relief, I realized it wasn't Nico. I was glad to see it also wasn't Greg. From what I could see, it wasn't any of the group of kids that I'd met yet.

So, was it murder? Or was I going to be blamed for the young man slipping and hitting his head on the anchor? There was the oar to consider though. I stood up and walked away. I'd seen all I could stand to see. Tears were brimming in my eyes. I looked up and saw Penny hovering at the door. Three more police officers had entered the store, and Dwayne was giving out orders.

I walked numbly to Penny's side. "I need coffee." I spoke between clenched teeth, trying to hold back my tears. She put an arm around my shoulder and led me quietly to her shop.

Perhaps I should have stayed, but at the moment, I just couldn't think straight. Somewhere in my mind I thought I remembered Dwayne telling me that the shop would have to be closed for the day. I heard an ambulance in the distance, and I shuddered.

The young man on the floor of my shop was beyond needing help from the medics.

CHAPTER SIX

An hour later, I was still sitting at the Cup 'n' Cake counter. I could finally feel my heart slowing down. We hadn't heard any more from Dwayne, but several other officers had gone into the bookstore. Penny was giving me plenty of space but stayed close in case I needed her.

Every time the bell over the door rang, I looked up, expecting to see Dwayne, but I was more than glad when Nico walked in the door.

"Hey, what's going on at the bookstore?" he asked. "I couldn't get near it with all the police officers."

I waved to him to come to the counter. I noticed he wasn't wearing his pirate outfit. "Where's your costume?" I asked.

"I don't know. This morning it was missing. I thought maybe Greg had grabbed it as a joke, but I just saw him, and he swore he didn't. I'm not sure I believe him though. He was acting pretty weird. After he denied taking it, he ran out of the room. I haven't seen him since."

I patted the seat beside me. He came and sat down. "Listen, Nico. Someone was in the shop today, dressed in your costume and. . .well. . .he's dead." I knew blurting it out like that was shocking, but I wasn't sure how else to tell him.

His eyes opened wide. "D-dead?"

"Yes." My voice dropped. "I thought it was you." A tear slipped down my face.

Nico was quiet.

"How did he die?"

I actually was taken aback at that. I wasn't really sure, but I remembered blood near the young man's head. I assumed he'd been hit. "I think he was hit over the head."

"So, murder?" Nico sounded as if he couldn't believe it.

I nodded.

"I'm pretty sure no one is trying to kill me." He seemed to be rolling thoughts over in his mind. I remembered what Bill had said about him, but I just didn't believe Bill could kill anyone.

"Maybe whoever had on my costume was robbing the book-store and he thought if anyone saw him in the shop, they'd think it was me and not be concerned."

That was all I could imagine that made sense too. Had anyone looked in the window earlier and seen the young man in costume, they wouldn't have given it a second thought. But if someone was trying to kill Nico, they also would have seen the person in the store and assumed it was him.

"Well, I'm glad it wasn't you. It wasn't Greg either. However, now that I think about it. . .the young man died in the back room, not robbing money from the till."

"Is there anything in the back room worth money?"

"Not that I know of." I didn't mention the box of books from Boston, which still needed to be looked at. That was information for Dwayne.

Nico thought for a while. "There's been that guy hanging around campus, you know the one I overheard telling Greg to find something? He gives me the creeps. But I just saw him a few minutes ago, so it's not him."

A memory of the man speaking to Greg flashed through my mind. I was pretty sure he was the same one who'd been in the store looking around at books.

Nico got up and paced. "That guy must have talked someone else into breaking in. I assume he had him dress up as a pirate so if anyone saw him, they'd think it was Greg." Nico thought for a moment more, trying to make sense of it all. "But why is he dead?"

I shrugged. It was so confusing.

"I can't imagine what anyone wants in my shop. I don't keep much money there, so did the dead young man find something I don't know about?" Nico wasn't really listening anymore, so I was basically just talking to myself.

I felt awful for the young man who was dead, and I was also worrying about the future of the store. A murder happening inside it wasn't going to go over very well in this small town. There might even be people who would never come to my store again.

Suddenly Nico said, "Listen, I'm gonna find Greg and bring him back here. We need to find out what he knows."

I thought he should stay and wait to talk to Dwayne, and even though I told him that, there was no stopping him. Before I could even suggest a different plan, he'd headed out the door.

Penny stepped out from the kitchen. "I noticed you talking to Nico." She kept her voice low so the other two customers couldn't hear her.

"Yes. I was glad to see him. He's going to find Greg. We think he may know what this is all about." I picked up my cup of coffee and took a sip. I was definitely feeling better, but now I had to worry about where Nico was going and if Greg would come back with him.

———

A half hour later, the door opened again, and Dwayne finally walked in. I spun around on the stool.

"Your shop is clear. We took the body and will have someone at the morgue try to identify him."

"That's good." I kept my eyes on his face. I wanted a hug more than anything, to comfort me, but I didn't know Dwayne well enough to ask for that, so instead I said, "Nico was just here a little bit ago. He didn't have any idea who had his costume, but he headed off to find Greg."

Dwayne frowned. "You shouldn't have let him go."

"I tried, but he ran out before I could convince him to stay." I felt a bit offended at his words. He must have realized that by my tone.

"I'm sorry, Lily." He sat on the stool next to me. "You've had a rough morning."

"I'm not used to dead bodies in my shop." I spoke in a low voice. I could feel the tears pressing on the back of my eyes. Dwayne put his arm around my shoulders and pulled me toward him. I turned my head and rested my face against his shoulder. It was very comforting, and I was glad he had initiated what I so desperately needed.

We both drank a cup of coffee then Dwayne drilled me with questions, trying to figure out why anyone would want to break into my shop.

"Do you have any books worth a lot of money?"

"No," I insisted. "At least not that I can think of. There were books in the shop when I got there, because it used to be a different bookstore. But I inventoried all of them, and nothing was worth much. I don't think I could have missed something." I dropped my head into my hands, sighing. "I'm exhausted from all this."

Dwayne lifted my head with a finger under my chin. "Is there any hope I can get you to go home for the day?"

Weariness had taken over my entire being, so I agreed. I suppose anyone who would come to the shop would simply be looking for information on what happened, and I had no answers for them.

Dwayne leaned over and pressed his lips to my forehead. It was more of a consoling kiss than anything else. I was too tired to read anything more into it but tucked it away in the back of my mind to consider later.

"I'll just walk over to the shop and clear a few things up. Then I'll go home."

Dwayne frowned. "But no opening the door for anyone. At the store or at home."

I crisscrossed my heart. "I promise."

Penny asked if I wanted her to come with me, but I assured her I'd be okay. Dwayne walked with me and stayed as I entered the bookstore. I had to admit, it was a bit eerie, being in a place where someone had been murdered.

I moved into the back room and glanced down where the body had been. The floor was wet, but there was no blood. Dwayne must have had the other officers clean it up.

I began to look around. Finally, my eyes settled on the other box of books from Boston. I frowned as I got closer to it. It had been opened. I rushed over, calling to Dwayne, and looked inside.

I couldn't really tell what, if anything, was missing. There did seem to be a space, which could have held a book or a small box.

"Will you have to take this for evidence?" I asked.

"No. You have no idea if something is missing, and if it is, the box won't help us. I suggest you inventory it as soon as possible though and send me a list of what's in it. I can also collect fingerprints off of it, so only touch it with gloves on."

We agreed Dwayne would come over and get fingerprints first thing in the morning, then I would do the inventory, but we'd both had enough for the day. Dwayne waited for me to turn off the lights and walked me back to my car.

"Lily, I'm sure that right now is not the time, but I want to tell you that I really like you and once we solve this case, I'd like to take you out to dinner."

I swallowed and nodded. "I'd like that." My words came out quietly, but I'd sincerely hoped he would ask.

Dwayne opened my car door and helped me in as I slid into the front seat and closed the door. He stood on the sidewalk and watched as I drove away, and in my rearview mirror, I saw him waving at me. A warmth spread through my insides. It felt good to be cared for.

———

The following morning, I arrived at my shop early. I wanted to begin on the inventory of the items in the other box before I was interrupted by customers. I'd sent Dwayne a message, and he was willing to meet early.

As I opened the door, I heard someone rushing up behind me. I turned, a bit frightened, and was glad to see Dwayne. "Morning. I wanted to get here before you," he called out as he got closer. "Let me go in first."

I stepped to the side. Dwayne strode into the shop and moved around it, checking to make sure no one had returned. I entered the shop and stood by the front door and watched as he went into the back room. I shuddered at the memory of the young man lying there.

When Dwayne returned, he gave me an apologetic smile. "All clear. Can never be too careful."

I wanted him to know I appreciated his thoughtfulness, but all I could think to say was "Should I run next door and get us some bagels and coffee?" I was unwrapping the winter scarf I had around my neck while I spoke.

His endearing grin spread across his face. "Please. I'll get the fingerprints while you do that." He began to take things out of a sports bag he had carried in and set on the counter. I turned back to the door and headed over to Cup 'n' Cake. It was a rather frigid morning, and without my scarf tied around my neck, I could feel the cool air. I was glad the coffee shop was nice and warm.

When I came in, Penny looked up from the newspaper she was reading and waved me over.

"Morning, Penny. I need two coffees and two blueberry bagels to go."

She met my eyes. "Two?"

I nodded, blushing. "Dwayne is taking some more fingerprints at the shop."

Penny tapped the counter with an open palm, indicating for me to sit down. "Tell me all about it. I thought he was done with the fingerprints?"

I sat down. "Yes, he was, but last night we discovered a box had been opened in my back room. It was so late, we decided to let it wait until today. It's a box of books I bought at an estate sale in Boston. I'm not even sure what was supposed to be in it, so I won't have any idea if anything is missing." I thought about the books I'd purchased and tried to recall the actual shelves the books had been on. Was there something on the shelves that could have been worth someone dying over?

The image of small, intricate boxes flashed through my mind. They had been on one shelf with the books. There were at least two of them. Now I was anxious to get back to the bookstore and see if they were in the second box, because they had not been in the first one.

Penny brought out two cups of coffee and two bagels and packaged them in a bag with a handle. I could hardly wait long enough for her to put them in the bag before I grabbed it and headed out the door. As I hurried toward the bookstore, my heart was racing. I was anxious to see what else was in that box.

At the door, I came to a halt because Nico and Greg were standing there. It was obvious that Greg was not happy to be there, but Nico held on to his coat with a deathlike grip.

"Nico? Greg?"

The boys looked at me. Greg pulled away, but Nico grabbed him again. "Greg, you've got to straighten this out."

My eyes met Greg's. I could see a mixture of fear and sadness in his gaze. "Please, Greg, if you know anything about the young man who was killed, we really need your help." I reached out and placed my hand on his arm.

His shoulders sagged, and he nodded. They both followed me into the bookstore. Not wanting to alarm him, I called out, "Officer Forgione, Nico and Greg are here."

CHAPTER SEVEN

I heard a bit of a scuttling sound, and Dwayne appeared from the back room. I could tell he was trying to force a smile. "Glad to see you," he said, but his eyes never left Greg.

Nico moved forward. "I've coerced Greg into coming, but he knows who was killed."

My head swung around, and my mouth dropped open. "Who was he?" I hissed.

Greg sighed. "I think it's Roger Petlewski. At least I'm pretty sure that's who it is." He fidgeted as he spoke.

Dwayne moved closer. "Maybe? Start from the beginning."

"There's a guy who's been hanging around campus. He's older, about twenty-eight. Wears black jeans and a black hoodie all the time."

I nodded, knowing exactly who he was talking about but having no name for him.

"He must have overheard me telling someone that I won't be able to come back to school next semester because I can't afford it. I was hoping to get a scholarship if I'd gotten the lead in the school play, but that didn't happen."

I was surprised by this information and noted that Greg didn't seem to be angry about it. Just sad.

"Dude, why didn't you tell me?" Nico interrupted. "Man, I wouldn't have tried out."

Greg frowned. "I want to be an actor, and that's all part of the reality. I can't be the lead if I'm not the best."

The room was silent as we listened to Greg's story. My mind was already in a swirl, trying to think of ways I could help Greg make money.

"Go on." Dwayne's words pulled us all back to the immediate issue.

"So that guy asked me to break in here."

"For money?" I squeaked.

Greg's head shook back and forth. "Nah, he wanted some little box. He said you'd gotten it at some kind of sale in Boston and he thought it might be inside a hollow book or inside a box of books you bought."

"So that's why he was looking at all my books that one day."

Dwayne and I looked at each other. He nodded.

"Are you the one who broke in the first time?" I asked.

"No!" Greg insisted. "He did it, but he didn't have enough time, and he didn't find anything. That's why he started bothering me. He offered me a lot of money, and at first, I agreed, and he told me I better find it, but after coming in that one day and looking around, I realized I didn't want anything to do with the whole thing. I don't trust him. I did everything I could to stay out of his way."

"Do you know what's in this little box?" Dwayne demanded.

"I have no idea. He just told me it was a little box."

Nico turned to Greg. "Is that why you were in your room for so long?"

Greg sheepishly nodded. "I was trying to hide from him."

"I appreciate that you didn't want to work for him," I told Greg. "So how do you know Roger Petlewski is the young man who died?"

"I'm just assuming. I saw that guy talking to Roger the other day. Roger's the type to do something like what the guy was asking, just for the fun of it. He's in the room next to Nico in the dorm. He could have swiped the costume if Nico walked out of the room and didn't lock his door."

Nico nodded with a grimace. "Which, unfortunately, I often do."

Dwayne pulled out his cell phone. "I'll call it in. We can find out for sure if that's who it is. But do we have a name for the guy who hired him?" The boys both shook their heads. Dwayne moved into the back room to make his call.

I was feeling so confused. "Why don't you guys go sit in the teen section while we wait to hear what Officer Forgione has to say? There are some comfortable gaming chairs back there."

They agreed and moved away. After a few minutes I heard them laughing. I noticed them holding a book of pirate jokes. I shook my head. *No matter what age, boys will be boys,* I thought.

I moved to the counter and took off my coat. I was a bit worn out already, and the joy of owning my own store was beginning to wane, dealing with all this. I pressed my fingers against my eyes, blinking back some tears. I didn't want to break down.

A few minutes later, Dwayne came out of the back room. "I called the station. They're sending a squad car over to the campus to check on Roger. I better join them."

"Of course. Can you let us know when you find out?"

He took my hand and gave it a gentle squeeze. "I'll come back and let you know, but you need to finish going through that box and see if you can figure out if anything is missing."

I watched him walk out of the shop then moved into the back room even though it made me shake a bit when I stepped over the area where the young man had been killed. With determination, I lifted the box and carried it to the front counter. Nothing would stop me today from going through the box. Nothing, that was, except the front door of the shop opening. When I heard the bell over the door, I looked up and was surprised to see Bill. He gave a small wave as he moved toward me. "Hi, Lily."

I smiled. "Hi, Bill. What brings you in?"

He moved closer to the counter. "I just wanted to tell you the name of the next book The Butler Did It Mystery Book Club is going to read. Everyone will want a copy, and I'm pretty sure they'd rather buy from you than scrounge the internet."

I was pleased to hear him say that. The mystery club had grown to about twenty members, so that would be a nice sale. I jotted down the name of the book. While I was doing that, Bill turned around and scanned the room. From the corner of my eye, I saw him suddenly straighten up. "What's he doing here?" His voice was filled with anger.

I looked up and saw Nico. Greg must have gone to the restroom, because Nico was all alone.

"I thought I took care of. . ." His voice faded, and he turned abruptly and stomped out of the shop. I stood there in amazement, wondering what he was talking about. What could it mean when he said he took care of something? It had to be Nico—he thought he'd taken care of Nico somehow. Was Bill the one who killed Roger Petlewski, thinking he was Nico?

I stood staring into space, trying to imagine any scenario in which Bill could do that. I kept moving my head back and forth, shaking out the thoughts. I knew I should wait for Dwayne to come back and discuss it with him, but I rushed over to Nico.

"Nico, did you see that man who was just in the store?"

Nico nodded, but he didn't look happy. "That's the guy who was bugging me at Cup 'n' Cake."

"What did he say to you?"

"He told me to get out of town." Nico set the book he was looking at down on the table. "I told him to walk the plank."

My hand covered a giggle. "You didn't."

"I know it was rude, but then he grabbed my shirt and shook me and yelled at me, warning me that if I didn't get out of town, he'd make me." Nico blinked rapidly as he remembered the event. "The weirdest thing about it was that he called me by my dad's name."

I placed my hand on his shoulder.

"But then he stopped and acted sort of embarrassed. Said he was sorry and walked out of the coffee shop. We all just figured he was a bit confused, even though he wasn't too old." Nico stopped talking and looked at me. "You don't think that he...he thought it was me in the bookstore...and...and killed..." His voice faded into silence.

I wasn't really sure what to say. Although I couldn't believe it of Bill, that did seem a plausible scenario. "Why don't we tell Officer Forgione everything and let him look into it? Bill told me something about your dad causing him to lose three thousand dollars. He may just have you and your dad confused." I wondered if Bill was having bouts of early dementia, and decided that once we talked to Dwayne about it, I would call Miss Sylvia. If anyone would know about Bill, she would.

Nico ran a hand through his hair. "Wow, if that's true, I'm gonna get my dad to pay him back. I know my dad wasn't such a great guy when he was younger, but he's really changed since he gave his heart to Jesus." Just then, Greg returned from the restroom. We shared the turn of events with him, and he was equally confused.

The boys went back to the gaming chairs, and Nico pulled out a cell phone. I assumed he was calling his father. I took a deep breath. This thing was getting more and more confusing. A few moments later, Dwayne reentered the shop. Nico and Greg stood up, and we all met at the counter.

"So we're pretty sure the victim is Roger Petlewski. He's not in the dorm or anywhere on campus, and his parents haven't heard from him. I went to his dorm room and saw a few photos, which pretty much confirms it in my mind."

I squeezed my eyes together. "It's so hard to believe that anyone in this town would kill anyone. Especially a college student."

Dwayne shrugged. "There have been a few murders in our history."

I nodded at Nico. "Better tell Officer Forgione about Bill."

Dwayne turned with questioning eyes and faced the younger man. Nico told him the same thing he'd told me, then I explained about Bill and Nico's father. "And I forgot to mention that I saw Bill that morning, going away from the square, just as I arrived. He could have been at the bookstore."

Dwayne frowned. "That's pretty important."

"I know, but at the time, I thought he was just out walking on the coastline."

"Which may still be the truth," Dwayne added. "But we need to know for sure. I'll have to go and interview him, at least."

"I'd like to hear that interview," I said.

His frown deepened. "Lily, this was murder. You need to be careful and not purposely put yourself in harm's way." I met his eyes and was about to argue, but I could see that he wasn't going to bend. It was nice, in a way, to be cared for, but a bit frustrating because I really did want to hear that interview.

Dwayne had suggested Nico and Greg go back to the campus but stay close to their phones and to one another. The boys sauntered out of the shop together, and I was glad to see them that way. I was sure they could come up with a plan to help Greg get the money for college.

Dwayne wasn't far behind the boys. He gathered his bag and headed out of the shop.

I wondered if I'd ever see him in any other capacity than as a police officer. I really enjoyed his company and was one hundred percent open to dating him. However, now was not the time to discuss it.

With nothing else to do, I finally turned back to the box from the estate sale. A few customers were wandering around the shop. They weren't anyone I knew from town, so I assumed they were visitors to the area. No one in town got up so early to look for books. Even with a few customers, I knew there was no longer any excuse. I needed to empty out the second box and figure out what, if anything, someone wanted to kill for.

With one hand in the box, I heard the bell ring over the door. "Grrr." I actually growled. I looked up. Greg and Nico's friend, Kat, entered. She stepped in and seemed to search the room. Then she moved toward me. I was honestly surprised by how much she really did seem catlike. The way she moved, swaying slightly as she walked, with the drama of a movie star. At times, it even seemed as if she were on tiptoe, slinking toward me.

"Morning, Kat." I acknowledged her presence. She blinked at me but didn't speak. Her eyes darted over my shoulder to the back room. I assumed she'd heard about the murder and was just coming to see what she could see, but I wondered how she had heard. It wasn't general knowledge yet.

"Can I help you with anything?" My hand rested on the box as I anxiously waited for her to answer.

She seemed to awaken, as if coming out of a trance. "I was wondering if you had any work? I know Nico is doing the pirate readings, but I could help you shelve books, sweep up, open crates. Anything, really. I could use the extra money." Her voice dropped lower and lower as she spoke, and she moved closer and closer to the counter.

I felt sorry for her, but honestly, I didn't think I could hire every college student who needed money. I was doing well, but not well enough for an extra employee. I was just about to try and explain that to her when she added, "I could work today for free. Then you can see how it goes. If you decide that you don't like the work I do or that you don't need me, there won't be any hard feelings."

I straightened up. "I couldn't allow you to work for free, and I'm not sure I can take on another employee. How about I let you work today and the rest of this week for pay? I'm still trying to get a lot of books out on the shelves. But after that I won't have enough work to keep on a second employee."

She smiled. And yes, it sounds cliché, but I had to admit it was rather like a Cheshire cat's smile. It made me wonder if she was pleased with my offer or pleased with herself.

"That's great. I can empty that box for you." She pointed to the box on the counter, which I still hadn't removed a single book from. She took a step toward the box, but I reached over and slid it out of the way.

"Sorry, this box may have something important in it, and I need to get it emptied. If you wouldn't mind, there's a cartful of books over by the cooking section that need to be shelved. You just put them in order by the last name of the author."

She tilted her head, "O...kay." She sounded as though she was offended. I shrugged to indicate I was sorry. My tone had been a bit on the harsh side because I was feeling protective of the box. She probably thought I was daft.

She smiled again and made her way toward the cart with the cookbooks. I watched her for a few minutes and noted that she knew what she was doing and didn't seem upset about my behavior. After each book was placed on the shelf, she looked at me and met my eyes. It was awkward for both of us, and I wasn't sure if she was trying to show me that she knew what she was doing or if she was actually watching me. I turned slightly away so she could get on with her work and I could get on with mine. I reached into the box. It was time to get to the bottom of the mystery.

I started to remove the books, one by one. Several I could tell right away were worth only a few dollars, and others I had to look up on eBay. One book called *Howard Pyle's Book of Pirates* looked very interesting. I slipped it open and found it was a first edition. This was a real find. A quick search on eBay revealed that I could sell it for about eight hundred dollars.

Holding it up, I had to wonder if there was any chance someone knew about it and would have come all the way to Harbor Inn from Boston to try to steal it.

I bowed my head. *Lord, if there's something about this book or this box I need to know, please show me.*

It was so comforting to speak to God about my worries. Not that I always got an answer right away, but I did always feel a sense of relief from anxiety. I laid the book to the side and continued. It had been a great find, but I was really thinking that if there was anything of murder-the-young-man value, it had to be something else.

Finally, at the bottom of the box, my hand met with a square, hard item. One small box. I looked around. I didn't want anyone to see it yet.

CHAPTER EIGHT

I pulled the small box up and looked at it. I think I even took a deep breath. The box fit snuggly in my hand and was painted with a delicate pattern of roses all over it. It was definitely one of the two I'd seen that day at the estate sale.

I glanced around. Kat didn't seem to be looking at me anymore, which was good. I examined the box more closely and noted that there was a latch and a tiny hole for a key. I frowned, turning the box upside down, hoping to find a key taped on the bottom. But no such luck.

Well, Lord, that's just frustrating.

Several thoughts ran through my head. Was the second small box even packed and sent to me? Was the key to this box inside the other one? Suddenly, I remembered the dead boy's body, laid out flat with one hand extended. Maybe he'd found the other small box, assumed it was the only one, and was running out of the shop with it in his hand. Then a second person hit him with the oar, causing him to fall and hit his head on the anchor.

I grabbed my phone, slipped into the back room, and called Dwayne. I only had to wait one ring, and he answered. I was excited to tell him my thoughts but tried to keep my voice down so none of my customers would hear me. "Dwayne, listen. I found a small box that has a lock and no key. I'm guessing there was a second box, because I remember two on the shelf where I bought the books."

"That sounds reasonable," Dwayne assured me.

"I'm thinking the other box is probably what that poor young man had stolen and got killed for. Someone must have known he was in the shop, and when they saw him running out, they hit him with the oar."

"Lily, this is getting more and more dangerous. I think you should just close the shop for the day. I'll come over and get the box and put it in the evidence room."

My mind agreed, but the curiosity in my soul got the better of me. "Can't we at least open the box first? See what's so important?"

Dwayne cleared his throat, and my hopes dropped, but then he said, "I guess that's okay. I mean, it won't get the case solved sitting in a locker." My heart raced. "But wait until I get there and, please, close the shop."

I crossed my hand over my heart although he couldn't see the motion, "I promise." After a few more words, I hung up and immediately started moving around the shop, informing customers that I was closing for the day.

I realized that I had the box clasped tightly in my hand and anyone could see it. So I slipped it into my pocket. I moved back to the counter, opened the drawer under the counter, and placed the box in it. The drawer had a lock, and the key for it was on my key fob. I felt the box was safe until Dwayne got there. I set the empty cardboard box on the floor. My legs were trembling with excitement.

Kat stepped out from behind one of the bookshelves. I'd almost forgotten she was in the store. "Kat, Officer Forgione wants me to close the shop. Can you come back tomorrow?"

She frowned but nodded. "What's wrong?"

"Something has come up that might have to do with why that young man was killed."

Her eyes opened wide. "Really? That's exciting." Her voice didn't reflect her words. She spoke in a rather monotone voice.

I had walked up to the front door and was waiting for her to leave so I could lock up. My gaze moved outside, and I was shocked to see the man who had been talking to Greg. He was dressed in his black hoodie and black pants and was heading toward the shop.

I quickly turned the lock and switched off the OPEN sign.

"Kat, you can go out that way, if you don't mind." I pointed at the back room.

She looked up and blinked.

I hesitated. I didn't want to tell her anything more about the case. I knew she thought I was acting really weird. Finally, she turned and headed toward the back room.

"I'll let you out," I called to her.

She gave a small wave. "I can find the door." She rushed out, so I didn't need to follow her, and within seconds I heard the back door open and close. I didn't need to worry about locking it, because it automatically locked.

I took a deep, calming breath, but my stomach made a loud noise.

"I guess coffee and bagels don't mix with anxiety." I spoke out loud to no one and headed for the restroom. Once there, I splashed water on my face and tried to relax, but that only lasted a moment, because I heard a loud rattling sound and then the splintering of glass coming from the front of the shop. Someone was breaking in.

I jumped up and rushed to the bathroom door, but as I reached it, I heard a click. I grabbed the knob and turned and pushed, but it wouldn't budge. Someone had locked the door from the outside.

Now my stomach really started screeching, but it would have to wait. I pressed my ear against the door, trying to hear anything.

There was some scuffling of feet, and I heard the sound of drawers being opened and closed.

Whoever was out there must be looking for the small box. I hoped they hadn't found it. But how did anyone know about it?

I pulled out my phone and dialed Dwayne. It rang three times, but he didn't answer. I got a quick text message that said, "I'll call you back." I could hardly believe it. This was no time for him not to answer his phone. I listened at the door again. This time I heard a loud bang, which indicated that the back door had once again been slammed closed, and everything was suddenly quiet.

All I could think to do was call Dwayne again. This time he answered and I yelled, "Dwayne!"

"What's wrong?" My tone must have frightened him, because he sounded sharp.

"I'm locked in the restroom in my shop. Someone broke in again, and they locked me in here."

"Do you think the person is still in the shop?" Dwayne's voice grew very serious.

"No, but before I locked the front door, I saw that guy again, hovering outside. I made Kat go out the back door. Then I came to the restroom, and within minutes, I heard a window break, and then they locked me in. The worst part is I put the small box in a drawer, and I'm afraid whoever locked me in may have found it."

"Okay, I'm almost there. What was Kat doing there?" Dwayne asked. Then he said, "Oh, never mind. If you're safe for now, I'm gonna hang up and call for backup."

"I guess I'm safe, if whoever it is doesn't open the bathroom door again. I think the person went out the back door."

I hated when Dwayne hung up. There had been some comfort in talking to him. Now I felt completely alone. I stood by the door, listening and trying not to shake. I planned to remove the lock from the outside of the bathroom as soon as possible. I never wanted to be stuck in here again, but for now, I began to pray.

Lord Jesus. I'm afraid, but I know You're with me and that You're protecting me. Perhaps this locked door is for my protection. I put myself and my bookstore into Your hands.

The prayer was silent, but it helped me get through the next few anxious minutes. I could almost feel God's comforting hand holding me.

Time drifted by slowly. In my mind I heard an imaginary clock ticking away. Dwayne should have been there by now. I wondered where he was. I pulled out my phone again and called Penny.

"Hello, Lily." Her voice was cheerful. She obviously didn't know I was locked in the bathroom in my bookstore while some unknown person was rummaging around. "Kyle and I were just talking about what book he'll read—"

I interrupted her sentence by yelling, "Penny, I'm locked in the bathroom at the bookstore."

Penny gasped. "What? How?"

"I don't know. Dwayne was supposed to come and help me, but he hasn't shown up yet."

"Hold on, Lily." Penny went silent, but I could hear her breathing heavily. I imagined her running from her shop to mine.

"Oops, Lily. There's broken glass all over the ground in front of the door. I don't think I should come in."

I sighed. "Better not." Not only did I not want her to risk getting cut, I knew it would disturb the evidence.

"Okay, I can stay here by the front door and keep talking to you," Penny assured me. That made me feel better, but wondering where Dwayne was niggled at the back of my mind.

"Lily, I hear something at the back of the shop. Should I go look?"

"No! Absolutely not. As a matter of fact, you better go back to Cup 'n' Cake. I'm not sure if the person who locked me in is actually gone, and the more I think about it, the more I realize you could be in danger."

I heard Penny gasp again. "I'll get Kyle."

Penny didn't end the call, and I could hear her steps as she trotted back to the Cup 'n' Cake and started calling for her husband. Even though Kyle was a writer, they ran Cup 'n' Cake together.

All of a sudden, the lock on the bathroom door began to turn. I pushed myself up against the wall. As the door opened, I could feel a scream surfacing. I squeezed my eyes closed and waited.

CHAPTER NINE

L ily?" It was Dwayne's voice. I opened my eyes.
"Dwayne!" I ran toward him and ended up with his arms wrapped around me.

"It's okay, Lily." He patted my back. After a few seconds I stepped back, embarrassed. I was very happy to see him, but throwing myself in his arms might have been a little too much.

"Sorry, Dwayne. I was so afraid."

He smiled. "That's okay. You're safe now."

I stuck my hand on my hip and glared at him. "Why are you smiling? Do you think me being locked in this bathroom by a potential killer is funny?"

His smile disappeared. "Not at all. I just liked having you throw yourself into my arms."

I couldn't help staring at him. That was not the time to pursue that conversation. "What took you so long to get to me?"

"That's the good news. I caught the guy." He turned, took my hand, and led me away from the bathroom. We moved toward the front of the shop. I was still feeling a bit shaky and leaned on the counter. "Really? Who is he?"

"His name is Tony Kleeman. I caught him coming out of the square. He claims to be innocent of any wrongdoing."

I looked toward the front door and noticed the broken window then quickly remembered the box I'd put in the drawer. I reached down, expecting to find the drawer broken, but it was still closed and locked. I pulled my key fob out of my purse, which was on the floor under the counter, and opened the drawer. The box was still there.

"Dwayne. He didn't get the box." I shouted across the room because Dwayne had walked toward the front door. He turned around, and I could see a frown on his face.

"This is good news," I said.

He nodded. "Yes, but I was in such a hurry to get to you, that when I came in the door, I didn't notice this." He pointed at the ground.

My gaze followed his finger. I couldn't see anything.

I guess he could see the confusion in my eyes.

"The glass is broken from the inside out," he explained. "That means whoever broke it was already in the store and wanted it to look like someone broke in. The glass is all on the sidewalk outside."

My jaw dropped in shock. No one else had been in the store. At least, I didn't think so. I'd heard Kat go out the back. My mind whirled with different thoughts. Finally, I realized that I hadn't seen Kat go out the door. I'd only heard the door close. Maybe she had stayed inside the shop.

"What?" Dwayne asked. "I can see you've thought of something." He walked back to the counter.

I explained to him how Kat had come in and asked for a job. How she'd been there when I found the box and how I'd sent her out the back door after speaking to him on the phone. "I can't believe she would have anything to do with this. I mean, she's just a college kid."

"I think I need to talk to her." Dwayne said. "But for now, you, Nico, and Greg better come to the station so we can find out what Tony Kleeman has to say about all of this. Do you want to ride with me?"

I was actually ready to go home and climb into my bed and sleep. The day's activities had worn out my soul. "I'll ride with you," I murmured. "What about this box?" I held it up.

"Bring it along. We'll open it at the station."

I tucked the box into my purse and joined him at the front door. It was obvious now that all the broken glass was lying outside the store, which meant for sure that it had been broken from the inside.

I tried to imagine what Kat could have to do with this, but nothing came to mind. Sure, she'd acted a bit weird, but nothing to make me think she had any nefarious thoughts against me.

Penny and Kyle had come out of Cup 'n' Cake. "Sorry it took so long. Kyle was on a call, and I had to get his attention. Are you okay?"

I nodded. "Dwayne got me out of the bathroom. We're going to the station to talk to a suspect."

Kyle gave a long whistle. "Wow, that's exciting. Wish I could tag along. Might be fodder for my next novel." He looked toward Dwayne with hopeful eyes.

Dwayne just shook his head.

Kyle's shoulders sagged. He and Penny headed back to their shop. I knew I'd have to make it up to them by giving them as many details as possible about my day and what happened at the police station.

Dwayne posted another officer in front of the bookstore, and as we walked to the car, the air seemed more frigid than earlier, but I assumed it was just my mood. I sighed heavily. Surely this wasn't going to be good for business. First a break-in, then a murder, and now someone trying to rob me. If the citizens of Harbor Inn learned about all this, my shop could die on the line before I could even haul all of the local readers in.

Shaking my head at the image, I moved closer to Dwayne, hoping to absorb some of his warmth. He helped me into the front seat of his police car then got in on the driver's side. It wasn't any warmer, but he gave me a sweet smile as if to say he was sorry for everything. That began to warm me from the inside out.

When we reached the station, Dwayne led me to a room with a large table. I sat there for a while alone. A few minutes later, Nico and Greg showed up, and Dwayne ushered them into the room as well. The boys seemed pleased that I was there, although I could tell they were nervous. We all sat and waited about five more minutes, then Dwayne brought Tony Kleeman into the room. He seemed surprised to see us and slouched into a chair that Dwayne pointed at.

Dwayne stood behind him. "Now, Mr. Kleeman, can you please explain what you have to do with the break-in and murder at the By Hook and by Book Bookstore?"

Kleeman glared at each of us. Then he sat back with a shrug. "Listen, all I'm guilty of is the very first break-in. But I didn't take anything."

Dwayne moved closer to him. "We need more information than that. We know you actually tried to hire Greg to break into the shop."

Kleeman growled at Greg, "I told you to keep your trap closed."

Greg winced as if he'd been hit. The room was silent for a minute then Kleeman shrugged again. "Okay, so I tried to hire him"—he nodded at Greg—"to break into the shop and look for the two boxes from an estate sale in Boston. When he wouldn't do it, I hired that other kid. Roger."

"And when he found one of the boxes, you killed him?" I knew immediately by the look on his face Dwayne wasn't happy that I'd spoken. I closed my mouth.

Kleeman tilted his head. "Nope. I never saw him again. He was supposed to find the boxes and bring them to me. He never showed up. He's dead?"

"Yes, he's dead." I tried, but I just couldn't keep quiet. "What's in the boxes?"

Realizing that Roger was dead must have made things much more serious to Tony. He knew he had to cooperate now, so he said, "One box has a key to open the other box."

"And in that box?" Dwayne asked.

"A jade ring worth about a hundred thousand dollars."

Greg whistled. "Man, I could have been arrested for grand larceny if I'd done what you wanted."

Tony didn't seem repentant about anything. He scowled at Greg.

"How do you know this?" Nico, who had been silent until then, spoke up.

Dwayne huffed, but I guess he was just glad that Tony was talking, so he didn't say anything to Nico.

Tony ran his hand through his long hair. He seemed to be an old hippy, about thirty.

"It belonged to my great aunt. I visited her once when I was a kid, and she showed me the two boxes. When she died, I went to the estate sale, looking for them because I was pretty sure no one would know about the ring and there aren't any other family members she could have left it to. She also wasn't the type to make a will. I was out of the state when she died, so I wasn't contacted until after plans for the estate sale were made."

We were all listening attentively now.

"When I got to the sale, late, by the way, the boxes were already gone with everything else on the shelf. I searched the house, but they weren't anywhere, so I knew they had to be with the books that had been on those shelves. I mentioned to the person in charge that I had been interested in one of the books. She gave me the address of your bookstore."

Dwayne's arms were crossed over his chest. I didn't think he believed Tony's whole story, but I did.

"Officer Forgione, can we open this?" I pulled the small, intricate box out and held it up.

Tony jumped up, his hand stretched toward me, but I pulled the box back. He smacked the table with his hand.

"That's mine."

Dwayne moved closer. "Kleeman, sit down. If this is the ring, it will have to go into the court system, where it will be determined who has a claim to it."

Dwayne nodded at me. "Go ahead and open it," he said.

"I hate to damage the clasp." I looked it over, but Dwayne walked out of the room then came back with a thin, flat screwdriver. I handed the box to him, and he pried it open. Everyone in the room leaned in.

As he opened the box, I could feel everyone's attention riveted on it. Sure enough, there was a ring inside. I really know nothing about jewelry, so whether it was worth a hundred thousand dollars or not, I had no idea, but it was one of the loveliest I'd ever seen.

I could see Nico and Greg's eyes were wide. "Wow, that's really something." Nico's voice was low, impressed.

"I told you so," Tony muttered. "Now I'll never get it."

I sat back and replayed his explanation. Then I leaned forward and asked, "What about Kat, did you hire her?"

"Kat who?" Tony actually sounded confused.

"What about Kat?" Nico asked. "What does she have to do with this?"

I was about to explain, but Dwayne stopped me. "Let me get Tony booked first. He admitted to breaking into your shop, so I can hold him on that until we get this all figured out."

When Dwayne left, Greg and Nico leaned in. "Tell us everything," Nico said.

I proceeded to tell them all about Kat coming to the shop, being locked in the restroom, and the broken glass.

"So you think Kat is responsible?" Greg asked. I could tell he was really surprised, which indicated that they weren't working together.

"I'm not sure. How would she know about the boxes in the first place? You could see that Tony didn't know who we were talking about when we mentioned her name. It's obvious that whoever locked me in the restroom was looking for the box, so could it be Kat?"

We all sat quietly, thinking.

After a few minutes, Dwayne returned. "Well, there's nothing more we can do about this today. Without more evidence, I can't book Tony for murder."

I really didn't think Tony had murdered Roger, but it was even harder to think Kat had done it. Not that I knew either of them at all. At this point, I wasn't sure if I was very good at reading people.

"Lily, I'll drive you home in a few minutes," Dwayne assured me. Then he left the room again. I looked at Nico and Greg. "How well do you all know Kat?"

They both shrugged. "She's cool, hangs around all the drama students, but I guess I don't know her at all." Nico looked at Greg as he spoke. "She's pretty good at acting the part of a pirate."

Greg shook his head. "I only met her in drama class. Since I've been hiding out most of the semester from Tony, I haven't gotten to know her at all."

That was frustrating. I'd hoped the boys might have some insight into Kat's personality, but it seemed they didn't know much at all. A few minutes later, Dwayne returned and told the boys to go back to school and stay available. Then he and I headed toward the parking garage.

Dwayne drove me to my mother's house instead of the bookstore, which was fine with me because I just wanted to sleep. When I got out of the car, my mother, who had only returned from her cruise that day, slipped out the side door, a worried expression on her face.

"Lily, what's going on?"

"Nothing. Well, lots, but I'm too tired to tell you tonight. Let's talk tomorrow over lunch."

She glanced at Dwayne, who gave some kind of nod that seemed to satisfy her. She turned and went back into her house, but I knew she'd be making calls all over town to find out what had been happening while she was gone.

"I'll board up that door on the shop for you, and you can reopen tomorrow."

"Thank you. It will be freezing if it doesn't get boarded up. Do you think it'll be safe?"

"Well, since we have the ring, there doesn't seem to be any reason for anyone to break in again." He stepped closer and pulled me into his arms for a hug. "You're shivering. Get inside."

"Yes sir, Officer," I joked. I made my way up the stairs to my apartment. With the least amount of effort I could manage, I was soon in bed and asleep.

The next morning my mother drove me to the shop and dropped me off. She knew almost everything before I even woke up. Dwayne had boarded up the door, and I knew I had to make some calls to get it fixed. I shuddered just looking at it and remembering the events that had led to it being broken.

I hadn't heard any more from Dwayne since he dropped me off the evening before, so I didn't know if they'd gotten ahold of Kat yet or not. I was just glad that Nico and Greg had nothing to do with any of it. Nico was supposed to do a reading at the shop today. So far, the murder had been kept quiet, so I expected our usual crowd of kids and parents.

Story time wasn't my favorite thing. There were always a few toddlers who wouldn't sit still for the readings, and parents often allowed them to wander around and pull books off shelves. So far, nothing had been ruined, but it was a job to clean up after them. However, our local library didn't do readings for kids, so I thought I should offer it.

When I turned on the lights, I got the same special feeling I did every time I opened the shop. Owning By Hook or by Book was my dream come true, and with all the twinkle lights that were placed strategically throughout the store, including those that highlighted the large, corrugated clouds I had hung throughout the building, the place had a calm feel to it.

I stepped into the shop and made my way to the counter. When I looked down, I saw that several drawers were pulled out and there were some papers and books strewn around on the floor. I'd almost forgotten that whoever had broken in and locked me in the bathroom had rummaged through things. Plus the police would have had to come look it all over again. I had some cleanup to do.

An hour later, the shop was in good order again. I added the books that had come from the Boston estate sale to the shelving cart, except for the one that was worth the most money. That one, I would take photos of later and list on eBay. I would also put it in the store, in the locked glass bookcase, but the chances of someone from Harbor Inn, Maine, buying it were not very good.

My phone rang. It was Dwayne.

"Good morning," I said.

"Morning. All okay there?"

"Yes, thanks for boarding up the window. I'll have to hire someone to fix the glass. But for now, the boards will work."

"I was wondering if you'd like to go to lunch with me after church this weekend?"

I gulped. He was asking me on a real date.

"There's a great little place called Flo's Hot Dogs."

That sounded good. Nothing too fancy. "Sounds intriguing. I'd love to join you."

"Great," Dwayne answered, and then the line was silent. I wasn't sure what else to say, and I expected Nico to arrive in about ten minutes, but then I heard the bell over the door jingle. I looked up. A woman had entered, but her back was to me as she'd turned to close the door behind her. I watched in fascination as her hand reached up and turned the lock on the door.

I gulped, knowing already who it was. I hurriedly tossed the phone on the counter. I wanted both hands free in case she charged me.

The woman, or rather, young woman, turned. Sure enough, it was Kat.

CHAPTER TEN

Kat stood there, glaring at me.

"Kat." Her name on my lips caused me to tremble inside, but I didn't want her to know it. "Did you come back to finish shelving the books?"

Laughter, a most bitter sound, came from deep in her throat. "No, I didn't come to shelve books. You know what I came for."

I was actually shocked by her tone. I stood there blinking at her, and she suddenly moved forward and grabbed my arm. "Stop standing there like an idiot and get me that box." She shook me.

I tried to pull away. "Kat, I took the box to the police station yesterday. It's not here."

A hissing sound came from her. "You expect me to believe that? You would take a box with a ring in it that's worth a hundred thousand dollars to a police station and leave it there? I'm not an idiot." She pushed me behind the counter, her eyes wild. "Open that drawer." She pointed at the one I had locked the box in the day before.

I wasn't sure if I should open the drawer or not. If she saw I didn't have the ring, she might just leave, but then again, she might kill me. I was silently praying and asking God to help me.

"How did you know about the ring?" I probed, hoping that if I could get her talking, someone might walk by the shop and see her inside and. . . Well, I don't know what, but something.

"I overheard that guy talking to Greg. He was offering him some good money just to get a box, but he didn't tell Greg what was in it. After that, I kept an eye on the guy, and when he talked to Roger, he told Roger all about what was in it. He was so eager to get the box, but he never said anything about there being two of them. He had no idea I overheard the conversation though. I know how to keep from getting caught."

I kept my voice calm and steady. "So you followed Roger here, and when you saw him running out of the back room with the box, you. . ." I didn't want to say it out loud. "Assumed it was the box with the ring in it and took it from him?"

She laughed again. "That's a gentle way of putting it. I don't know what came over me. I saw him running with the box, so I grabbed the oar and smashed him over the head. I thought it would knock him out, but then he fell and hit his head on the anchor you have sitting there." She pointed, and I cringed, remembering the blood from Roger's head.

"I didn't mean to kill him." Her voice shook a little.

I looked toward the front of the store. Nico was looking into the shop window. I mouthed the word *help*, and he nodded then ran off. I hoped Kat hadn't seen the exchange, but she seemed lost in thought, remembering how she'd hit Roger.

"I'm sure you didn't, Kat. The police will understand. Why don't you let me call Officer Forgione? He's very helpful."

She slammed her hand on the counter. "No, I want that ring. I need money to finish school."

She was so far into denial, she didn't even realize that there was no way she could attend any college after what she'd done, but I tried to reassure her. "That's all right, Kat. Maybe I can talk to Officer Forgione about letting me sell the ring and give you the money."

Her eyes lit up, and she nodded. "Yeah, that's a good idea. But first, open that drawer and prove to me the ring isn't there." She pointed again. I was glad her back was to the front door, because now I noticed Penny and Nico hovering near it. I shook my head to warn them not to come in.

Nico had his phone pressed against his ear. I hoped it was a call to the police.

"I need to get the key out of my purse to open the drawer," I explained. I reached over and pulled the leather satchel closer to me. I began searching. My purse was a minefield, and finding the key fob with the small key took a few moments with my trembling hands.

Lord, help! The key won't reveal what she wants. I need to get out of here. Help me get away.

Finally, I leaned over and put the key into the hole and opened the drawer. Kat actually pushed me away so hard, I nearly fell. My foot hit the anchor, and my hands waved around wildly for a second. If I hadn't put my hands out to stop myself from falling, I could have been another casualty.

"There's nothing here!" Kat yowled. It sounded like a cat crying. I actually started backing away, toward the door. The girl looked crazed, and I wasn't about to get in her clutches.

Suddenly Kat looked up. "You!" she shouted, and began to move toward me.

I turned and ran, slamming into the back door, but pushing it open at the same time. I wasn't sure if I was screaming or if it was Kat's voice following me, but my mouth was wide open as I ran. Once out the door, I brushed by someone who was standing there. I thought it was Dwayne, but all I could think to do was run.

When I reached the parking lot, I stopped, trying to catch my breath and looking back over my shoulder. I expected to see Kat chasing me, but no one was anywhere around. Dwayne's police car was parked near my car, but he wasn't in it.

I took in a huge breath. I *had* seen Dwayne. Now I was worried something might have happened to him. Had I knocked him over when I ran out the door? Did he go inside, and was he in there with Kat right now?

I decided to run around to the front of the building. Maybe Penny and Nico were still there. I moved quickly but kept looking around in case Kat had come out of the building. I couldn't believe how frightened I was of a young college girl.

When I reached the front of the building, Penny and Nico were still hovering near the front door. I sidled up to them.

"Lily, what? How? Are you okay?" Penny stumbled over her words.

"Yes, I ran out the back, but I'm afraid Dwayne is in there with Kat and well, she's sort of a psycho."

Penny frowned. "I'm sure Dwayne can handle her. He does have a gun."

I nodded. That only made sense.

"I called 911, and there should be some backup here pretty soon," Nico said. At just that moment, I heard the sound of a siren. Tires screeched to a stop, and two officers joined us.

"We got a call about a hostage situation," one of them announced. He began herding us away from the door.

Hostage? It took a moment for me to realize that Nico must have called and told them Kat was holding me hostage.

I moved forward again. "Officer Forgione was at the back door. I think he's in the bookstore with a young woman named Kat, who is the main suspect in a recent murder."

The officer, who probably had never done more than direct traffic before, gasped, and his eyes widened. He faced the front door, hesitating.

I explained that the front door was locked from the inside, and he began pushing on it. All I could think was that the entire door would snap if he applied his full weight.

Luckily, the door was suddenly opened, and Dwayne was standing there. His eyes seemed to seek me out. "Are you okay, Lily?"

"Yes, you?"

He nodded then started talking to the other officer. I couldn't hear everything he said, and I wondered where Kat was, but after about five minutes, he disappeared for a few seconds then returned to the door, holding on to Kat's arm. She had her hands cuffed behind her back.

"She's handcuffed," Nico whispered loud enough for us all to hear.

As they stepped out into the courtyard, Kat glared at me. I really felt sorry for her but wasn't sure what I could do for her. Maybe, in the future, I could write to her and tell her about Jesus, but for today, I didn't think she was going to be open to anything like that.

Dwayne handed Kat over to the other officer, who beamed at being given the responsibility and began to lead Kat to his car.

I felt my head spinning, and I must have stumbled forward because, without knowing it, I actually fell into Dwayne's arms. For a moment, I blacked out.

Dwayne tapped my cheeks. "Lily, Lily, are you okay?"

I opened my eyes, and they met his. "What? What is it?" I stood up straight.

"You fainted." Penny came up beside me. "Let's go get a cup of coffee."

Dwayne put an arm around me, and we followed Penny back to Cup 'n' Cake. We settled on the counter chairs, and Penny filled mugs with coffee. I allowed the warm liquid to soothe me.

"Ah, that's what I needed." I set the mug down. "Now, Dwayne, can you tell us what happened?"

He tilted his head and smiled. "Sure. You ran out of the building like a wild woman, almost knocking me over. I ran in. Kat was screaming and chasing after you. When she saw me, she got even crazier and started swinging punches at me. Kicked and scratched too. Sort of like a wildcat."

I was nodding in understanding. Penny and Nico were listening attentively.

"It took a bit for me to get her into cuffs, but once I was done, she started spilling the beans. She told me all about overhearing Tony hiring Roger to find the box, how she hit him with the oar and he fell and hit his head on the anchor. She even told me about pretending to leave the bookstore then breaking the glass on the door to make it look like someone had broken in. She's the one who locked you in the bathroom."

Penny and Nico were entranced by the story. I was just weary. If anything else happened, my bookstore wasn't going to survive. I laid my head down on my arm.

"Lily, you need to go get some rest. This has been too much for you." Dwayne rubbed my back gently. All I wanted was to go to my mom's house and take a nap in her guestroom, which used to be my bedroom.

I raised my head. "What do you think will happen to Kat?" I asked.

Dwayne shrugged. "I don't know. She's sort of crazy, so she might plead insanity and go to a special facility. She didn't mean to kill Roger."

"All that for a ring," Nico blurted out. "I need money as much as any college student, but I'd never go as far as she did to get it. I don't even mean murdering someone. She didn't plan to do that. She was a thief, I guess. I couldn't imagine even going that far!"

Dwayne stood up. "That's enough for now. Lily, you are going home and getting some rest. You, Nico, are going back to your dorm. I'll post a CLOSED FOR THE DAY notice on the door of the shop."

The young man stood up. "Okay. I'll be back to the shop on Wednesday for the next reading." He headed out the door.

Penny picked up the coffee mugs and carried them into her kitchen.

Dwyane and I looked at each other.

"You know, I prayed to get away from Kat, and God worked it out by allowing me to get out the back door. You being there was a miracle."

"What was really a miracle, Lily, is that you didn't hang up your phone when we were talking. I heard Kat and realized I needed to get to you quickly."

I leaned on him a bit. "I'm glad you were there."

CHAPTER ELEVEN

A few weeks later, The Butler Did It Mystery Book Club met at my store. Unlike any other meeting, they asked Officer Forgione and me to attend. Once there, they asked us to run them through the entire case. Then they had a vigorous talk about how each of them would have handled things differently. Dwayne sat back with his arms crossed over his chest. I could tell he was laughing inside.

Several times I almost spoke up, but Dwayne touched my arm and shook his head. "Let them talk." He smiled and took my hand in his. Enjoying the warmth that spread through my body at his touch, I sat back.

The entire story of Roger's death and Kat's break-in made the local news, which brought many curious people into the shop, many of whom ended up purchasing books. And now that the calendar was filled with upcoming readings, group meetings, and other special activities, I was pretty sure there would be enough income to keep the shop going.

Nico's father had come to town and met with Bill. I'm not sure if he paid the three thousand dollars or not, but he'd made amends that seemed to satisfy our town's taxi driver.

As to the jade ring, it ended up that Tony Kleeman was the only living relative to his great aunt's estate. So the ring belonged to him after all. Of course, he was going to have to go through the legal system before he could make any kind of claim on it.

Glancing around the shop, with the twinkle lights lit, the huge anchor now set up next to a small stage where meetings such as this one were being held, and all the other pirate paraphernalia placed strategically throughout the building, I felt honestly happy. It all seemed so perfect.

Dwayne leaned over and pressed a kiss on my cheek, which added to my good mood. It was nice to know he still wanted to see me and it wasn't all just about the case.

"Lily, let me ask you something."

My mind was feeling dreamy as I looked up into his eyes. "Yes?" I was expecting to hear him say something sweet.

"What did the ocean say to the pirate?"

My eyes opened wide. I couldn't believe he was telling a joke right now, but I realized I was going to have to get used to it.

I blinked. "I don't know. What *did* the ocean say to the pirate?"

Dwayne smiled. "Nothing. It just waved."

TERESA IVES LILLY's ninth-grade teacher inspired her writing by allowing her to take a twelfth-grade creative writing course during the summer. After that, it has been her passion and dream to write; however, until her salvation in 1986, when she discovered the genre of Christian Romance, Teresa did not even try writing. Since then, she has gone on to write over thirty novellas and novels including several published by Barbour Books. Teresa lives in San Antonio, Texas. Teresa believes God let her be born "at such a time as this" to be able to write and share her stories of faith. Follow or contact Teresa at www.teresalilly.wordpress.com.

To read more stories by Teresa that take place in Harbor Inn, Maine, find these titles on Amazon:

Coffee and Cake: Harbor Inn Romance Series
Cocoa and Christmas: Harbor Inn Romance Series
Diary and Death: Harbor Inn Mystery Series
Donations and Demise: Harbor Inn Mystery Series

THE MISSING CHAPTER

BY MARILYN TURK

CHAPTER 1

The bell on the door jingled as I walked into Bayside Books and Reading Room. It took a moment for my eyes to adjust to the dim light of the store after the bright sunshine outside.

"Can I help you?"

I turned toward the voice and spotted an older woman sitting on a stool behind an old-school counter to the left of the door. She was focused on her hands and didn't look up.

Behind her, a huge orange tabby cat lying on the top shelf of a bookcase stretched and yawned.

"Yes, I'm sorry I didn't see you there for a minute," I said, putting my sunglasses on the top of my head.

She looked up with a frown. "It's too dark in here, I keep telling Jep." She pointed to a desk lamp illuminating her hands behind the counter. "I need more light when I'm doing needlepoint."

I peered over the counter to see. "What are you working on?"

Holding up her work, the woman said, "Bookmarks. I needle-point these." She pointed to a display of colorful bookmarks under the glass countertop.

"Those are lovely! And such tiny stitching! You made all these?" I peered into the display, admiring bookmarks adorned with butterflies, cats, sayings, and even a lighthouse.

Nodding, she said, "Yes. Got to do something to stay busy. You needlepoint? If you do, Nellie's Needles is down the street. That's where I get all my thread and canvas. You know what the Bible says about idle hands."

"Um, I'm not sure I do." But I was pretty sure she was about to tell me.

" 'Idle hands are the devil's workshop.'" The white-haired woman with pale blue eyes studied me. "You're the new girl in town, aren't you?" She took one hand off her needlework and extended it to me. "Matilda Thompson, but everybody calls me Tilly."

I accepted her hand. "Kelly Stephens. I'm opening the shop across the street."

Tilly squinted toward the window. "Oh, yes. Some kind of artsy stuff. I sure hope it lasts longer than the last place that was there."

I hoped so too. This venture was a real stretch for me, and I'd invested my life savings into it. Having worked for other people all my life, now I only had myself to answer to. "It was a boutique, wasn't it?"

Tilly rolled her eyes. "So-called. It had the most outlandish clothes that nobody around here would wear. And the prices were outrageous!"

"Well, I'm planning to sell locally made arts and crafts, so if you know anyone who creates such things, send them my way."

Another customer entered the store, and Tilly shifted her attention to him, temporarily ignoring me. I took the opportunity to survey the place. It was quaint, with the usual rows of shelves marching toward the back of the store. On one side of the room was a seating area with a couple of well-worn sofas, mismatched oversized chairs, and end tables with lamps. In the middle of the area sat a large round coffee table strewn with magazines. An older man with a scruffy white beard sat reading a book, a cup of coffee beside him on the end table.

The aroma of coffee filled the air, and I saw the source on a table along the wall behind the sitting area, a large coffeemaker like I had at home. On the wall were some open shelves displaying a variety of coffee cups in all shapes, sizes, and colors. I sure could use a cup of coffee. Was I supposed to help myself?

"See ya, Walter. I'll be sure and tell Jep." As Walter left the store, Tilly remembered me.

"Kelly, isn't it? Where were we? Oh yes, where are you from?"

"I moved here from Atlanta."

"Oh my. What a big city! I could never live in a place that big! No, Bayside is big enough for me. My husband, when he was alive, used to travel for his job, and he would tell me stories about all the traffic and hustle and bustle in those big cities. He once had an opportunity to move to one of them, and I said, 'Not on your life! You go if you want to, but you'll go without me!'"

I nodded. "It's definitely a slower pace here. I rather like the change."

"Well, of course you do! People around here call our little town paradise." She looked me up and down, apparently trying to figure out if I fit here. "Got any relatives in the area?"

"I have a distant cousin who lives in Destin." Did this woman need to know everything about me?

Tilly shook her head. "I stay away from that place. Too many tourists. Too much traffic."

I'd heard other people in Bayside say the same thing, that they refused to go to the beach during tourist season for those reasons. I'd been surprised to hear that at first, since the Destin beach was only twenty minutes away. But I acted like I agreed. I certainly didn't want to argue with her. I needed allies if I was going to make it in this town.

"I'm sure that's true during the summer. I've had enough traffic in Atlanta." To be honest, if I could have afforded it, I would have liked to open my shop in Destin where there were sure to be more customers, but the cost of renting space in that area was beyond my means. Hopefully, there would be enough business here in Bayside to keep me afloat, making the town a paradise for me as well.

"Hey, Jep! Coffeepot's empty!" Across the room, the bearded man stood, holding the empty coffeepot aloft.

"All right, Mac. I'll put another pot on. Just a minute." My gaze traveled to the voice and spotted a nice-looking man who looked about my age walking toward Mac. He wore a button-down blue chambray shirt and jeans and black-rimmed glasses that tried to hide his eyes. But his rather unkempt chestnut hair fell across his face and did that.

"That's Jep. He's the store owner." Tilly faced Kelly with raised eyebrows. "Are you single?"

My face heated, so I must've blushed. "Um, yes I am." Still single, unlike all my friends who had gotten married since college. After a long-term relationship that went nowhere, yes, I was still single.

The door burst open, and a curvaceous woman in pink skin-fitting tights and exercise bra bounced in. Her long blond hair fell over her shoulders. The cat hissed as she blew past, and I got a whiff of a fruity fragrance. Giving the feline a frown, the woman said, "Hush, Samson."

"Morning everybody!" she announced as she strode over toward Jep with a broad smile showing too-white teeth. She closed the distance and left little space between herself and the man. Batting overly long false eyelashes, she said, "Hi, Jep."

"Hi, Bunny." Jep gave a perfunctory smile as he put a new filter in the coffeepot. "How's it going?"

"Great! Hey, call me when the coffee's ready. I need to find a certain book."

She bounded over to the shelves and disappeared behind them.

Tilly grimaced, crossing her arms. "That's Bunny Wilson. She owns Bunny's Body Beautiful gym across the square." She leaned closer and lowered her voice. "But if you ask me, she didn't get that body at a gym. She bought it with lots of money. She's got the hots for Jep, been flirting with him since she moved here a year ago, but he's got enough sense to not pay her any attention if he can help it."

Bunny Wilson. Could it be? Not *the* Bunny Wilson from high school who stole my boyfriend in the twelfth grade. Boy, did she look different now. Why, she wasn't even blond in high school! I never did like her, especially after what she did. Would she recognize me? After all, we had both changed in the last ten years, her the most. And I used to wear glasses, but now I wore contacts. But really, how many people are named Bunny?

"Funny, I went to school with someone named Bunny Wilson, but she looked a lot different," I said in a low voice to Tilly.

"I guess so, with all that work she's had done. Her face doesn't even look natural with those big lips in a perpetual pout. Mac calls her 'duck face.' He doesn't like her much. In fact, most people around here just tolerate her. But she has the only gym in town, if you're into that type of thing."

About that time, Bunny bounded back into the seating area with a book.

"Coffee's ready," Jep said.

"Great! I would truly love a cup." The way she stretched out the word *love* made the simple response sound provocative.

Jep lifted a pink mug from the shelves and filled it with coffee. Handing it to Bunny, he said, "Here you go." He carried the pot over to Mac. "Refill, Mac?"

"Do squirrels eat nuts?" Mac held out his cup while Jep poured fresh brew into it.

Bunny plopped down in the chair beside Mac, and he harrumphed. She drank some of her coffee then put the cup down on the table that sat between them.

"Jep! Come over here. I want you to meet our new town entrepreneur." Tilly waved him over.

Jep glanced our way and strode over, extending his hand. "Jep Pennington. You must be opening the art store."

I took his hand, and I could've sworn a bolt of electricity traveled up my arm. What on earth? Taking a deep breath to act normal after that, I said, "Kelly Stephens, yes, I'm opening Artistic Adventures."

"She just moved here from Atlanta." Tilly seemed eager to fill him in about me.

"That so?" He looked like he was about to say more, but Bunny interrupted from across the room.

"Did you say Kelly Stephens? Is that really you, Kelly?"

Bunny started to get up but searched for her phone purse and opened it first. A puzzled look on her face, she stood, took two steps, and grabbed her throat. Then she teetered and toppled face-first onto the floor.

Tilly and I both gasped as Jep ran toward the prone body and placed two fingers on Bunny's neck. Then he felt her wrist. "No pulse. Tilly, call 911."

CHAPTER 2

As the EMTs loaded a dead Bunny onto the stretcher, Chief of Police Chuck Chaney scribbled some notes on a pad while questioning Jep.

"You say she was here less than ten minutes?"

"Yes, Chuck. That's right." Jep ran his fingers through his thick hair in an attempt to pull it away from his face. "Like I told you, she came in, spoke to everyone, then went to get a book. She came back, and I gave her a cup of coffee."

Chuck nodded and repeated his standard response. "Uh-huh." Then he said, "Did she grab her head or her stomach when she stood up?"

"I didn't notice."

"Did she have any enemies that you know of?"

Jep crossed his arms. "Come on, Chuck. You know how most people felt about her."

Chuck looked over the top of his glasses at Jep. "You tell me."

Tilly spoke up. "Chuck, you know nobody particularly liked her."

Chuck turned his attention to Tilly. "And you, Tilly. Did you like her?"

Tilly opened her mouth to speak then snapped it shut and shrugged.

"Tilly, any thoughts you'd like to share?" Chuck persisted.

"I didn't really know her. She just came in here for a few minutes pretty much every morning and drank a cup of coffee from her pink coffee cup."

"That so? So she was an avid reader or book buyer?"

Tilly twisted her lips. "One or the other."

I hadn't been in town that long, nor did I know Tilly that well, but I could tell she was exercising great self-control. My guess was Bunny came in often to see Jep, but Tilly didn't want to say anything that might get him in trouble.

The police chief turned his attention to me. "What is your name?"

"Kelly Stephens."

"New in town?"

I nodded. "Yes, I'm opening the store Artistic Adventures."

"Uh-huh." He scribbled, keeping his head down. Then, looking me in the eyes, he said, "Did you know the victim?"

Did I? Not now, that is, if I ever really knew her. "I think we may have gone to high school together."

"You think? Wouldn't you know? A couple of patrons in the store said she called out your name before she fell."

Which patrons? Mac?

"I'm not sure if she's the same person I knew. She looked so different than the Bunny Wilson I knew in high school. But we didn't get a chance to talk. She had just stood up, so I thought she fainted."

"So, assuming this is the same Bunny Wilson, what was your relationship?"

"Relationship? There wasn't any. I haven't seen her in about ten years."

"Were you friends in high school?"

How could I answer that question honestly and not incriminate myself? I glanced outside where people clustered in groups while casting glances toward the bookstore. This must be the biggest news that ever happened in this town. What would this do to my business?

"Ma'am?"

"Oh, sorry. We knew each other but didn't hang out together." Hopefully, that answer would suffice, and the chief couldn't read minds. The fact that Bunny stole Chris, my high school boyfriend, from me right before the senior prom haunted me for a couple of years. But I had moved on and now had to deal with Kyle's betrayal. Those situations were in my past, where I wanted them to stay.

"Isn't it odd that you both moved here to Bayside and knew each other from high school?"

I shrugged and offered a smile. "Quite a coincidence, isn't it? As they say, 'small world.'"

He snapped his notebook shut. "That's all for now. But don't leave town. I may have some more questions for you."

The chief walked over to his forensics team, who were dusting and marking the floor and the chair Bunny sat in.

About that time, Mr. Universe, or a good wannabe, burst into the store. "Where is she? Where's Bunny?"

The guy wore gym shorts that revealed tremendous thigh muscles and a T-shirt stretched to the limit over a buff chest and arms. His hair was cut stylishly short, and his chiseled face reminded me of an ancient Greek god.

The chief turned away from his team to approach the man.

"And you are. . .?" the chief asked, sizing him up.

"Adam Miller. Why? What happened?" He glanced around frantically.

"How do you know Bunny Wilson?" The chief pegged him with a stern gaze.

"She's my business partner. And fiancée. Why? Where is she? Tell me what's going on!"

"I'm afraid your fiancée has died."

Wide-eyed, Adam Miller covered his mouth. "No! How?"

A young lady with long dark hair I hadn't noticed before approached him and put her arm around him.

"And who are you?" The police chief turned his attention to her.

"I'm Jennifer Tucker. Bunny and Adam are my friends." Turning to the now-sobbing Adam, whose massive shoulders were shaking, she muttered, "I'm so sorry, Adam. I'm here for you if you need anything."

"Please tell me what happened," Adam implored the chief.

"Your fiancée just collapsed here in this store. Do you know if she was feeling ill?"

"I told her not to overdo it. She was just getting over a bout with the flu, but Bunny wouldn't slow down." He sniffed and wiped his eyes. "She wouldn't listen to me."

"Mr. Miller, stay in town. We may need you again for questioning." Adam nodded then lowered his head while Jennifer consoled him with her arm across his back.

Chief Chaney glanced around. "Who else was here?"

I noticed Mac sidling around the room as if trying to go unnoticed. Jep saw him and said, "Mac was here."

Mac, wearing a cap that said Mac's Fish and Tackle, scowled at Jep as the chief walked over to him. "Hi, Mac. What did you see?"

"Nothin'. She just got up from that chair and keeled over."

It was obvious Mac didn't want anything to do with the whole incident.

"And what was she doing before that?"

"Nothin' special. Just drinking coffee with a book, jes like I was."

"She didn't act sick or anything?"

"Not that I noticed. I didn't pay her much attention."

"All right. Let me know if you think of anything else."

"Sure, chief. I need to get back to the store now." Mac hurried out the door into the group of onlookers.

Tilly leaned over to me. "Last time I saw this many people in town was the Fourth of July parade."

"So Bunny was engaged to Adam Miller?" I asked Tilly.

"First I heard of it. I knew they were partners in the gym, but I never saw more than that. In fact, I don't remember seeing her wear an engagement ring."

"I got the feeling she was interested in Jep."

"She acted like it, didn't she? Guess she didn't take her engagement too seriously."

"Okay, everybody. You can go now. Just stay around in case I need to question you some more. I'll let you know what the coroner's report says." The chief nodded at Jep then left, dispersing the crowd outside. I could hear him saying, "Y'all go on back to what you were doing. Show's over here."

Jep walked up, shaking his head. "I'm sorry about all this. Not the way we usually welcome people to town."

"I'm sure it's not. And she looked so healthy."

I saw Tilly roll her eyes, and I bit back a smile.

"You never know, do you?" Jep paused. "Maybe she had a heart condition."

I wanted to respond with a sarcastic remark. The Bunny I knew definitely had a "heart condition," like maybe missing one. She sure seemed to like toying with other people's hearts, at least in high school, and maybe here too.

"I suppose I better get back to my shop. I'm expecting some deliveries," I said.

"Well, nice to meet you. Maybe next time you'll be able to stay long enough to have a cup of coffee and visit. Do you like to read?"

"Yes, I do. Oh, as a matter of fact, one of the reasons I came by today, in addition to meeting you, was to look for a book on local birds."

"Birds? There are several species that are on the feeders right now, plus some migrating through."

"Actually, these are birds you see around the water. I took my kayak out in the bay the other day and saw some I'd like to read about."

"Oh, waterfowl. Sure, we have plenty around here—herons, gulls, osprey. Just a minute, I'll go get one of the books we have about them." Jep strode away, leaving me and Tilly at the front counter.

"So you like to kayak?" Tilly asked.

"I do. I'm relatively new at it, but I enjoy it when the water's calm."

"Jep used to kayak too. Maybe he can show you around sometime."

Tilly was quite the matchmaker. Jep was certainly attractive, but I wasn't ready for another relationship anytime soon.

Tilly shook her head. "Poor Jep. Too bad Bunny had to drop dead in his store. He's had enough to deal with since his wife disappeared."

CHAPTER 3

The next day, I returned to my shop, still mulling over the events of the previous day and really curious about the disappearance of Jep's wife. I placed a sign in the window that read LOOKING FOR LOCAL ARTISTS then crossed my arms to gaze around the square. Nellie's Needles wasn't open yet, but Del's Donuts had a steady stream of customers going in and out. Donuts weren't on my self-imposed no-carb diet, but the thought of fresh donuts made me forget diet and propelled my feet over to the shop.

When I stepped inside, the sweet aroma of sugar assaulted my sense of smell, and the list of donut varieties made my mouth water. Immediately, I was transported back in time to my childhood. On Sunday mornings, Daddy would say, "If you hurry up and get dressed, you can help me pick out the donuts before we go to church." That was motivation enough, so Daddy and I went to the donut shop while Mother finished getting dressed. Daddy let me pick out whatever I wanted, so I chose all the pretty donuts, knowing if it were up to him, they'd all be plain, heaven forbid.

"Can I help you?" A woman's voice interrupted my memories. Startled, I glanced at the person behind the glass counter. Short, curly red hair framed her round, pleasant face.

"Oh, I'm sorry. I just got lost in all the varieties."

"You're the new lady who's opening the artsy store, aren't you? I'm Kay Dean Hamner. My husband Del and I run this place." She glanced over her shoulder at the man in the kitchen behind her, visible through a little window in the wall. Hearing his name, Del looked up and nodded. "This is our retirement home." Kay Dean gave a wry smile, lifting her eyebrows.

"Nice to meet you. I'm Kelly Stephens, and yes, I'm opening Artistic Adventures."

Wearing a white apron, Del stepped through the door carrying a tray of donuts. He crossed to the display case and opened the door to slide the tray inside. "Hi, Kelly. Kay Dean told me she heard you were at the bookstore when Bunny Wilson keeled over."

I nodded. "Yes, I'm afraid I was. What a terrible thing. I wonder if they've figured out what killed her."

"Not that I heard of. Too bad it happened at Jep's place. Poor guy, he doesn't need another investigation," Del said.

Before I could ask about what other investigations Jep had been involved in, Kay Dean spoke. "Bunny had come in earlier and gotten her usual daily donuts." She shook her head then focused on me. "What can I get you, honey?"

So Bunny liked donuts too. Guess she wasn't that much of a fitness freak. "I can't decide whether to get a lemon-filled or a chocolate covered."

"Oh, get them both. It's on the house, since you're new to town and all."

This place was going to be my downfall and the possible cause for a size up in clothes.

As Kay Dean wrapped the donuts and put them in a bag, I asked, "Another investigation?"

Del, a bigger version of his wife but with less hair, answered. "Oh, that's right. You weren't here when all that happened. When

Jep's wife disappeared, a lot of people suspected him of killing her and burning down his house to cover it up."

"Oh my. How awful."

"Yeah, that house was magnificent. A mansion right on the water too. You know, he comes from old money around here."

No, I didn't know. But my first impression of Jep had not been someone who was wealthy. He was way too low-key and humble, in my opinion. Of course, I didn't really know him.

"So did they find out who killed her?"

"No. Well, they never found her body. Wasn't in the ashes of the house. And I don't think Jep would've burned down the house. He'd built it for her dream house, but she was a big-city girl and was bored with our small town, people heard her say."

"So Jep wasn't charged with anything?"

"Nope. No proof."

I hid my relief, although I didn't know why I felt relieved to know Jep wasn't guilty.

Kay Dean handed me my donuts. "You want some coffee to go with those? We have some."

"Sure. That'd be great. Can you make a vanilla latte?" That had been my go-to in Atlanta, but I didn't want to appear too citified, a possible detriment to my reception here.

"Will do!" Kay Dean prepared the latte with vanilla flavoring and milk, added coffee from the brewer, then poured it into a disposable cup and put a lid on it. She picked up a couple of sugar packets. "Need extra sugar?"

"No, thanks."

Kay Dean handed me the cup. "Enjoy your donuts and coffee!"

"Thanks. I'm sure I will. Oh, and if you know any local artists, please send them my way."

"Actually, I think Belinda's cousin is an artist. I've seen some of her stuff, and it's pretty good."

"Belinda?"

"Belinda Collins. She runs Hair We Are, the hair salon."

"Okay, thanks. I'll go talk to her."

After taking my unhealthy breakfast back to the shop, I indulged myself, my eyes rolling back in my head as I tasted the sweet deliciousness of the donuts. I would need to fast the rest of the day to make up for it. I arranged a display of art supplies then decided to go to the hair salon and talk to Belinda about her cousin. I needed to get some local art in the shop.

The aroma of hair products hit me as I stepped inside Hair We Are. The salon's interior design was a colorful combination of children's pictures and frog knickknacks.

"Hi!" A little lady with a mass of black-and-green-tinted curls grinned at me as she stood behind an elderly woman sitting in the salon chair. "I'll be with you in a minute. Do you need an appointment, honey?"

I glanced in the mirror at my straight hair. Did I?

"Um, not today. I'm Kelly Stephens from Artistic Adventures, the new shop across the square."

"Oh, I've heard about you! Welcome to Bayside! I'm Belinda." She combed and snipped white hair from the woman in the chair. "This is Sadie Butler. Sadie's been my customer long as I've been here."

Sadie cut her eyes toward me instead of moving her head, and offered the hint of a smile.

"Nice to meet you ladies." I glanced around the room at the pictures pinned to a bulletin board or stuck on the mirror. "Are all of these your children?"

Belinda giggled. "Heavens, no! I don't have that many! Well, I did have six, but most of these are my grandchildren, nieces and nephews, and their kids. We have a pretty big family scattered all over the county."

"And you like frogs too, I see," I said, remarking on the frogs of different shapes, sizes, and materials adorning every available space.

"Can you tell? My customers have given me most of these since they know I collect frogs."

"Kay Dean at the donut shop told me you have a cousin who is an artist. I'm looking for local artists to display and sell their work, maybe even give some lessons in the shop."

"Ooh! Yes, my cousin Nita Sue is a fabulous artist! She did that picture over there of the frog. I'll call her today and tell her to come see you right away!" She lowered her voice, and her face drooped. "Oh, hon, I heard you were in the bookstore when Bunny passed. How awful!"

Apparently, everybody in town knew where I was yesterday at that time. "Yes, it was very sudden."

"My husband, Duke, he runs the car repair shop around the corner, he thinks Jep had something to do with it. But he also thinks Jep did away with his wife."

"I just met Jep, but it's hard to believe he would be guilty of something like that." Here I was, defending a man I barely knew.

"Oh, I don't think he killed Bunny. Besides, how would he have done it? It's not like she was stabbed or anything."

Thank goodness for that. I can't imagine what the scene would have been if that were true.

"So you think she died of natural causes?" I asked. "Her fiancé mentioned something about her getting over the flu. Maybe there was something wrong with her heart."

"Ha! How could it be her heart? The woman ran a gym! She taught classes and exercised like a maniac. I've seen her running up the hill on her way to work!"

"So you think someone killed her?" I hadn't considered Bunny had been murdered. I mean, I saw the whole thing. Didn't I? "Who do you think would have a motive?"

Belinda lowered her voice as if anyone besides the people in the shop could hear her. "I'll put my dibs on that fiancé. I've seen them arguing before. Plus, I think he was really jealous. He hated the way she flirted with other men."

"Enough to kill her?"

"You know how some people are. If they can't have them, nobody can!"

"But how. . .?"

Belinda shrugged. "You never know."

"Guess we won't know until the coroner's report comes back." I hated to end this delightful conversation, but I was actually pretty tired of all the conjecture. And accusations. "Well, I better get back to my shop. Please tell your cousin to contact me. Here's my number." I handed her my card and gave a cursory smile to Ms. Sadie.

Belinda studied my hand as she took my card. "Honey, you know we do nails here too. Looks like your nails could use some love."

Couldn't we all? But yes, my hands needed help. I picked at my cuticles all the time, and the nails had taken a beating from opening boxes. I wanted to hide them, but it was too late. "I'm sure you're right. Maybe after I get everything moved in and set up in the shop, I'll schedule a manicure."

"Sounds good." Belinda smiled as she returned to curling Sadie's hair with a curling iron. "And you should get those split ends cut off while you're here too."

Stepping outside of the salon, I turned and glanced at my reflection in the window and wondered just how badly I needed a cut. Turning back around, I paused to study the white concrete fountain in the middle of the square. At the top was a big fish standing on its tail and spouting water. Surrounding the pool below it were other concrete fish doing the same. Park benches on four sides faced the fountain.

"Right purty fountain, ain't it?"

I spun to find the origin of the voice and saw Mac standing nearby.

"Oh, hi. Mac, is it? Yes, it's a very interesting fountain."

"Yep, there was a lot of arguing about what we'd put in the middle of the square. Some people wanted local heroes, but we really didn't have any. Others suggested the city founders. Since they were Jep's relatives, he voted that down, saying they wouldn't want a statue of them. So since we're by the water and a fishing community, we decided to put fish in it. We used to have some real fish in the bottom, goldfish, you know. But the herons came and had a meal out of them, so we didn't put in any more."

The mention of herons reminded me of the book I'd gotten at the bookstore.

"So when are you going to come into my store?" Mac nodded in the opposite direction.

"You have a bait and tackle shop, right?"

"Yes, ma'am. Got everything you need to catch fish around here."

"I'm afraid I don't fish. But I do like to go kayaking."

"Well then, I might have something you need for that. You know, a lot of people fish from their kayaks. I've got nets, life vests, whistles, bait boxes—anything you need."

"I never considered fishing from a kayak. I'm afraid I'm not coordinated enough."

Mac grinned. "It does take a little practice. Some of the guys have the kind you pedal, so they don't have to worry about paddles getting in the way."

"Really? I've never heard of that." What else didn't I know about kayaking? "What would I need a whistle for?"

"You know, if you get lost or need help or something."

"Oh, I see." I sure hoped that wouldn't happen, but maybe I should get one for good measure. "I'm learning something new every day."

Movement across the square caught our attention. A woman jogged down the sidewalk toward Body Beautiful. She looked like she was trying to catch up with someone in front of the building.

Just outside the door, she grabbed the arm of Adam Miller, turning him to face her.

"I wonder what's going on there?" Mac said.

Where had I seen the woman before? I shielded my eyes to get a better look. When she flipped her long ponytail behind her, I realized it was Jennifer Tucker. Wonder what the hurry was about?

CHAPTER 4

I got up early the next morning so I could go kayaking before I went to the store. I really wanted to explore the place some more, plus I enjoyed the peaceful atmosphere out on the water. The night before, I'd studied the bird book and was eager to spot some of the birds in it. I wished I could bring my dog, Beau, with me. Golden retrievers like water, but I was afraid my seventy-pound dog would tip me over in the kayak. Besides, he was still too young to sit for long. Plus, he'd probably bark at all the birds and scare them away.

I drove to the boat ramp and slid my kayak out the back of my little truck. It felt good to be able to do something outdoorsy like this by myself. After spending most of my life in the city, I was ready to embrace this coastal scene. The sun was just coming up over the horizon as I climbed in the kayak and paddled away from the shore.

What a beautiful place. Birds were waking up and singing as I moved slowly along the shore and into the bayou, what the people here called a small bay off the larger one. On one side of the bayou was the undisturbed natural park, while on the opposite shore were homes, many that appeared to have been there for years with moss-dripping oaks surrounding them. Every house had a boat dock with a boat by it, and I was glad to get out on the water before all those boats stirred it up. In fact, I was right proud of myself for doing this on my own. I'd taken lessons in Destin when I bought the kayak and had only flipped once during them. But now that I got that fear out of the way, I felt like a pro. As long as there weren't any waves.

I wondered what Kyle would think. But why was I even thinking about him? I was done with him and didn't appreciate him invading my mental space again. But still, I bet he'd be shocked to see I could handle this by myself.

A shrill cry overhead made me look up. A rather large bird with a white underside circled above the water. I watched it soar in wide circles, then suddenly it flew down into the water, dipping its talons in and snagging a fish. The bird flapped its wings, lifting from the water with its prize, then flew to the top of a tall pine tree and settled on a large nest resting on a branch. Another adult bird perched on the edge of the nest began to tear the fish apart and feed it to the little bird head that popped up. What an awesome sight. Thinking back to the book, I decided the birds must be ospreys.

I inhaled the fresh air, loving everything about this place. Ahead I saw ripples in the water. What kind of creature made those? Fish, turtles, an alligator? Heaven forbid. I heard that in Florida, anywhere there's water, there's a gator. I shuddered at the thought. What if I fell out of my kayak and the gator got me? What if it bumped my kayak and made me tip over?

I was being silly. There were no gators around here. My attention shifted to fish jumping out of the water closer to shore. I wondered why they jumped. Were they trying to get away from something? *Stop it, Kelly! Get a grip!* Sometimes fish just jump for fun. At least that's what my grandpa used to say. He said they got tired of being underwater and wanted to get out sometimes and take a look around. Whether that was true or not, it sounded good to me.

I paddled along the park side of the bayou, observing the wildlife, then reached the place where the shoreline curved like a horseshoe and the houses began. Wouldn't it be wonderful to live beside the water like that and see this view every day? It was evident that this was the "high rent" district, with large, manicured lawns, palm trees, swimming pools, and shiny new boats.

I'd love to live in one of those houses, but I didn't see that happening. Not unless my store took off and made scads of money. Who was I kidding? I would be happy if I could make enough to pay my bills.

I paddled on, the wind blowing in my face and making it a little more difficult to manuever the kayak. After passing yards with nice lawns, I came to an area where the shoreline was just reeds. Maybe the land wasn't buildable in that spot. But something caught my eye, and I paddled closer to see what it was. A weathered gazebo with intricate carvings and a pagoda-like design was hidden among the tall reeds. I was amazed at its dilapidated condition, forgotten and taken over by the vegetation. Why would somebody let that happen? I mean, if they went to all that trouble to build a fancy gazebo, why let it go to ruin?

Had the previous owner died, leaving it to deteriorate afterward? But then, why wouldn't the property be sold so someone else could build on it? As I neared it to look closer, I spotted a big blue-gray bird sitting on the very top. My paddle splashed the water, and the bird took flight, squawking at me for bothering him.

"Sorry, buddy. Didn't mean to disturb you," I said to the bird, a heron, I thought.

I was tempted to sit in the gazebo, but I wasn't that adept at getting in and out of kayaks. So I paddled away, keeping my eye on the interesting structure and looking back beyond it to see if there was a house that might belong to it. But I couldn't see one. However, the land appeared to go uphill from the water, so I lifted my gaze to see if there was a house farther away. I gasped when

I saw two towering chimneys at the top of the hill but no house. The chimneys looked charred, as if they'd burned. So this was all that was left of the house?

Wow. That house must've been huge! I felt like I'd landed in the novel *Rebecca* and I was looking at the ruins of Manderley, a gothic mansion in England. Who had lived there? I determined I would find out. Maybe this place wasn't as peaceful as I thought. First, someone drops dead in the bookstore, then I run across a burned-down mansion and an abandoned gazebo. Thinking of the bookstore, I remembered what somebody said about Jep's first wife disappearing and his house burning down. Was this it? Still, I couldn't believe Jep had anything to do with that. Did he? I thought he was a nice guy, but I couldn't claim to be the best judge of character. Look at how my relationship with Kyle turned out.

But was Bunny killed, or did she have a heart attack? People were pointing fingers, but how did they know? Why did people want to suspect Jep? She sure had a lot of people who didn't like her. But dislike and murder are not the same thing. And now even I had a connection with her! One I didn't want and wished I didn't have. I didn't like her years ago, but I never gave her another thought after high school. Goodness, no. I was happy to leave high school drama behind.

But had I ever wished she was dead? Well, if I could be convicted by my thoughts from high school, I'd be in big trouble. I had shot many negative thoughts her direction. Good thing I wasn't on Facebook or Instagram back then. I wasn't the best at keeping my thoughts to myself. Not in high school, anyway. So why had Bunny acted happy to see me at the bookstore, coming to greet me when she died? I wasn't happy to see her.

Anything but. Here I was, trying to start a new life after leaving the corporate world and my failed relationship with Kyle behind, and out of the blue, my high school past slapped me right in the face. I hoped I didn't have to tell the police any more about our past.

Hearing a splash nearby, I jerked my head toward the water. A young man wearing jeans, a T-shirt, and a ball cap over shoulder-length hair stood in a small boat about twenty feet away. I watched as he pulled in a net and dumped some fish into a cooler. He looked up, saw me, and waved.

With his net in one hand, he tipped his cap to me with the other. "Morning."

"Good morning," I returned. "What kind of fish are you catching?"

"Mullet." He gathered his net then tossed it back out onto the water in a perfect circle. A minute later, he began drawing it toward himself. When it reached the boat, he lifted it out and dropped a few more fish into the cooler.

"Wow. I didn't realize you could catch such large fish with a net like that. I suppose that beats baiting a hook and catching one at a time." I hoped I didn't sound too stupid, since my fishing knowledge was pretty limited. In fact, the nets I was most familiar with were the kind they use in a pet store to scoop out fish for an aquarium.

"Cast-netting is the best way to catch mullet. They're pretty hard to catch with a rod."

"Oh." A large fish jumped nearby, hurling itself through the air and slapping the water as it landed. "Is that a mullet?"

He grinned. "Sure is. You're new around here, aren't you?"

How could he tell? "Guess that's pretty obvious. I'm Kelly Stephens, and I just moved here. I'm opening Artistic Adventures up on the square."

He cocked his head. "Oh yeah, I saw something new going in there. I'm Lucas Jones. Lived here all my life."

So he must know about the gazebo and the ruins.

"Nice to meet you, Lucas. Do you fish for a living?"

"Pretty much. I sell these to the local market and seafood restaurant."

"I noticed that old gazebo back there in the reeds. Do you know anything about it? It looks abandoned, and I didn't see a house near it."

He nodded as he threw the net out again. "Yeah. A rich dude in town owns all that property." He waved a free hand in the direction of the gazebo. "Some woman got killed there, and the guy let the place go to pot."

I glanced in that direction. "And those chimneys up on the hill? Looks like there was a fire."

"Oh yeah, that's part of his cover-up, everybody says. They say he killed his wife and then burned down the house to get rid of evidence."

He had to be talking about Jep. I sure wanted to find out more about Jep's story. I glanced at the fitness tracker on my wrist and realized I'd been out an hour already. I needed to go to work if I was going to make it as an entrepreneur. Although it was still early, I couldn't afford to waste any more time away from the store.

I waved goodbye to Lucas and headed back to the boat launch. Maybe I would take up fishing someday, but not with a net. How on earth did Lucas stay balanced standing in the boat and throwing a net?

As I loaded the kayak in the truck, my mind flashed back to the way Bunny went down at the bookstore. She grabbed her throat before she fell. If she'd had a heart attack, she wouldn't grab her throat, would she? *Wonder when they'll have the autopsy report?* And why did people always jump to the most negative conclusions? *Ouch.* I've had my fair share of those.

It was time for a new start with new friends. Jep kept coming to mind. He intrigued me and seemed like a nice guy—the mild-mannered, get-along-with-everyone kind of guy. Even if he did come from money, he didn't act like it.

CHAPTER 5

After leaving the bayou, I went home and changed into jeans, a T-shirt, and tennis shoes, fed Beau, and walked him around the block. Why couldn't I take him to the store with me? I was the boss after all.

I carried some artwork I'd already procured for the store to the truck and put it in the back then covered it with a blanket. Then I told Beau to get in the front seat, which he energetically did. He might be disappointed when he discovered we weren't going to the woods where he could run but to a store where he would be cooped up all day. But I thought he'd rather be cooped up with me than left alone at the townhouse. Dogs are unconditional love personified. Too bad people aren't like that.

I backed into a parking place in front of the store then got out to unlock the door. Of course, I could've parked behind the store, but this way, people would notice something was going on and maybe it would generate future business. After I opened the door, I carried the artwork in and propped it against a wall. Beau barked to remind me I'd left him in the truck, so I went to fetch him before he annoyed someone or summoned animal welfare. After clipping his leash to his collar, I led him out. I glanced around to see who else was out and about and which stores were open. Feeling eyes on me, I looked toward the bookstore and, sure enough, Tilly was watching me, taking mental notes, no doubt. I waved and smiled, and she returned the gesture.

About that time, Jep walked in the door of the bookstore. Seeing Tilly's focus on me, he turned around, left the store, and came over. My heart did a little happy dance for some unknown reason. Okay, he was really good-looking, and I welcomed the attention.

"Handsome dog," he said, leaning over to pet Beau, who instantly claimed Jep as his new best friend. Tail wagging, Beau lifted his paw to put on Jep's arm. I held him back to keep him from jumping up and kissing the man like he wanted to. Not a bad idea, actually. *Oh stop, Kelly.*

"Thank you. Sorry, he's a bit overly friendly," I said.

"No problem. One of the things I like about dogs is their unprejudiced way of liking people."

"I agree, but he only likes nice people." Did I say that? But really, it was true. Beau barked or growled at suspicious characters. But Jep liked dogs? Another stroke in his favor. "Do you have a dog?"

Jep continued to pet Beau, who now sat on the man's feet and leaned against his legs.

"Not now. My old dog, Swimmer, passed away last year, and I haven't been ready to get another dog. He was a red-coated golden retriever, not pale blond like this one. What's this guy's name?"

"Beau. He's three years old, so just about to leave the puppy stage. I thought he'd like to come to work with me instead of being left at home."

"Good idea. He'll probably be deluged with affection. Everybody loves dogs here."

Another reason to like this town. I glanced up and saw Tilly waving. "I think Tilly's trying to get your attention."

He turned and saw her. "Excuse me, please. I'll come back later."

I didn't want to stare after him, but he did say he'd be back. So, if I went inside the store, would that send a message that I didn't want to talk to him anymore? I waited a few minutes, looking elsewhere while Beau strained at the leash to follow Jep.

"Not now, Beau. Maybe later, if you're a good dog, you can go visit." Beau looked at me as only a golden can, with tilted head and quizzical eyes, like he was trying to figure out what I said. He wagged his tail as if to say, "Okay, Mom!"

Jep returned a few minutes later, his expression more serious than before. "The coroner's report came back." He paused, frowning. "The police chief said it looked like a heart attack but also showed signs of upper airway edema, which is a swollen throat that can lead to asphyxiation and can cause a heart attack."

"I don't get it. Did she have a heart attack or was she asphyxiated?" I told Beau to sit.

Jep shook his head. "The chief said it looks like she may have had an allergic reaction to something that brought on the other symptoms."

"Allergic reaction? To what?" I became aware of people watching us. "Let's go inside my store and talk." I nodded toward the door. "Come, Beau." We went inside but didn't flip on the lights because it seemed bright enough with sunlight coming in the front windows. "Sorry, I don't have a place to offer you to sit."

Jep shook off my apology then continued talking about Bunny.

"I wasn't aware of any allergies she had," he said. "Of course, I didn't know her that well, but I don't remember her ever mentioning it. Tilly might know if she had."

"I was thinking just this morning that she grabbed her throat before she fell. So that would confirm an allergic reaction, I think. I wonder if her fiancé knows of any allergies she had."

"You would think so, wouldn't you?"

Seemed to me Jep didn't think too highly of the fiancé, maybe even doubting the relationship.

"Yes, you would. I guess he's been told?" No doubt the police would've called Adam Miller first since he was going to marry Bunny.

"Probably. The chief called me since it happened in my store. Then I assume he'd call the next of kin, although I'm not sure who that is. I don't think she had any relatives here in town."

"So, I guess this clears you of suspicion, since she died a natural death." I watched Jep to see if he was relieved.

"Yes, it does. I just wonder what might be in my store that she would be allergic to?"

I was thinking the same thing. "She came in pretty regularly?" He nodded.

"Have you changed anything or added anything new?" Maybe he had inadvertently exposed Bunny to an allergen.

He shook his head. "No, just some new books."

I raised my finger, and he said, "And no, the book she had in her hands was not new. We've had it for years."

"Just curious. What was the book?"

He smirked. "*How to Win Friends and Influence People.*"

My eyes widened as I exercised great restraint to keep from bursting out laughing. I wanted to ask if she had read it before, but I kept my mouth shut. I glanced away to avoid eye contact, crossing my arms across my chest to hold in the giggles. This was not a laughing matter, for Pete's sake. Someone had died.

Seeing work I needed to do, I said, "Well, I guess I better start getting this place in order so I can open it for business."

He took the hint. "Right. Sorry to hold you up. I thought you might like to know about Bunny, though, since you were there when it happened. I'll leave you to it. See you later."

He smiled and left the store before I turned around and faced Beau. "Well, Beau, what new surprises await us now?"

Beau was doing an inspection of the store, sniffing everything in sight. I had brought his water bowl, so I filled it from the sink in the bathroom and set it out of the way. He slurped it up appreciatively.

Behind me, the front door opened, and footsteps sounded on the concrete floor. I turned around to see who it was. A young lady with unnaturally vibrant red hair falling across her shoulders stood there with a shy smile. She wore a white T-shirt with something like graffiti on it and jeans that had more holes than fabric.

"Um, hi," she said shyly in a soft voice. "I'm Nita Sue, Belinda's cousin. She told me to come see you and show you my art."

"Oh yes!" Belinda moved fast. I strode forward to greet her with a welcoming smile, eager to see her work. "I saw your frog picture at Hair We Are. It's quite good. What else do you have?" I looked down at the large portfolio she carried. "Come set it down over here." I motioned to a large, pub-height wooden table.

She opened the portfolio, took out a handful of watercolor pictures, and spread them out. They were very nicely done and rather whimsical in a rainbow of colors.

"These are great!" I said, eyeing each one. "Are these all you have?"

"No, ma'am. I have lots more at home. These are just my biggest. I have some small ones also."

"Well, I'd love to see those too. We can definitely display them here in the store. Do you have any idea what you'd like to charge for them?"

She shook her head. "No, ma'am. I never sold any before."

"Okay, well let me think about it, and I'll come up with some prices. I'll take these on consignment and pay you half of whatever price they sell for. Okay?"

"Yes, ma'am. I'll bring more tomorrow."

"Great! I'll get a contract ready so everything's on the up and up." I made a mental note to bring my computer and printer from home.

"Yes, ma'am." She looked down at Beau, who had come over to check her and her paintings out. Something intriguing smelled good on her shoes, apparently. "Does he bite?"

"No, he's cool. But he sure is interested in your feet."

"Must be my chickens, Mable and Bitty. They're my pets."

"Oh, no wonder he's interested. I don't think he's ever met chickens before."

"May I pet him?"

"Sure."

She put a tentative hand on Beau's head and barely patted him. He sniffed her hand as if trying to decide whether it smelled like her feet or not. His tail wagged slowly, as though he wasn't sure.

Nita Sue looked up at me. "I heard you saw Miss Bunny die."

Hmm. That was one way to put it, but not preferable. "Yes, I was there."

She showed the saddest face as she cast her gaze down, and in a quiet yet angry voice, said, "She killed one of my chickens. Ran over it with her car." Then she looked up at me with interest. "How did she die? Was it horrible?"

I felt like she thought I'd witnessed a terrible car wreck and wanted details. "Shocking more than anything else. She just fell over."

"I'm sorry to hear that." I got the feeling that not only was Nita Sue not sad to know Bunny died, but that she was sorry her death wasn't more horrific.

Apparently grief-stricken over the loss of her chicken, she turned to leave, seeming to be disappointed that I didn't have more gore to share about Bunny's death.

"Bye," I said. "See you tomorrow."

When Nita Sue left the store, I exhaled. She was a strange one, for sure, her bitterness toward Bunny surprising. But at least her artwork was good, and I now had something to display in the store. I'd have to rummage through my collection of frames and get to work mounting these to hang on the walls. My stomach rumbled, and I remembered I hadn't had anything to eat yet, since I got out early to go kayaking. The memory of the gazebo and the ruins came to mind. Should I ask Jep about them? I wanted to, but I didn't want to. How would he take it if I asked questions about his property, considering the suspicions surrounding it?

I was sure I could ask Tilly, but was now a good time? Actually, I wanted a cup of coffee. I'd need to bring my coffeemaker from home. Or I could go to the bookstore like everybody else. Or the donut shop. But I really shouldn't eat a donut every day. Then a thought reverberated through my brain. Kay Dean had said Bunny ate a donut there daily. Did Kay Dean know about Bunny's allergies? I decided to lock up for a short break and go have a donut and coffee. Maybe they had a healthy whole-wheat one, although those were not the kind I usually craved. I hoped they wouldn't mind if I brought Beau.

Putting Beau on the leash, I went out, locking the door behind me, then strode down the block to Del's Donuts. Peeking my head in, I said, "Hi. I've got my dog and better not bring him in, but I wanted to get a donut and coffee. Okay?"

Kay Dean grinned. "Sure, hon! What do you want? I'll bring it to you. Board of Health won't let us have critters in here."

"I figured. Have you got anything healthy, whole wheat or something?"

"How about a carrot cake doughnut?"

Carrots were healthy, weren't they? "With cream cheese frosting?"

Kay Dean nodded. "Of course."

Even better. I'd get dairy too. My mouth watered as I said, "That sounds wonderful."

"Be right out with it. Coffee too?"

"Yes, please."

I parked myself at one of the little round tables outside the shop. A couple of minutes later, Kay Dean came out with my food and handed it to me. "Brought a little doggie doughnut for your friend too, if it's okay."

"Sure. This is Beau."

"Here you go, Beau." She handed a doggie treat to Beau, who snapped it up. Then she sat down on the other chair at the table with a cup of coffee for herself. "Guess you heard about the autopsy report."

How had she heard that so soon? News traveled at warp speed in this little town.

"Yes, I did. But I'm not sure what it means. Do you think she had an allergic reaction to something?" I took a bite of the carrot cake doughnut and moaned with pleasure.

"She could have. She asked us if we used peanut oil or put peanuts on any of our donuts, because she was allergic to them. A lot of food establishments use peanut oil to fry things in, you know. We told her we didn't and wouldn't because many people are allergic to peanuts. She asked what other ingredients we used too, saying she was very allergic to avocados as well, but we wouldn't make avocado donuts. Yuck! Can you imagine?"

"You mentioned before that she got donuts the morning she died."

Kay Dean's eyes widened. "Why yes, but they were her usual ones, chocolate iced and cream-filled. Those never caused her a problem before. I hope no one thinks one of our donuts caused her reaction."

"Maybe it wasn't food. Maybe it was some other kind of allergy, like an insect bite or sting. Spiders?"

"Hmm. That could be a possibility, but it seems like they would've found it during the autopsy," Kay Dean said, her elbows resting on the table.

"Well, at least it was a natural death, so Jep can't be accused of killing her." For some reason, I wanted to make sure everyone knew that.

She sipped her coffee. "Yes, I'm thankful for that. Poor guy."

I leaned forward. "Kay Dean, I wonder if you can tell me something."

"Sure. What do you need to know?"

I told her about my kayak trip, what I saw, and what Lucas Jones told me. "Was that Jep's property I saw?"

She nodded. " 'Fraid so. It used to be beautiful. Too bad it's in the condition it's in."

"So Lucas told me people thought Jep's wife was murdered and he set the house on fire to cover it up."

She shook her head. "Yeah, that nonsense story has been going on around here for years, ten in fact, since she disappeared."

"So she really didn't die?" For some reason, I was relieved to hear that.

"No one knows what happened to her. Her body never showed up."

Did the woman disappear into thin air?

Kay Dean continued, "We think she ran off with another man. She hated Bayside."

"So if Jep didn't start the fire, who did?"

"Lightning. It just happened to coincide with her disappearance. Frankly, we were glad to see her gone. She was snooty to all the locals."

"And Jep? Was he glad to see her go?"

"No, I don't think so. Even though she made his life miserable. First he built the mansion for her, then the special gazebo, but she was never satisfied. I know he loved her, though, so it must've hurt when she disappeared. And losing the house too. And then, on top of that, he was accused of killing her and setting the fire himself."

"That hardly seems fair. I wonder why he never rebuilt?"

371

She shook her head. "He just locked the gates and walked away. He lives in a little old craftsman cottage he bought from a fisherman over on the bayou, but not near his old house."

I pictured him in that big house all alone. And even though there was an answer to the cause of the fire, people still liked to gossip. He didn't even have his dog anymore. I sure wished I could do something to cheer him up, but it seemed that he just attracted bad luck. And I sure didn't need anyone else's problems. Why did I want to fix things for him? That was how I got into the disastrous relationship with Kyle.

A thought suddenly occurred to me. If Bunny knew she had allergies, wouldn't she carry an EpiPen? I remembered seeing her look in her little phone purse. There certainly wasn't any room on her clothes to put anything in. I wondered if the police checked the purse. If I knew I had allergies like that, I'd certainly carry an EpiPen. My friend Shannon in Atlanta was very allergic to peanuts, so she always carried an EpiPen in case she came in contact with food that had been near peanuts. So why wouldn't Bunny have one?

CHAPTER 6

Just to be nosy, I decided to go to the gym and check it out. I didn't have a lot of time to waste, but I really needed to know about the allergy Bunny had. I headed that direction then remembered I had Beau with me and wouldn't be able to take him inside.

I stopped outside the glass windows and looked in at the equipment where hopeful individuals ran on treadmills or lifted weights. Adam Miller stood behind a counter in the front of the store, looking at a computer screen. He was buff enough to be on the cover of a fitness magazine, and definitely good-looking, but a little too narcissistic, in my humble opinion. He glanced up, and seeing me standing there, staring at him no less, gave me a sparkling-white toothy smile.

I smiled back, but my face warmed from embarrassment from being caught looking at him. He probably thought I was admiring him instead of studying him, which was my real reason. He motioned for me to come in, but I pointed down at Beau and shrugged. He spotted my dog then came around the counter and out the door.

"Hey! I'm Adam." He extended his hand, and I shook it. "Nice dog."

"Thanks."

"You new in town? I don't think we've met." He obviously hadn't noticed me at the bookstore.

"Yes, I moved here recently. I'm opening Artistic Adventures over there." I motioned with my head toward my store. "I thought I'd check out your gym, but I forgot I had the dog with me. But from what I can see, it looks very nice."

"Sure. Well, come in when you can. We've got a great deal on a new membership."

He sure was happy for someone who just lost his fiancée.

"Thanks, I will." As I turned to leave, a man stopped and said, "Hey, Adam. Sorry to hear about Bunny."

Adam's face changed so radically, it was like seeing a chameleon change colors from green plants to brown wood. His mouth drooped, his eyes lowered, and even his chest deflated. If he wasn't grieving, he was a pretty good actor.

"Thank you. It's still quite a shock."

The man walked on, and Adam lifted his gaze to me. "My business partner died suddenly yesterday. Heart attack."

Business partner and not fiancée? "I'm sorry," I said. Sounded to me like he wasn't that close to her. And heart attack? Guess that was simpler than explaining an allergic reaction. This wasn't the time to interrogate him about Bunny. But I really wanted to know if he knew what her allergies were and if she carried an EpiPen.

Beau and I walked back to the store, where a stack of packages waited by the front door. I shouldn't have been gone that long. I missed the delivery man and didn't have a chance to check the merchandise to see if it was what I ordered. I unlocked the door and let Beau walk in then grabbed the top two boxes, pushing the two underneath inside the door with my foot as I entered.

After finding some scissors, I cut the tape then tore the boxes open. The largest box was a table I needed to assemble. The smaller ones were display racks and stands of different sizes. I plopped down on the floor and tried to figure out the instructions to put the table together. Unfortunately, I didn't read Chinese, so I had to study the pictures, wishing I had someone to help me. I wasn't mechanically inclined, but I wasn't helpless either. Surely I could do this.

While I worked to assemble the thing, I didn't hear anyone come in until Tilly's voice rang out, and I jumped through my skin. I was going to have to put a bell on my door too.

"I didn't mean to surprise you, Kelly. I took a break and came to see how it's going."

It was going well enough until she startled me like that. I gave her a wry smile as I looked up from the floor. "It's getting there, soon as I figure this thing out."

"You need a man to help you."

I bristled at her remark. "I've almost got it now." No, I did not need a man. Now I was more determined than ever to put this thing together. I thought about men like Adam Miller and his reaction when offered sympathy. I almost felt sorry for Bunny, if her so-called fiancé could be so romantically detached.

"Tilly, I'm sorry I don't have any chairs for you to sit on. I need to remember to bring some from my townhouse."

"That's okay. I'm not staying long." She glanced at the table where Nita Sue's paintings lay. "I see Belinda's cousin has been to see you."

"Yes, she has. I like her stuff. I'm going to frame some of it and sell it."

"She's a strange one, if you ask me."

I didn't, but I sort of agreed. "She's unique, but I didn't talk to her that much."

"Her family's bayou people."

"Isn't everyone around here?"

"No, we're not. I mean back bayou people, you know, more country and less citified."

I did not wish to engage in this conversation, so I asked her about Bunny. "Tilly, apparently Bunny had an allergic reaction to something. Were you aware of her allergies?"

"Oh yes, she told me about them. Carried one of those pens with her everywhere in case she had an attack."

"She did? I didn't see one. Where did she keep it?"

"In that little phone purse thing she wore."

"Yeah, I remember her looking in it before she stood up. But she didn't take anything out. Do you know if the police took the purse?"

"Probably. I didn't notice."

"But if she had it with her, wouldn't she have used it?"

Tilly frowned. "Maybe the reaction came on too fast for her to get it."

"Maybe." Or maybe she couldn't find the pen when she looked for it. I needed to ask the police, but how could I without calling unwanted attention to myself? But what if someone removed the EpiPen from the bag? In that case, we'd be looking at murder. But who would've done that? Who had the opportunity when Bunny wasn't wearing it?

My suspicions ran back to Adam Miller. Surely he had the opportunity, if he was close enough to her. It had to have happened that morning, so where had she been?

I ruled out the donuts. I didn't know Del and Kay Dean at all, but I doubted they'd do something as hateful as putting one of Bunny's allergens in the donuts. What would they have to gain by doing that? And how would they get the EpiPen from her?

After going to Del's, Bunny went to the bookstore, got a book, drank coffee, then died. Could something have been put in her coffee? But if there was, wouldn't Mac have mentioned it tasting odd? Besides, Jep had just made the coffee in front of everyone in the store. So what else could've set off the reaction? Where else did she go?

"Well, I guess I better get back to work." Tilly glanced over toward the bookstore. "Oh, I wanted to tell you there's going to be a craft show over on Navarre Beach this weekend if you'd like to go check out the artists there. Might find something you'd like to sell in your shop."

"That sounds great. Thanks, Tilly. Are you going to sell your bookmarks at the show?"

"I thought about it but didn't want to spend the money for a booth. I'd have to sell a lot of bookmarks to make it worth the investment."

"Where do I find the address?" I didn't even know where Navarre was.

"Just look up Navarre Crafts Show online, and you'll find it."

"I will." Should I ask her? "Tilly, would you like to go with me?"

A slight smile crossed her face. "Sure. My sister Nellie would go with me, but she has to stay and mind the store."

Nellie? Oh, Nellie of Nellie's Needles, of course. I glanced down at Beau. "Do you mind if I bring Beau along?"

"No, he seems well behaved."

"Then great! Give me your phone number and address, and I'll pick you up Saturday morning." I paused. "Will Jep let you off?"

She chuckled. "I make my own hours, so I'll take off Saturday. He can handle the sales by himself."

I smiled, thinking how much Tilly reminded me of my grandmother.

"But we need to leave early. It'll take an hour to get there, and we want to beat the beach crowd and find a good parking place," Tilly added.

"Of course. What's early? Seven o'clock?" Early was relative, of course. I was guessing.

"Not that early. The show probably opens at nine. How about seven thirty, to be safe."

I was close.

"Okay. Seven thirty then."

Tilly left the store while I thought about the craft show. I definitely wanted to go. I hadn't planned on hanging out with Tilly, but I thought she wanted to go and not by herself. Besides, she seemed to know everything and everybody in town and would be a good source of information.

I was getting frustrated with the table, so I decided to work on the display racks instead. A few minutes later, Jep came in the door, carrying two folding chairs. "Thought you could use these."

"Did Tilly make you do this?"

He laughed and shook his head. "She strongly suggested it. But really, I don't need them. They were just taking up space in the back room." He set the chairs up near me then eyed the abandoned table. "Can I help you with that?"

I shrugged. "If you can read Chinese, go for it."

Jep laughed, lighting his face in a very nice way. "I've put one of these together before, so it should be easy."

He set to work on the table while I continued to work on the display racks. I was dying to ask him about what Lucas and Kay Dean had told me. "I went kayaking this morning."

"You did? I haven't done that for a while. Where did you go?"

"In the bayou with the park on one side."

He nodded, focused on the table. "How was it?"

"Really nice and calm. I loved looking at the scenery." I wondered if he did too.

"So did you recognize any birds from your bird book?"

"I did. I saw an osprey land in the water and grab a fish. That was pretty cool."

"Yeah, I like watching ospreys too."

Well, we had that in common. "And I saw one of those big grayish-blue birds, a heron, I think. It was on top of an old gazebo in the reeds."

I watched him for a response, but none came. He picked up the table and stood it on its legs. "There. That should do. Where do you want it?"

"Just leave it there for now. Thank you. You know, it was such a cool gazebo. I'm surprised the owner let it get grown over like it is." Okay, I'd given him a chance to fess up if it was his property.

He shrugged. "Guess the owner doesn't think it's important. Or maybe he forgot about it."

Why wouldn't he take the bait and admit it was his property? I should've asked Tilly.

"That's too bad. I was tempted to get out of the kayak and explore it, but I was afraid my balance wasn't that good. Or maybe I would get shot as a trespasser if I did?"

Jep quirked an eyebrow. "I doubt that would happen."

Well, so much for that. I figured I shouldn't mention the chimneys.

"Maybe someday I'll get a place on the water. I couldn't find anything that fit my budget now, so I found a townhouse a few blocks from it. At least the water isn't far away, wherever you are in this town."

He nodded. "One of the perks of living here. I live on the water in a little fisherman's cottage. Maybe you can find something like that sometime, although I have to say, people who live on the water usually don't move. Unless a hurricane comes and wipes the place out. But that doesn't happen very often here. If a storm hits here, we get some damage, but not like they do over at the beach, where they get the full force of it."

So the man owned property on the water, a large chunk of land actually, but didn't use it. Or sell it. He obviously didn't need the money. Or maybe he was still sentimentally connected to it. But he didn't seem to want to volunteer any more info about it, so I let it rest. He must have really wanted to leave the past behind. I didn't blame him for that. I wondered again what really happened to his wife. As much as I wanted to know, I couldn't ask him about that either.

"Oh, Tilly told me she knew about Bunny's allergies and that she carried an EpiPen in case she felt a reaction coming on."

"She did? Well, that's news to me. I didn't talk to her much." Jep glanced back toward the bookstore like he was looking for an exit. "Well, she couldn't have been allergic to the coffee, since she drank it at the store on a regular basis."

"Unless you changed brands?"

He frowned at me like I was accusing him. "I didn't."

Trying to create some levity, I said, "And apparently she wasn't allergic to books either."

Jep studied me a moment, either thinking about my comment or wondering why I made it.

"Well, I'll leave you to your work. See you later." He turned to go.

"Thank you for the chairs. And for putting the table together."

He smiled and waved as he left.

I sure struck out as a detective. I knew absolutely nothing more than I had when he came in. He couldn't possibly be a killer. What would be his motive anyway? To get rid of a curvaceous customer? That was doubtful. Most men appreciated a beautiful woman's appearance even if they didn't like her personality. So he didn't know about Bunny's allergies, but Tilly did. Tilly didn't like her, but would she go so far as to kill her? I couldn't see Tilly doing that either.

Who else was in the bookstore when it happened? My memory sparked, and I remembered Mac. He didn't like Bunny, but did he dislike her enough to kill her? He certainly was in the vicinity. Could he have put something in Bunny's coffee? Certainly not while she sat next to him. But what if he put something in her mug? I remembered Tilly saying the pink mug was Bunny's. So maybe he walked by the shelves of mugs and slipped something in, knowing she'd be coming in the store soon. But what about the EpiPen? How would he have taken that out of her purse?

The display racks finished, I scanned the room to see where to put them. A few that would hold larger displays could stand on the floor. The others would be on the table until I found something else to put them on. I needed more furniture; even something old would do to display artwork on. A visit to the local thrift store was in order.

"Come on, Beau. Let's go get something to eat, then I'll take you home."

Beau's ears perked up at the mention of his name, and he stood, looking at me with those expressive brown eyes. Although I tried to stay away from fast food, I'd heard the local burger joint was good and cheap, so I drove through and picked up my lunch, giving Beau a french fry on the way home. Sometimes I just couldn't resist those eyes. I dropped him off at home then drove to the thrift store I'd passed by on the way to the square.

The store was a repository of garage sale items. The owners were probably the people who arrived at the sales before they were open. I remembered when that happened in Atlanta and I had a garage sale before I moved. People were parked out front and walking around the driveway before I'd even gotten dressed. It was creepy. Some of the things were in my garage, and opening the door to it was like inviting strangers into my house. If I ever decided to have another one of those events, I wouldn't do it alone.

I strolled the crowded aisles, examining things while wondering who had owned them before and why they parted with them. My habit of creating a story to go with each piece was sometimes a distraction to what I was doing. I could even bring tears to my eyes as I imagined someone having to say goodbye to a family heirloom. All right, I was a little loony. I spied an old hutch that was scratched up, one door hanging crooked. It would be perfect.

All I had to do was sand it a little, rehang the door, and if I wanted to, paint it someday.

No one would come into my shop looking for furniture unless I found a local woodcrafter who made some unusual handmade furniture. They'd be looking at what was displayed on the hutch, not the hutch itself. I spotted a farmer's table that had remnants of old paint on it, but that added to its shabbiness, something a lot of people would want and perfect for the things I'd be displaying. Near the table were two old wooden chairs, so I nabbed them too. That was about all I could fit in the truck, so I haggled with the man who owned the stuff then bought it for what I thought was a fair price.

With his wife's nagging, he helped me load the items into my truck. I thanked them, promising to come back another time and inviting them to visit my store. I probably would need to come back, but I'd be surprised if they came to my store. I wasn't going to give my merchandise away.

I hauled the furniture to my store, backing in before I unlocked the door. How I was going to move that hutch, I had no idea. I really didn't want to ask anyone, especially Jep, who had already done enough favors for me. I resented being a weak female, but I didn't even have another female to help me. I lowered the tailgate then grabbed a chair under each arm. I made it to the entrance with only slight difficulty and set them down to unlock the door. The table was going to be a bit tricky.

"Hey. Can I help you with that?"

I glanced behind me and saw Lucas, the mullet fisherman.

"That would be great. Thanks."

I stepped aside, and he climbed up into the truck. He lifted the table then carried it to the back edge of the tailgate and set it down. I reached to help him with it, but he hopped down and said, "I've got this."

Moving out of his way, I watched him hoist the table over his head and carry it to my door. There, he lowered it carefully then maneuvered it inside while I held the door open. I set the chairs inside before returning to the truck. The hutch would be a bigger challenge. We stared at it for a few minutes, trying to figure the best way to get it out of the truck.

"I think we can just tip it on its side and carry it in that way. I'll get the front end if you can get the back," Lucas said.

"Sure." That was how the thrift store manager and I got it into the truck in the first place. He climbed back into the truck. As I waited for him to position the hutch, another voice spoke over my shoulder.

"Let me help with that, Lucas," Jep said.

Lucas glanced at him, and a look of disapproval crossed his face before he shrugged. "Sure, Jep."

I got the distinct impression the two men didn't like each other. Based on what Lucas told me about the "rich dude," he must've been referring to Jep and didn't have much respect for him. The two finagled the hutch inside the store.

"Where do you want it?" Lucas said.

"Over there." I pointed. "I need to clean it up before I can use it."

Jep helped him move it, then they moved the table as well.

"Thank you, gentlemen," I said.

Casting a brief glance at Jep, Lucas said, "No problem." He acted as though he might want to hang around longer but didn't seem to want Jep's company. He stepped toward the door. "See ya around. Let me know if you need any more help."

"Thank you, Lucas," I said.

After he left, I looked at Jep. "You keep turning up to help me out. I'm beginning to feel a bit codependent."

"You can thank Tilly for keeping me informed about what's going on outside the store. However, I welcome the excuse to get some fresh air. It can get a bit stuffy in the bookstore."

"Well, tell Tilly thank you too."

"You know Lucas?" Jep asked.

Surprised at his question, I said, "Yes, I met him when I was kayaking and he was fishing for mullet. He was near that gazebo I asked you about."

Jep frowned. "Is that right?"

"Yes, why?"

He shrugged. "No reason in particular."

CHAPTER 7

The rest of the week I spent cleaning furniture and setting up displays. Some merchandise I'd ordered from other craftspeople arrived, and I placed it in the store. All was ready for customers, but I needed more. So by Saturday, I was ready to head to the craft show to scope out more products to sell. This would be a good outing for me, and Beau as well, since I wanted to see more of the area.

I arrived at Tilly's neat little patio home in a shaded community of similar homes at seven twenty Saturday morning. On the way to the show, Tilly filled me in on the local scenery and history of the area. The towns around the bay had been inhabited by fishermen until developers saw the area as a desirable place for retirees. Subsequently, many of the communities were now owned by them or snowbirds who only lived there half a year. Tilly's home was in one of those communities. We arrived at the craft show just as it was opening, getting a good parking place near the entrance.

We strolled along, taking plenty of time to see all the booths and artisans before they got too busy and it got too hot. At one booth, I met Genevieve, a jewelry designer who had some unique earrings and necklaces made of stainless steel and local shells. I bought several pieces and set up a deal with her to sell more of her wares in Artistic Adventures. She didn't live very far away, so she promised to bring more to the store. Of course, Tilly knew of her family through old connections.

In another booth I met Archie, who made really cool pottery. I particularly liked the sea-related designs in lovely shades of blue and green he had, so I bought a dish that looked like a crab was holding it, along with little crabby bowls. I also bought a chip-and-dip tray, a vase, and a large salad bowl with a fish embossed in the center. Archie was also interested in selling more for consignment, so he said he'd come by with more items the next week.

Everyone wanted to pet Beau as if they'd never seen a golden retriever before. Of course, he is the prettiest dog ever. Not that I'm biased. I kept my eye out for a booth that made dog treats or toys so I could buy him something too. Maybe I could find him a squeaky plush toy. He really liked them and carried them around in his mouth.

I turned the corner at the end of the aisle and stopped, seeing Adam and Jennifer locked arm in arm, strolling along. Tilly paused next to me and saw what I was looking at. We watched as the couple laughed and carried on, obviously enjoying each other's company.

"Looks like he got over losing his business partner and fiancée in one fell swoop," Tilly said.

"I suppose his time of mourning is over," I said, adding to the sarcasm.

As if feeling eyes on them, they turned and looked our way. Would they recognize us? They'd probably know Tilly, but would they remember me? Beau tugged the leash, and I looked down at him. Adam would certainly remember Beau.

Adam turned to Jennifer, said something, and then they moseyed on down the row. Well, that confirmed my thoughts about him. What a jerk.

"Well, ain't that special?" Tilly said. "I doubt this relationship just started."

"Do you think they could've been in cahoots to get rid of Bunny?"

"Maybe. Bet having her out of the way made it easier for them to be together," Tilly said.

"How would they benefit from it? Would he get the business all to himself?"

"More than likely. But she died from an allergy. In the bookstore. How could they make that happen?" Tilly asked.

"I don't know. But the last thing she drank was the coffee in the bookstore."

Tilly faced me with scorn. "Are you saying you think Jep did it?"

"No, no. I don't believe that at all." The words rushed out even though I wasn't sure of Jep's innocence. But I wanted him to be innocent. "Could someone else have put something in her coffee?"

"When? Nobody else was around. And folks only use their own cup that we keep for them and don't pick up somebody else's." Tilly huffed. "You were there. Did you see anything strange?"

"No, which means it had to be something she'd come into contact with that morning, something that might have taken a while to act."

"But if it took a while, then she would've had time to use the EpiPen."

"If she had it with her," I said.

"And if she didn't, who took it?" Tilly crossed her arms, frowning.

"We've got to find out if there was a pen in her purse."

"Have you considered that it might have been accidental, that she was around something she was allergic to, had a reaction, but had forgotten to bring her pen with her?" Tilly asked as she examined a quilted potholder in the next booth.

"Of course, that's what the killer would want us to think." Was I just going down rabbit trails? Why did I believe so strongly that Bunny was murdered? What was I missing here? Was no one else concerned about the truth? If that was the case, I guessed I was on my own.

Tilly walked up to a booth displaying stained glass, and I followed. She fingered some wind chimes with dragonflies and butterflies. "I like these," she said.

"I do too." I went over to speak to Tiffany Young, the artist, and pretty soon, I had a few to display with the promise of more to come. "I think I'll hang this on my back patio," I said, holding up one with stained-glass dolphins.

"What if your neighbors don't like the noise?" Tilly asked. "Some of those things are downright annoying."

"I don't think anyone will complain about this. It tinkles." I tapped the clapper in the middle, and it swung out and hit the tubes, emitting a pleasant sound. "You know what they say, 'Every time a bell rings, an angel gets its wings.'" I quoted the line from *It's a Wonderful Life.*

"You believe that stuff?" Tilly frowned at me as if I'd lost my mind.

Shrugging, I said, "I don't know. It's a nice thought though."

"Well, I don't think God made any angels without wings."

I never thought about the comment that deeply, but Tilly was more of an expert on godly matters than I was.

"So, Tilly, tell me what you know about Bunny. She moved here by herself?"

"Far as I know. Nobody around here liked her much. Even Samson didn't like her, so that should tell you something. And that *fiancé*," she said with a note of sarcasm, "didn't show up until later. Right after she opened the gym, she started renovating an old house over on the bayou. Seems like that's when he appeared."

"Oh? Where is the house? I might have seen it when I was kayaking." We moved on to the next row, and the smell of fried food hit my nose.

"You might have, if you went all the way to the end of the bayou. She changed the old place a lot and made it real modern with lots of glass. It doesn't fit in with anything else around here. It's the last residential property before you get to the back bayou country."

Back bayou? Where had I heard that before? Oh yes, she'd said that was the area Nita Sue lived in. "Sounds like it was expensive. She must've had some money when she moved here." I followed the aroma of food down the aisle. "Are you hungry?"

"Gettin' there."

At the end of the aisle, set a few hundred feet away from the vendors, was a row of food trucks. Bingo.

"Let's see. What do we have here? Funnel cakes, gyros, Hawaiian poke bowls, subs, fried shrimp baskets. A pretty big selection."

"I'll have a funnel cake," Tilly said, pointing to the respective truck.

"Wow, I like all the choices. I was thinking funnel cake, but now that it's closer to lunch, fried shrimp sounds good." Boy, was I killing my diet.

"Those people have a restaurant too. It's pretty good." Tilly turned toward the funnel cake truck. "I'll go get mine and meet you back here."

As I headed toward the shrimp truck, I saw Adam and Jennifer in line in front of the poke bowl truck. A flashback of Jennifer coming into the bookstore to console Adam came to mind. She told the police she was Adam and Bunny's friend. But come to think of it, she didn't seem too upset about her friend Bunny.

When I got in the line for shrimp, a man's voice behind me said, "I see you like shrimp too, Ms. Stephens."

I whirled around to find the police chief standing behind me. "Yes, I do. I hear these people cook it well."

"They sure do. Good french fries too." He rocked back on his heels, fingers hooked in his bulging waistband. "I eat at their restaurant at least once a week."

A walking advertisement for fried food. "I'll have to try the food there sometime."

I started to turn around, but it felt rude to turn my back to him. Meanwhile, Beau was checking out his shoes.

"Yep. Wife says they have good salads too, but I don't eat rabbit food." He chuckled at his own joke.

Speaking of rabbits. . . "That reminds me. Did the police happen to pick up Bunny's phone purse?"

He shrugged. "If she was wearing it, sure. Why?"

"Well, I was thinking that if she was allergic to things, she probably carried an EpiPen with her, so I wondered if she had one in her purse. I have a friend who has allergies, and she always has her EpiPen with her in case she accidentally comes in contact with an allergen. They can save your life, you know."

"Hmm. I'll check." He grabbed his phone and punched in a number. "Hey, Bob. Chaney here over at the craft fair. Say, did you pick up a phone purse when you got Bunny Wilson's body?" Pause. "Okay, good. Any note of contents?" Pause. "I see. That's it? Just a phone?" Pause. "No, I heard she might be carrying one of those anti-allergy pens, since she had allergies, you know." Pause. "All right. Thanks. See you later." He disconnected the call, stuck his phone back in his shirt pocket, then shook his head as he faced me. "No pen."

I held my hand to shield my face from the sun as I looked up at him. "Don't you find that strange?"

He shrugged. "Maybe she forgot it that day."

Knowing how diligent my friend was to have her pen with her, I found it hard to believe Bunny simply forgot it. But who else would know if she had it with her? Adam?

"What if she had it with her but someone took it out?"

The chief frowned, pursing his lips. "Are you suggesting someone set her up to have a reaction, but had removed the pen so she'd die?"

"I've considered that."

"So you're suggesting a homicide?"

"Just looking at the possibility."

"You a detective or something?"

"Not professionally, no. I just think there might be more to this than we know."

"Well, you're wasting your time. You'd have to come up with somebody who had motive and opportunity to expose her to something and take the pen out of her purse. Good luck with that."

Chief Chaney was obviously not happy that I questioned his department's conclusions. But if he wasn't interested in pursuing this, I would. It wasn't that I owed anything to Bunny, not at all. I just wanted the truth to come out, and if someone got away with murder, I wanted them found out. I mean, what if that happened to me? Of course, I wasn't allergic to anything but dust, and that certainly hadn't killed me, if you look at my house. But if I were, and somebody used that to kill me, well, it just wouldn't be right.

CHAPTER 8

After visiting every booth at the fair, Tilly and I headed back to Bayside, both tired. I pulled into a drive-through to buy some iced coffee to get me through the rest of the day. Tilly dozed as I drove, listening to my favorite '80s music. Even though it was popular before I was born, my mom played it all the time, so it became my music too.

After I dropped Tilly off at her home, I decided to check out the area a little bit, i.e., find Jep's former home and maybe Bunny's too. I knew they were on the water, so surely I could find a road that ran along the bayou. The closest one to town would be Jep's, so I turned down a road that looked like it had water behind the houses. I had to make a few turns because the neighborhoods didn't follow the water exactly, but I ended up on a shaded road with older, large houses, and I could see the bayou behind them.

The lots were huge, going from the street and sloping all the way back to the water. What a nice area to live in. I drove along the winding road until I saw two wrought iron gates between two huge concrete columns. The gates were padlocked, but behind them halfway to the water were the remains of a mansion, its chimneys charred while weeds overtook the ruins. Stopping in front of the gate, I gazed, awestruck at the sight. The home must have been magnificent.

Then I noticed the iron letters on the gate—on the left gate the letter *J*, and on the right gate, the letter *P*. Yes, it was definitely Jep's place. I got out of the truck and walked to the gate to see if I could see the gazebo down by the water. It took me a minute, but finally, I spotted a heron perched on the rooftop. Guess the bird had claimed that spot permanently. An uneasiness crept down my back. Was I being watched? Glancing above the gate, I spotted a camera. So much for being discreet. I wondered who had placed it there.

I climbed back into the truck then proceeded along the road until it ended. But I could tell I wasn't at the end of the bayou. So I turned onto another road and kept weaving back toward the water until I found another neighborhood. This was a new one. Based on the lot sizes of the last neighborhood, I assumed this land had formerly been part of a larger estate that was now being subdivided into streets and houses built close together. After driving through this new treeless area—how sad that builders had to cut down every tree to build the neighborhood— I knew Bunny's house wasn't in it.

Once again, I drove out and looked for a road that led back to the water farther down. Finally, I spotted a private drive with a sign that said No Trespassing. I contemplated the danger for about two seconds then went for it. I drove slowly, hoping I wouldn't get shot for trespassing. After a mile or so, the road opened onto a large, landscaped lawn that led to the water. Sitting closer to the water was a very modern-looking house. I crept along as I checked it out, unsure if anyone was there or not.

Then I saw it—a shiny black sports car parked in the circular drive. Two guesses whose car that was, and the first one didn't count. It had to belong to Adam Miller. I was afraid to drive in any farther, but I could see through the house to the pool behind it.

And there by the pool were two people I had seen earlier that day. They must've finished their craft show shopping sooner than I did.

Beau whined, and I knew he needed a potty break.

"Wait a minute, Beau," I said, and tried to back out, an activity I am not very proficient at. But I couldn't drive down the driveway and turn around by the house where I'd be seen. How would I explain that? A wrong turn? Unlikely. I crept back, keeping an eye on my back and side mirrors, trying to stay on the road. Finally, I got to the end—or beginning—of the road and stopped, opened the door, and let Beau out.

He did his business right away then took off through the woods. Oh no, he was chasing squirrels, thinking we were there for a hike.

"Beau!" I called his name but had no idea where he was. "Beau!" There was no way he was coming back soon after being cooped up in the truck for over an hour. What if Adam Miller decided to leave and found me parked there? Good grief, what was I going to do? I'd have to wait, but would Beau find me? This was a new place to him, and to me. I walked into the woods a ways, calling his name again. Then I heard him barking. He must've treed a squirrel. I followed the sound until I spotted him, and called him again. When that didn't work, I whistled. One thing I learned from my grandpa was how to make that loud, earsplitting whistle that will summon the dead, or so it seemed.

The barking stopped when he heard my whistle. But before he came back to me, I heard a gunshot. I jerked my head around, looking for someone with a gun. Was there a hunter here? I had no idea exactly where I was. I had lost sight of Beau again. I whistled again, heard a noise coming through the underbrush, and then Beau was at my side, panting. I grabbed his collar. "Beau! Do not run away from me again!" I started going back the way I hoped I'd come.

We'd only walked a few more steps when a man stepped out of the woods in front of us. He held a gun in one hand, and three dead squirrels hung by their tails from his belt. I shuddered and froze. Had I stepped into a scene from *Deliverance*? Beau growled.

"This here's private property," the man said. "You're trespassin'."

"I'm sorry. I didn't mean to. I stopped on the road to let my dog go to the bathroom, and he ran off."

"Good thing I didn't shoot him." I didn't think the man was much older than me, but he was big and scary. I'd expect him to wear a plaid flannel shirt if we were up north, but here in Florida, he wore a dirty T-shirt, jeans, and an old beaten-up cap with faded letters that said MAC'S FISH AND TACKLE. His long dark hair stuck out beneath the cap, and his beard and mustache met each other somewhere on his face. So this was what Tilly had meant by "back bayou" people. I felt a little guilty for judging the man, but running into a stranger in the woods carrying a gun had unnerved me.

"Um, thank you for not shooting him. I just moved here, and I'm not familiar with the area." Were those No Trespassing signs for Bunny's property or this man's? "I was looking for a friend's house." That was kind of true.

He frowned. "That woman what lives over there in that house by the water?" He motioned with his gun.

"Um, yes. Yes, that's right. Bunny Wilson."

"She's dead." The finality of his tone was like a bell tolling.

"Yes, yes, I know." I didn't tell him I saw her die. "I, uh, hadn't seen her in a long time, and somebody told me she lived out here, so I wanted to see where her house was, since I'm new to the area." I rambled on like a schoolchild caught looking at her neighbor's test paper. Well, at least I wasn't lying.

"She stole that property from my family," he said. "Been ours for hunderds of years."

What was I supposed to say? "Oh, I don't know anything about that." I so wanted to get out of the woods. A mosquito buzzed my face, and I slapped at it. "Well, I better get out of here before the mosquitoes eat me alive. Which way is out?"

He stepped aside and pointed. "That way."

"Thank you," I said, and hurried past, bent over and holding Beau's collar. Boy, I wish I'd brought the leash. As I passed the man, I caught the odor of fish from his clothes. After I got ten feet or so beyond him, I finally took a breath. Then I heard his voice behind me.

"Hey!"

I froze and turned slowly around. What had I done now? "Yes?"

"You're that lady openin' that art place, ain't you?"

I tried to make my face smile. "Yes, that's me. Kelly Stephens."

"I'm Zeke. My sister Nita Sue told me about you. You gonna sell her pictures, ain't you?"

"Yes, yes I am. She does lovely work." I didn't say "nice to meet you," because it wasn't.

He shrugged.

"Well, see you around!" I hurried back to the truck as fast as I could, a crick in my neck from holding on to Beau's collar and looking up to see where I was going. When we got to the truck, we both jumped in, and I drove away as fast as I could.

On the way home, I'm not sure who panted more, me or Beau. There was certainly no love lost between Bunny and Nita Sue's family. But would they dislike her enough to kill her? They didn't seem like the subtle type. If they wanted to kill her, they could just go to her house and shoot her. Much as I'd like to add them to my list of suspects, they really didn't fit the scenario of exposing Bunny to an allergen and stealing her EpiPen. But they certainly had motive to kill her, with her stealing their land. And then I remembered Nita Sue said Bunny ran over one of her chickens.

They had a double motive. But would they be able to pull off the allergy death?

I wondered what Zeke thought about Adam Miller. I was sure he knew Adam was at the house. Did Adam know who Zeke was and what the story was about Bunny stealing his property? If Zeke disliked Bunny so much, he probably wouldn't want Adam around either. Maybe Adam should be concerned for his safety.

CHAPTER 9

I slipped into the church on Sunday and sat on the back pew, trying to be invisible. I had never been to this church, and I wasn't sure I would return, but I needed to get back to my habit of attending church on Sundays.

Scanning the congregation, I looked for people I recognized. Up near the front were Kay Dean and Del, looking so different not wearing aprons and dressed for church. On the side aisle, I spotted Mac with a woman beside him. His wife? In the center aisle was Tilly, sitting with Nellie.

Some of the others present looked vaguely familiar too, although I didn't remember their names or where I'd seen them before. We stood to sing the opening hymn, and a man near me said, "Excuse me. Is this seat taken?"

I jumped at the sound of Jep's voice. I turned toward him and smiled, scooting over so he could get in the pew. My heart skipped a few beats at the sight of him, not to mention the closeness of him. I tried to keep my focus on the hymnal, offering to share it with him, but when he took it and his hand touched mine, I almost jumped again. Any suspicions I'd had disappeared. Who would suspect this nice, church-going man of evil deeds?

When we sat down, he leaned over and whispered, "Good morning."

My face warmed. "Good morning."

I worked very hard to listen to the preacher and pay no attention to the handsome man who was inches away from me. The sermon was about forgiveness and how holding on to grudges was not healthy, nor was it God's will. Naturally, I thought about Bunny and who held a grudge against her enough to murder her. Surely not someone in church. I scanned the pews again, this time taking note of who wasn't there. Did that mean anything, or did they just go to a different church? After all, there was more than one church in this town.

Then it hit me. I hadn't forgiven Bunny either. Good grief. The preacher said that Jesus equated hate with murder. Oh dear. Maybe I was just as guilty as the person who poisoned her. Looked like I had some praying to do.

Next to me, Jep bowed his head. Was he guilty of unforgiveness too? It seemed to me that he was the victim in his wife's case, taking the blame for her disappearance. That just wasn't fair. I hadn't been around him that much, but I hadn't seen him be rude to anyone, even if they were rude to him.

When the service was over and everyone stood to leave, Jep nodded at people who passed down the aisle. More often than not, they eyed me with questionable gazes, wondering, no doubt, who the woman was with him. He introduced me as the new person in town who was opening the art store. I felt like I should be wearing a sign so he wouldn't have to say it so much. When Tilly and Nellie came by, he said, "Good morning, ladies." Tilly smiled and glanced at me, nodding with a slight wink.

After everyone walked out, he turned to me. "Would you like to go have lunch somewhere?"

My palms sweated on the top of the pew where I held on for dear life. "Yes, that sounds great. Where do you suggest?"

"We could go to the seafood restaurant over on the bay. Of course, that's where most of the town will go if they don't eat at home. Or we could go to Destin, if you don't mind the drive and would prefer not running into everyone else, although it's probably busy this time of day too. It's up to you."

"Big decision." Did I want the whole town to see me with him? "I suppose I should meet the rest of the town or at least become a familiar face, so let's go to the local place. Do you like the food there?"

He nodded. "Oh, yes. If you like fresh seafood, Sammy's Seafood is the place to go. It's all caught in this area. Or, if you don't want seafood, there's a Mexican place, an Asian buffet, and the burger place."

I remembered that Lucas said he sold his mullet to the local restaurant. It must be Sammy's. "Seafood sounds great. Fresh seafood is not something I had often in Atlanta."

I followed Jep in my truck to the restaurant. It was packed, so we walked along the water on the dock outside as we waited for our buzzer to go off. The breeze off the water was wonderful, and the company even better. About twenty boats were parked at the nearby marina. "Do you like to sail?" Jep asked as we watched a large sailboat pass by.

"I have to admit I never have. It looks like fun though."

"It can be a lot of work too, depending on the size of the boat and the weather. I used to own one."

"You did?"

He nodded. "I hardly ever used it, so I sold it. Unfortunately, that's the case with many folks around here. They buy a boat, use it a year or so, then quit for one reason or another."

"I hope that doesn't happen with my kayak. I really enjoy it, but once my store opens, I may get too busy."

"Then we'll have to make sure that doesn't happen. I'll get mine out and show you around the water. There are so many bayous and bays to explore."

We? I hadn't expected to hear that. I tried not to act too surprised and to keep my cool. "Mac says people fish from their kayaks. I don't think I'm that coordinated."

"Yes, a lot of people do. It's much easier to launch a kayak than a big boat, especially if you want to fish around here. Of course, if you want to go out to the deeper water or to the Gulf of Mexico, you'd need a bigger boat."

Our beeper buzzed, and Jep said, "Looks like our table is ready."

Once we were seated and handed menus, I noticed "Fried mullet special" featured. I chuckled. "I guess this is the mullet that Lucas caught."

Jep nodded. "Well, he's one of the mullet fishermen around here. There are others as well. Have you ever eaten mullet?"

"No, I haven't. Is it good?"

"If it's fresh and fried, yes."

"Seems like I've eaten a lot of fried food here lately."

"It's a favorite way to cook seafood. But you can get broiled fish as well. My favorite dish here is the shrimp and grits."

"That sounds good. I think I'll try it too." He placed our order, and I noticed a lot of customers looking our direction. "I feel like I'm on display," I said.

"Sorry about that. You know, small town. Everybody wants to know everything about the new woman in town and why she's with me."

"Maybe I should wave."

"Smiling will suffice. We'll be interrogated later."

"Speaking of interrogating, how did you get the name Jep?" I asked.

He sighed. "My birth name is Jonathon Edward Pennington, so my initials are J. E. P."

I remembered the letters *J* and *P* on the iron gate. Should I mention that I saw them, or would that sound like I had been snooping, which I was? "Oh, I get it. Well, it's different, that's for sure."

Shrugging, he said, "I've been called that ever since I can remember, so I don't think about it being unusual."

I glanced around the restaurant and recognized some people from church. "I liked your church. Everyone seems friendly, and the sermon was good too, even if it did step on my toes."

He quirked a brow. "How so?"

"He talked about forgiveness, and I realized I had some forgiving to do."

"Don't we all? I think he was talking to me too."

Before I could stop myself, I said, "It seems somebody couldn't forgive Bunny for something she'd done."

Jep cocked his head. "You think she was killed for revenge?"

I leaned forward. "Why does someone kill another person?"

"Hmm. Revenge, jealousy, anger, hate?"

"Do you know of anything she ever did to anyone around here, something that would make them angry enough to kill her?"

He shook his head slowly. "There was a little land dispute when she built her house. The people who lived on the neighboring property claimed the land was theirs. But she bought it legally. I don't think they knew where the property lines were."

A memory of Zeke crossed my mind. "I think I met one of them."

"You did?"

I nodded reluctantly. "Yes. After I dropped Tilly off at her house, I drove around to look at the area. Beau started whining to get out, so I parked by some woods, let him out, and he ran off. I had no idea where I was, much less where he was, but I followed him into the woods, calling him. I ran across Zeke, who told me I was trespassing. He was carrying a gun and apparently hunting squirrels, if the dead ones hanging from his belt were any indication."

"Good ole Zeke. He is kind of scary-looking."

You could say that again.

Jep continued. "Yes, they're the ones who got angry with Bunny. Do you think he had something to do with her death?"

"It sounds to me like they had a motive, but I don't know how they would've been able to expose her that morning to something she was allergic to. I doubt they went to her house, and even if they did, wouldn't she have had a reaction long before she reached the bookstore, especially if she went someplace else first? Also, they would have to have known she carried an EpiPen with her all the time and get it away from her."

He shook his head as the servers came with our food. "You've done some investigating, I see."

"I can't help it." I waited until the server placed our food on the table before I said any more. "I feel like I owe it to Bunny to find out. I remember now that she was an only child, and I think both her parents passed away while she was in college. So she doesn't have anyone who cares."

He stared at me a moment then nodded as if he agreed. "May I say grace?"

Surprised by the question, I said, "Please do."

He reached across the table and took my hand, sparking warmth up my arm. Did he have any idea how he affected me? Hopefully not. Bowing his head, he said, "Lord, thank You for this day of worship. Thank You for this good food, and this new friendship Kelly and I have. Please help us to find out the truth about what happened to Bunny, and please help us to forgive others the way You forgive us. Amen."

"Amen." Our "new" friendship had a nice ring to it.

The food was wonderful and so was the conversation, once we changed the topic. Maybe this relocation was a "God-thing" as some people called it. I hoped so.

CHAPTER 10

After lunch, I went home full and happy. But I started thinking of all the work I had to do, so I took my laptop and Beau to the shop, sat at the large table, and started entering my inventory into a database. It took several hours to enter each item, categorize it by vendor, and price it. I didn't have a lot of inventory yet, but if I didn't get it cataloged soon, I'd fall behind.

I glanced up and stared out the window. The square was quiet since everyone in town closed on Sunday. My mind went back to Bunny and how she had been killed. I retraced her steps. First, she went to the donut shop and ate two donuts. Then she went to the bookstore, where she got a book and coffee and sat down by Mac. Before she got up to come toward me, she grabbed her throat, looked in her purse, didn't find the EpiPen, then died.

What was I missing? Kay Dean and Del didn't take the pen. Neither did Jep or Mac. But something told me she had it when she left home. Surely she would have checked to make sure. Could she have gone somewhere else before she got to the bookstore, like maybe her gym, Bunny's Body Beautiful? Maybe it was taken there. If Adam was there, he could have had access to it. Was there anyplace else she could've gone? And where was she exposed to the allergen? And how?

Whoever exposed her to the allergen must've known how long it would take before it affected her. Did the killers expect her to die at the bookstore? If so, they could have been setting Jep up to take the blame. It made sense if she went someplace else between the donut shop and the bookstore. But where? And who could confirm she had?

I stood and stretched. A big lunch then sitting on my bottom for hours didn't help my figure. Beau stood too, looking at me expectantly and wagging his tail. "I know. You want to go walkie," I said in dog language. Beau's ears perked up. They always did when he heard the "walk" word. I had to be careful not to say it unless a walk was imminent.

"Okay, but wait a minute."

I wiped off the hutch and laid Genevieve's earrings on it. They'd look nice there after I got a jewelry tree of some type to display them better. On the shelves above the jewelry, I would set examples of Nita Sue's smaller pictures among pieces of Archie's pottery.

Where was I going to put Tiffany's stained glass? I wanted to hang it from the ceiling, but the ceilings were too high. I'd have to get help. I hated to ask someone to do things for me. Besides, no one could see them up there. I needed something like the rack the vendor had at the show. And I needed more items to sell.

Beau barked, and I looked outside the store window. "Okay. Let's go." I glanced around at what I'd accomplished. It was beginning to come together. Tomorrow, I'd put frames together so I could hang Nita Sue's paintings on the wall. "I guess that's enough for this afternoon." I attached Beau's leash to his collar. I had no intention of a repeat of yesterday's close call with Zeke. Not that I was near the woods, but I couldn't chance Beau getting me into more trouble. I grabbed the leash and my laptop then turned out the lights and went outside, locking the door behind me.

The sun was showing off as it descended, painting the sky in brilliant streaks of oranges, yellows, and reds. I could imagine how amazing that sunset would look over the bayou. Too bad I wasn't beside the water now, but I was afraid I'd miss most of the display if I took the time to drive there. I sighed. Another day, I'd catch it, I promised myself. Could Jep see it from where he lived?

Across the square, I noticed a black sports car parked in front of the gym. I guessed Adam needed to do some work today too. I wondered if Bunny had ever worked on Sundays. Was Adam the sole owner of the place now that Bunny was gone? The more I thought about him, the more convinced I became that he was behind Bunny's death. He had motive, opportunity, and an alibi. Besides, how did he know she was at the bookstore? Had she told him that was where she was going? And if so, when did she tell him? He had to have known enough ahead of time to remove the EpiPen. Could he have exposed her to something before she got the donuts? How would he know when the allergen would take effect? Or maybe he didn't, and he thought she'd die soon after she ate the donuts. That way, Kay Dean and Del would look guilty. Either the bookstore or the donut shop could take the blame. Should I take my suspicions about Adam Miller to Chief Chaney? If I did, would he believe my reasoning or just brush it off?

I arrived at the store early Monday morning, ready to get to work. I'd brought my framing materials from home—hammer, nails, screwdriver, wire, and a little saw. As I measured each piece of art, I jotted down the figures on a notepad, compiling a list of frames I needed to make. Thankfully, most were the same size. I studied each piece and its name. Which one should I frame first?

Nita Sue's watercolor of a blue heron was my favorite. It was a large, vertical, life-size painting of the bird standing in tall reeds. I'd hang it in a place where customers would spot it first thing when they entered the store. It was the perfect piece to tie in with the local environment and reminded me of the heron I'd seen on the old gazebo.

I decided to go ahead and frame that picture first so I could hang it right away. I put my earbuds in to listen to music while I worked and was so absorbed in putting the frame together, singing along with Lauren Daigle, that I didn't hear when Jep came in.

"Hello!" He spoke loudly as he placed himself in front of me.

I jumped then put down my tools and turned off the music on my phone. Taking the earbuds out, I said, "I'm sorry, I didn't hear you."

He smiled and handed me a cup of coffee. "I hope this is the way you like it. Tilly said you like vanilla latte, so I asked Kay Dean to make you one. I thought you could probably use a cup by now. I saw you arrive this morning, so I know you've been at it a while."

I tilted my head as I looked at him. "Thank you. How thoughtful of you." I took a sip. "It's perfect."

"I hated to interrupt you, especially since I liked listening to you sing." He glanced around at the store. "It's coming together."

Oh my stars. He heard me sing. My face must have gotten beet-red. "No one's supposed to listen to me while I work. I just enjoy the music, and it helps pass the time."

He raised his hand. "Don't worry. You have a nice voice." He pointed to the picture I was working on. "May I see it?"

"Sure. I just finished it." I held up the heron picture.

"Nice. Nita Sue did that?"

"Yes. It reminds me of the bird I saw on that old gazebo the other day. Of course, it's perfect for this coastal area."

He looked thoughtful as he gazed at the picture. "Where do you plan to put it?"

I turned and pointed to the center of the back wall. "There. I'll just have to get the ladder."

"I'll get it for you. Are you ready to hang it?"

"Yes, but. . ."

Before I could stop him, he had grabbed the ladder and was placing it in front of the wall. I had attached the screw eyes and hanging wire to the back of the picture, so I handed Jep the hammer and a heavy-duty hook and nail. "Let's hope you find the stud," I said.

Jep climbed up the ladder and placed the hook and nail on the wall. "Does this look centered?"

I stood back and mentally measured the space. "A little to the left."

He moved them over. "How about this?"

"Okay. That's good."

He nailed the pieces in, I handed him the picture, and he hung it on the wall. He adjusted it to make it level. "Is it straight?"

"Perfect."

He stepped down off the ladder then walked to the front door and looked back at the picture, resting his hand under his chin to appraise the job. Then he gave me a thumbs-up, and I felt like I'd accomplished something major.

"Thanks, Jep. Once again, you come to my rescue."

"I'm your knight in shining armor."

Boy, was he. I held back from saying, "My hero," lest I overplay the situation. Instead, I said, "One down, and many to go."

"Okay, I'll leave you to your work. Just call me or come get me if you need another picture hung that high."

"Will do." I got back to work and finished six more frames before I decided to take a break from what I was doing. I framed and arranged six pictures then hung them on the wall at or above eye level. The pictures were all of the natural landscape around the area, with birds flying, fish jumping out of the water, and moss-hung trees silhouetting the moon over water.

The next batch of pictures were more whimsical. One had a wide-eyed imp peering from behind a tree. The picture was titled

Woods Elf. Another had a similar creature perched on a tree limb, but this one had iridescent wings, and it was named *Tree Fairy.* The creatures were all quite enchanting, and I wondered if Nita Sue believed they really existed. But then I found a couple of pictures that were more disturbing. One of them was called *Mourning Fairy* and depicted a fairy with sad eyes and big teardrops running down its face. Another was of a very angry elf with a deep frown, holding a pointed stick like a spear. It was named *Warrior Elf.*

I framed and hung these in a grouping separate from the nature pictures. However, I was confident they would all sell because they were well done. I just needed to get the customers to come in, and the sooner I finished, the sooner I could open, hopefully by the end of the week. Of course, I would continue to seek new artists and merchandise to sell. And I also wanted to start offering lessons of some type, once I got the store going.

Brushing off my hands, I decided to get some fresh air. I walked outside and inhaled a deep breath. With my hands on my hips, I watched people walking from one store to the next. It seemed pretty busy today, and I noticed out-of-state tags on the cars parked along the street. Apparently, a lot of traffic came through Bayside on the way to or from the beach. Even more reason to hurry and get my shop open.

One place I had not visited yet was Fran's Fancy Flowers. Maybe now would be a good time to do that. I walked around the square until I reached the store. The lovely aroma of a profusion of flowers hit me when I entered. I was immediately captivated by the beautiful colors and varieties of arrangements placed around the store. A glass cooler containing vases of fresh flowers ran along the wall on one side.

"Hello!" A pleasant-faced woman with chestnut hair twisted into a knot on top of her head approached from behind the counter. "Can I help you?"

I smiled and introduced myself. "I'm Kelly Stephens. I'm—"

"You're the one who's opening the art store," she finished. "Nice to meet ya. I'm Fran."

"What a lovely store you have." I gazed around the room, admiring the selection. "I'll have to get an arrangement for my store when I open."

"We've got lots to choose from. Just let me know what you like."

The phone rang, and she ran to the counter. "Fran's Fancy Flowers," she said when she picked up the phone. "Yes, I'll be happy to. No, Belinda, I don't know when the funeral will be. Whenever the coroner releases the body, I guess. All right. Bye."

She disconnected the call and put the phone down, facing me. "I wonder when they're going to bury that woman."

I didn't have to think hard to figure out what woman she meant. "Bunny Wilson?"

"Yes. Poor thing. I heard you were in the bookstore when it happened."

"Unfortunately, I was." I leaned down and sniffed a blue flower in an arrangement. "Who's planning the funeral?"

Fran shook her head. "I assume her partner Adam is doing it. But I can't make the arrangements until we know when the funeral will be."

"You've had lots of orders?"

She shrugged. "More than I expected. I guess people are just trying to extend their sympathies in some way."

I wanted to ask who had ordered flowers, especially since she wasn't all that well liked, but that was really none of my business. I suppose the townspeople were just trying to show their respects, like Fran said. Would the killer order flowers for the funeral?

CHAPTER 11

B efore I went back to my shop, I decided to stop by the bookstore and ask Tilly about something. She was sitting at the counter as usual, eating from a plastic container, while Samson sat a few feet away, watching her. When I greeted her, Tilly stopped eating and looked up. "Sorry, I'm taking my lunch break now. Leftovers." She nodded toward the cat. "Samson thinks I'm going to share some of my tuna casserole with him." She scowled at the cat. "But I'm not."

"Meow," the cat replied, whether arguing or pleading, I wasn't sure.

Speaking of lunch, I hadn't thought about it. If I had any groceries in my house, I'd bring something from home. But I had grabbed an apple for an afternoon snack on the way out. Guess it'd be my lunch instead.

"Sorry, I didn't mean to interrupt you," I said.

She shook her head. "Don't worry. I could've gone to the back room to eat, but I prefer to stay out here. What can I help you with today?"

"I was just at Fran's, and she got a call for a funeral arrangement for Bunny. Have you heard when the funeral will be?"

"No, not yet."

"Do you know who's planning the funeral? Adam?"

Tilly glanced from side to side then shrugged. "I guess so."

"Fran said she's gotten several calls for funeral flowers, more than she expected."

"Most people around here are pretty nice, you know."

"Of course." I just hadn't gotten used to small-town dynamics yet. "Tilly, do you know what happened to the book Bunny was reading before she died?"

She nodded. "*How to Win Friends and Influence People.* It's here. The book has been out over fifty years, but our copy is a recent edition. Guess it still has good advice."

"The police didn't take it?"

"No, guess they didn't need it. But we're going to throw it away. Someone tore a chapter out of the book. Imagine that, tearing up a book."

"May I see it, please?"

Tilly shrugged. "Sure. I kept it to remind Jep to reorder it." She climbed off her stool. "Hang on, and I'll get it for you." As she hurried away, I wondered why Bunny was reading such an old book. And who would tear out a chapter in a book, much less one they didn't own?

Tilly returned moments later with the book and handed it to me. "I'm not sure if she knew the pages were ripped out when she was looking at it. I don't think she had time to rip them out before she took it and sat down, then died."

I flipped through the book and found the missing space. Glancing at the table of contents, I looked to see what was missing. From what I could tell, it was the section titled, "A Sure Way to Make Enemies and How to Avoid It." Strange. I looked more closely and noticed the pages weren't torn out, they had been cut out. Now that was even more strange. If someone was going to take the pages out, why not just tear them?

I pictured someone standing in the aisle, trying not to be seen and taking the pages out of the book. Tearing them out would make noise, and noise would call attention to themselves. Cutting them out would be quieter, especially if they used something sharp like a razor. But why take them out and leave the book? Or if that part was the only part they didn't like, why not buy the book and then remove the pages?

But what if it was a ruse to get someone to come look for the book? Someone like Bunny? Maybe there was some type of residue in the book that would be an allergen and they wanted Bunny to find it?

"Tilly, I think the police need to take a close look at this book."

"Police? Why?"

Jep walked up, his eyebrows knit in a frown. "What's this about?"

I explained my suspicions to him. "I think the police need to examine the book for signs of some type of allergen. Remember, when Bunny came into the store, she said something about looking for a certain book. Somebody might have suggested to Bunny that she come get the book so she would be exposed to it."

Jep rubbed his chin in thought. "You might have something there." He took a look at the book where I pointed to the missing part. "I'll call Chuck."

"Now we have to figure out who would have told her to come find the book."

"We?" Tilly said. "Seems like you've turned into a one-woman detective agency."

"All right. Maybe I have. But don't you see? Whoever got her to come get the book was the same person who took her EpiPen."

"Makes sense," Jep said. "And if you're right, someone got away with murder."

"Not yet, they haven't," I said.

Jep motioned for me to follow him, and we went outside. "Hey, I've been thinking," he said. "Why don't we knock off early this afternoon and take our kayaks out?"

My heart did a little flutter dance. "Um, I don't know. I still have some work I wanted to finish today. I was just taking a little break."

"What do you need to do? I can come over and help you."

I chewed on my lip. I needed to stop doing that. "I want to frame the smaller paintings, price everything I have on display, and hang the stained glass."

"Two people can cut the time in half. Do you have all you need for that?"

"I think so. But don't you have work to do here?"

"Nothing that can't wait. Let me finish what I was doing and call Chuck, then I'll be over."

He seemed pretty determined, so I agreed. A niggling feeling crossed my mind. What if he was the killer and I was getting too close to finding out the truth? What if he planned to take me out on the kayak and arrange an accident? Maybe that was how his wife had died. But they never found her body, did they?

Kelly, stop it. Remember the man goes to church. He seemed like a good man, didn't he? He had talked about forgiveness like I had. And he prayed before meals too. But for every good thing I thought about Jep, another negative thought followed. Was I losing my mind over this thing?

On the other hand, it sure would be nice to go out kayaking with him. He could fill me in on the area. But I had a store to get ready to open. However, I was my own boss, and I could give myself permission to leave. Would that little time delay my opening that much, especially if he helped me finish what I needed to get done?

I finally quit arguing with myself and organized the items I needed to work on in the store. Jep came over a little while later, and I put him to work hanging the stained glass, using suction cups with hooks. Then I got busy on the small frames, handing the rest of that job over to Jep when he finished with the stained glass, so I could finish making price tags. The work went quickly, and I was relieved to see so much accomplished. We sure did make a good team.

We were almost finished when a man came in I recognized from the fair. I had given him my card. Neil Stokes was a woodworker, and he'd made a bunch of signs with cute little wood-burned messages like "What's a weekend?" "Gone Fishin'," "Beach Bum on Duty," and others. I thought they'd sell, so I agreed to carry them in the store, took twenty of them, and signed a contract.

When Neil left, Jep and I looked at each other and smiled.

"Not a bad day's work," he said.

"Not bad at all," I agreed.

"So are you ready to close up shop and go kayaking?"

"Yes, I am."

I grabbed my computer bag and water bottle, we walked out, and I locked up.

"Why don't I come to your place, and I can pick up your kayak? No need for both of us to drive to the launch," Jep said.

"Okay, I need to change." I looked down at my clothes. "I don't plan on wearing jeans."

"Me either," he said. "Let's pick up a couple of subs and have a picnic while we're out." He glanced down at his watch then up at the sky. "We might get to see the sunset, if we time it right."

"Sounds great." Better than great. A picnic with a swoon-worthy man and a sunset too. I gave him my address, and he said he'd be over in twenty minutes. I got in my truck and drove home, ready for a new adventure. Hopefully, my instincts about this guy were right. But what did I know about this man? He owned a bookstore, had been married before, but his wife disappeared, his house burned down, and he came from old local money. But other than that, I didn't really know him. Yet he was always very nice to me and to others too, from what I could tell. The mild-mannered

Clark Kent kind of guy. I'd never seen him get angry with anyone, just mildly perturbed. But what if my instincts were wrong? I'd sure be disappointed if they were.

Disappointed or dead.

For Pete's sake, Kelly. Give it a rest.

———

Jep arrived soon after I changed clothes, and Beau was all over him as if his best friend had just appeared. I tried to pull him off, but Jep said, "Don't worry. I appreciate the welcome."

"I wish I could trust him in the kayak, but I don't think that would work. But I've seen other people with dogs on kayaks."

"Yes, I think that'll take some training, if not age. He's still mostly puppy."

"I guess you're right."

I had dragged my kayak to the parking area so we could load it on top of Jep's SUV. He lifted it with no trouble, and I was of little use, since I wasn't tall enough to reach the top of the car. He strapped it on with some bungee cords and turned to me. "Ready to go?"

I nodded. "Sorry, Beau," I said through the window of my townhouse. Then I climbed into Jep's car, and we drove off. After stopping at a sub shop, we put our sandwiches in a small cooler Jep had brought. I felt like I should have contributed something to the event but wasn't sure what was needed. We drove to a local boat launch, and Jep pulled the two kayaks off the vehicle and retrieved the paddles from inside. I grabbed the handle of my kayak and slid it down the grass to the launch. Jep followed suit then parked the car and joined me with the cooler in hand.

He held my lime-green kayak steady while I climbed in then pushed me off. That sure was easier than doing it myself. The water at the launch was shallow enough that I could have gotten in the water and climbed in, but with his help, I didn't need to.

He climbed into his tan kayak and shoved off to join me. "Follow me," he said. "We'll stay fairly close to the shore and keep out of the wind until we get around the bend."

I followed his instructions, my eyes scanning the shore to see the variety of homes and gardens. What a peaceful community. Who would think a murderer lurked in their midst? But for now, I'd focus on enjoying this pleasant experience on the water, especially thankful to have someone to share it with.

CHAPTER 12

He was right about the wind. It was difficult to keep the kayaks going straight until we turned the bend, and what a difference. Calm water greeted us, making our kayaks glide easily through the water. He paused and let me catch up with him. "This is better, isn't it?"

"Yes, much." I looked back toward the bend we'd passed. "I'm surprised there are no houses there. It seems like a great location."

"It is, as far as views are concerned. However, it's also the first place a hurricane hits. There's been more than one house built on that spit of land, but every one of them got wiped out. If the wind didn't blow the house away, the flooding swamped it. So the property owners got tired of dealing with rebuilding until the next storm arrived."

"What a shame." It seemed like such a good place for a house. "How often do you have hurricanes here?"

"Big ones, about once every ten years, but we've had some minor ones that still do damage to places on the water—depending, of course, where on the water they are." He pointed to the shore near us. "Over here out of the wind, the houses aren't hit too badly, but the water might tear up their docks. On the opposite side, though, the houses get a direct hit. That's why you see more new houses on that side made of different materials. After the last couple of big hurricanes, the state passed building codes on material and construction that new homes have to meet."

"Do you know everyone who lives in these houses?"

He nodded. "Mostly. The homeowners who have been here a while, I've known all my life. But some of them died or moved away, and I don't know who all the newer owners are."

"So you never lived anywhere else?"

"Only when I was in college. Then I moved back here to help my parents run the bookstore and took it over when they passed away. Actually, the bookstore was my mother's baby, and my father was a doctor in town, but when he retired, he helped her run it."

When did he get married, I wondered? He was leaving out a missing part, a missing chapter in his life. But it was none of my business to ask about it.

"So what made you move to Bayside?" he asked.

Uh oh. It was my confession time. "I grew up in a small town outside Atlanta, went to college, then began my career in marketing there. I was with the same company ten years when they went through a merger, and a lot of my colleagues got fired or jumped ship. My personal life was going downhill as well, so I decided to make a clean break." I hated mentioning the personal stuff, but it was part of the reason I moved. "I took my severance package, sold my condo there, and moved to Florida to start my own business. I thought Destin might be the place to start, but everything cost so much there. I looked here and liked the area. I'm not sure about the retail market here, but I'm going to give it a try."

"I think you'll do well," he said. "I'll do what I can to help."

I appreciated his vote of confidence more than he knew.

"Thanks. You've been a lot of help already."

He put his finger to his lips and pointed ahead. "Look."

Following his direction, I gazed at the water ahead of us. A silver animal spouted and rolled into the water face first, then another did the same nearby.

"Dolphins!" I rested my paddle across my legs and pulled my phone out of its waterproof pouch. Focusing it on the scene, I held it to get the right moment. This time, there was a smaller silver creature between the other two. "It's a baby!"

Jep smiled and nodded. "Looks like a family. They're feeding in this bayou."

"I thought you only saw them in the ocean," I said, mesmerized by the animals rolling through the water in synchronization.

"Oh no, they come in here all the time. They'll feed a while then move out to another location. But with the small one, they'll stay closer to land for a while."

"How cool. I love it." Eventually, the dolphins moved on until I didn't see them anymore.

We began paddling again, and I followed Jep over to a park-like area on the shore where picnic tables were. I watched him paddle his kayak right up onto the sandy bank then step out into the shallow water. He dragged his boat farther up and waited for me to do the same. Once I climbed out of my kayak, I followed him to the picnic tables, where he motioned for me to sit while he put the cooler down and opened it up.

He handed me my sub, a bag of chips, and a bottle of water, took out his own, and sat down on the bench across the table from me. Reaching for my hand, he bowed his head and said, "Lord, we thank You and praise You for this wonderful place. Please bless our food and time together. Amen."

"Amen," I said, then took a much-anticipated bite of my sandwich. We ate in silence while taking in the view of the water and watching the clouds change color as the sun began to lower. The silence was so calming, I could hear every birdcall as the water's small waves gently met the shore. How could something so evil as a murder happen in a place like this? And how long would it take for the police to discover something unusual in the remaining part of the book? However, I didn't voice my thoughts to Jep. I didn't want to spoil the moment.

"This is such a beautiful place. I don't know why you aren't out here every day," I said.

"I was just asking myself that same question. It's a shame how we can get so busy, we forget to take time to enjoy life. It would be nice to be able to be out here all the time. But if we need to work, we can't afford that luxury."

I was surprised to hear he needed to make money, based on what I'd heard of him being from old money. "Some of us have to work, for sure."

"The bookstore was Mother's hobby, and it never really made money, but Dad didn't care, as long as she was happy. So he kept paying the bills and letting her do her thing. But when he passed, I had to turn the store around or close it."

"Well, I'm glad you decided to keep it. Hopefully, you've made it profitable."

"It's holding its own. Have to compete with that 'big box in the sky,' you know, the big A, but folks around here still prefer the personal touch."

I let my gaze wander down the shoreline in the opposite direction and spotted the rooftop of the gazebo. "That gazebo makes me sad. I hate that it's been abandoned."

Jep turned toward me and pinned me with a serious expression. "I need to make a confession."

My heart leaped. Was he going to tell me he killed Bunny? I waited, holding my breath.

"That gazebo belongs to me. So does the property it sits on and the property behind it. I once lived in the house at the top of the hill, the one that's only chimneys now."

I swallowed, unable to reply.

He blew out a breath. "I met a girl in college, fell in love, and married her after we graduated. We moved here, and she wanted to live in a grand house on the water, so I had it built the way she wanted. She also asked for the gazebo by the water. But she never liked it here in Bayside, even with the big house. She was from a large city and couldn't adjust to small-town life. She wanted to move, and I didn't. I couldn't.

"She started having an affair with a man who owned and rented beach property in Destin but lived in Chicago. I didn't know this until she disappeared and mailed me a letter sometime later. I didn't know where she'd gone, but she left without even saying goodbye. The night she left, we had a bad thunderstorm, and lightning struck the house, burning it down. I just barely got out before part of the roof caved in, and I didn't realize she was gone. I went back in to look for her but never found her, and I had to get out before the rest of the roof collapsed on top of me. Afterward, the fire inspector didn't find a body."

I could only imagine how terrified he had been to think his wife was in the house during the fire. Thankfully, he got out before he was a victim.

"I'm sure you've heard the rumor that I killed her and burned down the house. But after I got her letter and knew what happened to her, I decided to keep it to myself and let others believe what they wanted to believe. I suppose the truth hurt more than the rumor. So I just closed off the property and moved somewhere else. It's been that way for ten years. I suppose you could say that's the missing chapter in my life."

I reached out and put my hand over his. "I'm so sorry."

Our eyes were focused on our hands.

"That's okay. It's in the past now, and actually, it feels rather freeing to tell somebody," Jep said.

Why tell me? I was flattered that he felt comfortable enough to confide in me though.

He lifted his gaze until his eyes met mine. "I guess we all have something in our past we'd like to leave there," he said.

Ouch. He was right, and I was ready to leave my past behind as well.

The sky streaked with shades of orange, pink, yellow, and red behind the descending sun.

"Ooh. What a gorgeous sunset," I said.

"God's handiwork. He's still in the business of creating, isn't He?"

I nodded. "Yes, He is. And recreating too."

"We better get back before it gets too dark," Jep said, standing.

I jumped up too. "I sure don't want to be on the water in the dark."

We paddled back to the launch site with only the gentle splash of our paddles accompanying the changing colors of the sky. It felt like a gate had opened between us, and now we could go through it. Jep opening up to me felt like I'd walked through the iron gates with the *J* and *P* on them and seen his life.

CHAPTER 13

B y the end of the week, I had received, priced, inventoried, and displayed enough merchandise to fill the store sufficiently to open. I'd scheduled a decoupage class for the next week where the attendees could make coasters and plaques using small seashells. To add excitement to the opening, I decided to advertise a grand opening on Saturday, complete with refreshments.

I made flyers and placed them in shops around the square, bought balloons and posters for the street, and told everyone I knew to tell all their friends. I bought a tray of mini donuts from Del's and bought a gallon of lemonade and cups from the grocery store. On Saturday morning when I arrived at my shop, a huge, colorful bouquet arrived from Fran's Fancy Flowers. I couldn't imagine Fran had sent them, so I wasn't entirely surprised to read the attached card.

Best wishes for your success, Jep.

My heart warmed at his thoughtfulness as I placed the arrangement in the center of the big table where it could be seen and smelled with its delicious scent wafting through the store. Excitement rattled my nerves as I waited for the first customers, turning the sign on the door of Artistic Adventures to OPEN FOR

BUSINESS. Soon, people began arriving, many of them tourists who saw the advertising on their way through town. I got so busy greeting folks and running around helping people, that I realized I should've hired help. Who knew I'd be so busy?

Just when I was about to come unglued, a handsome man walked in and began helping customers. Dear Jep, always there when I needed him. How could I have ever suspected him of murder? How could anyone? Sales were going like wildfire, and I couldn't believe it. We'd only been open a couple of hours when I noticed the refreshments were running out and I had no backup plans.

Then another local angel arrived to save the day. Kay Dean came in the door with another tray of mini donuts, and Del followed her with a jug of lemonade. I ran over and hugged them both. "Oh my goodness, you two are lifesavers!"

They smiled, then Del said he had to get back to their shop and hurried out the door. Kay Dean took a spot by the table, pouring lemonade and handing it out to customers. Could the people in this town be any nicer?

When Adam Miller walked in with a handful of flyers advertising the gym, I didn't protest. If he was advertising my store with my flyers in his, then it was only fair I returned the gesture. Kay Dean frowned, but I shrugged and took the flyers, setting them on a small table in the corner after Adam left.

After business slowed, Tilly and Nellie came in together. They took refreshments and milled around the store. I hadn't realized Jep was gone until I saw Tilly was there.

"Jep told me to come over and see the store," she said. "From all the folks I've seen going and coming, you've been pretty busy."

"Yes, we have, thankfully." I glanced around to see if anyone needed my help. "I didn't even get to tell Jep thanks for helping earlier."

"I'm sure you'll have your chance when he comes back. He just wanted to give me a break so I could come over and see all the commotion for myself."

Nellie sidled up to me and took my arm. "Word is you two have been spending quite a bit of time together." She smiled at me. "I know Bunny had her eye on him—she even got all gussied up that last day she came to see him at the bookstore."

I looked at her, confused. "What do you mean, she got gussied up?"

"I saw her coming out of the hair salon that morning," Nellie said. "It wasn't her normal day to go, so I figured she had something up her sleeve for Jep."

Now how had I not known Bunny went to the salon?

I said something about getting to know Jep as a friend and hurried to greet the next customer. There wasn't another moment for me to breathe, and I wondered once again how I'd gotten so lucky. One by one, every shop owner on the square dropped by to congratulate me and check out the store themselves. Even Mac harrumphed his way through the store before spotting the "Gone Fishin'" wooden plaque and buying it. "This is meant to be in my store," he said.

Belinda popped in later in the afternoon, the aroma of beauty products following her as she flashed her sparkling purple nails. "Everybody's talking about your store," she said. "I think all my customers were coming here today."

I admired her nails, glancing at the pitiful condition of mine. "Maybe I can come in next week for a manicure," I said.

"You certainly need one. And we've got several products that can help build them up too."

No doubt I needed them. Fortunately, my customers didn't seem to mind my poor nails. As a matter of fact, I couldn't remember any artists with nice nails. Belinda spotted one of the stained-glass ornaments with a frog sitting on a lily pad. "I've just got to have one of these!" she said, bringing it to me.

"I thought you might say so," I said as she paid me. It helped to know what people liked. I was about to ask her about Bunny coming to the salon the day she died, but there was a long line waiting to check out behind her.

After Belinda left, things were beginning to slow, so I thanked Kay Dean and told her she could leave. I plopped down in one of the chairs, my eyes scanning the room to see what had sold and where there were spaces that needed to be filled. My gaze swept to the front door as Nita Sue slipped in quietly, glancing around like a timid mouse looking for a cat.

I stood. "Nita Sue, come in!"

She jumped at the sound of my words, then saw me. "Oh, hi. I heard you opened today."

"Yes, we did! We've been very busy!"

She continued glancing around. "We? I thought you were by yourself."

"I am. I don't know why I said 'we.' However, several people have helped me today. I don't know what I would've done without them."

"Oh."

"I sold several of your paintings." I pointed to the wall where they were displayed. "Do you have more you can bring me?"

She nodded, running her hand along the wall as she walked, looking at each picture. "When do you pay me?" she asked.

"Oh, I haven't had a chance to calculate it yet. How about I pay you when you bring me more pictures?"

"Okay. I'll do that Monday."

"Fine. I'll have it ready." She didn't seem to be in any hurry as she studied each item in the store. I, on the other hand, was tired and ready to call it a day. "Belinda came in earlier. She bought a frog ornament." I pointed to the stained-glass display. She moved over to that area and studied each piece.

Nita Sue looked up. "I worked there today."

The girl acted strangely—quiet, and keeping her head down as she glanced around in a furtive kind of way. I was beginning to feel uncomfortable around her. My mind flashed back to the dead squirrels Zeke carried. "I'll take this one," she said, reaching for one of the ornaments. Before I could get there to cut the tag off, she pulled a small knife from her pants pocket and sliced it off herself.

Putting the knife back in her pocket, she reached in her other pocket and retrieved a ten-dollar bill. "Here," she said, handing it to me.

"Okay, thank you," I said, trying to sound cheerful to mask my uneasiness. "Would you like me to put that in a bag for you?"

"Okay."

I scrambled to find a small bag to fit, placed the ornament inside, and tied the top together with some green ribbon. "Here ya go," I said, handing her the bag.

She took the bag and studied the ribbon. She turned to leave, but something she'd said made me curious.

"Where did you say you worked today?"

"Belinda's. I clean up for her."

Based on her appearance, I couldn't imagine her cleaning up for anybody. But at least she had a paying job.

"Oh, I see. Well, then, bye. I'll see you Monday."

She walked out the door. I was about to lock it behind her, but Jep walked up before I could.

I stepped back and opened the door for him. He smiled then studied my face. "Is something wrong?"

"No, I'm just tired. And Nita Sue was just here."

"Oh, I see. Nita Sue is different, but I think she's had a rough life, being poor and raised by her brother Zeke and all."

"Oh dear. Poor girl. She told me she works for Belinda."

"Yes, she helps clean up, sweeps, washes the towels, etc. Sometimes she does some work for me too."

I thought my eyes would pop out. "She does? Doing what?"

"Same thing. General cleaning, dusting, etc."

"I had no idea," I said.

"She needs to earn money somehow. Maybe selling her art here will help her out."

No wonder she asked about being paid. She needed the money.

I rubbed the back of my neck. "Nellie told me when she was in here that Bunny went to Belinda's salon before she came to the bookstore that morning."

Jep held up his hand. "No. We're not going to discuss anything heavier than how cute Beau is tonight. In fact, why don't I take you out to eat?" Jep's sudden change in the conversation caught me off guard.

"Okay, but nothing fancy. I'm beat."

"Nothing fancy. Do you want Thai food or Mexican?" The man certainly was accommodating.

"Thai. I haven't seen a Thai place around here."

"It's a tiny place between the post office and the hardware store. But it's good food." I'd have to take his word for it.

"Right now, anything would be good. Thanks."

"Okay, are you ready to close up for the day?"

"Boy, am I! Thankfully, tomorrow is Sunday, a day of rest. At least it will be for me unless I spend the afternoon doing paper-work to square my sales and inventory."

"You will rest." He waved his hand in the air. "All that other stuff can wait until Monday."

"If you say so," I said. I really wanted to go home later and figure out my sales, but it could wait. Besides, I was so tired, I didn't think I had enough brain power to do it anyway.

I locked up and walked to my truck with Jep following me to the car door. "Do you want me to pick something up and meet you at your house? I bet you'd rather just go home and put your feet up."

"How did you guess?" This man was a mind reader. Hopefully, he didn't read everything I thought about him. "That would be great. I don't know what they have, but my tastes are pretty simple. I'll take stir-fried rice with chicken and an order of egg rolls."

"Hot or mild?"

"Mild. I don't feel like fighting with my food tonight."

He laughed and opened the door for me. "Okay. You go home and get comfortable, and I'll be there with the food as soon as I can get it."

If I were keeping a chart on him, he'd just scored extra points.

CHAPTER 14

Sunday at church I was greeted by many people who had become my friends since I opened the store. I recognized most of them, but I didn't remember any names, even though they acted like I should. Wow. I had gone from the stranger in town to one of the locals. It felt good to be accepted, but now I also felt more responsible, like I had to do well to gain approval.

Jep and I sat together again, but this time, he picked me up at my place instead of meeting me there. We were beginning to feel like a couple, and much as I liked the idea, it also scared me because I hated the thought that it might not work out. After already being burned, I was hesitant to throw myself back into the fire.

While I sat in church reflecting on the past week, I reveled in the opening success of my store. Would the business continue to do well, or was this just a one-time event? One thing for sure, I had to keep plenty of inventory.

As we were leaving church, a woman came up to me and said, "I know this is a bad time to talk business, but I just wanted to tell you I make dog and cat toys you could sell in your store. Here's my number if you want to call me about it this week."

I thanked her and promised to call. I was sure Beau would approve. He loved his doggie toys, but I hoped she made some that were durable, since he could chew them up in a heartbeat.

"Kelly, are you interested in going for a ride on a pontoon boat?" Jep asked at lunch. Like last week, he had asked me to lunch again. A weekly habit I could get used to.

"A pontoon boat? When? Where?"

"A friend of mine has one at the marina and said I could use it. We could take a relaxing ride across the big bay to Destin. It's a nice ride, and you don't have to do anything but relax. It even has a canopy if you want to get out of the sun."

"Well, since you won't let me work today, that sounds like a nice way to spend the afternoon."

"Okay, I'll drop you off so you can change into your swimsuit, just in case you want to jump into the water. I'll be back after I go home and change."

He took me home, where Beau's bark could be heard greeting us. "Poor Beau. I leave him every day."

"Bring him. There's plenty of room."

The pontoon boat worked out well for all of us. Beau could walk around on it, stand, sit, or lie on a cushion. The ride was smooth and comfortable with occasional splashes when the boat hit a big wave. I lounged on a cushion on the way, keeping an eye on Beau and enjoying the view of the wide expanse of blue water. When we got to Destin, we visited the famous Crab Island, a shallow area where lots of boats park and party. We enjoyed people-watching, although Beau did his fair share of people-barking, saying "hello" in dog language.

The water was a gorgeous aqua color, and I could see the sand on the bottom, so I got in and walked around a little bit, the water not coming up past my waist. We even got Beau in the water with us, and he dogpaddled around, but was eager to get back on the boat, where he shook off enough water to shower in. After a couple of hours there, we boated back to Bayside.

While we were en route, I sat up front with Jep and we talked about the day. But something was bothering me. "Jep, did you hear anything back from the police department about what they found in the book?"

"Oh, I meant to tell you. They found residue of soap or shampoo, which anyone could have had on their hands. But the surprising thing they found was peanut crumbs."

"Peanut crumbs?"

"Yes, like you'd find if someone had been eating peanuts when they read the book."

"Bunny was allergic to peanuts."

"I know. So do you think someone put the crumbs there intentionally?"

"It sure seems likely, doesn't it? But wouldn't that make you suspect, since it was in your store?"

He nodded. "It could. However, why would I cut pages out of a book I wanted to sell? And how would I make sure she picked up that particular book?"

"That doesn't make sense. But what if someone cut them out to mark the spot they wanted Bunny to look and be exposed to the peanuts?" I paused before putting to words the niggling thought that had been hiding from me since yesterday.

"Someone who wanted to make me look guilty?"

"Or maybe just point the authorities in another direction instead of at the real culprit. Nita Sue carries a knife. She had it on her at the store yesterday."

"But there's no crime in having a knife. Unless you kill someone with it."

"Or you're an accomplice to a murder."

He quirked an eyebrow. "Do you think Nita Sue could have been an accomplice to Bunny's murder? Why?"

"I have a hunch. But I need to ask you something. You said Nita Sue worked for you sometimes cleaning up. Was she there the morning Bunny died?"

"Let me think." He rubbed his chin. "You know, I think she was. She's so quiet, she often slips in and out without speaking to anyone. But it seems like I saw her that morning."

"So she had opportunity."

"To do what? Cut pages out of the book?" He frowned.

"And add peanut crumbs," I said.

Jep shook his head. "I can't imagine Nita Sue doing that. Why would she?"

"Because someone else told her to."

"I don't get it. But who? And why would someone ask her to do that?"

"To keep the authorities from finding what really killed Bunny."

"But how do we know it wasn't the peanut exposure?"

"I've been thinking about that," I said, putting my hand on his arm. "Jep, I don't think she ever opened the book. She had only just sat down when she heard my name and got up to come toward me. That's when she collapsed. So she had to have been exposed to something else beforehand."

Jep blew out a breath and ran his fingers through his hair. "Do you think you know what and how?"

Remembering what Nellie had told me the day before, I said, "I have my suspicions."

But proving them was something else. First thing in the morning, I needed to make a call to Kay Dean and find out if she knew where else Bunny went the morning she died. And then I was going to make a hair appointment.

———

I arrived at the shop around seven thirty Monday morning and got busy on my spreadsheet, calculating Saturday's sales and how much I owed each vendor. I promised Nita Sue I'd have her money, and I intended to keep my word. Most of the other shops hadn't opened yet, except for Del's Donuts. An hour later, the gym was open and so was Hair We Are. I called, and Belinda answered on the first ring.

"Hair We Are!" Belinda said cheerfully.

"Hi, Belinda. This is Kelly Stephens from Artistic Adventures. Can you squeeze me in today?"

"Just a second, let me look at my calendar. What do you want to do? Something with your hair, or your nails?"

"How about both? I need a trim, but I also need a manicure." I might as well go for it.

"Can you come in the next thirty minutes? I can get you in before my first regular appointment."

"Sure. That'd be perfect. I just finished my bookkeeping so I can pay Nita Sue. Is she there?"

"Not yet. She'll probably come in while you're here."

"Good. I'll be able to pay her while I'm there. That'll save us both some time."

"Okay, honey. See you soon!"

I made a couple more phone calls then left for the hairdresser.

When I entered Hair We Are, Belinda came out to meet me and escorted me to her work station. She pointed to her new stained-glass frog hanging from the mirror. "He's just perfect there, isn't he?"

"He sure is. Fits in like he's right at home."

Belinda stood behind me as we both faced the mirror. "What are we going to do with your hair?"

Since lately I hadn't been doing anything with it except letting it hang straight or pulling it back in a ponytail, I had no idea. "I'm not sure what I want to do with it now. Could you just cut off a couple of inches and shape it? It's just so limp and needs to be in better condition."

"If that's all you want to do now, then fine. It's up to you," Belinda said, but I think she really wanted to do something dramatic to it. "Let's get you shampooed first." She opened a cabinet, took out a towel, and wrapped it around my neck. Then she put a plastic cape over it, tying it at the back. She led me to the adjoining room and pointed to a shampoo chair, so I sat down in it.

I lay back in the chair, and Belinda ran the water to warm it up, then she hosed my hair to get it wet. Above my head, she reached into a cabinet.

"This shampoo is really good for limp hair like yours. It's made from avocado oil and has all the nutrients your hair needs. We also have the avocado conditioner we like to use after we shampoo. I use it on all my customers now."

The aroma of the hair product reminded me of the last time I'd smelled it, the morning Bunny walked in the door to the bookstore. I tried to act relaxed, but my stomach was tense. If I was right, a killer was washing my hair.

Belinda started talking to me about the grand opening I'd had while she scrubbed my scalp.

"Hi, Nita Sue," she said, indicating her niece had arrived. "Miss Kelly here says your paintings sold well on Saturday."

"I brought your check," I said, although I couldn't see the girl yet.

When Belinda finished washing my hair, the front door of the salon opened, and the police chief walked in, a deputy following. I exhaled a sigh of relief.

"Why, Chief Chaney, what are you doing here this morning?" Belinda raised her eyebrows in surprise. "I don't think I have you down for a haircut today."

"Belinda Collins, you're under arrest for the murder of Bunny Wilson." The deputy moved behind Belinda and pulled her arms back to put handcuffs on her.

Her eyes widened, and her mouth dropped open. "What are you talking about, Chuck Chaney? That woman died of a heart attack, and you know it!"

"No, she died of an allergic reaction to avocados because she was exposed to them here at your shop when you intentionally used an avocado shampoo on her, knowing she was allergic."

"Now that's nonsense." She huffed, acting annoyed. "If that was true, why did she die at the bookstore?"

"You made sure she went to the bookstore to find a book you recommended so she'd be exposed to peanuts, something else she was allergic to, so when she died, it would be in the bookstore and someone else would be responsible."

"You can't prove that." Belinda glanced around nervously.

The police chief held up a piece of paper. "Search warrant." He put on gloves and started scrounging through drawers and cabinets. When he walked to the cabinet where the towels were kept, he opened it and began taking towels out. He stretched to reach the back of the cabinet and pulled out an EpiPen. He held it up for Belinda to see and then dropped it in an evidence bag. "You knew she would have a reaction, and you made sure she didn't have this to counteract it."

"I did no such thing!" Belinda's eyes flashed with anger, and she glanced back where Nita Sue had been standing, but she wasn't there. Another deputy came in the back door with Nita Sue in handcuffs. "Found this one sneaking out the back."

"That's true," the chief continued, "because you told Nita Sue to take the pen out of Bunny's phone purse while you shampooed her hair."

Nita Sue focused on the floor.

"I want a lawyer," Belinda said as she and Nita Sue were escorted out the front door.

The chief nodded at me as he walked out. "Thanks for the tip," he said over his shoulder.

Jep had arrived in time to witness the arrest. I stood there with wet hair, watching the two women being hauled off to jail. Jep turned to me and winked. "Nice hair."

I punched him. "Drastic times call for drastic measures."

"So you were right. Belinda was behind the murder, and Nita Sue was her accomplice. So what was her motive?"

"She hated Bunny for a number of reasons, jealousy for one, but also revenge. Belinda and Nita Sue believed the property Bunny built her fancy house on was theirs and that she had no right to be there. Then when she ran over Nita Sue's chicken, Nita Sue became angry enough to seek revenge too, so she agreed to help Belinda get rid of Bunny."

"But why cut the pages out of the book?"

"I think Belinda told Bunny she needed to read the book to help her business. So Bunny went straight to the bookstore after she got her hair done that morning and found the book. By then, the allergen had kicked in, but when she looked in her purse for the EpiPen, it was gone, so she died of the reaction."

"Pretty clever. And it would have worked if you hadn't been such a sleuth."

"It just didn't add up, and I had to figure it out," I said.

"So I guess now we can put that behind us and move forward, just as I'm doing with other stuff in my life. I'm ready to move forward, are you?"

"Frankly, I'm ready to dry my hair."

Award-winning author **Marilyn Turk** writes historical fiction flavored with suspense and romance. Marilyn also writes devotions for *Daily Guideposts*. She and her husband are lighthouse enthusiasts, have visited over one hundred lighthouses, and also served as volunteer lighthouse caretakers at Little River Light off the coast of Maine.

When not writing or visiting lighthouses, Marilyn enjoys boating, fishing, gardening, tennis, playing with grandkids, and her golden retriever Dolly.

She is a member of American Christian Fiction Writers; Faith, Hope and Love; Advanced Writers and Speakers Association; and Word Weavers International.

Connect with her at

- http://pathwayheart.com
- https://x.com/MarilynTurk
- https://www.facebook.com/MarilynTurkAuthor/
- https://www.pinterest.com/bluewaterbayou/
- Amazon:https://www.amazon.com/Marilyn-Turk/e/B017Y76L9A
- Bookbub: https://www.bookbub.com/profile/marilyn-turk
- Email her at marilynturkwriter@yahoo.com

YOU MIGHT ALSO ENJOY...

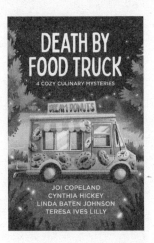

DEATH BY FOOD TRUCK
FOOD TRUCKS CAN BE MURDEROUSLY GOOD

GET A TASTE OF MURDER AND MAYHEM IN FOUR COZY MYSTERIES.

Birch Tree, Maine, is experiencing a rash of deaths, all mysteriously linked to food trucks that frequent the Birch Point Lake Park. Mey's noodle truck was her ticket to a new life, until her ex-boyfriend threatened to take it away. Angel's new donut truck was doing great, until deathly rumors started. Shanice thought she had customer support when taking over her grandpa's potato truck, until one started complaining. Marissa's taco truck was a fixture in the park, until linked to a food judge's death. What could have led to such foul-tasting murder and mayhem in an idyllic community?

Paperback / 978-1-63609-594-3

You Might Also Enjoy. . .

Gone to the Dogs Series of Cozy Mysteries

The town of Brenham, Texas, has gone to the dogs! The employees of Lone Star Veterinary Clinic link arms with animal rescue organization Second Chance Ranch to care for the area's sweetest canines. Along the way, there are mysteries a'plenty in this series of six books by authors Janice Thompson and Kathleen Y'Barbo-Turner.

Book 1: *Off the Chain* by Janice Thompson

Marigold Evans' first attempt at rescuing an abandoned pooch lands her in the underground sewer lines of Houston's Buffalo Bayou. . .and almost in jail, until Parker Jenson comes to her defense. Then a bad day only gets worse as the Lone Star Vet Clinic, where they both work, is vandalized and the list of suspects starts to climb. With the help of her fellow employees, Marigold sets out to simultaneously solve the crime, rehab the rescued dog, and help more dogs in crisis. But why would anyone continue to work against all their good efforts?

Paperback / 978-1-63609-313-0

Book 2: *Dog Days of Summer* by Kathleen Y'Barbo,
978-1-63609-394-9

Book 3: *Barking up the Wrong Tree* by Janice Thompson,
978-1-63609-451-9

Book 4: *The Bark of Zorro* by Kathleen Y'Barbo,
978-1-63609-517-2

Book 5: *Every Dog Has His Day* by Janice Thompson,
978-1-63609-587-5

Book 6: *New Leash on Life* by Kathleen Y'Barbo,
978-1-63609-662-9

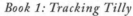